BACKFIRE

Backfire

CATHERINE COULTER

DOUBLEDAY LARGE PRINT HOME LIBRARY EDITION

G. P. PUTNAM'S SONS, NEW YORK

This Large Print Edition, prepared especially for
Doubleday Large Print Home Library, contains
the complete, unabridged text of the original
Publisher's Edition.

PUTNAM

G. P. PUTNAM'S SONS
Publishers Since 1838
Published by the Penguin Group
Penguin Group (USA) Inc.,
375 Hudson Street, New York, New York 10014, USA

Penguin Books Ltd, Registered Offices:
80 Strand, London WC2R 0RL, England

ISBN 978-1-62090-034-5

Printed in the United States of America

This is a work of fiction. Names, characters, places, and incidents either are the product of the author's imagination or are used fictitiously, and any resemblance to actual persons, living or dead, businesses, companies, events, or locales is entirely coincidental.

This Large Print Book carries the
Seal of Approval of N.A.V.H.

*To my splendid other half, Anton,
with your sharp brain and, thankfully,
ultimate knowledge of all things medical*

ACKNOWLEDGMENTS

I would like to thank the following consummate professionals for their infinite kindness and patience in making *Backfire* richer, and, super-important, accurate. Thank you all so very much for coming into my life. I worship at your feet.

Let me add that if there are any factual goofs in the book, it's my fault. I mean, I'd like to blame someone else, but alas, it's on my head.

Deputy U.S. Marshal Dave Key—your experiences and exploits are amazing. Perhaps even more amazing is that you're still alive and smiling and ready to take on more.

Marshal Donald O'Keefe, U.S. Department of Justice, U.S. Marshals Service, Northern District of California—El Jefe, your willingness to provide me with everything I needed is appreciated.

Chief Judge James Ware, U.S. District Court for the Northern District of California—you are thoughtful, eloquent, and you answered every one of my crazy questions, and even some I hadn't thought of.

Ms. Uyen Trinh, judicial assistant for Chief Judge James Ware—you are the great facilitator. I appreciate all your assistance and your wonderful enthusiasm for my books.

Lieutenant Donald Wick, Marin County Sheriff Department—I was told you were The Man, and I find I must agree. You added richness and verisimilitude to the Marin County scenes.

Ms. Angela Bell, FBI Office of Public Affairs, Hoover Building, Washington, D.C.—thank you for your plot-saving idea to get the letter into the lobby of the Hoover Building without breaking any rules, and for telling me the CAU moved to the third floor.

Mr. Alexander DeAngelis, director, China Office, National Science Foundation—I'm not just saying this because you're my brother-in-law. Your brain and succinct insights are a pleasure to behold. Thank you for providing me accuracy in all things Chinese.

1

Sea Cliff, San Francisco
Late Thursday night
One week before Thanksgiving

Judge Ramsey Hunt listened to the lapping water break against the rocks below, a sound that always brought him back into himself and centered him. He stood at this exact spot every night and listened to the waves, as unending and as infinite as he knew he wasn't. Only the sound of the waves, he thought. Otherwise, it was dead silent, not even a distant foghorn blast from the huge cargo ship that was nearing the Golden Gate through a veil of low-lying fog.

A light breeze ruffled the tree leaves and put a light chop on the ocean below. It was chilly tonight. He was glad Molly had tossed him his leather jacket on his way out. A week before Thanksgiving, he thought, a week before he would preside over the turkey carving and feel so blessed he'd want to sing, which, thankfully, he wouldn't.

Ramsey looked up at the low-hanging half-moon that seemed cold and alien tonight. His ever-curious son, Cal, had asked him if he could sink his fingers into the pitted surface. Would it be hard, like his wooden Ford truck, he wondered, or soft like ice cream?

At least his day had ended well. In the late afternoon, he'd met Molly and the twins at Davies Hall to hear Emma rehearse Gershwin's *Rhapsody in Blue* with the San Francisco Symphony, smiling and nodding as they listened. Ramsey had long thought of her as his own daughter, and here she was, a prodigy, of all things. He had to be careful or he'd burst with pride, Molly always said. Remarkably,

Cal and Gage hadn't raised too much of a fuss at having to sit still during the rehearsal. Well, Cal did yell out once, "Emmy, I want you to play 'Twinkle Twinkle Little Star'!" which had brought warm laughter from the violin section.

They'd enjoyed enchiladas and tacos an hour later at La Barca, the family's favorite Mexican restaurant on Lombard, always an adventure when the three-year-old twins were anywhere near chips and guacamole.

Ramsey rested his elbows on the solid stone fence built when his boys had reached the age of exploration a year and a half ago. Better than nightmares about them tumbling off the sixty-foot cliff into the mess of rocks and water below.

He looked out across the entrance to the bay at the Marin Headlands, as stark and barren as the half-moon above them. Soon the winter rains would begin to green things up, as green as Ireland in some years, his second favorite place on earth after San Francisco. It was a blessing that this incredible stretch was all a national recreational area so he would never have to look at some guy sipping a nice fruity Chardonnay across from him on a condo balcony. He noticed a Zodiac sitting anchored below him, nearly as still as a small island in the ocean. There were no other boats around it that he could see. Who would be out so late, anchored in open water? He saw no one aboard, and for a moment, he felt alarmed. Had someone fallen overboard? No, whoever motored over in the Zodiac could easily have swum or waded to the narrow beach. But why? Not to get a suntan, that's for sure. He wondered if he should call 911 when he heard Molly open the family room door behind him. "Goodness, it's cold out here. I'm glad you're wearing your jacket. Is your favorite sea lion talking to you again?"

Ramsey smiled. Old Carl, that was the name he'd given this giant of a sea lion that liked to laze about in the water below. He hadn't seen Old Carl in several days now. He called back, "He's probably at Pier Thirty-nine, stretched out on the barges with his cousins. What's up?"

"Gage had a nightmare. Can you come and tell him the spinach monster isn't

lurking in his closet? He doesn't believe me."

He turned to her, grinning. "Be right
there—"

Molly heard a shot, cold and sharp as
the moon, and saw her husband slammed
violently forward by a bullet. Molly's
scream pierced the night.

2

Criminal Apprehension Unit (CAU)
Hoover Building
Washington, D.C.
Earlier on Thursday

Denny Roper from Security came into Savich's office and handed him a plain white legal-sized envelope. Savich studied the big black block-printed handwriting: DILLON SAVICH, CRIMINAL APPREHENSION UNIT, THIRD FLOOR. That was it. No address.

Roper said, "A visitor told Briggs at security check-in in the lobby that he noticed this envelope propped against the outside door on the Pennsylvania Avenue entrance. Briggs wanted me to look at it before it came to you, just in case.

"We put it through the X-ray, checked it out for biologics. There's nothing gnarly like anthrax on the envelope or on that one piece of paper—but it's curious, Savich. The person who sent it knows not only the name of your unit but your location—third floor."

Savich unfolded the single white sheet of paper. The same black block printing: FOR WHAT YOU DID YOU DESERVE THIS.

"I hope you've got some idea what that clown is talking about."

Savich said, "Not a clue. Tell me you have the visitor who handed over the envelope to Briggs."

"No, the guy walked away while Briggs was looking at the envelope. You know there are lots of tourists coming in this time of morning. Briggs called out, but the guy was gone, disappeared in the crowd. But we've got lots of good camera coverage of him, a close-up when he's speaking to Briggs. You think he was the one who wrote it?"

"Since it isn't possible to get into the

lobby without a thorough security check, why not do it this way? Hey, I found this envelope, not a clue what it is or who left it."

Roper said, "Would you like to have a look-see at this surveillance video?"

Savich nodded.

"Since he spoke to Briggs, we also have his voice on tape, nice and clear. He looked and acted like an ordinary guy, according to Briggs, but I wanted some of you experts to double-check it for us." Roper paused, looked up at all the faces focused on him and Savich, not more than two feet outside of Savich's office. "It looks like your people are already interested. I'll get things set up in the conference room," and Roper walked out, waving the disk at the agents as he passed them.

Savich read the note again:

FOR WHAT YOU DID YOU DESERVE THIS

He sat back in his chair, closed his eyes, and thought: *What* had he done? Exactly *what* did he deserve? It was clearly a threat, but from whom? It had been only two weeks since they'd brought down Ted Bundy's mad daughter, Kirsten Bolger. There was her mother, her stepfather, and her aunt Sentra to think about. Anyone else? Well, there was the family of her lover and partner Bruce Comafield, but both families were solidly middle-class, with a great deal to lose. When he'd met with them after Comafield's death and Kirsten's capture, they'd been in a state of shock. Sometimes shocks like that upended a person's whole world, but no, those folks just didn't seem likely.

Who else? Behind his closed eyes, Savich saw a kaleidoscope of tumbled vivid memories of blood and death and brutal faces, too much and too many. *We're a failed species,* he thought, not for the first time. He opened his eyes to see his wife, Sherlock, standing in front of him, her eyes on the open sheet of paper.

Sherlock said, "Denny's got the DVD ready, said we might all want to see it. What's going on? What's in that letter?"

"It's a weird threat. What I don't like is

that it was delivered personally. Come on, let's have a look at the guy who gave it to Briggs in the lobby."

He watched Sherlock shove a thick corking curl of hair behind her ear. He'd give it two seconds before another curl worked its way out of one of the clips and sprang forward. The clips never seemed to work very well. She said, "Everybody watched Denny come in and give you this envelope. Good thing you're involving all of us, or you'd be mobbed in here."

"That's what Roper seemed to think. It shouldn't take very long. We'll see if that brainpower can figure something out." She gave him a long assessing look, then turned and walked out of his office. He watched her walk in that no-nonsense stride, a traffic-stopper in those sexy black boots of hers. She was wearing her signature low-cut black pants and white blouse. He felt his heartbeat quicken. Could Sherlock be in danger because of something he'd done?

When Savich walked in with the envelope, Sherlock said, "Okay, Dillon, tell everyone what's in the letter before we watch the video."

Savich unfolded the single white sheet and said in an emotionless voice, *"For what you did you deserve this.* That's it, nothing else. Now, let's see what we've got, Denny."

There were nine agents, including Shirley, a gum-chewing grandmother and the unit secretary, with bright red hair this week, and one of the two unit clerks who would bet on anything with you and usually win. Denny Roper hit play and they all leaned forward to watch the sharp, high-res picture. Lots of tourists in the security line, all of them talking, dozens of conversations overlapping. The two security guards behind Plexiglas greeting and questioning everyone, handing out IDs, a smooth, practiced routine. Roper paused the DVD. "It's exactly nine-fifteen this morning. Here he comes."

A man—or a woman; it was hard to tell—came through the Pennsylvania Avenue entrance ahead of a dozen or so tourists. He stood in line, speaking to no one. When he reached the Plexiglas, he handed the envelope to Briggs. He was wearing loose jeans, an FBI hoodie pulled up over his head, and sunglasses, all of which would have had to come off if he went through security, which he'd had no intention of doing. He, or she?

Roper said, "I had them filter out everything but Briggs's voice and the man's. Listen again."

"What can I do for you, sir?"

"I found this envelope propped against the glass right outside. I brought it to you before it got trampled or tossed or whatever." A low voice, not particularly deep, but clear as a bell. A nice voice, really, calm, unhurried. And young.

Briggs accepted the envelope, studied it for a second, and the man blended into the group of tourists behind him. They saw him walk out the Pennsylvania Avenue exit and disappear. Roper said, "All slow and easy, not a care in the world. And that's it." Roper turned off the video.

Dane Carver said, "You've figured out his size?"

Roper said, "He's five-eight, weighs about one hundred thirty-five pounds. So what do you think?"

Ruth Warnecki Noble said, "I'd like to watch this a dozen more times, but first impression? He's slight for a guy, but I'd say he's male, twenty to twenty-five."

Dane said, "Or a pretty average female. But I agree, the walk makes you think man. But who knows? He never took off his hoodie and sunglasses."

Savich said, "We'll get the DVD to Operations Technology at Quantico. They'll enlarge, enhance, depixelate the face, do some reconstruction for us. The lab at Quantico can work on the audio recording."

There was a knock on the conference room door. It was an audio tech, Chuck Manson, who swore every single week he would have his name changed, but he never did. Savich suspected it was because he really enjoyed the attention. "Ninety-eight percent chance it's a man, and under thirty," Manson said, and disappeared.

"Okay, if Chuck says it's a guy, I'll take his word for it," Roper said. "I've asked for possible brands on the pants and hoodie, we'll see."

Lucy Carlyle said, "He has to look up when he speaks to Briggs, then his head goes down again. He knows he's on camera. It's a giveaway."

Savich's second-in-command, Ollie Hamish, said, "Denny, did you speak to the other security guard behind the Plexiglas? His name's Brady, right?"

Roper nodded. "Brady remembers the guy, what with the envelope delivery, but neither Brady nor Briggs can tell us much that's helpful."

"I'd like to speak to both Briggs and Brady myself later," Savich said as he stood.

Roper nodded. "I'll send both of them up."

Savich shook his head. "No, let me come down to the mezzanine to your turf."

Cooper McKnight sat forward. "Unless this guy's a loon, he's got to be from one of our cases. We could start with the most recent gnarly one—Bundy's daughter. Even though Comafield's close relatives seemed normal as apple pie, who knows? Maybe there's a nutso in there."

Roper looked at Savich. "I'll leave the video. Let me know when you want to speak to my people." He paused in the conference room doorway, a big man, built like a thick, knotted rope, Savich had always thought, and added, "I don't like this punk coming into our house like that. There are a lot of brains in this room, so take care of this for us."

Sherlock read the note again. *"For what you did you deserve this.* Something *you* did specifically, Dillon, so it's got to be a case you were personally involved with. There's Lissy Smiley, for example— that was up close and personal. But it could take weeks to make sure there's no one, absolutely no one, who would care enough about any of the dozens of perps we've brought down to do something this nuts."

Dane Carver said, "I wonder what the threat is, exactly? *For what you did you deserve this.* What is *this*? Is he targeting someone specific?"

All eyes turned to Sherlock.

Sherlock splayed her hands in front of her. "It doesn't have to be me. All right, all right, I'll be really careful. We've got the guy on camera, we'll get a good facial reconstruction. It's our best lead."

Savich saw everyone was looking at

him now. He tried to keep his face blank, but it was hard. He realized he was clutching his pen too tightly. It was Sherlock, he simply knew the threat was directed at Sherlock. Who else? He wanted to say something, but nothing came out. He couldn't stand himself. *Get it together.* He said, his voice sounding calm and in control, "If any of you come up with anything we haven't mentioned, let me know. I'm going down to the security section, speak to Briggs and Brady. Sherlock, you and Dane start work on this."

On the elevator ride to the mezzanine, Savich remembered the shoot-out in Mr. Patil's Shop 'n Go in Georgetown. Was it only three weeks ago? The woman he'd had to shoot, her name was Elsa Heinz. Who else knew Savich had shot her? Everyone, of course. It was in the papers, his name included. Was someone who knew her out for revenge against him? A loved one for a loved one?

He put her out of his head. Threats were part of the job. Both he and Sherlock knew that. They and the CAU would deal with it.

3

Georgetown
Washington, D.C.
Friday morning
Five a.m.

Sean leapt impossibly high, caught the football from his mother, and took off toward the end of a park that was really a baseball field, with Savich on his heels. Savich couldn't catch him because Sean's legs were stilt-long, eating up huge swathes of ground, and he was rounding bases for some reason, clutching the football tight to his chest, heading for home, and John Lennon was suddenly singing into Savich's left ear in his flat whiny-smooth voice about imagining people getting along, like that would ever happen.

Savich reared up in bed and automatically looked at the clock. *Five a.m. Not good. No telephone call was ever good at five a.m.*

He picked up his cell. "Savich."

"Dillon, you've got to come, quickly, it's bad, it's really bad, I'm afraid—" Molly Hunt's voice, choking and thick with tears and fear. Dillon thought, *Not little Emma, who'd survived so much—*

"I'm putting you on speakerphone so Sherlock can hear you. Tell us what's happened, Molly."

Sherlock was leaning up beside him, her face pale in the predawn, her hair tangled wildly around her face.

"Someone shot Ramsey in the back. I don't know if he's going to make it; he's in surgery. Everyone's here, but I need you and Sherlock. You've got to come and find out who did this to him. Please, please, come quickly."

Ramsey shot? Savich couldn't get his

brain around it. He hadn't seen Ramsey for six months, since he, Sherlock, and Sean last visited San Francisco. It had been more than five years, he realized now, since Ramsey had saved six-year-old Emma's life and hooked up with her mother, Molly.

Ramsey shot?

"Molly, take a deep breath. That's right. Now slow down and tell us exactly what happened." But he was thinking, *Why Ramsey? He's a federal judge, removed from that sort of violence—but a man who judged others was a man who gathered enemies.*

"He's in surgery," Molly said again. "The nurses say they don't know anything yet, but I know it can't be good. He was shot in the back—" she said, and broke off. He heard her breathing, harsh and fast, and then her voice, choked, frantic: "Please, Dillon, you and Sherlock, you've got to come."

Savich and Sherlock both asked questions and let her ramble, knowing she was trying to get it together. She told them Lieutenant Virginia Trolley was there with her, and they realized she was probably listening to their questions and Molly's answers. They'd met Virginia and her husband a couple of times when they'd visited San Francisco over the past five years.

"Molly, let me speak to Virginia." Virginia came on the line. "Dillon, the SFPD responded and arrived at Ramsey's house right after midnight. I arrived ten minutes later. Since it was dark, we didn't bother to look for footprints while I was there. No one wanted to mess up the crime scene bumbling around with flashlights."

"Have you spoken to Cheney?"

Virginia said, "Cheney arrived at Ramsey's house when I was leaving. He called me a couple minutes ago, told me he's assigned Special Agent Harry Christoff to lead the case, but he, Cheney, will be monitoring every detail. He wondered if shooting Ramsey was a revenge deal. It's too soon to know, but I'll tell you, it sure feels like it." Virginia's voice dropped lower. "Molly needs you guys. Can you come out here?"

"We'll be there as soon as we can."

When he punched off, he took Sherlock in his arms and held her close, stroking his hand up and down her back.

"He'll make it," Sherlock said against his neck. "Ramsey's got to make it. He's one of the good guys, Dillon. He will make it. How could this happen, and right on top of this threat to you?"

No, the threat's not aimed at me, it's aimed at you. Or Sean.

Cheney Stone called back as Savich was stepping out of the shower. He'd made it back to the hospital and learned that Ramsey had survived surgery and was in the surgical ICU. Molly, though, was a mess. "I asked the doc to give her Valium to calm her. You know what? He did. It seems to have helped her.

"Ah, here's Virginia. Let's go to speakerphone."

"Is Emma all right?" Savich asked.

Virginia said, "She was bordering on shock at first, with everything that was happening, but Emma's a tough little nut, she'll hold it together. When I was at the house I heard her tell her brother Cal she'd play him the theme from Harry Potter on the piano this morning—with variations—if he stopped shining a flashlight into Gage's eyes. Cal said he wanted to see if it would cause seizures." Virginia's voice hitched. "Where'd a three-year-old kid hear about lights and seizures?"

Savich said, "Don't ask. Our flight gets in this afternoon. You playing nice with Cheney? And Harry Christoff?"

"Oh, yeah, Cheney's a nice guy"—pause—"he'll throw us some crumbs, even though you FBI guys are going to have jurisdiction. All I hear about Christoff is that he came off an ugly divorce a year and a half ago, and he's been a nasty git ever since."

Savich heard Cheney say in the background, "Crumbs? You know what we know. Hey, and Harry's not a nasty git any longer, he's just nasty."

Virginia said, "And you, Mr. SAC? You're newly married. That means you're stupid happy all the time. Wait till you're married a few years, then I'll check back in with you. My guess is you'll still be stupid, but the happy part isn't a given."

Cheney said, "I'll be sure to pass that along to Julia."

Stupid happy? Savich liked the sound of that.

Savich said to Virginia, "Since you've known Ramsey for a long time, you know his habits, his friends. Cheney and Agent Christoff will see you as a valued resource."

Virginia gave a curiously charming snort. "Sure, like I'll expect to see that from any of his precious special agents." She sighed. "Every single cop in San Francisco wants to help get this crazy craphead, Dillon. You know Ramsey's a hero, even after five years, he's still Judge Dredd to all of us."

Savich remembered how Ramsey had been dubbed Judge Dredd by local and world media after he'd jumped down from the bench, black robes flying, and single-handedly took out the three gunmen who'd invaded his courtroom with guns and violence and death.

He said, "Keep repeating that to Cheney and Christoff."

"Just saying, Dillon. This is tough, really

tough. It's personal, not only for me but for most of the force."

"We'll get the crazy craphead together, then, Virginia," Sherlock said. "See you later today."

Ramsey, Savich thought, *who did you push over the edge?* And then he realized he and Sherlock would be three thousand miles away from the guy who'd written the letter to him. And they could take Sean with them, to stay at his grandparents'. That was a relief.

Cheney called again when they were on their way to Dulles. "Here's what I know so far. Ramsey postponed a hearing at a trial yesterday morning because he believed the federal prosecutor wasn't conducting the case properly, that he might have been threatened. He met with the federal marshal and the U.S. attorney, who are all in the same building with us, as you know.

"Now the prosecutor is a twelve-year veteran, Assistant U.S. Attorney Mickey O'Rourke. Ramsey had asked to speak to him in chambers, naturally, after he came to suspect Mickey might be purposefully jeopardizing the case. Mickey made an excuse. According to Olivia, Ramsey's secretary, Ramsey told O'Rourke he wanted him and his people at the meeting he was calling. Mickey didn't show, and none of his staff had any clue where he was. They hadn't seen him since Ramsey adjourned the hearing, and they were worried about him. His second chair said Mickey seemed off. But this? No one could believe it. In any case, we can't find O'Rourke. He's now officially missing. There's quite an uproar, as you can imagine."

"The name of the defendant?"

"There are two co-defendants, Clive and Cindy Cahill, up for the murder of a rich software geek here in Silicon Valley. Either the Cahills have lots of money stashed offshore or they have some rich friends, because they have hired a first-rate counsel."

But once the prosecutor was suspected, Savich thought, what would it matter which judge presided anymore? And O'Rourke's disappearance would mean only a delay. None of it made sense yet to Savich.

He asked, "Why are the Cahills a federal case?"

Cheney said, "Because there's espionage involved, that's why. The murder victim, Mark Lindy, was working on a top-secret project for the government, and was probably murdered because of it. That's why the FBI handled the case and not local law enforcement. We've got the Cahills pretty cold on the murder, but we could never find out the particulars of the project Lindy was into, because it involved national security. You know the CIA—they refused to tell us anything at all, even with CIA operations officers out here digging around.

"Even if a foreign government did set the Cahills on Mark Lindy, I don't know which one. I'll be speaking to O'Rourke's team again while you're in the air, see exactly what they have, if anything, that might help us find him."

"All right, Cheney, see you this afternoon," Savich said. He and his laptop MAX had a lot of reading to do about the Cahills on their way to California.

And flying with Sean was always a treat.

4

Before they left for the coast on the 8:19 a.m. United flight out of Dulles, Sherlock called her parents in San Francisco. "Lacey, you're flying into a real mess here," her father, Judge Corman Sherlock, said. "Ramsey's shooting is all over local TV, and everyone is out for blood. What with his martial arts heroics in his own courtroom five years ago, you'd think most of the media around here would imply he's unevolved and uncivilized. Go figure.

"There's lots of speculation, as you'd

expect, but no one knows a thing yet, and the FBI hasn't said a word.

"The police commissioner's got a press conference scheduled at noon. We'll see if she's going to try to squeeze the SFPD into bed with the FBI. It would be a good career move.

"I saw Ramsey yesterday. He was on his way out to meet his family to go listen to Emma practice with the symphony at Davies Hall." He paused. "I told him I'd heard he'd postponed the murder trial, but he didn't tell me anything, only shook his head, said it was too sensitive and too soon to talk about.

"We're looking forward to seeing all of you. Your mother and I will get to take good care of Sean, of course, while the two of you are out finding the people responsible. I know you'll nail whoever did this."

From Dad's mouth to God's ears, Sherlock thought.

"This is an awful thing, Lacey, an awful thing. I'm wondering if it has anything to do with the trial he postponed. Do you think that's possible?"

By the end of the very long flight, Sherlock and Savich agreed they would rather eat week-old frozen artichoke dip than compete against Sean in another computer-based adventure of *Atoc the Incan Wizard*, a young Incan boy who used numbers, magic, and nerve to unravel the knottiest arithmetic problems and bring down an endless number of villains. Sherlock called Atoc the Harry Potter of Machu Picchu. During most of the flight, she played with Sean while Dillon read files on MAX and Skyped Cheney, working out what the Criminal Apprehension Unit could do. Cheney said, "It would help us for MAX to work on trying to locate any offshore stash the Cahills might have, and what talent they could have called in on short notice. We've had no luck as of yet."

"Eggs all in the Cahill basket, Cheney?"

"No, but it makes more sense than some sort of foreign government conspiracy to shoot Ramsey. I mean, if a foreign government was paying the Cahills for Mark Lindy's top-secret materials, and they threatened to talk if they weren't somehow found innocent, said govern-

ment would more likely have them elimi-
nated, not a federal judge or a federal
prosecutor. There could be too much hell
to pay for that."

Savich said, "The Cahills are the obvious suspects, but what would it gain
them to kill Judge Hunt?"

"Maybe they were afraid O'Rourke had
already told Ramsey too much," Cheney
said. "But you're right. We're being thorough. We're looking at mail threats to
Judge Hunt, letters and emails going
back three years, and we've started a re-
view of his cases going back even further. I'm making sure the SFPD is in the
loop, passing along some assignments
to them. We can use the manpower." He
sighed, then added, "There are already
endless complications, since Ramsey isn't
an anonymous federal judge like most
of his confederates. Nope, he's Judge
Dredd, superhero. The mayor, the police
commissioner, the major news outlets,
even the conductor for the San Francisco
Symphony have called me, wanting to
know what progress we've made. The
police commissioner is pushing for a task
force, composed of the SFPD, the FBI,

and the federal marshals, with the commissioner herself in charge. As if that's going to happen. I'm already getting an ulcer."

Savich asked, "Any progress on the missing federal prosecutor yet? Mickey O'Rourke?"

The answer was no.

When Savich ended the call, Sherlock said, "A federal prosecutor missing—it sounds like a spy novel. I'm very grateful my father wasn't the one judging the Cahill case."

"Mama, you weren't paying attention. I got you!"

Savich smiled, listening to Sherlock wail. "Oh, dear, Sean, how am I going to save myself this time? Atoc's shoved me in a pit of purple-headed Amazonian hippo snakes. Ah, here's what I'll do," and Sherlock walloped one of the writhing hippo snakes with a canoe paddle. Since she was the master Incan mathematician, Professor Pahuac, and rotten to the bone, she knew her end probably wouldn't be a good one.

5

San Francisco
Friday, early afternoon

Lieutenant Vincent Delion of the SFPD,
and a longtime friend, met them at airport
baggage claim. He told them he'd talked
Cheney into letting him come get them.
He told them the San Francisco Feds
didn't know squat yet, and neither did the
SFPD, and he told them about the task
force Police Commissioner Montoya announced she'd like to form, just a couple
of hours ago—with the FBI's assistance,

of course. He tossed Savich a copy of the *Chronicle*. "Read this." Savich and Sherlock looked at the big block headline: JUDGE DREDD SHOT.

Delion soon pulled his Crown Vic into the heavy 101 traffic north to the city. "At least Ramsey is holding on. None of us wanted a murder case, particularly not his. I can't imagine what would happen to Emma, Molly, and the twins if he died." There was a punch of hard silence, then, "No, they won't lose him, they can't."

Delion shook his head, lightly stroked big fingers over his pride and joy. He smiled, remembering Sean Savich telling him in grave confidence at the baggage carousel, "I think your mustache is shinier than Hercule Poirot's."

Delion told Sean he was a fine judge of mustachios and that his was particularly shiny this morning in honor of meeting the bigwigs from Washington, D.C., their kiddo included.

Delion plowed his hand through his hair. "I'm hoping Ramsey will be ready to speak to us soon at the hospital."

Sherlock said, "How's Molly?"

"She's trying to show she's solid for the kids' sake." He paused for a moment, then added, "After what happened to Emma years ago, they all try to watch out for each other."

"Is Uncle Ramsey all right, Mama?"

They'd told Sean they were coming to San Francisco because Ramsey had been hurt, nothing more. "He will be all right, Sean. He's injured, but he's going to start getting better now." *Please, God, please, God.*

"Is Emma okay?"

"She's fine, Sean. She's watching Cal and Gage."

"No wonder," her five-year-old said. "Cal and Gage are babies. They need all the watching they can get. I'll help her."

Sherlock said to Delion, "When we flew out here for Memorial Day weekend six months ago, Sean spent three hours with Emma and the boys, and announced to us he was going to marry Emma and help her teach Cal and Gage about life. I asked him about Marty Perry, his girlfriend next door, and the love of his life. I also asked him about Bowie Richards's daughter, Georgie, also the love of his life, up in

Connecticut. Sean just smiled, didn't you, kiddo?"

Delion said to Sean, "I agree with you, Sean, Emma's a champ. As for Marty and Georgie, they sound pretty cool, too. Hey, kid, the older you get the more you look like your old man."

Sean considered that. "Mama says I'm more handsome than Papa, since I have her smile. She says that makes all the difference."

Delion laughed.

"Handsome is as handsome does," Savich said, and Sherlock saw Sean repeating his father's words to himself. She rolled her eyes. She leaned over and ruffled Sean's thick black hair.

Sean said, sounding a bit worried, "I hope Emma didn't forget she's engaged to me."

"Not a chance," Savich said. "Do you think your mama could have ever forgotten she was engaged to me?"

"Not a chance," Sean said.

When they passed by Candlestick Park, Sean said, "That's where Dwight Clark made *The Catch* way back in the old days, right, Papa?"

Savich grinned. "It sure is."

Sherlock said to Delion, "Can you believe he remembers that?"

Delion said, "Yeah, well, his hard drive works better because it isn't as full as ours."

All the adults realized any more discussion about Ramsey's shooting had to wait. Delion was talking about the upcoming 49ers-Seahawks game when Sean said, "Marty asked me when I was going to have a sister because she's going to have a new brother in March."

Now, that was a conversation starter.

6

San Francisco General Hospital
Surgical ICU
Friday afternoon

Savich didn't want to count all the lines that tethered Ramsey Hunt to life. There were IV lines in his neck, and an oxygen mask on his face. Savich recognized a kind of suction device connected to the end of the tube coming from Ramsey's chest, a Pleurovac, they called it. Ramsey lay on his back, still and pale, his immense life force badly faded. At least it wasn't extinguished. A light sheet was pulled to his chest, not quite covering his wide white surgical bandages. He was breathing lightly and steadily, a relief, but his eyelids looked bruised, perhaps from when he'd fallen. Savich hated it.

The SFPD guard outside the cubicle had given them the stink eye before Lieutenant Trolley introduced them to Officer Jay Mancusso of the SFPD. Since only two visitors could go into the small cubicle at a time, Savich went in first to stand beside Molly. She didn't look away from Ramsey, merely took Savich's hand in hers and squeezed hard. "Thank you for coming so quickly. The Valium Cheney suggested the doctor give me—it's magic stuff. It's helped unparalyze my brain. I'm sorry I lost it when I called you."

"Don't worry about it," Savich said. "Ramsey's breathing is solid and easy, Molly; that's a good sign."

Ramsey had told him once that Molly's hair was as vibrant a red as a sunset off the Cliffs of Moher in Ireland, and Ramsey was right. You'd think Ramsey was describing Sherlock's hair, but it wasn't the same color at all.

She turned into him, and he closed his

arms around her. She felt fragile. It was odd, he thought, but Molly's hair didn't feel the same as Sherlock's hair, and didn't smell like her hair, either—it was jasmine he was smelling, jasmine mixed with lemon, not the faint rose scent of Sherlock's. "He'll make it, Molly," he said against her hair. "He'll make it. He's strong and determined, and he wants to stay here with us."

She pulled back in his arms and smiled up at him. "I think he will, too. But I'm so scared, Dillon. What if—"

"No what-ifs. Has he been awake at all?"

"In and out, mumbling words I can't understand for the most part, then saying Emma's name over and over. I think he's remembering back to the time he found her unconscious in the forest near his cabin."

"Has Cheney come in yet?"

"Yes, we spoke briefly. I told him what I could, which wasn't much of anything at all, and he said he'd see me later today after Ramsey was awake and the doctors were satisfied he was going to be okay. I think he wanted to give me more time to consider who and why, but I can't think of a single person who would want to kill him. Cheney told me about the Cahills and how Ramsey had postponed the trial and how that federal prosecutor was missing. Ramsey hadn't said a word to me, but in all honesty, there wasn't time." She walked away from him, then turned, her hands fisted at her sides. "No, there was time, but damn him, he's always trying to protect me. He knew something hinky was going on, and he kept it to himself. I will have to seriously consider hurting him for that."

She picked up Ramsey's limp hand. "He's so strong," she said, more to herself than to him, "so tough, always a rock, you know?" A beautiful man, she'd always thought, with his dark hair and brilliant dark eyes, and his laugh, his seductive laugh. "Can you believe we've been married for five years? Goodness, Emma's eleven and the boys are three. The boys are scared, Dillon, they don't understand." Her voice hitched, then smoothed out again. "Emma's taking care of them. She's more their second mother than their older sister. The babysitter, Mrs. Hicks, is with them, too." She raised wet eyes to Savich's face. "They won't let the boys come see him, Dillon, and that only makes them more scared."

Ramsey moaned deep in his throat.

She leaned over him, lightly kissed his cheek. "Ramsey? You have a visitor. Come, wake up now."

His eyes opened slowly, blind and empty of knowledge, but they cleared slowly and focused. Savich leaned close. "I'd rather we were fishing in Lake Tahoe and I was catching that four-pound trout and you weren't."

An attempt at a smile, but he didn't quite make it. "I don't remember it just like that."

"Okay, I'll give you the trout since you were the one who fried the sucker. It's nice to have you here with us, either way."

Ramsey whispered, "Molly?"

"I'm here," she said, squeezing his hand.

Ramsey looked back at Dillon, and now his voice was stronger, some of the familiar steel sounding through. "I remember now, someone shot me."

Molly said, "You were turning when I

called out to you and someone shot you in the back."

"I went down like a rock, lights out," he said. He looked thoughtful. "I was shot once before in the leg—and, you know, wherever you're shot, it doesn't feel too good." He closed his eyes against a vicious lick of pain. "My chest feels like it's been flattened by an eighteen-wheeler."

Savich put the morphine plunger in his hand. "Squeeze this, it's your PLA, and it'll cut the pain."

Ramsey had never seen one before. He closed his eyes in gratitude and pressed the button. They both waited silently until he said, "That's better already. I can control this if I don't move too much."

Savich said, "I'm glad you turned when you did. Do you know what direction the shot came from?"

Ramsey looked blank. "The direction? I suppose it had to be from the ocean. Someone in a boat? It's hard to imagine someone firing at me from a boat, what with all the motion from the waves. That would take a professional, and still I can't imagine it'd be a sure thing."

Savich said, "Did you see a boat?"

Ramsey looked perfectly blank, not totally with them, and then pain hit him again, and he went stone silent.

Savich said, "You feel a little muddled, Ramsey, don't worry about it. The important thing is you're alive, and you're going to get better every day."

"The Cahills?"

"It's possible. We're checking."

"I don't know why, Savich. Do you?"

"We don't know yet, either."

"Have they found the prosecutor, Mickey O'Rourke?"

"Not yet."

Molly lightly shoved Savich away when Ramsey's eyes closed. She whispered next to his cheek, "I want you to think about healing yourself, Ramsey. Think about tossing me and Emma around on the mat—you need to get better to do that. And you need a shave."

He managed a rictus of a grin.

ICU nurse Janine Holder said from the doorway, "I like the dark whiskers. They make him look tough and dangerous. Dr. Kardak is here to see you, Judge Hunt."

Savich introduced himself, stepped

back to let Dr. Kardak examine Ramsey. He was an older man, tall and thin as a whip handle, and he looked tired, like he'd gone ten rounds with death and just barely won.

When Dr. Kardak noticed Ramsey's eyes on him, he said, "Ah, Judge Hunt, you're awake and with us, excellent. My trauma team and I operated on you last night, and I've come to check how you're doing." Without waiting for an answer, he started to examine the IV lines and the fluid in contraptions Ramsey was tied to. All the while, he kept up a running monologue about what they had found at surgery, the broken ribs, the torn lung, the blood in the chest cavity, as if it were all business as usual and nothing to be worried about. When he at last listened to Ramsey's chest and examined his dressings, he said, "You sound good, Judge Hunt. I'm hopeful your lung will stay fully expanded and that we can pull out the chest tube this weekend. You need it for now, but I know it can hurt like the dickens."

When Dr. Kardak straightened, Savich

asked him, "How close a thing was it, doctor?"

Dr. Kardak said, "Tough to say, but he got to us—a level-one trauma center—in what we call the golden hour." He touched long, thin fingers to Ramsey's pulse. "Your major risk was blood loss, Judge Hunt, and that's behind you. You're going to live. That's not to say you're going to be happy for a while, but it beats the alternative."

"Amen," Ramsey said. "Thank you."

"Make full use of the morphine. We can give you something else if it doesn't hold you."

Ramsey pressed the button again. "Now that I know about this magic button, I'm thinking I'll empty it pretty fast."

Dr. Kardak said, "Not a problem. Three of us worked on you in the OR, Judge Hunt. Dr. Janes kept reminding us you were Judge Dredd and we'd be tarred and feathered and ridden out of town if you went down on our watch." He gave Ramsey a fat smile, then turned to Molly and took her hands in his. "Your husband is strong and healthy, and, trust me, the team here is excellent. Try not to worry. Oh, yes, I forgot to tell you. I heard your daughter play Bach's *Italian Concerto* at the children's concert with the symphony two years ago. My wife still remembers how well she played it. In fact, I remember she wept when Emma played the second movement. I read she'll be playing Gershwin with the symphony in early December. Congratulations. She is incredible. Now, Agent Savich, Judge Hunt should rest."

Ramsey said, his voice low, a bit slurred, "Special Agent Dillon Savich is a longtime friend of ours. He knows all about gunshot wounds, and he's here to help."

"Is that so?" Dr. Kardak shook Savich's hand again, even though he'd already met him. He said, "I met your wife in the hall. Hard to believe two FBI agents married, as in to each other. How does that work?"

"I'm her boss. It's up to me to make it work."

"And how do you do that? Men everywhere would like to know."

"I tell her to suck it up when she disagrees with me."

This brought a laugh and a "Good luck with that" from Dr. Kardak. He said, "I'll be in the hospital all day if you have any questions or concerns."

Molly grabbed his sleeve. "Why is that? You said Ramsey would be all right."

"Yes, I did. I mentioned my being here, close by, only to help you feel confident and supported. It will be just me you need to ask for, no residents or medical students. Judge Hunt, if you want to sleep, simply close your eyes and everyone will go away."

Dr. Kardak was a very nice man, Savich thought. "Molly, do you think you and Sherlock could trade off for a while?"

Molly didn't want to leave, it was plain to see, but she did after kissing Ramsey and promising to bring him a pint of his favorite pistachio ice cream.

7

San Francisco General Hospital
Friday afternoon

U.S. Federal Deputy Marshal Eve Barbieri leaned against the hallway wall, outside the SICU, her knee bent and her
arms crossed over her chest, waiting for
her turn to see Judge Hunt. His surgeon,
Dr. Kardak, had told everyone Judge Hunt
was doing fine, but she still wasn't over
the soul-wrenching fear she'd felt when
she'd been called at four a.m. to be told
Judge Hunt had been shot. *Would he
live?* Her boss, Carney Maynard, didn't

know, but Hunt had survived surgery and he had a chance, he told her matter-of-factly, because Judge Hunt was made of pure titanium. *Thank all the powers that be, and thank Dr. Kardak's team.*

Maynard had told her the SFPD would be part of the protection detail along with the U.S. Marshals Service while Judge Hunt was in the hospital, but she was to stay close, as any questions about coverage or assignments would be directed to her. When Judge Hunt was discharged, she would be officially responsible for his and his family's protection. She looked through the windowed door of the SICU at Officer Jay Mancusso of the SFPD, seated by Judge Hunt's cubicle, and watched him study every face that came near. He looked angry, like most other cops she'd met since Judge Hunt had been shot. She wondered if every single law enforcement agency in the city would try to be involved in hunting down the man—or woman—who'd tried to kill him. Judge Hunt was a big deal, an American hero. She closed her eyes for a moment, thankful Ramsey would live and thankful for how well she had gotten to know him and his family over the years. When he was shot, she'd promised a real biggie if he would live—to be pleasant to her ex-mother-in-law if ever she saw her again, something she hoped would never happen. Eve and her ex-mother-in-law's son, Ryan, had been married for about half an hour before Eve booted him out. She could still hear the woman's outraged voice: *A good woman would forgive her husband his small transgressions.*

As she waited, she asked herself again for at least the twelfth time—had the Cahills hired the shooter? If so, it meant their defense attorney, Milo Siles, had to be in on it. How else could the Cahills have gotten hold of the talent and money so fast? She'd met the prosecutor, Mickey O'Rourke, several times, on the volleyball court. She remembered his laugh when his team had won—a really big laugh. He didn't laugh in the courtroom, though, he was all business, a veteran who wielded a bullwhip. He had a good conviction rate. But none of that mattered now. He was missing, simply gone, no word, no emails, no nothing. She sighed, wishing just this once she was FBI and had the assignment to lead this case.

She pushed off the wall and began to pace, aware that Mancusso was watching her through the window. She wanted to see Ramsey, see for herself he was breathing, that his excellent brain was working behind his smart dark eyes, but it was one cop after the other trooping in. Lieutenant Virginia Trolley, SFPD, was in and out because she was also a trusted family friend. Eve knew it made Molly feel better to have Virginia close, another trained body to protect Ramsey. And those two FBI agents from Washington had been in, Savich and Sherlock were their names, a husband and wife, and wasn't that a kick?

Eve looked up to see two men approaching—yeah, they were definitely Feds; you couldn't mistake their private club dress code—dark suits, white shirts, usually dark ties. They were striding toward her, self-assured and arrogant as toreadors entering the ring. She recognized both, of course; she'd been introduced to the new SAC, Cheney Stone, but not the other agent. She'd seen the other one driving out of the parking garage a couple of times, but that was it.

She moved to stand against the wall again, waiting, all indolent and loose-limbed. Let them come to her. She whistled between her teeth. She wondered who'd cornered the market on the federal wingtips.

She heard the agent walking beside Cheney Stone say, "That picture we found in the bushes, the newspaper clipping of Judge Dredd with an X through his face— it's like he's sticking it in our faces and laughing."

Hmmm, there was a clipping of Ramsey left at the crime scene? It was the first she'd heard of it. Not that she expected to know much about what the FBI had found, since she'd never even been inside the locked door on the thirteenth floor in the Federal Building. No, that space was inhabited only by the San Francisco FBI tribe. The U.S. Marshals Service occupied the twentieth floor, their digs only one floor above the senior federal judges' offices and courtrooms. She didn't care much for that FBI attitude, one of the reasons she hadn't considered signing on with them six years before. She'd heard too many stories about some of the special agents—and wasn't that a self-important title? For the most part, the FBI got results, but too often, it was their way or why don't you take a leap from the Golden Gate Bridge? Were they prepared to deal with her, or would they try to plant their big Fed feet on some part of her anatomy? She'd see. She'd go around them, or through them, if necessary.

Cheney Stone stopped. "And here's Deputy Marshal Eve Barbieri."

He remembered her name, and that was a surprise. Eve shook hands with Stone. "Congratulations on becoming special agent in charge, Agent Stone."

Cheney gave her a grin. "Thanks. It's already been two months and I'm still alive and breathing, for the most part. But my once predictable life now consists of herding pit bulls."

Eve could only agree, her opinion clear on her face even though she kept her mouth shut.

"Since we'll be working together on Judge Hunt's shooting, call me Cheney."

First name? Nice smile, white teeth, seeming sincerity, but with a new SAC, it was wise to be cautious. She nodded, too soon to offer up her own first name.

Cheney said, "Eve Barbieri, this is Agent Harry Christoff. Harry, this is Deputy Marshal Eve Barbieri. She's worked with Judge Hunt for three years and is a friend of the family."

8

Eve took a good look at Special Agent Harry Christoff. He was in his early thirties, tall and lean, with dark brown hair and bright green eyes. He kept himself in very fine shape indeed. Although he was dressed in the obligatory dark suit and white shirt, he wasn't wearing wingtips. Instead he wore black boots that looked as old as he did, but the ancient boots sported a high shine. As for his tie, it was bright yellow with black squiggles. A rebel? She didn't think such an animal existed in the Big Machine.

So the new SAC was trying to herd

Christoff—good luck. She'd heard of him before, most had. He was known as a loose cannon, and that sparked her interest. He looked as mean as any of the other pit bulls, like he could kick the crap out of you while chowing a pepperoni pizza and washing it down with a Bud. But he had to have something going for him in the brain department, since SAC Cheney Stone had assigned him to this case.

"I know you by rep," Eve said. "They say you're a wild hair."

"Good to know," Harry said, and stuck out his hand. Eve shook his hand, strong, with tanned, long fingers.

Cheney continued to Eve, "You guys are fast. We've already started looking at those boxes of threatening letters to Judge Hunt you sent over."

She nodded, but she was still distracted studying Christoff, still evaluating—was he smart? Intuitive? Did this particular pit bull have any common sense? Did he have nerve?

She realized, of course, that Agent Harry Christoff was looking her over as well. "Ever have any problems before?" Christoff asked her.

Eve shook her head.

"Looks like the first time a problem cropped up, none of you were around."

Nice shot. She said on a yawn, "Guess I was out drinking grappa in North Beach, not camping out in Judge Hunt's back-yard, stroking my Glock."

Not bad. Harry eyed her. She hadn't taken the bait, hadn't tried to belt him. He liked attitude, wanted to grin at her amused in-your-face, "you're not worth my time, Agent Moron" look. He'd seen Barbieri before and thought she was a real looker, but he'd never seen her up close. The close-up reality surprised him. With her long legs in black pants and her black boots that put her close to six feet tall, she nearly reached his eyebrows. They were really shiny black boots, too, maybe shinier than his. Nah, probably not. She wore a raw-looking red leather jacket over a black turtleneck, topping off the tough U.S. marshal look.

But her face spoiled the effect. Despite the outfit, she looked like she should be serving ice cream and cake to kids at a birthday party, smiling and tending them, her blond ponytail bouncing. She was real pretty and sweet-looking and— wholesome was the word, like some former Ohio State cheerleader, like the girl next door voted beauty queen at the state fair. Until you looked at her eyes, dark blue stormy eyes that weren't at all trusting, and the U.S. marshal showed through again. They were eyes that had seen a lot, though the good Lord knew she couldn't have seen more than he had in his eight years with the Bureau.

Harry stuck out his hand, wondering if she'd bite it, but she shook his hand, hers cool and dry, all business.

"Why are you grinning?"

"I was wondering if you would bite my hand."

She arched a dark blond eyebrow. "Only if you try to feed me."

Harry said, "So you think I'm a wild hair, do you? There's a story around about you, too, Barbieri. Something about a fugitive in a shopping mall in Omaha last year who tried to take a hostage in a Macy's women's room? And you ended up sticking the woman's head in the john and not letting her up until she dropped her gun?" He grinned at the visual. "Talk about the pot and the kettle."

Cheney laughed, couldn't help it, watching the two of them. If they could manage to avoid bloodshed, they might work well together. Barbieri could stand up to anybody, and as for Harry, well, despite his reputation, he had gotten some remarkable results, and that's why Cheney wanted him on Judge Hunt's shooting.

Cheney said to Eve, "Your boss told me you'll be heading up Judge Hunt's protection team."

Eve nodded.

"Good. The media is gathered in the lobby. I don't doubt they'll try to sneak up."

"We've got that covered," Eve said. "Just look at Mancusso's face—show him a lurking reporter and he'll stuff him into one of the laundry carts."

"We've also had Agent Dillon Savich, chief of the CAU back at the Hoover Building—that's the Criminal Apprehension Unit—and his wife, Agent Sherlock, fly out to help us with the case. You'll be working with them as well."

"Yes, I know," she said. "I saw you with them earlier." Eve had watched Cheney hug the woman with the rioting red hair and shake the big man's hand, all chatty and full of bonhomie, best buds.

Great, Harry thought, he'd be working with Savich and Sherlock from Disneyland East, too, as if there weren't already enough noses eager to poke under the tent.

Cheney said, "Harry, do you think you can manage to work with Barbieri? Work *with* her, not make her want to knock your teeth down your throat? Given it's Barbieri we're talking about here, she probably wouldn't hesitate."

"You're recommending caution around Suzie Cheerleader? Not a problem. She's only heading up the protection detail, so that's not a lot of work we'll need to do together."

Suzie Cheerleader? Eve gave him the fish eye. "I'll get the job done, whether you work with me or not," and she shrugged as an eyebrow went up. "The question is, will you, Christoff?"

"In the FBI, we have cases, not jobs."

He held up his hand and said to Cheney, "Like I said, there's no problem here. I can work with anybody, even cute little cheerleader types."

Cheney eyed them both, wondering if he was making a mistake. No, but he'd talk to Harry again privately, and ask Marshal Carney Maynard to make sure Eve Barbieri would work with Harry, not go haring off on her own. He had to admit there'd been a time or two when he'd wanted to rip Harry's face off himself. He said, "Deputy Barbieri, Harry will be point man on this. Your boss has asked that you assist him, as time allows. No hotdogging from either of you, especially you, Christoff, all right?"

Harry said, "Me, hotdog? Not a single lick of yellow mustard on me."

Eve took one last look at Harry, gave a little finger wave to Cheney, and turned away down the hall.

Cheney said, "I'm serious about this, Harry. Not only does she know Judge Hunt, she knows about most everything that goes on inside and outside the courtroom. You want to use her."

Harry nodded. "Sure, but bottom line, she's just the protection." He gave his boss a maniacal grin and strode off. "Hey, Barbieri, wait up! You and I got stuff to work out here."

9

San Francisco General Hospital
Friday afternoon

The first thing Eve heard when she slipped into Ramsey's cubicle was the sound of machines, some beeping, some humming. Then she saw all the lines running into and out of his body. She couldn't imagine trying to rest like that. She saw Molly standing over Ramsey, her head lowered, speaking to him quietly. She looked up when Eve came in.

"Eve, it's good to see you. Do come in. Ramsey, it's Eve."

Thank the good Lord he was awake. Eve nodded to Molly, leaned over Ramsey, and felt her throat clog. Not a single word could get through without risking tears. She stared down at him, taking everything in.

Ramsey saw her fear, and he wanted to reassure her, at least smile at her, but it was hard to make his mouth muscles work. He felt oddly detached from his own body. He thought it was all the drugs that were making it hard to focus his mind on anything. But there was no pain, and that was a profound blessing, thanks to the magic morphine pump. He felt her clasp his hand and squeeze, felt her warm breath, like lemons, he thought, when she leaned close. "You're looking good, Ramsey. I gotta say I'm really happy about that."

For a moment, he couldn't find words. Where were the words? "So are you, Eve. Don't worry, I'm going to pull through, Molly told me so. And don't cry. I don't want to walk into the men's room and read 'Barbieri's a weeping wuss' scratched on the wall. What would that do to your reputation?"

She started to say she never cried, but that lie would perch right on the end of her nose. His voice was thin, insubstantial, and that scared the bejesus out of her. The last thing he needed was for her to fall apart. "We got a regular hoedown outside, FBI everywhere. They're all huddled together, so I slipped in to see you."

"I'm glad you did."

"I can't imagine why anyone would want to shoot you, of all people."

Ramsey frowned. Eve squeezed his hand again. "I know, why shoot the judge?"

"Can you tell me what happened, Ramsey?"

Surely he could try to do that again for Eve before his lights went out. "It was late, nearly midnight. I was out back, staring up at the stars and over at the Marin Headlands, and I was remembering Cal asking if he could sink his fingers into those pits on the surface of the moon."

Was it her imagination or did he sound stronger? Pits in the moon? This hard-as-nails federal judge was wondering about the pits on the moon?

"I didn't hear a thing out of the ordinary, nor did I see anything or anyone.

One shot and I was down and out." He paused, and the pain suddenly surfaced. He jerked, gritted his teeth, but it didn't lessen, it was pulling him down. He pressed the morphine button.

Molly said, "If I hadn't called out to him, Eve, he wouldn't have turned and moved, and the bullet would have hit him in his chest." Saying the words broke the dam. Molly burst into tears.

Ramsey said, "No, sweetheart, I'll be okay. No need to cry." He hated to see her cry, but there was nothing he could do, only lie there helpless, wanting to howl. "Eve—I remember now. There was a boat. A Zodiac, pulled up near the beach. I saw it."

Eve's heart speeded up. A Zodiac— now they had a place to start. She saw his eyes were squeezed tightly shut, his mouth in a thin seam. "Just a moment," he said, and she watched him press the button again. But she couldn't stand it. She went to get the nurse, but when she came back he was out again.

Molly was huddled over him, her shoulders shaking. It nearly broke Eve's heart.

10

Sea Cliff
San Francisco
Late Friday afternoon

Emma Hunt pushed back her piano bench and rose. She couldn't concentrate on Gershwin's *Rhapsody in Blue*, though she loved the sheer romantic exuberance of it, how the music built and built until its grandeur, its firecracker opulence, made her fingers tingle and her heart beat faster. But not today. Emma sighed. Ever since her dad was shot the night before, she'd felt deadening fear.

She heard Cal and Gage squabbling in the next room, speaking their twin talk, taking pleasure in knowing their mother had no clue what they were saying. Neither did she, but the two of them understood each other perfectly. Did they realize no one else could understand them? Oh, yes, she'd bet a week's allowance on it.

"Emma?"

She turned to see her mother standing in the doorway, holding Cal and Gage's hands. Both of them looked grubby from playing underneath the big oak tree outside the music room door. Her mother looked frazzled, but she was trying to pretend she was fine.

Emma smiled, though it wasn't easy. Her brothers didn't need to see that she was afraid—no, not just afraid, she was terrified—their father would die. "Mama, do you need me to do something with the boys?"

"No, sweetie, I'm going to clean them up myself. I wanted to tell you the Gershwin sounded wonderful. Do you know I listened to Gershwin himself playing *Rhapsody in Blue* on iTunes and sometimes you sound just like him? Maybe better."

Emma rolled her eyes. "You're my mother. Of course you'd say that. You know I'm not as good as Gershwin. Mrs. Mayhew says he was brilliant."

Molly said, "Ellie will be here soon to watch the boys so you and I can go back to the hospital." She glanced at her watch. Emma knew her mother hadn't wanted to leave her dad at all, that she'd rather have stayed beside his bed, holding his hand, telling him he would be all right. But it was better for the twins that she came home to see them. The hospital staff always patted Emma's head, her shoulder, telling her every other minute that her father would recover. She was grateful everyone cared so much. She closed her eyes for a moment. Her father's stillness scared her the most. He was never still, always in motion, laughing or using his hands when he talked. She always clutched her mother's hand when they were with him.

Cal and Gage pulled away from their mother and ran to the corner of the music room, where they had stacked piano music into two equal piles, one for each of them. What on earth did they plan to do with those piles? They knew better than to tear the pages; she'd yelled at them too much about that over the past year. The boys were arguing now, and about what? Emma said, "I wonder when they'll start speaking English to each other?"

Molly smiled. "They already say your name and *Mama* and *Papa* to each other."

"And ice cream."

That got a small smile. "And ice cream. Don't worry about the Gershwin, you're ready to play for the audience and the orchestra. You know they love listening to you. The concertmaster, Mr. Williams, told me you were a miracle. Naturally, I agreed."

"That's because Mr. Williams doesn't have perfect pitch and he wishes he had mine," Emma said matter-of-factly. "I sure hope Giovanni will like my *Rhapsody in Blue.*"

"Of course he will. Emma, I really don't think you should be calling the conductor of the San Francisco Symphony Orches-tra by his first name. Maybe best to call him Mr. Rossini. You're eleven. You want to show him respect."

Emma was silent for a moment, a frown between her eyebrows, identical to her mother's. "I know I'm only a kid, but he asked me to call him Giovanni. He said he'd like me to go to Milan to study with Pietro Bianci." She said the name slowly, careful to get the pronunciation right.

Molly went on alert. "When did this happen?"

"Yesterday at Davies Hall, while you and Dad were trying to get Cal and Gage to behave—before Dad—" Emma swallowed. "He doesn't think Mrs. Mayhew is the right teacher for me anymore."

Molly, momentarily distracted, said, "Not only does Mrs. Mayhew know every single serious piece of music for the piano in the universe, she's played most of them, including Gershwin, both in Paris and London."

"Mrs. Mayhew is very old, Mama; that's what Giovanni—Mr. Rossini—said. He told me her teaching isn't what it used to be."

Emma's eighty-two-year-old piano

teacher had elegance, style, and immense talent and goodwill. She had
known George Gershwin. Who cared if
she didn't play as well as she did fifty
years ago? As for Emma going to Italy to
study at her age? Not a chance. She
wanted to tell Emma she wasn't about to
let her out of her sight until she was
twenty-one, maybe even thirty-five, not
after what had happened five years ago,
but the words fell out of her head. She
swallowed. She would have a talk with
Mr. Rossini, but even that didn't seem
important now. Ramsey was fastened to
more high-tech machines than she'd ever
seen in one place. He could still die. Tears
gushed up into her throat, and she had to
swallow to keep them down.

But Emma knew, of course. She rushed
to Molly, squeezed herself against her.
"Dad will be all right, Mama." She pulled
away a bit. "I had a dream about him on
Wednesday night, the night before—it
was Thanksgiving, and we were all sitting
around the table and he was carving a
turkey about as big as our backyard, and
he was singing 'Roll out the Barrel.' He

looked really good, Mama. He looked happy."

Molly drew in a deep breath. Thanksgiving was six days away. She was not going to lose it again in front of her child. "I've never heard your father sing that song."

"Neither have I, but he sang it in a big deep booming voice. It was sort of catchy."

"I wonder how much that turkey weighed," Molly said. "Do you think Safeway will have one that big?"

Emma smiled. "Not a chance. That turkey must have weighed one hundred pounds. I think we'd eat leftovers for a year. I hear Mrs. Hicks."

Molly called out, "Cal, Gage, would the two of you stop trying to break each other's heads? Are you ready to go, Em?"

But Emma wasn't looking at her mother, she was staring out the window.

11

Harry smoothly turned his beloved dark blue Shelby Mustang onto Geary Street.

"Why don't you tell me about the old newspaper photo of Judge Dredd with an X through his face you found at the scene?" Eve said.

He whipped around and looked at her. "How'd you know—well, yeah, I'm surprised that bit got out. Yeah, that's what we found. Sitting under the big hydrangea bush in the backyard."

Eve wasn't about to tell him she knew because she'd overheard him and Cheney talking about it. "The shooter rubbing our noses in it?"

"That's what I think." He gave her another surprised look.

Eve said, "So we're going to meet the two FBI hotshots at Ramsey's house in Sea Cliff, check out how the photo got in the hydrangea? Check out the beach for signs of the Zodiac?"

"The forensic team couldn't find anything on the beach, so no need to traipse down there," Harry said. "You ever hear of Savich and Sherlock before?"

"Who hasn't? Only two weeks ago they were front and center on the Kirsten Bolger case, and can you believe it, Bolger grew up right here in San Francisco?" She'd savored the colorful reporting, even felt a good dollop of envy, although she'd never admit it, at least to an FBI agent, particularly this FBI agent.

Harry said, "At least the local coverage has finally run out of juice on Kirsten Bolger's family. They'll be taking a rest until the trial begins next year, when they'll light up their torches again."

Eve marveled at the two agents—married. What could two people in such stress-filled, dangerous jobs possibly have to say to each other after, say, a violent shoot-out, like the one with Bolger in a North Carolina tobacco field? *Hey, sweetie, you want to go get a beer to celebrate we're still alive?* She wondered if Sherlock painted her toenails, and imagined a nice French. And Savich was big, tough, hard as nails, good-looking. "Is Savich as fast as he looks?"

Harry nodded as he braked for a red light. "He is. He's a fourth-degree black belt. Sherlock is a first-degree, a *shodan*—"

"Yeah, yeah, I also know when you're a sixth *dan,* you wear a red-and-white belt. I mean, come on, why care so much about the color of your freaking belt? One big show, a business, that's all it is. The bottom line in the real world is to beat the crap out of your opponent, however you can."

"How do you know about a sixth *dan*?"

"From a book I saw at my boss's house."

"At Maynard's?"

"Yep. He hosts these big barbecues, feeds all hundred of the deputy marshals regularly."

"That's a lot of spareribs." Harry shot a look at her. "Cheney is new at his job, but

I wouldn't mind if he picked up on the barbecue ribs idea from Maynard. So that's what marshals do? What about fighting?"

She gave him a fast smile, gone in the next instant. "We've got martial arts experts of our own, with all sorts of belts and colors. Lots of our deputy marshals are scrappers who like to show off their ripped-up knuckles and bruised kidneys."

"And you're not into martial arts?"

"Don't know about that. I fight dirty, real dirty. Like I said, you want to put your opponent on the ground, his knees around his neck, as fast as possible." She started to ask him if he'd like to visit her in the marshals' gym, wear a couple of his prized belts, then remembered her boss telling her, *Play nice, Barbieri, play nice.* She cleared her throat. "So Savich is a computer expert, right?"

She fought dirty? He thought of her toilet adventure in the Macy's women's room in Omaha and smiled. "Give Savich a motherboard and he can make bread with it in no time at all."

"Hey, that was sort of sweet."

"Sweet? Hey, I tell you what. Let's mix it

up one of these days, Barbieri. I'll get you feeling a little respect for the discipline. Because you're so cute with that blond cheerleader ponytail swinging around, I'll go easy on you."

She batted her eyelashes at him, very effective, since she was so damned pretty. "Your best shot is I'll be dazzled by your multicolored karate belt. Turn right here, we're nearly there."

When Harry pulled his Shelby into the Hunt driveway a few minutes later, he couldn't help it, he gawked. "Some digs."

"It's got about the best views in Sea Cliff—the ocean, Marin Headlands, and the Golden Gate Bridge. Looks like all the news people have left. So has the SFPD. I don't like this; someone should be here." She pulled out her cell, punched in Carney Maynard's number, and then she dropped her cell and pointed. "Hey, that's Emma—she screamed!"

Eve was out of the car before Harry could turn off the motor, her Glock 22 in her hand, her long strides eating up ground.

12

Molly jerked open the front door, saw them, and thought she'd collapse in relief. "A man, he was staring in the window at us! He ran over toward Mr. Sproole's backyard!"

Eve shouted, "I'll take care of it. Get back inside, Molly!"

Eve saw a man running, a blur of black. And he was carrying something black—a gun? He had jumped the fence into the neighbor's backyard. Harry started to yell for her to wait up, but he didn't waste his breath. He watched her leap the stone fence smooth and high, like a hurdler. He ran after them.

"Federal agents! Stop!" Eve shouted.

But the man didn't stop. He ran straight for the fence at the back of the neighbor's yard, vaulted over it, and disappeared.

Eve didn't hesitate. She jumped that fence, too, right after him.

A scratchy old voice yelled from the yard, "Be careful or you're dead!" He turned to see Harry running toward the fence after them. "Hey, fellow, there's a snaking little trail down to the water, but it isn't safe. Who's the guy she's chasing? You're all federal agents? Is that the guy who shot Judge Hunt?"

Harry waved off the old man and jumped the fence, stumbled on some loose rocks beyond it, and nearly fell on his face. He windmilled his arms, and managed to gain purchase. He looked down—at least sixty feet to the beach— not a beach, only a thin strip of dirty sand covered with a mess of black rocks and huge boulders.

Below him, Eve was tacking back and forth down the side of the cliff, shortcutting the windy little path. She stumbled once, and Harry's heart seized. She caught herself, but she had to drop her Glock to do it and stopped to pick it up before she started down again. Harry saw the man had reached the beach and looked up to see Eve coming toward him. He scooped up a rock to hurl at her, thought better of it, and ran. Eve yelled back at Harry, "Call it in! I'm going to get him!"

She would catch him, Harry didn't have a single doubt, even though she was a good twenty yards behind him. Harry dialed 911. The SFPD would get here faster than the FBI.

He watched Eve jump onto the strip of dirty sand and rocks and sprint after the man. Was that a gun in his hand? Then why hadn't he shot her instead of picking up a rock? Surely the guy could tell, even from this distance, that she was moving way faster, gaining on him quickly. The putz looked like he was going to drop, he was breathing so hard. In that moment, Harry felt kind of sorry for the guy. He had no clue what was in store for him in about twenty seconds.

Eve felt the wind sharp and cold off the

water, and was happy to see the guy in front of her was flagging big-time. She shouted, "Stop it right now, or I'll shoot you in the leg. Do you hear me?"

The guy looked back at her, faltered, slowed, and finally stopped. He bent over, trying to catch his breath.

"Well, now, isn't this easier?"

"I didn't do anything!" he managed to say between breaths.

Eve jogged up to him, her Glock pointed at his chest, and threw him to the ground. She went down on her haunches beside him and ripped a camera from his hand. "That was for making me chase you, you brainless moron. Do you realize it looked like you had a gun? And, oh, my, would you look at this—it's a really expensive camera you're carrying."

Harry was grinning when he climbed back over the fence and saw the old man again, a golfer's cap on his head, a newspaper spread open on his lap, stretched out on a red-and-green striped chaise longue.

Harry said, "She's trying to prove she's tougher than I am."

"I gotta say she proved it, since you're not screaming she's dead. That fence is there to keep idiots from flying off the edge, but that first idiot headed to it like a homing pigeon. Didn't even see me, he was moving so fast. You said you're federal agents?"

Harry pulled out his creds, introduced himself.

The old man said, "FBI Special Agent Harry Christoff. I think I've seen that girl before. Who is she, another FBI agent?"

"She's a U.S. marshal, and a friend of the Hunt family."

"Yeah, I've seen her over at the Hunts' house. I'm Decker Sproole. You people are here because of Judge Hunt, aren't you? Was that guy the one who shot him? Why would he come back? I haven't ever understood that old saw about a criminal returning to the scene of the crime."

Harry said, "I don't know who he is yet. We've got to wait until she brings him up." They heard voices from over the fence, and watched Barbieri heft a young man over it, his hands cuffed behind him. He was skinny as a flagpole, a baseball cap pulled low over his forehead, his black clothes bagging off him.

Harry eyed the guy. He didn't look much like a professional killer. He said to Eve, "Glad you didn't break your neck."

"No thanks to this pathetic bozo," she said, and smacked his shoulder.

Mr. Sproole said, "Is he the man who shot Judge Hunt?"

"I didn't shoot anybody! She knows it!"

"Yeah, I guess I do. After all my running around, it looks like I didn't haul in our perp. What I landed was a would-be paparazzo. Imagine this fine upstanding young man wanted to take pictures of the grieving family."

"I'm not young, I'm older than you are! I'm a professional photographer."

"Yeah, and a trespasser who resisted arrest." She pulled the camera from his hand again. "After I remove the memory card and press delete a few times, you'll be all set to go sneak around someplace else and cause aggravation."

Harry said, "What's your name?"

"Robert Bacon. Like I said, I'm a professional, a freelance photographer. These photographs might be worth something, though there aren't that many, since Emma Hunt saw me and yelled her head off."

"Well, Robert Bacon, did you know there are laws against doing that on private property?"

Bacon stood tall and proud. "I'm a professional. Have you ever heard of freedom of the press?"

Eve smacked him again on the shoulder. "Quiet, Bobby." She quirked an eyebrow at Harry. "Bobby Bacon? We got us the real live Bobby Bacon, the photojournalist."

"I go by Robert. Hey, if you give me back my memory card and take off these cuffs, I'll shoot a couple photos of you, you know, doing your job," and he looked at Eve hopefully.

"Thanks, Bobby," Eve said, "but I don't think I'd take such a good photo right now, since I'm all sweaty and windblown because of you," and she slapped him on the back of the head with her open palm.

He staggered, then straightened. "Listen, a photo of Emma Hunt playing the piano, I coulda paid my rent for two months, what with her history."

Eve put her hand on Bobby's shoulder.

"Bobby, you don't want to mess with Emma or her family. Don't you know who her grandfather is?"

Bobby Bacon looked blank, then pointed to Mr. Sproole. "This old guy?"

"Nope. Her grandfather is Mason Lord. Look him up. If you got a photo of Emma published he didn't like, he'd carve out your pea brain and make you eat it."

Bobby swallowed. "But I didn't think—"

"Well, now you know. If you've got a brain, you'll stay away from Emma."

Harry introduced Eve to Mr. Sproole, who eyed Bobby Bacon. "If I had my daddy's Remington, I woulda blasted you between the eyes, shooting Ramsey in the back like that."

"You crazy old duffer, you know I didn't shoot anybody. I'm a professional photographer."

"Yeah, well, I would have shot you on spec. Maybe you carry that camera around as camouflage. Maybe you got a gun hid in your shorts."

"I didn't wear shorts today. I'm commando."

Mr. Sproole said, "I got a feeling I don't

wanna know what that means. You tres-passed on my private property, too, and for calling me crazy, I'm going to press charges myself, put your skinny butt in the slammer."

"I was only trying to make a living. I'm sorry I called you crazy. She's the one who's crazy. I mean, who would come rocketing down that path like that over some photographs? I practiced climbing that trail twice in case I had to use it."

"And where did you think you were going to go from there, Bobby? Swim to Marin?" Eve said.

"You're a wuss, Bobby," Mr. Sproole said. "This little cutie brought you back, all trussed up." He eyed Eve. "And look at you, Deputy Barbieri. I've got to say, you're prettier than any of my four grand-daughters ever were."

Harry wrote down Mr. Sproole's num-ber and address, gave him a salute. They walked through the garden gate and back to the sidewalk with Bobby Bacon, his wrists now uncuffed, clutching his cam-era, minus the memory card, walking be-tween them.

Harry said, "Prettier than any of his four granddaughters? He must like cheer-leader types."

"Shut up," Eve said.

"All of them?" and Harry laughed.

"Hey, he's right," Bobby said. "You are pretty. Your hair is a nice natural blond. So how come you're such a bitch?"

"That's Deputy Marshal Bitch to you, Bobby."

They kept him on the sidewalk until three squad cars, sirens blasting, rolled into the driveway. Six cops jumped out, guns drawn.

"That was fast," Harry said, his creds raised high over his head.

Molly said, "It's because everyone knows it's Ramsey's address."

There was pandemonium before every-thing got sorted out. They watched two officers drag Bobby Bacon to a squad car, Bobby yelling about police brutality and freedom of the press. He was still yelling as one of the officers shoved his head down to get him into the backseat. "I want my memory card back."

Eve grinned, tossed it to one of the officers.

When Eve and Harry walked to the Hunt home, Molly was standing in the doorway. Behind her stood Mrs. Hicks, the babysitter. She looked ready to kiss them. They heard Gage and Cal talking up a storm, and Emma's voice over theirs, telling them to be quiet, but they didn't.

Eve took Molly's arms in her hands, steadied her.

"He's a paparazzo. He didn't get any photos. The cops have taken Mr. Bacon downtown, where he'll be booked for trespassing and trying to escape a federal marshal."

Gage shouted, "Was that bad Bacon man here to shoot us?"

Eve went down on her knees in front of Cal and Gage, gathered them to her. "Listen up. That guy was a rude photographer, nothing more. The policemen hauled him off to jail. He wasn't here to hurt anyone."

Cal said, "But why'd he want to take our picture, Aunt Eve? Daddy's not here, he's in the hospital."

For the almighty buck. "You and Cal are so cute, I'll bet he was going to hawk them in Union Square. I bet he could get a buck each for them, at least. Hey, I'm glad you're speaking English today."

They gave her an identical look. Gage said, "We're not stupid, we have to if we're talking to you. I think he wanted to see Mama cry, didn't he, Aunt Eve? He wanted to take a picture of her crying." Cal shook her sleeve.

"Maybe, but we don't have to worry about him anymore. Now, this man is Special Agent Harry Christoff. He's FBI, and he's going to help me find out who hurt your dad."

"But he's a stranger, he could be another Bacon—"

Emma rolled her eyes. "You guys want some ice cream?"

Once Emma herded the twins out of the room, Mrs. Hicks, looking stalwart, following after them, Molly said, "They were terrified the man was here to shoot them."

"So were we," Harry said.

Molly blew out a breath. "The jerk. What will happen to him?"

"Probably not much," Harry said. "A bail hearing. Maybe a plea bargain."

Eve said, "Now that the excitement's

over, Harry and I can start taking a look around outside. Agents Savich and Sherlock will be here any time now. If you want to go back to the hospital, Molly, go right ahead."

Harry said, "I think it'd be a good idea for you guys to have some protection right now, not wait until Judge Hunt is home from the hospital. They can keep the Bobby Bacons of the world out of here."

"The media, too," Eve said. She'd assumed there'd already be coverage here. She'd been wrong. She pulled out her cell phone.

13

Sea Cliff
Friday afternoon

It was late afternoon and chilly, with only a few wispy tails of fog coming through the Golden Gate when Savich and Sherlock joined Eve and Harry in the Hunts' backyard. Sharp gusts of wind blew off the water. It was too cold to think much about the incredible view.

Savich said to Harry, "The SFPD out front aren't fooling around. They stopped us and looked us over pretty closely since they didn't know who we were."

Harry said, "There was a paparazzo here who caused a commotion only a half-hour ago. The police are here to keep everyone else off the property. Deputy Marshal Barbieri here—Eve—will be heading up security."

Savich said, "Good to know. I can see from that police tape and the height of the stone wall pretty much where Ramsey had to be standing when he was shot. He said he saw a Zodiac anchored off his little slice of beach. He didn't mention hearing anything, which means the shooter had to have motored in before Ramsey came out, and waited. Ramsey is about my height, and he was shot from the rear under his right shoulder blade, with the exit wound higher." He looked over the wall and studied the terrain below. "Maybe sixty to seventy feet up from the rocks, with a steep angle down."

"Have you heard about the rock with a newspaper photo of Judge Hunt tied to it, his face marked through with an X?" Harry said, and pointed.

"We've heard," Savich said, looking over at the bush.

"The conundrum is, do we have two

people, the shooter from the beach and someone else who dropped the rock up here? Seems like an awfully risky thing to do just to leave a message. There's an active neighborhood watch, according to Mrs. Hunt, that she herself helped start five years ago. Even though it was near midnight, there's a chance one of the neighbors would have seen a second perp."

Eve said, "You can bet someone in a neighborhood like this one would have gone on alert if they saw a stranger near Ramsey's property. I'd wager my Sunday hat if the shooter dropped the message, he came up the trail from the beach on Mr. Sproole's property next door and over his fence into that backyard, since that's the only trail for a good distance. And if he risked Mr. Sproole seeing him, then why would he bother to shoot him from down below in the first place? Why not right here, then drop the rock and head back down to that Zodiac? It's a conundrum, like Harry said."

Sherlock said, "Show me where they found that rock."

Eve touched the leaves about halfway

down the huge hydrangea and pushed them aside. "I wasn't here, but that flag marks the spot, there."

Sherlock turned to Harry. "You were here when the rock was found. Tell me how the rock was set under the hydrangea. Did it look carefully placed, or like it was simply tossed there, like an afterthought?"

Harry said, "The note attached to the rock was actually upside down and set partially into that soft soil. It looked freshly placed, not covered by any dirt or leaves. The forensic team didn't find it until it was full daylight, because the rock was under the hydrangea."

Sherlock stuck her hand in among the leaves, felt around with her fingers. Then she went down on her haunches and continued to carefully poke around inside the hydrangea.

She looked up and cocked her head to one side, something Savich had seen her do many times, a sure sign she was picturing what had happened. "How did the shooter know Ramsey would be outside, by himself, late Thursday night? Surely he didn't simply hang around to see if his target happened to come outside? So did Ramsey have a habit of coming out here at night by himself? To look at the Marin Headlands, the Golden Gate?"

Eve pulled her cell out of her pocket and dialed. "Molly? Did Ramsey have a habit of spending a few minutes outside every night, before bed?"

She listened. "Thank you. That helps. I'll tell you later, I promise. We're still out here at the house trying to make sense of how this all happened. I'll see you soon."

She punched off, slipped the phone back in her red jacket pocket. "Yes, every night. Molly said it was a ritual, that Ramsey came out sometimes even in the rain. She said it made him feel blessed to be able to look out from his own Wuthering Heights, like it was the center of the world."

Harry said, "That means the shooter, or the people who hired him, knew that. They had to know his family well, or they had to be watching his house long enough to be sure he would be there. Are the Cahills even a possibility? Could they have found out a detail like that about Ramsey's habits from jail?"

Eve said, "You're right. How many people could have known about Ramsey's habits at night, in his own backyard? And Ramsey was shot within twenty-four hours of his closing down the trial. That's a small window of opportunity for the Cahills."

"So what is it you've been thinking about down there, Sherlock?" Savich asked.

She pulled her arm out of the hydrangea bush. "I've been thinking about why the picture, why the message. Someone seeing it sitting handily under the bush, not twenty feet from where Ramsey fell, might conclude we've got two people involved, as Harry said. But if the second man's job was to plant the picture for the police to find, to make some sort of statement, why on the ground under the bush? And what message were they sending?"

"The first impression it leaves," Eve said, "is that Ramsey was shot because of what he'd done as a judge, because of his reputation and what it means to people. The crossed-out picture is a sort of in-your-face sneer; that's what Harry thought."

"I suppose," Harry said, "that it could be some kind of misdirection, to point us away from the trial or from some personal motive."

Sherlock nodded. "Here's the deal. I agree the Xerox itself could be misdirection, but what about where it was found? It makes it seem like there were two people involved, but the fact is there was only the shooter, and he was on the beach."

Harry said, "Then how'd the rock get here? Did the guy climb up the cliff to drop it under the bush, then scramble back down to the beach and climb back aboard his Zodiac before the cops got here?"

Sherlock smiled. "There's a freshly broken branch inside that bush, and I doubt it was one of our forensic team who broke it. Something heavy broke it from behind, from the rear, and it's maybe two feet directly up from where the flag on the ground marks where they found the rock. That means the rock wasn't just laid on the ground under the bush, it hit the bush hard."

Savich said, "So it came from a distance." He looked down over the wall again. "It's too far down to throw it up and hit the bush with much force. But a small rock could easily be shot up here with a slingshot, say. One of those leather Trumark models they use to hunt jackrabbits and such. It would reach up here easily, aimed at the hydrangea, a nice big target. Good going, Sherlock."

Eve stared at her. "How'd you think to even look for that?"

Sherlock said matter-of-factly, "There had to be a solution to Harry's conundrum, and this was the only one I could think of. The shooter was careful, he studied Ramsey and picked his spot carefully, so it didn't make sense he'd give up that advantage by climbing up the trail to drop a message."

"Amazing," Eve said. "So much for our second perp." But Harry wasn't convinced.

Sherlock said, "Answer me this, Agent Christoff. If there was a second man, why didn't he come out from his hidey-hole to make sure Ramsey was dead? No, what the shooter wanted was to kill Ramsey, and didn't care too much if he missed with that rock. In the grand scheme of things, that attempt to sneer at us, to misdirect us, or whatever, wouldn't have worked if we didn't find the rock. So what?"

Everyone chewed on that. Harry said, "Okay, one shooter, then. I can't get over the timing—Ramsey postponed the trial and he gets shot. It's got to be the Cahills behind this, or someone they're involved with. The timing makes it too coincidental, and I, for one, don't believe in coincidences."

"I don't, either," Savich said. "But as Sherlock pointed out, a stranger couldn't predict Ramsey would be standing out here exactly when he needed him to, and so someone's been studying him for at least a week, I'd say."

Eve rubbed her hands over her arms. "Someone who followed him around for a week? That's hard to take in."

Harry said, "Okay, say it isn't the Cahills. But the timing is still what it is—even if it was planned for some time, someone may be cashing in on a wonderful opportunity, since the Cahills are hanging over the crime scene like a black cloud."

"Judge Hunt closing down the trial was

mentioned on the local news at noon yesterday," Eve said. "If someone had already planned to kill him, they moved very fast."

"There's another big question with the Cahills," Savich said. "The way it looks now, there'll be a mistrial because the federal prosecutor may have been compromised, and now he's missing. Ramsey's being shot doesn't change that. It will all begin again for them, with a different set of players."

Eve said, "Molly said that was one of the first things out of Ramsey's mouth when he woke up. Why shoot him? A judge's job is to be impartial, unlike the prosecutor who'd spent months preparing for the trial. What difference did it make to the Cahills who was sitting up there in the black robe?"

Eve looked over at the crime scene tape that marked where Ramsey had fallen. "Whoever it was made one big fat mistake."

Everyone looked at her.

"The shooter didn't manage to kill Ramsey. He failed. Now what's he going to do? Try again? If it was the Cahills who targeted Ramsey, for whatever reason, they've already won, because he's out of the picture for the near future. What if it was someone else?"

"That's why we've got to protect him, Eve," Harry said.

"No one will hurt Judge Ramsey Hunt on my watch," Eve said. "No one."

Sherlock said, "I'll be checking on the Zodiac, and Cheney has feelers out for any word about a shooter for hire."

"We need to talk to the Cahills," Eve said. "Regardless, they're certainly people of interest. It's a place to start."

14

Judge Sherlock's home
Pacific Heights, San Francisco
Friday evening

Sherlock's eyes were closed as she listened to Emma play George Gershwin's *Rhapsody in Blue* on her parents' magnificent Bösendorfer grand piano, which had been purchased for Sherlock when she was about Emma's age. When Emma hit the final notes, there was a long moment of silence, then applause, Sherlock's parents the loudest.

"It's been too long since I've listened

to you play," Judge Corman Sherlock said. "Thank you, Emma."

Harry couldn't believe what he had just heard. An eleven-year-old kid, her thick dark brown hair veiling her face, had knocked his socks off. How could those small hands play with such passion and purity, even reach all those racing chords, those endless runs and trills?

Evelyn Sherlock was still smiling. "That was grand, Emma. Thank you for the preview. We'll be there to hear you at the symphony, of course."

Emma gave them a small smile, but it soon fell away. "I don't know how well I'll play with Daddy in the hospital." She looked down at her clasped hands. "He smiled at me this afternoon, but it was so hard for him, and I knew it hurt him."

Eve said, "Say your dad can't be with you at Davies Hall. We'll fix it so he can be listening to you on a live feed."

"But what if something happens? What if he's still in the hospital? How could I play then?"

Eve said, "If he isn't home—and believe me, that's unlikely, since your daddy's such a tough dude—we'll take the live feed to the hospital and hook it up there. Can't you see all the nurses and doctors, all the other patients cramming into his room to see you play? Believe me on this. Wherever your daddy happens to be in a week and a half, you know he'll be right onstage with you."

What a perfect thing to say, Savich thought. Eve didn't even hint that Ramsey could possibly be well enough to actually attend her performance, and that was smart. He squeezed Sherlock's hand.

Emma tried to smile at Eve. "That means I can't make a single mistake."

"You never do," Eve said.

Sherlock said, "Do you like the Bösendorfer, Emma? My parents got it for me a very long time ago."

"It's too bad you aren't here very often to play it," Emma said. "Mrs. Mayhew— she's my teacher—she says a piano has to be played or it goes stale."

"Do you think the Gershwin sounded stale?"

Emma shook her head. "No, it sounded perfect. I'm used to my Steinway, but I like this piano, too. I wish Mama were here."

Eve said, "Look at the big picture, Emma. Your daddy needs her attention right now more than we do."

Emma thought about that and nodded. She touched middle C. "The action's perfect."

Evelyn Sherlock said, "Emma, would you like to have Lacey play for you?"

Emma's eyes shone. "Oh, yes. Do you know Bach's *Italian Concerto*?"

Sherlock rolled her eyes. "I haven't played that killer in a long time. I can feel my fingers yelling at me not to try it."

Harry said, "Tell your fingers to man up. I'd sure like to hear you play, Sherlock."

Sherlock took Emma's place at the black piano bench. She played some scales, ran some chords, and realized the feel of the keys on this magnificent instrument was a deeply embedded memory that came back quickly. Still, she wasn't about to try the first movement, far too wild and hairy without practice. She played the second movement, slow, evocative, and sorrowful. As she played, she felt the power of the music burrow into her. When she finished, Sherlock slowly lifted her hands from the keyboard, letting herself settle for a moment, another embedded memory she would thankfully never lose.

Emma jumped to her feet. "Oh, goodness, that was beautiful. I can play that movement, but not like that, not like it makes everyone want to cry."

"The last time you played that second movement for me, I cried," Eve said.

"You're easy, Aunt Eve," Emma said, and gave her a fat kid grin.

"Yeah, your music is my downfall."

Sherlock hugged her. "You're eleven years old, Emma. You'll make everyone weep when you have more life under your belt."

Molly arrived at nine o'clock to take the children home. Savich brought down Cal and Gage, both deeply asleep, one draped over each shoulder. He saw Molly speaking quietly to Sherlock. Molly even managed a smile. *Excellent.* Then it was his turn.

An SFPD black-and-white was parked across the street to follow Molly home.

Sherlock asked, "What were you talking to Molly about, Dillon?"

"Ramsey was more lucid this evening. He described the Zodiac to Molly again." He cupped his wife's face in his big hands. "Cheney will find it. Now, I don't think I woke Sean up when I fetched Cal and Gage, but he's got ears like a bat; we should check on him again."

15

Russian Hill
Friday night

It had been a lovely evening, Eve thought, as she unlocked the front door of her condo on Russian Hill, only a ten-minute drive this time of night from the Sherlock home on Mulberry in Pacific Heights. She couldn't get over Agent Sherlock playing the piano like that. She pictured Agent Savich—no, Dillon, he'd told her—his eyes never leaving his wife's face. He said that after you shared a dinner of barbecued pork spareribs and finger licking, only first names sounded right. "But you're a vegetarian," she'd said to him. "You didn't eat any of those delicious ribs."

He said, "Licking your fingers is the operative image here."

Eve wondered what Harry had thought of the odd evening—an FBI agent playing Bach, and no talk of who had tried to kill Ramsey. When she'd mentioned that to Dillon, he'd said only, "Don't you think your brain does better when it gets to stir a different kind of stew for a bit?"

Good people, she thought, full of life, so much of it. Some people seemed to have more of life in them than others, and that included Sean, brought downstairs after dinner, beaming at all of them in his Transformers pajamas.

She saw Harry in her mind's eye, frankly astonished when Emma had played Gershwin's *Rhapsody in Blue.* Then he'd closed his eyes and leaned his head back on the chair cushion as he listened to Sherlock play that incredibly sad second movement.

She heard a noise, something close, something dangerous—she jerked around, her hand going to the Glock at her waist. Harry said, raising his arms, palms toward her, "Don't shoot me. It's only ten o'clock. I thought we should talk. Sorry to alarm you, I thought you saw me following you here."

Her heart was pounding. She couldn't make him out clearly, but she recognized his voice. "I can't believe I didn't hear you sooner. I can hear ants nesting. I never noticed you behind me, and here you were driving that hot Shelby."

"How can you protect Judge Hunt if you don't pay more attention to who's on your tail?"

He got her, curse him. "Yeah, you're right, but that'll be the last time. Talk would be good. Come on in. I'll put on some coffee. So it's only ten o'clock? What does that have to do with my shooting you?"

"No shooting until after midnight, that's the rule."

"Haven't heard that one. I think it's smart to talk about the case."

"So what do ants sound like when they're nesting?"

She grinned at him over her shoulder as she unlocked the door to a small lobby with a black-and-white tiled floor, black mailboxes set against a stark white wall, and a half-dozen palm trees in green and blue pots stationed in the corners. She waved him in. "The elevator's a 1920s job that creaks and groans all the way up. Scares most people, but I love it. Still, I prefer to walk up. Keeps yummy things like spareribs from making a home on my thighs." They walked steep, wide stairs to the third and top floor.

"I'm on the end." The corridor was wide, covered in a red carpet splashed with cabbage roses that should have made Harry bilious. Instead he found it curiously charming. She stopped in front of a blue door, unlocked it, and stepped in. She flipped on the light, waved him in.

Eve's living room wasn't what Harry was expecting, although he wasn't quite sure what that would be, since he'd only met her earlier in the day. Maybe a black leather sofa and chairs and lots of gym mats on the floor? No, the living room was light, airy, filled with color. There was a view of the city through the big windows and a sliver of a view of the bay. He followed her to the kitchen, streamlined but softened with fresh flowers in a vase on the two-seater kitchen table, herbs in small pots lining the windowsill over the sink. It was painted a soft yellow.

"Nice apartment."

"It's mine now, bought it when the building went condo five years ago. It's the right size for me."

Eve smacked the heel of her hand to her head. "I'm an idiot." After she turned on the coffeemaker, Eve pulled out her cell, and typed on the small Google screen.

"Well, okay, that's only because you aren't FBI. What are you doing?"

She stared at him.

"What? Oh, I'm picturing you lying flat on your back, out like a light, me standing over you rubbing my bruised knuckles."

"That's a pretty solid fantasy scenario. What are you doing really?"

She punched in numbers she'd looked up on her cell. "Calling the Port Authority to see if there were any cargo ships coming through the Golden Gate about midnight last night."

He hadn't thought of that. He guessed he was an idiot, too.

"Here we go." She dialed, got a message, punched off her cell. "It's late, no one there. I'll call in the morning."

She laid her cell phone on the counter. "Where do you live, Harry?"

"Over in Laurel Heights."

She knew it was a lovely area near the Presidio, with streets named after trees. "You have a house?"

He nodded. "After my wife left—" He cut off like a spigot run dry, nodded at the coffeepot.

As Eve filled two large mugs, a hank of her blond hair fell along the side of her face. He watched her tuck it behind her ear. "This is decaf, so we'll both have a shot at some sleep tonight. What do you take in your coffee?"

"Black is good."

When they were seated across from each other at the kitchen table, Harry waved his hand toward the window. "What have you got planted in that first pot?"

"Thyme."

"Yeah? You put that in birthday cakes?" Again, he saw her in a pretty swingy summer dress, long legs in open-toed sandals, serving cake up to a noisy herd of kids at a party.

"Not unless my specialty was pasta primavera cake."

He laughed. "I called the hospital on the way over. Judge Hunt is sleeping. No setbacks so far. I hope he makes it out of the hospital in time to see Emma play at Davies Hall."

"If he can make it without causing a stir and disturbing the audience, he'll be there," Eve said. "With the paramedics, if he needs them."

"He's a local hero. The paramedics would be thrilled. Emma blew my mind tonight."

"I guess I've heard her play so many times I'm used to it. It was Sherlock who blew me away. Made me feel inferior. Judge Sherlock told me she chose being an agent over trying to make it as a concert pianist. When I asked him why, he only smiled and shook his head. I wonder what happened."

"Who knows? Maybe in the pursuit of her blood?"

Eve said, "It's hard to imagine Savich and Sherlock are actually married."

"Cheney told me he's heard stories about Sherlock going toe-to-toe with

Savich when she disagrees with him, that she can be as stubborn as he imagined his mother-in-law would be if he had one. But despite that, he says what impresses him the most about Sherlock is her loyalty." He studied his coffee, swirled it in his cup. "Imagine that, loyalty in a woman."

Whoa. Best move right along.

"Tomorrow's Saturday," Eve said. "Virginia Trolley has asked to be part of our protection team. She'll have officers stick close to Ramsey's house, keep people from sneaking in when no one's home. Did you know Virginia Trolley is a long-time friend of Ramsey's? She's a good cop, too."

Harry said, "I met Lieutenant Trolley. She acted suspicious, didn't much like me."

"What did you do?"

"Nothing at all. I was my charming self."

"Yeah, I can only imagine."

"She's like you, wears a uniform."

"What does that mean?"

"Look at you, all in black with that kick-butt red leather jacket. I'll bet your socks and your underwear are black, too."

He'd nailed that one.

"You didn't tell me what you did to make Virginia dislike you."

"Strange, really. I only happened to mention that the San Francisco cops are really good at writing parking tickets."

Eve rolled her eyes, then grinned. "Yeah, no secret there. Got to raise money to support the city budget."

"Good coffee, even though it's decaf. Cheney told me he put Burt Seng with Sherlock on finding that Zodiac. Fact is, Burt could find a contact lens in a swimming pool. He'll be updating us at the meeting tomorrow."

"I hadn't heard about a meeting. Do you think I can be in on that? When? Tomorrow morning?"

He couldn't help himself. "That'd be okay, if you don't forget your place."

She leaped for the bait, coffee sputtered out. She wiped a napkin over her mouth and gave him a look to fry his liver.

He quickly raised his hand, smiling. "You gotta learn control, Barbieri. You can't lose it every time someone makes an innocent comment rubs you the wrong way."

The jerk, but he'd done it on purpose,

and she'd been ready to go for his throat. She dredged up a smile and a sneer. "And when do you interview the Cahills? Can I go with you for that?"

"Savich and I planned to do that in the morning. That actually is why I followed you home tonight, so I could ask you about the trial. I'd wanted to be there from the beginning, since it was my case, but something else came up. Since Judge Hunt isn't in any shape to tell me about it himself yet, could you tell me exactly what was happening to make him so suspicious about Mickey O'Rourke?"

Eve said, "Ramsey never talked to me about it directly—of course he wouldn't— but I can tell you what I saw.

"The trial was still in the final pretrial motion stage. They hadn't impaneled a jury yet. Milo Siles, the Cahills' defense attorney, had been making all sorts of motions for discovery. He'd demanded proof of everything the government accessed from the murder victim's computer, especially anything that was considered top secret. He kept going on about the *Brady* rules giving the defense the right to any documents it needs to defend their clients, even in the case of espionage. It was pretty obvious, really, Siles was trying to force the government to disclose exactly what Mark Lindy—the murder victim—did for them."

"Yeah, I know all about Mark Lindy, since it was my case, like I told you. So it sounds like Siles was trying to get the government to drop the case rather than have what Mark Lindy was working on compromised? That sounds nuts."

"Just you wait. There was a lot of talk then about the Classified Information Procedures Act that provides protection for the government and for defendants in these kinds of cases. There were a bunch of conferences, some of them in camera— that means in Ramsey's chambers—and after that, Ramsey started getting more and more hard-nosed with O'Rourke. You see, Ramsey had ruled some of that information admissible, but O'Rourke had repeatedly failed to provide it to the court. At first his excuses seemed reasonable, but then he had no more excuses, even bad ones.

"I'll tell you, it was quite a sight seeing Ramsey lambaste a federal prosecutor like that. He said the court would have to impose sanctions, possibly dismiss the federal indictment, and you could tell that really burned Ramsey, and that's when he suspended the trial, the same day he was shot."

Harry nodded. "Since Judge Hunt's known O'Rourke pretty well after working with him for years, he realized he wouldn't behave like that—ignoring the judge's directives time after time—if something weren't seriously wrong. No way would a federal prosecutor want a case dismissed, except if there was bad stuff going on, and he was directly involved. Yes, that fits nicely.

"Thanks, Eve. I've got a better handle on it now. About the Cahills: Savich wants to meet with them as soon as possible, before they have a chance to talk all this through with their lawyer. We're going to offer them a chance to spend some time together if they're willing to talk to us immediately, without waiting for Siles. They're going to want to see each other real bad, one reason is so they can both be sure they can still trust each other. A lot has happened in two days. Who knows what they know? What they've heard? What they're thinking? Maybe they're ready to deal."

"Maybe," Eve said.

Harry rose. "Gotta go. Thanks for the coffee."

She followed him to the front door. "Do you think I could go interview the Cahills with you?"

"That'll be up to Savich."

Eve didn't think her chances were that good. Besides, there was so much to do, best not to overload anywhere. She dropped it. "Hey, what tree are you heading for?"

An eyebrow went up, and then he grinned. "Yeah, yeah, my street name. I live on Maple—my house is in the center of the block. I'm really close to pizza and Szechuan, and the dry cleaner's. All the comforts, lots of people driving around, parking to shop or eat. The cops love to ticket in that neighborhood."

"Imagine Virginia not liking you when, I'm sure, you just happened to mention that to her."

She heard him whistling as he walked away down the corridor. She was in bed ten minutes later.

So his wife had left him the house on Maple and he'd stayed there.

16

Hall of Justice
850 Bryant Street
San Francisco
Saturday morning

Two guards walked Cindy Cahill over from county jail number two to the interview room on the sixth floor, where the men were housed in the Hall of Justice. She shuffled into the room ahead of the guards, wearing her prisoner's three-piece suit—cuffs, belly chain, and leg irons. She looked up and saw her husband, Clive, dressed as she was, sitting in one of the uncomfortable chairs.

"Clive," she said, and tried to move toward him, but the guards stopped her. Clive rose slowly, smiling at her. "Hi, gorgeous. I liked you in the blue suit Milo brought you to wear in court last week, but hey, orange looks great on you, too. You okay?"

"I'm okay, but I wish I knew what's—" Cindy shot a look at Savich and shut up.

Savich rose slowly as the guards seated Cindy beside her husband, then left the small room with Savich's nod.

Savich introduced himself and Eve to the Cahills. He said, "Before we begin, I'd like you to confirm you've both agreed not to have your attorney, Mr. Siles, present. Is that correct?"

"Sure," Clive said. "Like I already said before my sweet wife arrived, we don't need Milo for this. We didn't do anything wrong, and we have nothing to hide. And how could I pass up the chance to spend some time with Cindy? Even talking to you clowns is better than being bored."

He sat back in the uncomfortable chair, like a seasoned lounge lizard.

Savich asked, "Mrs. Cahill?"

"Okay with me," Cindy said. "So call me Cindy. I heard the guards talking about you, Agent Savich; said you were from Washington, and you were real important."

Clive said, "Hey, where's Special Agent Christoff? That boy needs manners, you know? He's a hard man, that one, not much fun at all."

Savich watched them look at each other for a moment—affectionately? Wondering if the other would spill the beans? He didn't know, but allowing them to be together in the same room without their lawyer present was a good start. With everything that had happened—suspension of the trial, the federal prosecutor O'Rourke gone missing, and Ramsey shot—Savich knew both of the Cahills would want to find out as much as they could about what the Feds knew. He doubted they'd fold their tents and want to deal given what had happened, but maybe they'd let drop something—anything—to give him some leverage, particularly with Milo Siles, since even on a good day the chances of getting the truth out of a defense lawyer were harder than getting a bipartisan bill out of Congress.

Savich said as he sat down, "You needn't worry. Agent Christoff won't be joining us. There will be only myself and Marshal Barbieri."

As Savich spoke, Cindy didn't look away from his face. She rested her cheek on her long white fingers, her fingernails not so lovely now. Those dark eyes of hers saw deep into a man's soul, no, not his soul, Savich thought, she made a direct connection to his sex, and the pull of her was powerful. He recognized he was new prey to her, and so Savich clicked away, knew she recognized that he'd turned her off, and hoped she would work really hard to snare him. He wanted to observe her methods.

When Cindy turned her eyes to Eve, with her fresh, very pretty face and blond ponytail, she didn't look happy, and he was pleased. What came out of her mouth pleased him even more. "Well, now, aren't you the cutest little thing? All blond and blue-eyed, like a little princess, and yet here you are, a big U.S. marshal all dressed up in red and black, like a hard-ass. I thought all you marshals did was chase bad guys who escaped from the real cops. Like Tommy Lee Jones."

"My hero," Eve said. She was pleased Savich had decided to bring her even though Harry had been major-league ripped until Savich had calmly said it was obvious Cindy would have the advantage with two male interviewers, plus she would be instantly wary of anything that came out of Harry's mouth, since he'd led the case against them and interviewed her at least a dozen times. Savich wanted to shuffle the deck, pull out a joker, and present Cindy with another woman. Hopefully Cindy hadn't noticed her in the courtroom. Unspoken to Harry was the message that since Eve Barbieri was a looker, why not try to rattle Cindy Cahill, who firmly believed she was God's gift to all men? Harry hadn't said another word. On their way to the interview room, Savich had said only to Eve, "Rattle her."

"And would you look, you've got a little holster where you carry your gun. Isn't that delicious? I always liked macho girls. I mean, men can be so difficult, don't you think? Tell me, Eve, what do you do with a difficult man?" And Cindy Cahill slanted Savich a sloe-eyed look.

Eve smiled at Cindy, recognizing pure sex on the hoof when she saw it. She was sure men vibrated to full alert when Cindy waltzed into their vicinity. She was also beautiful, despite so many months spent in jail. Her dark eyes were exotic, slightly slanted, full of sparkle and high-voltage tease. She looked at you with incredible focus, and that focus was now turned on Eve. Eve sensed a formidable intelligence behind those hot, dark eyes—and something else when Cindy looked at her— calculation, and hatred. *Hatred?* Was Savich right? Was this incredible woman jealous of *her*? She said nothing.

Savich smiled. "Maybe what we should be talking about, Cindy, is how you thought you could get away with threatening a federal prosecutor."

Direct attack, Eve thought, and took due note.

Cindy Cahill answered Savich, her voice dripping Southern Savannah honey, "Threaten the federal prosecutor? You mean Mr. O'Rourke? I'm sure I have no idea what you're talking about, Agent Savich. Do you, Clive?"

Clive said through a yawn, "Not a clue."

"What you both must have figured out by now," Savich continued smoothly, "is that your whole plan to get the murder charges dismissed has blown up in your face. Judge Hunt saw through it, and now there will be a mistrial. You will be tried again, with even greater security, and you'll be convicted. If you had anything to do with Judge Hunt's shooting or with O'Rourke's disappearance, we'll find that out, too. I would think two people facing the death penalty might be asking about a deal right about now."

Clive and Cindy exchanged glances. Clive said, "We already told you we had nothing to do with any of that. Mr. Siles has already told us to sit back and wait awhile, see what happens now. Right, darling?"

Cindy said, "Right. We wouldn't want to disappoint Mr. Siles."

Savich said, "You've got to know your lawyer doesn't want to end up in prison with you, if he was involved. If you could help us find Mr. O'Rourke, or to find Judge Hunt's shooter before he can do any more harm, I'm sure the U.S. attorney would be very interested in possibly removing the death penalty from the table, maybe even reducing your sentences. And I'm sure the government would very much like to know who you sold that information to from Mark Lindy's computer."

Clive said, "We don't know what happened to Mr. O'Rourke. I'll tell you, though, I think maybe he went off somewhere and had a heart attack. He was real intense, always impatient, always demanding. I saw him start shaking once in the courtroom, looked to me like the poor boy was about to fall apart. Do you know he threatened me? I laughed at him, because what could he do? I was already in jail."

Cindy said, "O'Rourke's a schmuck, no sense of humor. Clive's right, he's probably dead in a ditch somewhere of a heart attack. If he is, I sure won't miss him."

Eve said, "I guess you don't know

Mickey O'Rourke's a great volleyball player with a serve like a bowling ball, and he can spike the ball down your tonsils. His wife tells him he's a killer, then she punches him, and he laughs. He's a nice guy, loves his daughters. Did you know he has two daughters, teenagers?"

Clive shrugged and began whistling.

Cindy continued to study Savich, but Eve knew she was well aware of her. She'd come out swinging at her, Eve thought, something she had to admire. *Well, then, time to go for it.*

Eve said, "I've wondered exactly what you did, Cindy. I mean, you had sex with Mark Lindy—it's your tried-and-true method, isn't it? And then Mark did most anything you wanted because he was so pleased with himself that this beautiful woman was sleeping with him, telling him he was a stud. Did he let you look over his shoulder while he worked on a classified government project, never suspecting you were writing all his user IDs and passwords on your sleeve while you were cooing in his ear?

"And then you put him to sleep with a

nice cocktail you made with your own little hands, a bit of Rohypnol with a knock-
out drug, didn't you? Poor Mark, he didn't
have a clue that his sex goddess was
knocking him out so she could get to his
key fob to tunnel into his computer, and
access all his data. I'll bet you called in
Clive to help you with that part, didn't
you? This is all really Clive's deal, isn't it,
Cindy? He's the brain in your duo, right?
He does the planning, makes the deci-
sions, deals with the buyers, handles all
the money, doles out spending money to
you, his sex kitten?

"Do you even know who the buyers are?"

Cindy rose straight up, slammed her
fist on the table, rattling her chains. "You
bitch! I do the planning, I do everything,
do you hear me?" Clive grabbed her
hand. She shut up, even managed a
twisted smile at Eve.

Nice start, Savich thought. Cindy Cahill
looked like she very much wanted to kill
Eve. The investigative training the marshals were given at the marshals' acad-
emy at Glenco looked to be good; either
that or Eve had learned a few things grow-

ing up with a marshal as a father. Probably both.

Eve said, "Was it Clive who targeted Mark Lindy for you? Or did some foreign agent set you up with Lindy? Did you know, Cindy, that those top-secret materials were headed for a foreign government?"

Cindy Cahill didn't leap to the bait this time, but she couldn't keep the rage from her eyes. She tried on a sneer for size, but she couldn't mask the mad. "You're making up a story. The same story that ridiculous CIA operations officer told, too. Do all of you read off the same script?

"Listen up, little girl. What I mean is that Clive is my husband, my partner." She gave Clive Cahill an adoring look and patted his hand, making the chains rattle again. "He's my sweetie pie, not my boss, never my boss."

Eve arched an eyebrow, gave her a *yeah, right* look. "Your sweetie pie didn't mind you sleeping with Mark Lindy so long as there was a big payoff? Sorry, Cindy, but come on, now—that was your only role, wasn't it? That is, until something went wrong. What happened? Did

Mark Lindy realize what you were doing and threaten to call the police? And so you gave him the last cocktail of his life?"

Cindy gave Eve a girl-to-girl smile. "In my experience, guys usually prefer beer."

Eve sat back in her chair. "That wasn't a bad comeback, Cindy, but maybe Clive could give you a cooler line, since he's smarter. *Hmm,* I wonder what your folks would think about how you've grown up, what you've finally done."

17

Cindy Cahill never looked away from Eve's face. "Since dear old Dad started coming to my bedroom when I was eleven years old, I don't think he'd care one way or the other."

Interesting, Savich thought. Did the shrinks know she'd been abused? He started to rein it back, since he didn't want the Cahills to demand their lawyer, but he wanted to see what Eve would say next. He gave her a small nod.

Eve said, "Clive, if it wasn't you run-ning the show, what were you doing, anyway? Did Cindy have you fetch her coffee, slide her slippers on her dainty feet, make up her schedule of seduction for her?"

Clive was shaking his head, looking from his wife to Savich, then finally back at Eve.

Eve continued. "Then what is she doing with you, Clive? You're nearly old enough to be her father, aren't you, nearly as old as her father who abused her? Tell me the truth, now, Clive, I know it must be tucked in the back of your brain. You're afraid of her, aren't you? Afraid she'll tire of you, afraid she'll start seeing a guy who's younger than you? Afraid she'll take her chances and talk to us, leave you here by yourself on death row?"

Clive's pale face turned red. He yelled, heaving, he was so mad, "I am not afraid of her! She's my wife. She'd never do anything to hurt me! I'm the one who found her, who taught her everything—"

"Did you teach her how to kill? Probably not, since the scene at that murder was a mess, not well done of you at all. Poison doesn't always make a person just fall over and die. No, Mark Lindy fought when he realized what you'd done to him. He tried to take you down, but the poison got to him first, and it wasn't at all pretty, was it, Cindy? And that, Clive, led the police to both of you."

Cindy Cahill squeezed Clive's hand hard. "Don't you get all bent out of shape about anything, Clive. She's only trying to play you." She shook her head at them. "Aren't you two the cool team? How long have you worked this routine together? Have you ever had any luck with it?"

Eve sat forward now, clasped her hands in front of her. "Do you know, Cindy, one thing I'd never do is kill someone by poison. It's so—mean-spirited, cowardly, really, you know what I mean? And it's so tacky. So low-class. Give me a knife any day and let me face down the person I'm going to kill."

"I am not tacky!"

"No? Then what do you call using your body whenever Clive wants you to? Without the money, without the trappings, who would think you're worth any more than a fast in and out with a streetwalker against a wall in an alley?"

"You bitch! I'm not a whore. Sue thinks I'm perfect!"

Sue? Who is Sue? What is this?

Savich broke in, hard and fast. "And Sue is walking around outside in the sunshine while you two are on the road to a lethal injection. Was it Sue who tried to kill Judge Hunt?"

Cindy and Clive Cahill looked at each other again and pulled it together. Cindy studied her fingernails and sounded bored. "There is no Sue, it's a name I made up. As for Judge Hunt getting shot, I don't know any more than anyone else who saw the news on TV. I have no idea who shot him."

Eve said, "Come on, game's up, Cindy. Did Sue shoot Judge Hunt?"

"I'll tell you again—there is no Sue," Cindy said. "There wasn't even a reason for us to shoot the judge, was there?"

Savich said, "Are you so unimportant, Cindy, that Sue didn't even tell you why she wanted Judge Hunt dead?"

"There is no Sue," Cindy said yet again, calm as a stone now. "Like I already told you morons, why would we want the frigging judge dead? There's no payoff for us, you said so yourself. Me, I was sort of sorry to hear it. Judge Hunt was hot, the way he looked at me—" Her husband didn't say a word, only stared at the wall behind Savich's head. "I bet he doesn't look so hot now, does he?"

Eve wanted to leap over the table and punch her out. She forced herself to draw a deep breath instead.

Savich said, "Did Sue kill the prosecutor like you did Mark Lindy?"

Clive shrugged. "We don't know anything about the judge, and we don't know anything about the prosecutor. How could we? We're in jail, Agent Savich, not out drinking beer and dancing at clubs." He sat back in his chair and smirked. "That prosecutor, what a schmuck. O'Rourke would never have proven a case against us."

But Cindy was still enraged. "All the accusations—it's entrapment, nothing more. We didn't kill anyone—if that ridiculous judge hadn't stopped the trial, we would have been acquitted! Somebody else shot him—probably someone he put away." She turned to Clive. "You know what, darling? This has been fun, but we got to put an end to it. Agent Savich, we want our lawyer."

Eve wanted to kick herself. She'd been the one to screw it up, to push it too far.

Savich said as he rose, "I was hoping you two were behind the attempt on Judge Hunt's life, that you'd hired an assassin to kill him, with the help of your lawyer paying him from some offshore account we haven't found yet. Now I see that's impossible." He flattened his palms on the scarred table. "After spending some time with the two of you, the fact is I don't think either of you has the brains to pull it off by yourselves."

"We could do anything we wanted to," Clive shouted. "And what we want now is our lawyer!"

Eve rose and stared down at him, then at Cindy. "Why don't you tell us about Sue? You really don't have to take the fall for her, not if she approached you, not if she's the go-between to sell the material you stole off Mark Lindy's computer."

Neither of them said a word.

Savich said, "Do you know Mark Lindy always liked to say he wasn't a wackadoodle, like Sheldon on *The Big Bang Theory*. He was more like Leonard, funny and kind?"

They looked at Savich blankly.

Savich shrugged. "Mark's sister Elaine said he readily admitted he was a nerd, and he'd laugh, say he loved Spock as much as the next nerd, but she said Mark knew he saw people more clearly, interacted with them more easily, than most nerds did. But he didn't see you clearly, did he, Cindy? And it cost him his life."

Still no word from either of them.

How had Savich known that? From the murder file, of course. Eve said, "Did this Sue tell you to poison him, Cindy? Clive? Did she watch you do it?"

Cindy said, her voice vicious, "There is no Sue, you little dyke."

Eve smiled at Cindy, turned to the door, and said over her shoulder, "You could be a model, Cindy, but not for much longer. Not if you stay in here."

"I wouldn't want to be a model. What idiot would want to live on yogurt and look like a refugee camp survivor?"

18

Federal Building
450 Golden Gate Avenue
San Francisco
Saturday

Savich and Eve walked into the FBI conference room on the thirteenth floor of the Federal Building a half-hour later, straight-up noon. Half a dozen FBI agents were seated around the long conference table along with Lieutenant Virginia Trolley and Lieutenant Delion of the SFPD, and the U.S. Marshal Carney Maynard. Savich gave a little finger wave to Sherlock and Harry, who were eating pizza out of the same box. Pepperoni, Savich knew; it was Sherlock's favorite.

There were stacked pizza boxes, a ton of paper napkins, and cans of soda scattered across the table. SAC Cheney Stone swallowed the last of his Hawaiian pineapple pizza slice and waved to them. "Come on in. Help yourselves, lots of pizza left, and probably still warm. Savich, there's a couple of slices of veggie pizza for you if this crew hasn't scarfed them all down. Tell us how you made out with the Cahills."

Savich looked over at Marshal Maynard as he sat down. "Deputy Barbieri did an excellent job, sir, rattled them good. She got Cindy Cahill so angry she spit out a name—Sue. We're thinking she might be the operative who was the Cahills' handler."

"Sue?" Maynard said. "Sue is a foreign operative?"

Savich nodded at Eve as he picked up one of the three slices of Veggie Heaven pizza.

Eve said, "Well, Cindy implied she had a close—maybe an intimate—relationship with her, before she tried to deny that Sue exists."

Savich said, "Harry, you've been looking for their contact for months, haven't you?"

Harry said, "We thought there had to be someone working closely with them. Their backgrounds didn't fit high-level espionage. They've been talented grifters, that's all, who've been busy rolling drunks and using Cindy's charms to cheat some lonely men out of their money. This was way out of their league."

Savich nodded. "So now this Sue is our best bet for the one who made contact with the Cahills, maybe recruited them."

Cheney asked, "So this woman might be the shooter? You think the CIA knows about this and they didn't bother to tell us?"

"We can ask the CIA if they have a file on her," Harry said. "But so far the CIA hasn't even told us what it was the Cahills managed to steal. Only that it was in the area of cyber-security, quote/unquote. Maybe now we have something to trade them."

There were smiles around the table.

Eve said, "We might have gotten more out of them, but their survival instinct kicked in and they backpedaled like crazy and hollered for their lawyer." She sighed. "It was my fault, I handled it wrong, pushed them too hard."

Savich said, "You did good, Eve, lots better than Harry would have done. He'd have scared the crap out of them. This is good pizza, guys."

Sherlock, a slice of pepperoni pizza halfway to her mouth, said, "No last name? Only Sue, and Cindy Cahill just spit it out?"

Eve nodded.

Harry turned to Eve, his eyes narrowed. "What did you do? Swing your blond ponytail in Cindy's direction and watch her explode?"

"Close," Savich said.

Harry said, "Maybe she was making up the name Sue, playing you."

Eve could see he wasn't happy about having this sprung on him. He'd worked this case for more than a year, and he'd never gotten a name out of them.

Deal with it, Harry.

Eve took a big bite of her pizza slice.

"Tell you what, Harry, you can listen to our recording of the interview, make up your own mind. Sorry there's no video showing my ponytail."

Cheney asked, "Harry, your team never came across this name Sue in your investigation?"

"No, and believe me, our agents"—he nodded to several agents across from him—"we checked through their known associates for months, in and out of jail. Clive Cahill isn't stupid. He's always used prepaid cell phones we can't trace to him, for example. If he was making contact with some foreign corporation or government or intelligence service, whatever, we have no record of it."

Ten-year veteran Agent Burt Seng said, "The whole operation was skillfully done until the Cahills screwed up and ended up with a dead body on their hands, and got caught. To get any of the confidential information off Mark Lindy's encrypted computer, somebody in the operation had to know a good deal about the information security system Lindy used to access the project he was working on. Not just his user IDs and passcodes, but enough about the access algorithms and the project itself to know what was valuable and how to get to it without alerting the security oversight team."

Savich said, "It means this Sue was super-careful. She had to pay the Cahills some upfront money, but you haven't been able to find any stashed funds, right?"

"Not a dime," Burt Seng said. "This 'Sue' name, though"—he turned to Agent Griffin Hammersmith—"you ever hear of a foreign spy with the name Sue?"

Griffin shook his head. "I'm thinking it's got to be a code name. Maybe it isn't even a woman, who knows?"

Eve said, "Cindy didn't shout it out like it was a code name. It sounded like she knew this Sue person, and well."

Cheney was tapping his pen on the tabletop. "Savich, you agree with Barbieri?"

Savich said, "Yes."

Cheney said, "I'll call the CIA operations officers who worked on the Cahills' case, see if they recognize it."

Savich said, "I'm thinking I might throw out Sue's name to Siles, see his reaction, see if he recognizes the name. I told the

guard not to let either Clive or Cindy Cahill have any phone calls until after we
visit Siles today."

Cheney said, "Okay, let's shift gears for
the moment." He turned to Agent Seng.
"Burt has been waiting to give us follow-
up on what he and Sherlock found out
about that Zodiac Judge Hunt saw."

Burt Seng wiped his hands on a napkin, then clicked on the overhead to show
a Google map of Sea Cliff. He pointed.
"Judge Hunt's house is there on the point
of land. You can see there are big boulders scattered all over the beach. Since
Judge Hunt told us about the Zodiac, we
can forget about whether the shooter
drove down Sea Cliff Avenue, parked his
car or motorcycle near China Beach Park,
and made his way down to the beach."
Burt grinned. "Man or woman, this Sue
came in by water.

"If you've ever been on an inflatable
with an outboard motor, you know it's capable of speed. He could have motored
the Zodiac right up to the beach. He
didn't care if Judge Hunt saw the Zodiac,
since he planned to kill him. He walked
around the ocean side of the bluff and

positioned himself in the mess of thick rocks that stud the beach." He nodded to Sherlock as he put the photo of the Zodiac on the overhead.

"Now, a female Sue adds a new wrinkle to this," Sherlock said, "since Mrs. Moe, the owner of Bay Outings in Sausalito, says she rented a Zodiac to a man at two o'clock on Thursday afternoon under the name Bently Ames."

Burt said, "Mrs. Moe never questioned it was a man. She described him well. Here's our sketch." He projected the drawing on the overhead and passed around a sketch of a man described as five-foot-nine or -ten, on the slender side, wearing loose jeans, sneakers, an oversized blue Windbreaker, dark opaque sunglasses, and a Giants baseball cap.

"Bently Ames never took off the sunglasses or the cap. He had a flat voice, Mrs. Moe said, no particular regional accent she could identify. He was polite, paid with an AmEx. He needed the Zodiac only one day, wanted to do an evening run on the bay with his girlfriend, who'd grown up on Zodiacs in Hawaii, he told her. She remembered he was wearing a big honker diamond ring on his pinkie finger, could have been fake, she didn't know, but why would a man wear a fake diamond? Again, Mrs. Moe didn't question this was a man. She thought he was middle-aged, maybe even older.

"Now, Bently Ames returned the Zodiac Friday morning right on time. Mrs. Moe said they didn't even have to wash it down, it was so squeaky clean."

Sherlock picked it up. "We had our forensic team scour the Zodiac for any sort of evidence anyway, but like Burt said, Bently Ames was thorough in his cleaning, so we don't have anything."

Burt said, "We'll show this photo of the Zodiac he or she rented to Judge Hunt, see if he can positively identify it. That's unlikely, though, since Zodiacs look similar, for the most part."

Sherlock said, "We found the real Bently Ames in his Tiburon real estate office. He said his wallet wasn't missing. We asked him to check. Turns out his wallet was in his pocket, but his AmEx was gone. He said he'd had dinner with his sister at Guymas, a Tiburon restaurant on the water, on Wednesday evening. Then he remembered that after he paid the bill, he'd stopped in the men's room. He said there were maybe four guys in there using the facilities but for the life of him he couldn't remember anything unusual. Then he stopped cold, said a guy bumped into him in the small hallway outside the restroom."

"Bingo," Virginia Trolley said. "Was he wearing sunglasses and a ball cap?"

Burt nodded. "Yep, a Giants baseball cap. Again, Mr. Ames described him as a man.

"Since Sue had to park someplace, we checked the parking lot closest to Guymas first," Sherlock said. "No luck. We didn't think he'd use the parking lot next to the Tiburon Theater and take a chance of being seen, but we checked anyway."

Sherlock said, "The parking lot attendant in the big lot sits in a booth and takes the money." She gave a big grin. "Guess what?"

"He did park there," Harry said. "And the parking attendant noticed a license plate? Please? Please?"

"Nope, but this little freckle-faced kid struts out of the booth in his loose low-rider jeans and tells us sure, he remembered the dude, remembered the sunglasses and the baseball cap. Then Freckle-face told us he knew for sure it wasn't a rental, since it was a butt-ugly old Dodge Charger, with red paint chipping off. Unfortunately, no license plate, but Freckle-face did say it was a California license."

Cheney turned to Agent Griffin Hammersmith. "Griffin has been coordinating with the highway patrol and the local police departments to try to locate that vehicle. He's also got more news for us."

Sherlock thought Griffin Hammersmith was saved from being too pretty by his nose. It was off-kilter, probably broken when he was a kid. As for his eyes, they were bluer than hers. She wondered if he was used to women trying to chase him down. He said in his slow, melodic voice, "I tried to put myself in the shooter's shoes. If I came to San Francisco to murder a federal judge, I'd want to draw as little attention to myself as possible.

I'd probably want to stay outside the city, unless I had to be there. And I wouldn't stay anywhere near where I was going to snatch a credit card, like from Bently Ames in Tiburon. So, south of the city, probably near a major highway. A nice enough place but not big or fancy.

"So that's where we focused. And after a couple of hours of phone calls, we found a small boutique inn off Highway 280 near Atherton, called Pelican Eave. The manager remembered the man, and the car. Yep, the same car the parking attendant described to us. 'Overdue to be traded in,' she said. She said he introduced himself as James Connor and he always wore his sunglasses and ball cap—though she remembered it as an Oakland A's cap— even when he drank tea by himself in the front parlor. Since he paid in cash upfront, for two weeks, she never asked to see any identification. A pity.

"We have agents out there surveilling the inn. She hasn't seen him since Thursday, the day of the shooting.

"We've got an APB out for the car as we speak, and his drawing and description at the local airports and all the cop shops in the Bay Area. I don't think we'll find him anywhere close to Atherton."

Sherlock looked at Agent Griffin Hammersmith. "Why?"

"It's my opinion he's not about to take the risk of going back to the Pelican Eave." Griffin cleared his throat. "Well, I'll bet this guy is alarmed. I mean, he knows now Judge Hunt is alive, and if he wants to try again he has to stay in the area. He also knows it's riskier for him now, and I think he might dump the old Charger and stay closer this time, more in the center of things, where he can blend in with the tourists. If I were this guy or this gal, I might change how I look and stay at one of the dozens of small hotels and motels on Lombard Street or at Fisherman's Wharf." Griffin splayed his hands. "This is all a guess, guys, so—"

Harry laughed. "And your point would be, Griffin? Your so-called guesses are almost always right."

Griffin said, "The thing is, though, our guy—or this Sue—has been in and out of San Francisco for at least a week, maybe longer. That's long enough to learn how to keep out of sight.

"We've got agents canvassing the hotels starting on Lombard and at Fisherman's Wharf, with his drawing. Thanks to Lieutenant Trolley, we've got us a half-dozen SFPD to help." He nodded to her, and Virginia said, "Our pleasure."

Harry sighed. "I'm wondering why don't you just tell us which hotel Sue's staying at, Griff, so we wouldn't have to waste all this time?"

This time everyone laughed.

Now that he'd seen Griffin Hammersmith in action, Savich was wondering if he could get him to relocate to Washington. He bit into the last slice of Veggie Heaven, now cold, and said, "Honestly, I don't think putting that drawing through the facial recognition program will get us anything, what with the ball cap and sunglasses."

Cheney said, "Maybe we'll get lucky and Sue will drop the ball cap; then we could try the FRP. One last note: We still don't have anything about our missing prosecutor, Mickey O'Rourke. We've talked to his prosecution team, his co-workers, his family, his friends. We have him on camera leaving the Federal Building by himself late Thursday morning, though he never told anyone in his office he was going out. We're examining his phone records, his credit card bills, but as of yet we don't have anything very helpful. His wife, as you can imagine, is a mess.

"Her name's Melissa. She told us Mickey had seemed distracted the last week or so, but he wouldn't tell her what was wrong. She did remember he kept asking his two daughters where they were going and when they'd be home every time they stepped out of the door, which makes it sound like O'Rourke was frightened. Because of the Cahills or this Sue? We don't know if he skipped or if he was taken by someone, but the longer he's gone, the worse it looks."

19

Hoover Building
Washington, D.C.
Saturday afternoon

Agent Dane Carver studied the young man sitting opposite him and Agent Ruth Warnecki Noble in one of the small interview rooms on the third floor of the Hoover Building. Ted Moody was bouncing his leg up and down, and kept his eyes on his bouncing leg, as if afraid if he looked them in the eyes they'd shoot him.

Dane sat with his arms crossed over his chest, his expression hard. "You don't look like a street punk, Mr. Moody, but I've been wrong before. How long have you been doing crap like this?"

The young guy flinched, raised his head, his eyes blinking furiously. "I didn't do anything wrong, not really. I mean, I don't know why those agents came and forced me to come with them. I have to get to work or Mr. Garber will fire me."

Ruth said, "I spoke to Mr. Garber, told him you were assisting us, so your job is safe. But you did do something you shouldn't have done."

Dane said, "It's called a felony, and you're a criminal, Mr. Moody."

"No, I'm not, sir, Agent, I'm not a criminal. Maybe you think—no, I—nothing I did was wrong."

Ruth leaned over the table, put her hand over his and smoothed it out. He had long, slender fingers and fairly clean fingernails today, but his hand was moist with sweat, he was so afraid, mostly of Dane, who looked perfectly ready to shove his tonsils into his sneakers. *Good.* "Ted—may I call you Ted?"

He whispered, "My mama calls me Teddy even though I'm grown up and even have my own apartment now, since last April, over on Washburn Street. It's not much, but I pay the rent on it all by myself, and I've got a bed and a couch and a TV."

"Teddy, then," Ruth said in the same gentle voice she used with her eldest stepson when he lost a ball game. "We really need your help. We need to know who hired you to deliver that envelope into the Hoover Building and recite that story to the security guards."

"But I don't know, I mean—is it national security?"

Dane opened his mouth to blast him again, but Ruth gave him a look she made sure Teddy saw, and Dane made do with a silent message to Teddy: *Fear me.*

Ruth kept touching Teddy's hands, kept her voice gentle. "Teddy, was it a man or a woman who gave you the envelope?"

Teddy shot a look at Dane, grabbed Ruth's hand like a lifeline. "All right, ma'am, I'll tell you. It was a man. Look, I really needed money because I lost most of my pay in a poker game and I didn't want to have to ask my mom to help me with the rent. He offered me two crisp one-hundred-dollar bills, and all I had to do was deliver that envelope here. I didn't have to run over anybody or break any laws, nothing like that, which I wouldn't do anyway."

Ruth beamed at him, patted his hand. "Tell us about this man. What did he look like? Was he young, old?"

Teddy leaned really close to Ruth. "I never saw him, I swear."

Bummer. Both Dane and Ruth knew he was telling the truth, so there was no reason for Dane to pound the table and yell at him.

"Then how do you know it was a man, moron?" Dane asked him, sitting forward.

"He sounded like a man on the phone. I mean, why would a woman do something like that? Really, he sounded like a man— honest."

Dane said, "All right, then tell us how you happened to connect with him."

Teddy said, "You know I work at the Union Seventy-six gas station over on Bowner Avenue. Mr. Garber hired me because I'm real good at figuring out what's wrong with a car, so anyway, this guy called me on my cell phone—said he'd seen me work, said he'd heard people say they could count on me, that I was reliable." Teddy Moody tried not to puff up, but he did. "Really, ma'am, Agent ma'am, I don't know anything about him, but he said he knew I was good to the bone, and he surely admired responsible young people like me, that's what he told me, exactly. My mama's always telling me I was good, but you can't always believe your mama."

And that made all the difference, Dane thought. It was strange logic, but he understood it. A nerdy twenty-year-old kid with one shining skill and the guy had the brain to praise him, drew him right in. That was clever.

"So then he told me what he wanted me to do, and I didn't see anything wrong with it, I swear I didn't."

Ruth said, "He called you only once?"

Teddy nodded.

"Did he tell you his name?"

"I asked him who he was, and he laughed. He said people used to call him the Hammer, but his name didn't matter. He told me he would mail me an envelope inside another envelope, and in the second envelope there'd be two one-hundred-dollar bills and a script—that's what he called it, 'my script'—and all I had to do was tell the security guards in the lobby exactly what he'd written on the script."

"And that was, exactly?"

Teddy closed his eyes and repeated word for word the conversation Ruth and Dane had heard on the security tape.

"That's very impressive, Teddy," Ruth told him.

"The Hammer told me to practice the script in front of the mirror until I had it memorized and it sounded all natural, and so I did. That was all, Agent ma'am, I swear." Teddy's eyes shimmered with tears. "He promised I couldn't get into trouble. He said it was only a joke on this Agent Dillon Savich. He said no one would ever even find out who I was. How could they? I'm a law-abiding person, and I could just walk out. I believed him. I was in this knot of tourists and everything happened like he said it would. I simply slipped back into the crowd when the guards were talking about the envelope." He dropped his head again, studied his hands. "I wanted to believe him, you know? I mean, I really did walk out and nobody said a word to me. And there were the two brand-new hundred-dollar bills—I really needed that money. What was in that envelope? Was it bad?"

Ruth said, "Yes, very bad. The Hammer wasn't trying to help you out, Teddy, and deep down, you knew that, didn't you?"

Teddy swallowed. He looked scared and miserable. "Yeah, I worried about it, Agent ma'am, but it was two hundred bucks and I didn't think it could be that bad. I mean, it was only a dippy white envelope, nothing lumpy in it, like a bomb or anything. I'm sorry, I really am." He looked from one to the other. "Am I in real bad trouble?"

The kid looked so scared Dane hoped he wouldn't pee his pants. He said, "Let's see if you can redeem yourself. Agent Warnecki asked you if the guy sounded young, older, or really old. Tell us what you can and we'll see."

Teddy's head snapped up, hope beaming out of his eyes. "He sounded—well, I never knew my pa or my grandpa, never had either one of those, though I guess everyone has to, even if they've never met them, right?"

Ruth smiled. "So he sounded what, forty? Sixty? Eighty?"

"In the middle, I guess."

"Did he have an accent?"

Teddy shook his head. "No, he didn't sound like anything I recognized, and his voice was kind of raspy, you know, like a longtime smoker's voice, not very deep, but scratchy, like I said."

"Do you have the script the Hammer sent you?"

Teddy shook his head. "I'm sorry. He told me as soon as I memorized it I had to burn it, and so I did. It sounded kind of neat, you know? Kind of like I was a spy or something, and so I borrowed Mr. Garber's Redskins lighter and burned it out in back of the station."

Dane pushed over a sheet of blank paper. "Was the script written in pencil or pen, or on a computer?"

"He handwrote it—a pen. It was black ink."

Dane pulled out his pen and handed it

to Teddy. "I want you to copy his handwriting the best you can. Write the script down as close to the way it looked. Take your time, Teddy. This is very important."

Dane's unspoken message this time was *Do it well and I might let you live.* After five minutes Dane and Ruth studied the script. The lettering was cramped and slanted really far to the right, like the Hammer had fisted the pen and written nearly upside down. A left-hander? Or someone who was trying to deceive?

Dane said, "Not bad," and Teddy looked suddenly like he might survive.

Ruth said, "Now, Teddy, I want you to write down everything the Hammer said to you when he called you on your cell, from beginning to end. I know it's been a couple of days. Do the best you can."

Teddy scrunched up his face and labored. After another five minutes he had written phrases, some single words, and some complete sentences, enough for them to see exactly how he drew the kid in.

Ruth said, "Think a moment, Teddy. What was your impression of the Hammer? What I mean by that is what did you think while you spoke to him? Did he frighten you? Did he make you laugh? Was he sincere? Did you believe him?"

Teddy fiddled with Dane's pen as he thought about this. Finally, he said, "He sounded like I always thought my daddy would sound if I'd ever known him."

Good enough, Ruth thought. Confident, probably some hardnose expecting obedience, and he'd gotten it from Teddy Moody.

Teddy said, "I didn't think you'd ever find me. I mean, I know there are cameras everywhere, but I've never even been arrested for anything, and why would anyone in the lobby know me? The Hammer told me you'd never find me, since I was just another tourist. See? I wrote that down, right there." And he pointed. "How did you find me?"

Dane said, "An agent who watched the security video saw something black under a couple of your fingernails. Once we enlarged your hands, we saw it was something thick and oily. We had photos of you. All we did was show them around some of the gas stations and body shops in the area. There aren't that many. We found you on the third try."

Teddy Moody blinked. He looked from Ruth to Dane and back again. "That is so cool," he said simply. "I'd sure like to do stuff like that."

Ruth smiled at him as she patted his shoulder. "You're still too young, Teddy, but maybe in ten years or so, if you don't take any more money from strangers, you could try out."

Dane leaned over the table close to his ear. "You better keep your poker game stake at fifty bucks, Teddy, no higher. You don't want any more Hammers searching you out. If something had gone wrong, believe me, he would have slit your throat and walked away, whistling."

Teddy looked like he was going to faint. "But you're not going to arrest me or anything, are you, Agent sir?"

"Not this time," Dane said.

Teddy gave both Dane and Ruth a blazing smile. "I got rent money and I won't have to go to jail, either. What a great day."

Ruth and Dane's eyes met when the elevator doors closed on Teddy Moody and the security guard who was escorting him from the Hoover Building. They both smiled.

"That's one lucky kid," Dane said. "And so are we. I have an idea where to look for this guy."

20

California Street
San Francisco
Saturday afternoon

Harry carefully steered his Shelby into a parking space in the California Street garage of the Mason Building, which housed Milo Siles's law firm. He looked over at Eve. "Savich told me he hates driving that rental car, says it hurts his soul."

Eve laughed, flipped her hand one way, then the other. "Well, red Porsche, ucktan rental—tough choice."

Harry cut the engine, fiddled with his

keys. "Congratulations, by the way, on what happened with Cindy and Clive. You did good."

"It was Dillon who told me to rattle her. I'll tell you, though, when she spit out Sue I nearly fainted."

Harry fiddled some more with his keys. "I guess I never made her mad enough. Yeah, I scared her, but she never stopped trying to play me, and all the while Clive sat back and grinned like a fathead, and watched her work me over. What she did to the other agents who interviewed her was just as sad." He hit his fist hard against the steering wheel, then looked closely to see if he'd done any damage. Luckily, he hadn't. What, Eve wondered, would he do if he'd wounded his baby?

He looked out the window, watched Savich pull the uck-tan Taurus into a parking slot. "I'd like to have been there when she lost it."

Eve grinned. "She claimed right away she'd made it up, then she tried to provoke me back. She's really pretty good at it. What I liked best was when she asked me what I'd do with a difficult man, like Savich. He'd turned her off, you see, and she saw he wasn't interested, and couldn't stand it."

"You can tell me later how you answered that," Harry said, getting out of the Shelby. He said to her over the roof of the car, "But none of that means you need to be along on this interview."

She tilted her head, swinging her ponytail, and one of her eyebrows went straight up. "What? You don't want my incredible brain at work on Milo Siles? Hey, he might spit out Sue's name, too. How can you afford to miss out on that chance?"

Harry was being a dog in the manger. He knew it and wanted to punch himself out. He sighed and stepped away to join Savich.

Savich said, "I like the Shelby, Harry, it oozes style. How do you like driving a stick in San Francisco?"

"Newbies around here tend to pray hard when they have to stop on a steep incline, but not us old-timers. All we old-timers ever worry about is how often we have to buy new tires."

Eve poked him in the ribs. "You're telling me you never pray when you're stopped dead on one of those Pacific Heights inclines?"

He shook his head and gave a tug on her ponytail. "I guess you drive a wuss automatic."

"And I'm proud of it."

"Siles's law firm has the entire eighteenth floor," Savich said. "There are a total of ten equity partners, a gazillion assistants, lawyers, and secretaries on salary. I verified Siles is in, but I didn't make an appointment; better to catch him by surprise. It seems a lot of folk work on Saturdays, including Silas's secretary. Harry, this guy knows you very well. Eve, how about you?"

"The Cahills' trial is the first time I saw him in federal court. I doubt he'll recognize me. I always sat in the back of the courtroom."

"Harry, any advice?"

"He's fast on his feet, and trying to pin him is like nailing Jell-O to a tree."

Savich grinned. "We're here to try anyway. Harry, Cheney says you do contempt and scorn really well. Feel free. A little fear couldn't hurt, either. Eve, go with your gut, depending on how he reacts to you."

"And what will you do, Dillon?" Eve asked, as she swung her black bag over her shoulder.

He thought about that for a moment. "If you guys leave any blanks, I'll try to fill them in."

They were greeted on the eighteenth floor by a stylish young woman with dark hair, the only receptionist manning the large, curving mahogany counter on this fine Saturday.

Savich looked at her name badge, smiled, and showed her his creds. "Alicia, we'd like to see Mr. Siles."

Alicia drew back, alarmed. "Do you have an appointment, Agent? Ah, Special Agent?"

Savich said, his smile warm, "We don't need one. Isn't that handy?"

She looked at Harry, then at Eve. "Who are you?"

Eve and Harry showed her their creds. "But—"

"Point us to his office, Alicia."

They followed her along a wide hallway

with polished wooden floors to the end office, both Savich and Harry admiring her red power suit, her stiletto heels, and her walk. Eve poked Harry in the ribs.

Before Alicia could precede them into Siles's office, Savich gently pushed her to the side and opened the door himself. "Thank you, Alicia. Please hold his calls and any clients that show up."

Milo Siles shot to his feet when the three of them walked into his bragging-rights corner office with its magnificent San Francisco Bay view. The fog had burned off earlier, and it was a postcard day, warm by San Francisco late-fall standards, in the upper sixties.

Milo liked hypermodern, Harry saw, like his own ex-wife. Show Nessa any piece of furniture that combined glass and chrome in a weird shape, and she'd embrace it, while Harry hunched over with a belly cramp.

Savich introduced the three of them to Siles.

Siles said, "I recognize Deputy Barbieri. She sat at the back of the courtroom during our very short trial. I didn't know you were a marshal. I pegged you as a TV reporter.

"Of course I also know Special Agent Christoff. I believe I've seen him perhaps too many times." He looked hard at Savich. "You, however, I've never seen before. You're not with the local FBI, are you?"

Savich shook his head. "I'm from Washington."

"What may I do for the three of you?"

Somehow, Eve thought, Savich knew it should be she who answered, and he gave her a small nod. She said, smiling at Siles, who, even in his lifts, was a good three inches shorter than she was, "Cindy told us about Sue, but she forgot to give us a last name. Could you please provide that, sir?"

Savich wouldn't have seen the flash of horrified recognition in Siles's eyes if he hadn't been watching him closely.

Gotcha.

Siles paled a bit, too, if Savich wasn't mistaken, but for only an instant. Then Siles turned his back on them, got himself together, and said over his shoulder, "Would any of you like a glass of water?"

They all declined.

Milo Siles drank, or pretended to, then sat behind his impressive glass desk framed with a beautiful dark wood that looked like it should be on the endangered list. Black paraphernalia was set precisely on the top of the desk—a computer, a phone, a fancy black desk set that looked like an expensive Christmas present from someone who didn't know what else to buy for him but didn't want to cheap out.

Siles waved them to chairs. There were only two. Without hesitation, Eve fetched another chair. She noticed that all the chairs were lower than Siles's, so he could, quite literally, look down on them. She remembered clearly her father telling her once, "You don't have to hunt for red buttons to push with short guys. And short guys wearing lifts are the easiest of all."

Eve glanced at Siles and saw from his look that he seemed to have downgraded her to gofer, a pretty girl with no particular importance, even though she was a deputy marshal. And so she said to him, her voice deferential, "I have to tell you, sir, I admired watching you sparring with the prosecutor. O'Rourke didn't have a chance against you even though he's probably a good eight inches taller than you and doesn't have to sit on a stack of books."

Bravo, Savich thought.

Whatever Siles would have said stuck in his throat. He turned red, then yelled, "I do not sit on a pile of books!"

Harry said, his voice lazy, "Come on, now, Deputy Barbieri, no reason to insult him. I'll bet his dad was short, so what could he expect? It's not very nice to rub his nose in it. Look at his office. He's a very successful man. He could probably convince the devil to buy charcoal for a barbecue."

Siles tented his fingers, regarded each of them in silence, smoothing himself out. "You're all quite good. But these insults, they're rather immature, don't you think? I'm a busy man. What can I do for you?"

"Tell us about Sue," Savich said.

"I heard about your interview with my clients without my being present," Siles said. "I don't care that they told you it was all right, because it's not. If that happens again, I'll take it up with the court."

Savich said, "It seems to me a big part of the court is missing, and another part has been shot. So I'll repeat what Deputy Barbieri asked you for, a last name. We know Sue is very likely an agent of a foreign government. Attorney-client privilege won't protect you for long from Homeland Security and the CIA if you're abetting espionage against the United States."

Siles said easily, "Isn't there an old song about Sue? I wonder why Cindy mentioned a girl named Sue?" And he laughed.

Savich said, "Because Sue is involved, a go-between. The Cahills' handler. She probably hired the Cahills to help her get the classified documents from Mark Lindy's computer, or maybe the Cahills looked her up when they realized what they had. I'm sure you can tell us how this all worked. You don't want to be tried for treason, Mr. Siles."

Milo Siles sat forward, clasped his hands atop the huge black desk pad. "I have never heard either of the Cahills mention a woman named Sue. I don't know personally who this Sue might be, well, unless she was referring to my wife.

There is no question of treason or of selling any of Mark Lindy's computer data to anyone. The Cahills were being tried for murder, not treason." He sat back, grinned at them. "My wife, by the way, is a bitch, and I'm taking steps to see she won't be my wife for much longer. Trust me, I'd hardly be involved in some conspiracy with her."

His desk phone rang, and Siles picked it up, listened, and said, "I'll be there in a few minutes." He set the phone gently back into the receiver. "Poor Alicia. I'm a busy man, even on Saturday. She was afraid to put through the call. Are we done here?"

"And here I thought we've only just started," Eve said.

Milo Siles looked amused. He studied Eve Barbieri's very pretty face, her blond hair whipped back into a ponytail, showing off her well-shaped ears that sported small gold studs. Her red leather jacket was open, showing her black turtleneck. "When I first noticed you in the courtroom, Deputy, I thought you were real cute, all bouncy and clean like some of the female

TV anchors, all tits and no brains, a girl next door every guy dreams about marrying. But let me be honest here. You're not in Cindy Cahill's league. She makes men forget their names from twenty feet away. She'd have no reason to be disturbed by your looks, such as they are. And you're what, five, six years older than she is?"

She's got him taking shots at her, Harry thought. *Good work.*

Eve smiled at him. "I guess that'd place me closer to Clive's age, like I could hook up with him and it wouldn't look quite so obscene. Is that what you were thinking, sir?"

She watched him quickly rethink his approach. She saw when he'd decided how to deal with her, all in about two seconds. Siles had defended some of the smarmiest, most dangerous people on the planet, drug dealers, extortionists, and murderers. Few people could shake him.

Savich could, maybe, but she? To him she was nothing more than a fly buzzing around him.

Siles said, "Who cares about ages,

Deputy? They're a loving couple. Wouldn't you say you're being rather sexist?"

Eve shook her head. "Not me. You want to know what I think? I think Cindy drives the bus and Clive has been expendable for a while now. I looked at him and wondered how long it would take before she dumps him. Not that she'll get the chance now. I mean, she's never getting out of prison unless she talks to us, right?"

"I have a client waiting outside—" He looked down at his Piaget watch. "Do either of you gentlemen have anything to say, because I'm finished talking with Ms. Ponytail here—Deputy Marshal, ah, what did you say your name was?"

Savich said smoothly, "Mr. Siles, why don't you tell us what you think about Federal Prosecutor Mickey O'Rourke's disappearance."

"I don't know anything about it, Agent Savich. How could I? Mickey has never shared his emotional sensitivities with me. I did hear through the grapevine that he was having an affair with a law clerk last year, though I don't know if that has anything to do with this. Look. I know people are starting to get alarmed, since Mickey hasn't showed up anywhere. I'm as concerned as anyone else." He paused for a minute. "We all noticed he was behaving pretty strangely in the pretrial hearings, like ignoring Judge Hunt's direct orders to hand over needful documents so I could give my clients the best defense. I chalked all his balking up to the intense cutthroat competition in the federal prosecutor's office finally getting to him. They have about a hundred federal prosecutors, and they're always jockeying for position. Did you know the prosecutors themselves keep actual records of their wins, who gets the toughest prison sentences in the least amount of time for the least cost? This is a death penalty case, and Mickey was going to have to convince a jury without using any of that classified information, information I'll bet he couldn't even access himself, information he either couldn't or wouldn't turn over to me. Can you imagine the stress?

"I think when Judge Hunt finally called him on the carpet, O'Rourke panicked. Once he failed to show up in chambers without a good reason, his career was over. I wouldn't be surprised if Mickey took off, and kept going."

Siles smiled and sat back in his chair, his fingers laced over his Italian vest, obviously pleased with himself.

Eve said, "You said your wife's name was Sue. It isn't, sir. It's Marjorie. Her middle name isn't Sue, either, it's Ann. And she's divorcing you, sir, not the other way around. I understand finances are the big bone of contention between you. Seems you have reasons to feel stressed yourself."

Siles looked momentarily poleaxed, then wiped the look off his face. "Didn't think you'd know that," he said slowly.

"Yes, sir, I do. Why did you make that up?"

"A joke, Deputy, only a small joke." Siles looked at his Piaget again, and rose.

Savich said, "It's not a joke that Mrs. Siles's divorce attorney plans to strip you down to your boxers. With those very embarrassing photos they say they have, I'm wagering you know you're going to need a lot of money soon."

Harry picked it up. "And what better

way to get it than to join in a little conspiracy and earn a couple of million getting the Cahills off?"

"I'd like all of you to leave now," Siles
said.

Savich paused in the doorway. "I'm
sure if we find your offshore accounts,
Marjorie will be very interested. She'll
probably help us any way she can when
we tell her you're colluding in selling information to a foreign government."

Before he closed the door, Eve said
over her shoulder, "So many bad things
can happen in federal prisons, Mr. Siles,
you know that. And a lawyer who defends
traitors, who's maybe a traitor himself?
Can you begin to imagine what would
happen to you? I can't see you defending
yourself that well in prison." She paused,
turned back to him, and gave him her
card. "Think about it. Call me."

Siles found himself taking her card. He
said nothing, watched her blond ponytail
swing as she walked out his office door
in those kick-ass boots. He walked to his
desk and picked up his phone to dial his
divorce lawyer. He'd have had his big-
mouthed wife, Marjorie, killed months

ago, easy enough back then, before the spotlight. It was only his two sons, both of them now taller than he was, who had kept her alive. He'd waited too long for that now.

21

San Francisco General Hospital
Saturday, late afternoon

Morphine-induced euphoria was a fine thing indeed, but Ramsey didn't want to cruise around in oblivion anymore. It left his brain fuzzed and stupid, not at all what he wanted now that Molly and Emma were coming to see him. Without drugs he was better able to cast about his brain to figure out who had shot him. Had someone picked out a judge with a certain reputation, or was it something about him, specifically?

And then there was the other big question: What had happened to Mickey O'Rourke?

Ramsey felt an ache building behind his left eye, and he gritted his teeth against the pain. He looked up to see Emma and Molly standing at the entrance to his cubicle. He felt a leap of pleasure and set himself to forget about his chest and his headache.

He called to them, "No need to tiptoe, I'm not zombied out on drugs. In fact, I'm doing so well the SICU nurses and doctors don't want me around any longer. They need my bed for someone who really needs to be here, not a slacker like me. They're going to move me very soon now to the biggest private room in the hospital. They call it the Taj—can you imagine? They're gathering the troops right now." He didn't mention the long conference at his bedside that morning with Dr. Kardak and Marshal Maynard, debating the pros and cons of moving him. There was too much traffic through the ICU to suit the security team, and too many interruptions by law enforcement to suit the nurses and the medical staff. They had compromised by agreeing he would leave the ICU a bit early, for a secure room on one of the inpatient floors, with an extra staff nurse assigned to him.

He said, "Come here, Emma, and give me a big hug."

She ran to him, drew up short. Was she afraid to touch him? Probably so. She studied his face as she reached out her hand and lightly laid her fingertips on his forearm. When she realized his eyes were clear and focused on her, she seemed to accept that he wasn't lying to her because she was a kid. "If they're going to move you away from all these machines, it for sure means you're getting better." She moved her fingers to hover over his whiskered cheek.

"I don't want to hurt you, Daddy."

He grinned up at her. "Nah, no chance of that. Do you remember a long time ago when I told you I was tough and you could always count on me? Forever?"

She swallowed, nodded.

"Nothing's changed, Emma. I'm still the same. There's nothing here your old man can't handle."

He knew even a small movement might

hurl him into a well of pain, but he raised his hand to gently stroke her face. Slowly, Emma leaned down and hugged him. "Doesn't it hurt to lie on your back?"

"Not much. They wrapped me up like a mummy. Don't be afraid, Emma. Everything is all right now."

But how could everything be all right? Emma wondered. Whoever had shot her father was still out there, and he might try again. Would there be guards around him forever?

Emma said, "Officer Hughes told us he heard you laugh this morning. He said it was a good sign."

He'd laughed? He couldn't remember. Ramsey had probably been riding the morphine express to LaLa Land and heard a nurse say something funny, or not funny at all, it wouldn't matter.

"There you go," he said, looking over at Molly, who cocked her head toward Emma and nodded. She was pleased he was finally getting some alone time with his daughter. Emma's fingers stroked his face, as light as butterfly wings.

He said, "Your mom told me you're keeping a close eye on Cal and Gage in case she gets so worried about me she forgets to feed them. I tried to think what Gage would do if food didn't magically appear whenever he wanted some. It wasn't a pretty picture."

Emma laughed. "They'd both go next door to Mr. Sproole's house and out-cute each other so he'd clean out his refrigerator for them."

Ramsey laughed along with her and managed to hug her again, though the pain in the back of his chest spiked. Pain tasted foul, he thought, not for the first time, and how odd was it that you could actually taste pain? It wasn't coppery, like blood. Maybe like rotted asparagus? He said, "I know Mr. Sproole is an ice-cream junkie; he's always got some in his freezer. Do you think he'd break out his chocolate-chip cookie dough ice cream for Gage and Cal?"

"No, that's his favorite. He'd give them an old carton of vanilla. They'd be happy enough with that." She settled herself on the bed beside him, still clutching his hand like a lifeline. "Sean was over at our house this morning, playing with Gage and Cal while I was practicing. When I finished a piece he tapped me on the shoulder. He was real serious and polite, Dad. He said he wanted to marry me, and even though he would have three wives he could promise me that I'd be his number-one wife, since I was older than his other two. He said if I agreed, I couldn't date any other boys until he grew up and came to fetch me." Emma giggled.

A laugh spurted out of Ramsey's mouth. He couldn't help it, though it made him groan. He breathed slowly in and out, and when the pain settled into a steady throb again, he asked, "So what did you say about being Sean's number-one wife?"

"Sean wasn't done. He asked me if I wanted a big wedding. When I told him I probably would, he said he was going to have to get three jobs, since both Marty and Georgie wanted big weddings, too."

Emma looked thoughtful. "Maybe two other wives would be good, since they could keep Sean company while I was practicing, or away playing somewhere."

His practical girl. And that twinkle in her eyes. It wouldn't have occurred to her to dismiss a five-year-old boy and make him feel small. Lucky Sean. Ramsey said,

"I wouldn't be surprised if Sean grew up to be as cool as his daddy."

"And his mama."

"And his mama. Trouble is, your Aunt Sherlock told me she doesn't want her son to go to jail. Three wives could push him right into the slammer."

Again, Emma looked thoughtful. "That wouldn't be good. Sean couldn't work three jobs to support his wives if he went to jail."

A nurse appeared in the doorway beside Molly. "Judge Hunt, are you ready for your trip to your very own private corner room? It's the same room the president would be given if something happened to him in San Francisco. It even has Monet reproductions on one of the walls. There'll be room for half a dozen guards to buzz around you." She frowned at him, seeing that he was in pain and guessing he hadn't used the morphine pump recently. Then she sighed. She understood why. She smiled at Emma. "Your daddy's so buff and strong he'll be better in no time, so don't you worry."

"My dad's real tough, and he's going to have my back all my life; he told me so."

ICU nurse Janine Holder hadn't cried in the hospital for a long time because it never helped, but she felt tears come to her eyes. This beautiful young girl was hovering protectively over her father, and what he'd said to her, so simple, so heartfelt—Janine swallowed and smiled. "If you're ready, Judge Hunt, I'll call everyone in and get it done. Mrs. Hunt, you and Emma need to come with me."

Two days was long enough in the surgical ICU, Ramsey thought. Too much beeping and clanging and buzzing all day and night. At least he hadn't heard any flatline whines, hadn't heard anyone dying. He'd have some peace and quiet now, even if there would be half a dozen guards. If he wasn't yet ready to be released into the wild, at least he would have a more comfortable cage.

Ramsey heard Molly say outside his cubicle, "Emma, we'll go get some sandwiches in the cafeteria, then go to your daddy's new room and wait for him there. Did you know Uncle Dillon and Aunt Sherlock are outside? We can say hello."

Ramsey wasn't stupid—he pumped in some morphine for the move. No matter how careful everyone was, he imagined there would be jostling, and it wouldn't be fun.

Officer Mancusso came to stand in the doorway. "You're not to worry, Judge Hunt. Hughes and I will be accompanying you. Nothing will happen to you, sir."

Ramsey could only marvel at the odd mix of pride and promise in the young officer's voice. He realized he didn't know his first name, and asked him.

"It's Jay, Judge Hunt," Mancusso said.

It looked like an honor guard, Sherlock thought, when they finally got the bed wheeling down the hall toward the east elevators. Officer Eddie Hughes was on one side of the bed and Officer Jay Mancusso on the other side. Eve and fifteen-year-veteran Deputy Marshal Allen Milton walked at the head of the bed, and a muscular orderly with a big Fu Manchu mustache steered and kept an eye on the IVs dangling from the headboard and the chest tube pinned to the sheets. Ramsey had tried to smile at them as they wheeled him by.

Sherlock saw Ramsey's face was white

with pain. At least Molly and Emma weren't here to see him. But Ramsey would live, and they would catch his shooter. She wondered how she'd be holding up if Dillon had been the one shot and nearly killed. She gave him a fast kiss.

Savich, Sherlock, and Harry got in the back of the line behind Ramsey's bed. Eve stood beside him, her hand resting lightly on his arm. She leaned over for a moment to say something to him and her ponytail swung down to lie against her face. Sherlock smiled. After the interview with Milo Siles, Dillon had told her, "I learn something new every single day. Do you know there appears to be power in the ponytail?" And he'd grinned like a bandit.

When they reached the elevator, they looked up and down the now-empty hospital corridor. They watched the doors open, and five people squeezed into the elevator around the bed. The doors closed behind them.

An SFPD officer waited with them for the other elevator, which seemed to be tied up on the seventh floor, while yet another deputy marshal used the stairs.

They stood quietly, watching the arrow of Ramsey's elevator leave the fourth floor and hover at the fifth floor.

They heard a loud clanging noise and the sound of muffled gunfire.

Savich ran to the stairs door, yelling over his shoulder, "Sherlock, Harry! Find out where the shooter got access to the elevator! Get him!"

When he burst out of the stairwell door onto the fifth floor, he was greeted with the yells of hospital staff and the screams and shouts of patients standing at the doors of their rooms, staring at smoke seeping out between the closed elevator doors. Half a dozen hospital personnel were trying to pull the elevator doors open, but no luck. Savich ran to the fire extinguisher case and pulled out the ax. He shouldered through and slipped the edge between the doors and pulled down across the safety beam. The doors sprang open.

Thick black smoke billowed out. When it was cleared enough to see inside, Savich saw blood spattered everywhere.

22

San Francisco General Hospital
Fifth floor

A shout came out of the chaos. "The shooter's on the roof of the elevator! Officers down!" Officer Eddie Hughes stumbled out, panting and coughing, holding his bloody arm and trying to keep Deputy Marshal Allen Milton upright, blinded by the blood streaming down his face. Both men still had their guns in their hands.

SFPD officer Jay Mancusso staggered out, his Glock at his side, his eyes tearing from the smoke, coughing. He wheezed out, "He threw a smoke bomb down through the top of the elevator and opened fire. Barbieri, she's with Judge Hunt. I don't know—" And he bent over in a fit of coughing. At least he hadn't been shot that Savich could see.

The orderly was trying to pull himself up, blood soaking his white pants.

All of it had happened in seconds.

Savich was coughing, fighting to see through the gray haze of smoke still clouding the elevator. A frantic voice came through the chaos, "Judge Hunt! How is Judge Hunt?"

Savich managed to push his way in, and his heart stopped. Eve was lying stretched out on top of Ramsey, and she wasn't moving. He was afraid to touch her. "Eve? Answer me!"

Slowly, Eve raised herself off of Ramsey. She was in pain, obvious to Savich, but he didn't see any blood. She turned to look at the myriad faces staring down at her, then settled again on Savich's face. He helped her slide off the bed. She stumbled, and he helped her right herself. "Sorry, the bullets knocked me silly. I'm okay." She pulled away from him and looked down at Ramsey's white face. "Ramsey—talk to me."

He opened his eyes. "Hi, Eve."

"Are you all right?"

A doctor and a nurse squeezed into the elevator beside them and eased them aside to tend to Ramsey. "Yes, I'll live." He coughed and moaned. "All the smoke and gunfire. How is everyone else? How are you, Eve?"

"I'll live, too. He shot me three times in my back, missed my head, thank goodness, or I'd be a goner. The impact knocked the breath out of me, that's all." She gave a wild grin, even though she felt like she'd been whacked by a two-by-four too many times. "Thank the good Lord for Kevlar."

A doctor tapped Eve on the shoulder. Ramsey gave her hand a squeeze, and reluctantly, Eve released his. They wheeled him out of the elevator. He said to all of them, "I'll be all right, don't worry about me." Three doctors, including Dr. Kardak, panting from running from surgery to get here, hovered over him as they wheeled his bed down the hall, two SFPD officers and one deputy marshal flanking them.

They heard Ramsey say, "You'd be wheeling me down to the morgue in the basement if not for Eve. I'm going to kick her butt for taking such a chance."

Eve waved into the elevator car. "It looks like a war zone in here." She pointed up, nearly groaning at the pain in her back. "Would you look at the ceiling? Our guys shot the crap out of it. They fired nonstop, but I don't know if we hit him."

She closed her eyes. It had looked like the end, but no one was dead. She sent a prayer of thanks upward. "Please tell me you got this idiot."

Savich said, "Sherlock and Harry are on it; they'll be here soon."

Harry Christoff gently picked up an elderly man by his elbows and set him aside. He shoved two police officers out of his way and stood in front of Eve, panting from running down three flights of stairs. He took in her tearing eyes, her blond straggling ponytail, her smoke-blackened face. "Good grief, woman, look at you. You're all right, aren't you?" He saw that she was hunched over and touched her arm.

Eve smiled at him. "I'm okay, thanks to the miracle of Kevlar. We all survived."

Sherlock burst out of the stairwell, panting.

Savich said immediately, "Ramsey's okay. Everyone's alive. Is he still inside the building?"

She started toward Eve, but Eve said quickly, "I'm in one piece. Did you get the guy?"

Sherlock ignored the god-awful mayhem in front of her and forced herself to calm. "He made it out of the elevator shaft. We started a search, but we can't lock down the whole hospital. He's probably out on the street by now."

"How could he have pulled this off?" Eve asked.

Sherlock said, "Okay, he had to case out the elevators and hang out close enough to the ICU to find out when Ramsey was going to be moved. It looks like the shooter called both of the east elevators to the roof. There's an access hatch up there for servicing. He immobilized one of them and settled himself on top of the working elevator when it was called down. He loosened the ceiling hatch and waited. We don't know how long he was up there, but he must have cut this pretty close, otherwise someone would have called for service on the immobilized elevator, and he didn't want that."

"But how did he know?" Eve smacked the side of her head. "Am I an idiot or what? I'll bet even the dishwashers in the cafeteria kitchen knew when Ramsey was being moved."

Sherlock said, "It's even better than that. He didn't even have to look in. The shaft acoustics are incredible, so he could hear Ramsey being pushed into the car, got himself set. The moment the car started up, he shoved the hatch aside, dropped the smoke canister in, and started firing. He couldn't see any better than you guys could through all the smoke, but he must have seen where Ramsey's bed was, focused his fire there. Eve, what happened inside?"

Eve tried to straighten, but a jab of pain punched her ribs. She felt Harry's hand tighten on her arm. She said, "I didn't think; I threw myself on top of Ramsey, and right away three shots hit me in the back—in the blessed Kevlar. He kept firing, but our guys were firing back, so his shots were pretty wild. Whatever he hit was random after that. I'll tell you my heart nearly stopped while I was lying there, thinking of how helpless Ramsey was." She paused for a moment. "You know, I'm betting the shooter thinks he killed Ramsey."

Sherlock stared at the blood splattered on the elevator walls, stared at Eve and at Harry standing behind her. She knew that three close-range shots in the back, even through Kevlar, would make you feel like you'd been beaten with a baseball bat. "If you hadn't been wearing the vests, he'd have killed all of you." She felt such rage she was shaking with it.

Sherlock asked Officer Mancusso, "What about Hughes and Milton? How badly are they hit?"

Officer Jay Mancusso said, "Deputy Milton's head wound looked bad, but they always do. I heard one of the doctors say it was only a scalp wound, though.

Eddie Hughes—he got it in the arm, through and through. The orderly who got shot in the leg went right off to the ER."

A nurse, still looking on, called out, "Doug was pressing on his leg wound himself. You'd better believe he was hollering for the trauma team. He'll be all right."

Jay said, "Both Eddie and I got two shots in the Kevlar, but we're okay. We didn't get hammered like Deputy Barbieri."

Savich said, "Eve, tell us what else you remember."

"Jumping on Ramsey, covering him as best I could, screaming at the orderly to take cover. There was so much gunfire after a second or two, most of it from our guys, shooting wildly upward through the thick smoke, and then there wasn't any more return fire. The shooter was gone."

Sherlock patted her arm. "Yeah, he got out, but guess what? I've got some good news I haven't told you—one of you wounded him. I saw some blood drops on the top of the elevator car, bloody handprints on the shaft ladder, and a couple of drops on the roof and in the stairway. Then he must have managed to get himself bandaged enough so he didn't spill anymore. That means we can spot him on the security cameras, see how badly he's hurt, but best of all, we'll have his DNA." She cocked her head to one side. "Or Sue's DNA."

"Excellent," Savich said. "At last we've got a break."

Harry cupped his elbow around Eve's arm and said without looking at her, "You think you got any broken ribs?"

"They feel like they're in splinters. Don't worry, I'll get it checked out." She knew she wouldn't be up for smelling the roses for the next couple of days. Bruises would cover her back. She prayed no ribs were cracked. She wondered who'd managed to nail the shooter. DNA. Dillon was right, at last they'd caught a break.

The last people Eve wanted to see here came running up in the next moment. She walked toward them, away from the elevator, and said quickly, "Emma, Molly, Ramsey's all right. The doctors took him back to his new room. He wasn't hurt, I swear. He's okay."

Emma clung to her mother and swallowed, but she couldn't stop shaking.

Neither could Molly. Emma stared at Eve and the drifting dirty smoke, and then she looked toward the elevator. "How can everything be okay, Aunt Eve? I can see the blood."

"I'm not lying to you, Emma."

Emma still stared into the bloody elevator.

One very old man called out from a doorway, "Is Judge Dredd dead?"

Emma turned on him. "Don't you say such a thing! My daddy's fine."

Eve said, "Some people were hurt, Emma, but not your dad. I promise."

They looked up to see Dr. Kardak walking toward them. He said, more to Emma and Molly than to them, "Judge Hunt is well. We're all a little shaken, but we've checked him out thoroughly, and he wasn't injured. We're settling him in his new room." He gestured toward Molly. "I suggest, Mrs. Hunt, that you and Emma stay here a while longer before you come back.

"As for you, Deputy Barbieri, I understand you were injured. You need to come with me."

Once they stood in an empty hospital

room, Dr. Kardak said to Eve, "Take off the vest, Deputy Barbieri. Let's see the damage."

When Eve and Dr. Kardak came out a few minutes later, three pairs of eyes fastened on them. The doctor said, "She won't be having much fun for a couple of days; there's going to be a lot of bruising from the impacts. I didn't feel any cracked ribs, and that's good. We're going to get an X-ray to be sure." He pulled a pad out of his coat pocket and wrote a pain prescription for her. A nurse trotted over and handed her a pill. "Take this, it'll help." She closed her hand over Eve's wrist. "Thank you for saving Judge Hunt."

23

San Francisco General Hospital

Hospital security chief Ron Martinez walked into the small security office off the hospital lobby, where Savich, Sherlock, Harry, and Eve sat in folding chairs waiting for him. He loaded a disk into the office computer and almost immediately paused it and pointed. "We think this is our guy, based on when and where he left, but we can't be sure. I had the tech start this at the beginning, where we think he came in, because, unfortunately, that's most of what we got. He walks straight to the two elevators on the right, no hesitation, like he knows exactly where he's going. Less attention from anyone at the reception desk that way."

Martinez reversed the disk and paused it where the camera got a close-up.

They stared at a man of indeterminate age wearing loose pants, sneakers, a loose navy Windbreaker, dark sunglasses, and a Giants ball cap.

"Bingo," Harry said. "He fits the description of the guy we've been looking for."

"He's well disguised," Eve said. "He knows you're getting him on film. He's not even trying to avoid the cameras, and I'll bet he knows where every one of them is. He looks middle-aged to me. What do you think?"

"Maybe older," Harry said. "Thin, maybe about five-foot-nine. I can't see his face or his hair with the sunglasses and the pulled-down cap, but we get a glimpse there of part of his neck—does his neck look saggy to anyone?"

"An elderly assassin?" Martinez's eyebrow shot up.

Savich said quietly, "Listen, it might even be a woman."

Martinez's other thick black eyebrow shot up. "A woman? In a shoot-out like that?"

Savich said, "Since we've got DNA, we'll soon know everything about him or her, including the time of birth. That is, if he's in the system."

"Or about Sue," Eve said.

Chief Martinez pressed the play button again. "Sorry, guys, but we don't have cameras on the roof of the hospital where he accessed the elevators." He fast-forwarded. "The next time we have him on camera, he's exiting the west stairwell into the lobby and waltzing out of the hospital. This is within a couple of minutes of the shooting." A new camera angle showed the shooter walking quickly out of one of the hospital entrances on the west side.

"But look at this. He's holding his arm. That's got to be where they hit him."

Sherlock said, "Yes, and the Windbreaker covers any blood."

Chief Martinez told them the security

people, SFPD officers, and deputy marshals were showing hard copies of the photos of the shooter to everyone who might have seen him, questioning the garage attendants, even people on the street. It was plain to see no one held out much hope of that happening, but on the other hand, it was worth a try.

They left Martinez singing a happier tune about what the DNA might show, and all returned to Ramsey's room. They passed a deputy marshal and an SFPD officer sitting on each side of the door, talking about Deputy Marshal Allen Milton's head wound. "The bullet slicked along the side of his head. Allen's blaming his head, said if it wasn't so big he could have tucked it inside his vest where it belonged."

The big corner room—the Taj—looked north toward the city. It was blessedly quiet now, with only six people and Ramsey. Molly and Emma were standing on either side of Ramsey's bed, not speaking, merely holding his hands, staring down at him. Two deputy marshals had positions by the windows, and Dr.

Kardak and a nurse were speaking in low voices, reviewing Ramsey's chart.

Ramsey's eyes were closed. He knew his wife and his daughter were standing next to him, but his brain seemed to be operating on a twenty-watt. He decided that was okay for the moment, a fair trade-off for the pain in his chest being magically gone, thanks to a shot of morphine. He opened his eyes as they approached and said in a slurred voice, "Eve?"

Eve, still hurting despite the pain pill, made herself walk upright and not hobble to his bed. He looked shell-shocked, she thought, as if the wild shoot-out in the elevator couldn't really have happened. She understood completely. She placed her fingers on his forearm and smiled down at him. "I'm here, Ramsey. No need to worry about me. I might look on the scruffy side, but all my working parts are operating fine. Looks like you're okay, too.

"We have some news for you, if you haven't already heard. We shot him, Ramsey, and we found his blood in the elevator shaft, and that means we'll have his DNA. There's a really good chance we'll identify him." Eve looked over at Dr. Kardak, and raised a questioning eyebrow. The doctor nodded his consent for her to keep talking to Ramsey.

"Was it this Sue person?"

"We don't know yet, but it's possible. On the security video, he looks like maybe an older guy, but that could have been a disguise. I'm just glad we were all so lucky."

Molly touched Eve's arm. "I will owe you forever."

"Me too, Aunt Eve," Emma said, swallowing down tears.

Marshal Carney Maynard came running through the door, Virginia Trolley on his heels. Maynard studied Ramsey, then, satisfied, said, "There's a media frenzy downstairs. My guys and hospital security have cordoned off the elevators, and we're putting security stations around the floor. We'll hope it works to keep them out. And I called Cheney Stone. He'll be here any minute. Maybe we can talk him into making a statement."

Better him than me, Savich thought.

Virginia Trolley said, shaking her head,

"Our police commissioner will probably beat him to it. She's always eager to be the face of law enforcement in the city."

Savich said, "Ramsey."

When Ramsey focused on Savich's face, Savich continued, "I know you're close to floating up on the ceiling, but you're the one who had the unusual visual perspective, looking up. Can you tell us what you saw?"

Ramsey wondered for a moment—had someone said something to him? He looked at all of them, then focused again on Savich. Yes, Savich had asked him to speak. He had to think about that. He willed away some of the mental confusion, and everything became clear, too clear, really. "Eve had her hand on my arm, Eddie was talking about the Forty-niners, and then I saw the roof hatch lift and I caught a glimpse of a face staring down at me, but only for a split second, right before all the smoke and gunfire—" He lost himself in the words, but that was all right, because in the next second the rest of him was lost as well.

Marshal Maynard said, "Your forensic team has five slugs from the Kevlar vests, all of them from a Kel Tec PF-9, chambered for the nine-millimeter Luger cartridge. As you know, it's the lightest and flattest nine-millimeter ever made and has a single stack holding seven rounds. That means he had three or four magazines with him and he was fast changing them out."

Eve looked at her boss. "If you hadn't insisted on Kevlar vests for everyone—" She stopped, which was okay, because everyone in the room knew what she meant.

24

SAC Cheney Stone's office
Federal Building
Thirteenth floor
San Francisco
Sunday morning

Five-foot-nothing veteran forensic blood expert Mimi Cutler rushed into the room, her wrinkled lab coat flapping, her short spiked dark hair sticking up at odd angles where she'd run her fingers through it countless times throughout more hours than she wanted to count. But she was smiling, and that made Sherlock's heart leap. She looked ready to make everyone's day.

Cutler caught her breath, smoothed her hair, straightened her coat, and beamed at the people in the office. She waved a sheaf of photos in her hand. "After a wild and hairy all-nighter, here you go, hot off the press." She fanned herself. "Okay, let me back up. The very first thing we did when we arrived at the scene yesterday was collect all the samples of the shooter's blood. We processed some of the blood, then ran the DNA through the CODIS and bang!—look at this photo, it just came through my email." She beamed as she handed each of them a copy. "Here's our shooter."

All of them stared at an eight-by-ten colored police booking photograph of a young bruiser who looked like he'd lost a fight—his face was a mass of blotched purple-and-green bruises, his split swollen lips dark red with dried blood. His head was shaved bald and sat on a neck that looked wider than Sherlock's waist. The height chart behind him showed he was six foot four inches, and he looked like he had to weigh two hundred and sixty pounds. "His name is Paul, aka Boozer, Gordon. He's an amateur boxer, has anger management issues. It looks like he lost a fight the night he was booked, doesn't it? He's been arrested and jailed for assault three times to date. He lives here in the city, on Clayton." She beamed at them.

There was dead silence in Cheney's office.

"What? We've identified your guy! What's wrong?"

Harry said, "Sorry, Mimi, but we don't think this is our shooter. Our shooter is lots older, lots shorter, weighs maybe half what this guy weighs, and his neck is about as thick of one of this guy's wrists."

"But this is an exact match; the probabilities are off the wall. You've got to be wrong."

"I guess it's time to back up again, Mimi," Sherlock said. "I don't suppose there's a chance of a lab error, or a mix-up with the samples?" She added with a smile, "Maybe more than one person's blood?"

"Naturally not," Mimi said, not appeased by the smile. "I collected the blood myself, and we ran samples from three different sites. All the samples matched."

Savich said, "Let's find this guy. Cheney, can you get some people working on his last known address? And Sherlock, get on the phone to the hospital, find out if Paul Boozer Gordon was there this week, maybe as some kind of patient?"

Mimi grabbed her hair and tugged on it. "A patient? How would a patient's blood get in the elevator shaft?"

There was only one possibility, Savich thought, far-fetched, but still. He said slowly, "Mimi, did you happen to test the blood samples for traces of heparin?"

"Heparin? No, why?"

Savich said, "There's lots of blood in a hospital—in the blood bank, in the laboratories, at nursing stations waiting to be picked up. And that includes heparinized blood that wouldn't clot right away. You wouldn't be able to tell as easily if the blood was older, that it was planted there, would you?"

"Are you telling me the shooter brought the blood *with* him into the elevator shaft? Someone else's blood, to plant on the scene? That he added heparin to the blood to fool me? Do you realize that would mean this frigging shooter would understand *blood analysis*? You're saying he purposefully set out to mislead us? To mislead *me*?" She paused for a moment, her rocket brain filling in the possibilities. "Goodness, even if he actually managed to get hold of someone else's blood, think of how careful he had to be to leave blood splattered at the scene in a way that wouldn't be spotted by the forensic team as looking wrong. All that work, all that study and practice—for what? Nothing, really."

Savich said, "Unless this Boozer Gordon was shot in the elevator shaft, how else does this make sense?"

Harry said, "If that's true, Savich, the shooter had to know we'd see through the deception sooner rather than later. He couldn't have hoped to frame someone else for the shooting that way. It reminds me of that newspaper picture of Judge Dredd we found in his backyard. Another way to give us the finger again, not give *you* the finger, Mimi, but us. He wanted to show us how smart he is, and what tail-chasing loser dogs we are in comparison. Another thing, apparently the shooter wasn't wounded after all." Harry cursed under his breath.

Cheney was off his cell first. "DMV still has Boozer Gordon's address on Clayton Street. Now, you're saying our shooter somehow got some of Boozer's blood, enough of it to create believable blood splatter?"

Savich nodded. "Only explanation I can think of."

Sherlock closed her cell. "Medical records has Boozer Gordon discharged from the hospital late Friday morning, the day before Ramsey was attacked in the elevator. He came in through the ER, apparently looking beat up as badly as in that mug shot. I spoke to an ER nurse. She was not very happy with my question. She said no one had ever walked in and stolen blood from them, for heaven's sake, that it simply couldn't happen. Then Miss Manners got huffier, told me it was ridiculous to think someone could simply waltz in there or into a patient's room and draw his blood. Couldn't happen, never in this lifetime. But I agree with Dillon. I think that's exactly what happened, I'd bet my hair rollers on it."

"No," Savich said, "not the hair rollers."

Harry said, "So our guy put on a white coat, walked in, and drew Mr. Gordon's blood?"

Sherlock thought for a moment. "However he got it was an elaborate pretense, especially with the huge risk he took in that elevator shaft. I'm thinking that even if he'd planned Ramsey's murder for a long time, there was very little planning in that attack on the elevator, since of course he couldn't know he needed to play it.

"Would a professional take on an armed guard like that? We're working on the assumption that Sue is a professional, but, you know, this really feels like it's personal."

"Personal, or maybe desperate," Savich said. "An act of rage, or delusion."

Harry nodded. "And he didn't leave that blood behind on the fly, since he added heparin to make us think it was fresh. It's like some kind of crazy what-if scenario that he'd played through in his mind, maybe even read about and practiced. That would have taken time, and that could be the key here, he had to have time on his hands. Sherlock's right, why would Sue the master spy go to all this trouble?"

Sherlock's eyes locked with Savich's.

He said matter-of-factly, "You mean the shooter was in prison."

Harry said, "Until recently, I suspect. If Sue the spy has nothing to do with this, then we may be talking about a guy who came out of prison knowing exactly what he wanted to do, everything all laid out."

Cheney said, "And, bottom line, what he wants to do is to kill Judge Hunt."

"A guy," Harry said. "I'd just gotten my brain wrapped around this Sue. Doesn't matter, if he was in jail, we can find him."

Mimi Cutler, who'd been standing by the door, began pulling on her hair again. "Do you guys know I had to *cancel* a date last night—my first date in four and a half months—and the guy is *hot.* I didn't tell him what I do for a living, since he'd probably freak. He's a stockbroker and only sees blood if he nicks himself shaving. I gave him a lame excuse about a sick mother, and would you look at this—it turns out I couldn't even find my mom."

She shook Boozer Gordon's photo and ripped it in two.

Sherlock said, "Mimi, tell your guy you do blood analysis for DNA, that you were working on the Judge Hunt incident at the hospital yesterday—it's all over the news. He'll be so impressed and excited to know someone in the thick of things, he'll be camping out on your front porch. Trust me on this."

Mimi stopped pulling on her spikes of hair. "You think?"

At Sherlock's solemn nod, Mimi smoothed down her hair. "You don't mind if I tell him about Judge Hunt? Give him the gory details?"

"Like I said," Sherlock added, "it's all over the news, so why not cash in?"

Mimi left, fluffing her hair and humming "Girls Just Wanna Have Fun."

Harry stared after Mimi, shaking his head, marveling at how you could be in the pits one second and laughing out loud the next.

25

Near Nicasio, California
Sunday morning

He was glad for the drizzling rain, cold and wet on his neck. It made shoveling dirt over Mickey O'Rourke nice and easy. Finally he stepped back, studied the mound he'd made. Not good, too high, too easy to find. He began pounding the back of the shovel on the wet dirt, flattening it down, scraping some of it away. Once he had the dirt as flat as he wanted it, he dragged branches over to cover it.

"RIP, Mickey," he said, as he kicked a chunk of sod under a branch.

He stood for a moment, marveling at the near-perfect silence, the only sound the rustle of leaves and the rain dripping off his arm and striking a rock beside his booted foot. He could hear himself breathe. The air was heavy with wet and green, not even a whiff of an exhaust fume. And here he was, only eleven miles from the interstate and its endless stream of cars. Not a bad place to be dead, he thought, like in a faraway forest.

He would miss this place, home for nearly a year and a half now, especially his small apartment in San Rafael, just a block from the Mission San Rafael Arcángel. He'd visited the old church quite often, not to pray but to focus his mind. It was as quiet as a tomb in the dark of night, cool and peaceful, as if the spirits settled there knew their own worth, and kept order.

He considered what to do with the shovel. Not leave it in the trunk of his Jeep; that wouldn't be smart. He would dump the shovel, but not around these grassy hills, and not in these woods. They were too close to Mickey in his tatty shroud. No, he'd dump it in some thick trees on his way back to San Rafael. Maybe a hiker would find the shovel and think it was good fortune.

He turned his face to the sky, felt the cool drizzle seam down his cheeks. Then he shook himself like a mongrel and trotted the quarter-mile back to his Jeep.

26

Clayton Street
San Francisco
Late Sunday morning

Boozer Gordon didn't look so hot. The tiny black stitches on his chin running up his cheek to his ear looked like one-sided beard bristle. The bruises covering his face were now a faded purple, and both his eyes were still black. He was wearing an ancient green fleece bathrobe, and his big feet were in thick black socks. Boozer was very big. Savich had to look up at him.

"Yeah, what do you clowns want? It's Sunday; you're supposed to be in church or at least getting out the chips and salsa for the football games."

Sherlock gave Boozer her patented sunny smile. Savich thought, *We'll see if your smile is as powerful as the blond ponytail.*

"We're not just any clowns," Sherlock said, "we're FBI clowns, and we labor every day to bring criminals to justice—what you see is your taxpayer dollars at work. We have some questions for you about a shooting that happened yesterday." And she flipped out her creds. After a thorough study, Boozer looked at Savich. "You her bodyguard?"

"That's right," Savich said, and handed over his own creds.

"Just what I needed," Boozer said, and sighed. "Federal cops on a Sunday, doesn't that make my day. It will only get suckier if the Forty-niners lose.

"Listen, you're wasting your time. I'm innocent of anything that's happened in the past two days—look at me, I've been in the hospital. I got the crap beat out of me, not in the ring, but in a stupid bar. Four morons whaled on me. Don't get me wrong, I coulda taken them if I didn't have beer leaking out my ears."

"Six sheets to the wind?"

"Yeah." He smiled down at Sherlock. "Only lucky thing is I never get hangovers."

Savich thought, *You're only twenty-three. You just wait.*

Boozer stepped back and let Savich and Sherlock walk into a small hallway with a living room off to the right, a long, narrow room that, surprisingly, had a big window that gave a sliver of view of the Golden Gate Bridge.

The room, even more surprisingly, was neat, down to the Sunday *Chronicle* stacked beside a big black La-Z-Boy with a beautifully crocheted dark blue afghan hanging over the arm.

Boozer waved them to a pale green sofa with three colorful throw pillows set just so along the back cushions.

"Nice pillows," Sherlock said.

"My mom," Boozer said. "She comes by when I'm not here to water my plants, and she does stuff, like brings pillows and changes the sheets and dries out the towels."

"The ivy looks good, too," Savich said. "Sit down, Mr. Gordon. We need your help."

Boozer's look was disbelieving. "My help? I told you, I've been out of commission for the past two days. I've never shot anybody—well, I couldn't have even tried if this happened in the past two days." He eased himself down in his big chair and pushed up the footrest. He gently unfolded the afghan and pulled it over his legs and leaned his head back against the headrest.

Sherlock and Savich sat on the sofa, careful not to disturb the artful placement of the throw pillows.

Sherlock said, "You were in San Francisco General Hospital until noon Friday, isn't that right, Mr. Gordon?"

His head came up and his eyes popped open. "Listen, I didn't hurt anybody at the hospital, I was too out of it even to get pissed off at anyone, and, well, everybody was nice to me."

Sherlock said, "That's good to know. I'm nice, too. Now, Mr. Gordon, we need you to think back. You're lying in your room on Friday, you're by yourself. You've got some nice pain meds working, and you're feeling pretty good, right?"

"Yes, but it didn't last all that long, maybe four hours; then I hurt again."

Savich said, "This is very important, Mr. Gordon. While you were lying in your hospital bed did any hospital technicians come in to draw your blood?"

That roused Boozer. "Oh, man, did that torturer accuse me of having bad blood? Did the hospital send you over because I've got that avian virus?"

"No, your blood is splendid," Sherlock said. "No viruses. We need you to tell us about the torturer."

Boozer looked from one to the other. "Why should I? You're cops, like those other yahoos who hauled my butt to lockup for no good reason. My manager had to bail me out, and he was yelling at me, too, and there I was, hurting since I was the one that got knocked crazy, not those four other bozos who ganged up on me. At least the cops sent me to the hospital. Why should I tell you anything?"

Savich said, "We think the person who drew your blood has tried to murder Judge Dredd twice."

Boozer blinked raccoon eyes at them. "Judge Dredd? You're kidding me, right? I mean, they used to have a poster of Judge Dredd at the martial arts school since he used to work out there. You're telling me the dude who took my blood is the one who tried to shoot him in the elevator yesterday?"

"Yes," Sherlock said. "Judge Dredd is okay, for the moment, but we want to find the shooter before he tries again. You called the man who drew your blood a torturer. Tell us about it."

The front door opened, and a very beautiful woman strolled in. She was wearing a black pantsuit and low-heeled shoes, and she was as blond, porcelain-skinned and fine-boned as a storybook princess. She was carrying a bag of groceries under her left arm with what looked like a pair of folded boxers sticking out of the huge tote in her right hand.

"What is going on here, Paul? Who are these people? You're not one of those missionary groups, are you? If you are, you're out of luck. Paul's a devout Catholic."

"Oh, hi, Mom. These here guys aren't Christians, they're FBI agents, and they need my help to find the guy who's trying to kill Judge Dredd."

Now it was her turn to stare. "Goodness me," she said finally, and accepted their hands to shake and their introductions and creds.

Boozer said, "Oh, yeah, this is my Mom, Cynthia Howell. She doesn't have my name because she divorced my pa for being a mean drunk and married Daniel, my stepdad. He gave me that black Ford One-fifty last Christmas. You saw it in the driveway, didn't you?"

Savich said, "A fine machine."

"Well, that about sums it up," Mrs. Howell said. "My Paul can help you? Really?"

"Mom, it turns out I saw the guy who shot Judge Dredd in the hospital. He drew my blood."

"I see. Paul, you tell these agents everything you know about this man while I get you another pain pill. Oh, I brought over two homemade pizzas, with lots of pepperoni, the way you like it. I know you're hungry, but let me warm them in the oven for about ten minutes." And she walked out of the living room and into the kitchen.

His mother made him pizza? Pepperoni? Sherlock felt her mouth water.

Mrs. Howell came right back with a glass of water with three ice cubes and a slice of lemon wedged on the side of the glass. Boozer took the pill, drank the water, and gave a sweet smile to his mother. She gently cupped his face. "It doesn't look as bad this morning. I'll get your pizza in the oven now, sweetie. Don't wait for me. You can tell me everything later."

Sherlock said, "The tech who came to draw your blood?"

Boozer leaned his head back and looked at the ceiling. "He was a little guy."

Savich said, "Being as how you're on the tall side, what do you mean, exactly, by little?"

"I don't know, shorter than you, lots

less than six feet. Kind of scrawny, not all that much to him, you know what I mean?"

You're a behemoth. Even Dillon looks scrawny to you. Sherlock said, "Tell us about his face. What did he look like?"

"I can't tell you much about his face because he was wearing one of those surgical masks, you know, like he needed protection from me, like I was contagious or something. That's why I thought when you showed up the hospital had found something was bad."

Savich said, "No, Mr. Gordon, there's nothing wrong with your blood. How about his hair? What color?"

"He had a green scrub hat on his head."

"Could you see his hair at all?"

"I remember thinking the cap was too big for him. It covered his whole head, came down over his ears. If he didn't have that big needle in his hand, I would have said something, like why didn't the hospital give him caps that fit him, but I kept quiet."

Sherlock said, "How tall is your mom, Boozer?"

They heard a lovely voice call from the

kitchen, "I'm five-foot-nine, Agent Sherlock. Paul is tall, too; he takes after me."

Sherlock smiled at Boozer. "Picture the guy in your mind, he's standing by your bed. Is he taller than your mom?"

Boozer thought about this. "Nah, he's about the same as my mom, maybe a little bit shorter."

"Is there anything you can tell us about him that stood out when you met him? You called him a torturer. So he wasn't very good?"

"That's for sure. He would have really hurt me if I hadn't been a little looped from all the drugs. He had a real hard time getting the needle in a vein, had to go to my other arm. I don't know how many times he stuck me. I was wishing I could knock his block off, even with the drugs."

"But he finally got the needle in a vein," Savich said. "Do you remember how many blood vials he filled?"

Boozer shuddered, scrunched up his face like a kid. "I didn't want to look, but after a while I did. Three of those vacuum vials with the purple stoppers. I asked him what all that blood was for, and he said something like, 'I guess they want to make sure your insides didn't get as wrecked as your face.'

"I remember that because I thought it sounded kind of nasty what he said; then he left, didn't say anything else to me. I guess he was the only one at the hospital who wasn't nice to me."

Savich studied Boozer's face for a moment. He could see the pain meds were starting to work. Boozer was sitting more easily in the big chair, his muscles loose, his hands smoothing out the afghan. He said, "Go ahead and close your eyes, Mr. Gordon. Relax. Imagine you're watching him draw your blood. Is there anything unusual about him?"

"I heard him cursing under his breath when he couldn't find a vein."

"Anything else?"

"Well, he stopped in the door when he was leaving and turned around."

"Look at him, Boozer. Was he old?"

"Hard to say, over fifty, I'd say, somewhere in there."

Sherlock wanted him to compare his age to his mother's, but she wasn't stupid. She heard Mrs. Howell coming into the living room carrying a huge tray with a pepperoni pizza so hot you could feel the cheese dripping off your chin.

"I have another pizza in the oven, so there's plenty for all of us. Agents?"

Boozer had his slice of pizza in his hand when he said, "I remember now, the guy was wearing this butt-ugly ring on his finger, and another ring with a big diamond on his pinkie finger. I saw them when he pulled out those surgical gloves to put on his hands."

The same diamond pinkie ring Mrs. Moe described the man wearing when he rented the Zodiac in Sausalito.

Sherlock chewed a bite, then asked him, "How big was the butt-ugly ring?"

Boozer studied her face for a moment. "You have a piece of cheese on your chin, Agent Sherlock."

She laughed, swiped her napkin over her face. "Thank you. The pizza is delicious, Mrs. Howell. Now, the ring, Mr. Gordon?"

"It looked like a religious ring, you know. It looked real old and solid, with some dull jewels sticking up in the middle."

"Why do you say religious?"

Boozer shrugged. "I don't know, just a feeling, I guess, when I saw it. I was flying sort of high and it popped out of my mouth—'You an ex-priest?' He asked me why I thought that, and I pointed to his ring.

"He said, 'Nah, it's just a ring I won off this old guy in a poker game.' Nothing more, that was it. I didn't really care because I was worried about that needle in his hand and I wanted it over with."

Twenty minutes later, the pizza settling happily in their stomachs, Mrs. Howell showed them to the door. Sherlock simply couldn't help asking her, "May I ask you how old you are? You look like Boozer's sister instead of his mother."

Mrs. Howell laughed. "If I told you it might get back to my husband. It's the strangest thing, but it embarrasses him that I look so much younger than he does. The joys of cosmetic surgery, but don't tell Daniel. He thinks I'm perfect, and I don't want him to think otherwise. Isn't my Paul an amazing young man?"

As they walked away from Boozer's apartment, Savich stopped by their rental car, pulled Sherlock against him, and kissed her. "Yep, pepperoni."

"I got to eat all yours, too. Poor Mrs. Howell, she was mortified that she hadn't brought a vegetarian pizza, just in case. Do you think our shooter really won that butt-ugly religious ring in a poker game?"

27

Hyde Street, Russian Hill
Sunday

After four long knocks, Eve opened her door to Harry Christoff.

"I had this feeling it was you, but I was sort of hoping I was wrong."

"Why? You wanted maybe the postman? It's Sunday, no delivery on Sunday."

A laugh spurted out of her. "No, I'm not really up to acting all social and civilized. I'm sorry I missed the meeting this morning; you'll tell me everything?"

"I will, but you have to invite me in first. I figured you'd be in pretty bad shape, so I came bearing gifts." He held out a bakery bag and a covered go-cup that sent the aroma of dark roast coffee wafting to her nose.

Eve took the bag first, looked upward, and said "Thank you," then, "You're amazing, Harry, and you even brought coffee. No, you're more than amazing, you're a prince, Agent Christoff. Are there any glazed?"

He looked down at her scrubbed face, her hair hanging loose around her shoulders over a faded red robe, her bare feet. "You look like the homecoming queen on a reality show. I'm glad you slept in this morning. How's your back?"

She forced herself to stand up straight. "I'll be good to go after three donuts and this wonderful coffee. Come in, let's go to the kitchen. Are there maybe more than one glazed?"

"There are three, but I was hoping for one myself," he said, as he followed her into her kitchen. He still couldn't get over how streamlined and cool it looked, with pale green granite counters shot with black, and hanging copper pots over a small center island. He said, "My kitchen's right out of the forties."

"As long as everything's clean and works, who cares what decade it comes from? It's all about the food and the person making it, right? You want milk in your coffee? You don't want a glazed donut, do you? You somehow knew it was my favorite?"

"Nah, give me a chocolate with sprinkles. I'm a real man."

"How many donuts?"

"Six."

She set everything out on the small kitchen table, and they started in on the donuts and coffee, neither saying much of anything until only one donut, not glazed, was left on the paper plate between them. Eve wiped the sticky glaze off her mouth and her fingers, laughed, and leaned forward to flick a red sprinkle off his chin. She sat back and sighed, contented. "Thank you. Before you came, I'd just gotten out of the shower and wondered what I was going to make for breakfast. Nothing appealed, then you showed up."

She toasted him with her coffee cup.

He asked, "How'd you sleep last night?"

"In the arms of the angels, with the help of two aspirin and a sleeping-pill chaser. I'm trying to stay away from the codeine." She stretched, froze, then began, very slowly, to stretch again.

Harry stood up. "Let me see how bad the bruising is today."

She stared up at him. "You mean you want me to drop my bathrobe?"

"Well, yeah, but don't feel like you have to put on a show for me, even though I did let you eat all three of the glazed do-nuts. No, just show me your back. You know, if you can't think of me as your doc-tor, you can pretend you're an artist's model draped with a towel. Come on, Barbieri, I'm not going to jump you. You're safe. I'm not desperate enough, and, fact is, you're too pathetic-looking right now."

She stood up, turned her back to him, and let her robe drop to her waist. Harry pushed her hair out of the way, even though he didn't need to, and studied the shades of her green, black, and yellow back. "You got a modern art painter living with you?"

She tried to look back over her shoulder. "That bad?"

He lightly touched his fingertips to one bruise. She didn't flinch. "Do you have some muscle cream?"

She pulled her robe back up. "Yeah, I do, for all the good it did me. I can't reach the bad areas."

"Get it. I'll do it for you."

She gave him a look, then left him in the kitchen to finish his coffee and stare out at her small back garden with its six-foot stone walls and single cypress tree. Everything looked dormant now, but he imagined there'd be lots of color in the summer.

He ate the last donut since it was chocolate.

She came back into the kitchen in a minute, handed him a white tube. It was brand-new.

"It's supposed to be good stuff, not only for muscle soreness but for bruising as well. I bought it yesterday before I realized I couldn't reach anything."

She again dropped the robe to her waist. She grinned over her shoulder. "Am I really that pitiful?"

"Not quite; you combed your hair."

"Well, I looked in the mirror and nearly fainted. I had to do something."

Harry covered his fingers with the cream, stared at her long stretch of back, closed his eyes for a moment to get a grip on himself, and touched his fingers to her skin. *I'm a solid, consummate professional, doing my job.* He wished she did look pathetic, but the fact was, she didn't, not at all. He reminded himself he was looking at a deputy marshal's back splotched blue and green, but, unfortunately, that didn't help.

"Am I rubbing too hard?"

She said over her shoulder, "No, it feels grand."

"Would you like to lie on your stomach? Speaking as one solid professional to another?"

She laughed, then groaned. "Not a good idea, even speaking as a professional. You've got really good hands, Harry."

Really good *professional* hands. He

started whistling as he continued rubbing the cream on her back in steady smooth strokes, deepening when he realized he wasn't hurting her, and if his hands went a bit lower than the bruises, surely there were sore muscles at her waist, and the massage couldn't but help.

"You can't see the bruises now," he said. "You're all white since I've used half the tube on you."

"Feels like it, nice and hot."

He didn't want to stop, but he did. He stepped back. Slowly, she shrugged back into her robe. She turned. "Thank you. Look at me, I think I can straighten without groaning."

He went to the sink to wash his hands. He could feel the heat deep and knew it must feel good on her back.

"Tell me more about your meeting this morning with Cheney, Savich, and Sherlock."

So he told her, answering her questions until she had no more. His cell phone chimed.

"Yeah?"

"Cheney here, Harry. They found Mickey O'Rourke. Two kids in Nicasio

saw a man bury him. Thank God they had
the sense to keep quiet so he never saw
them. The Marin County sheriff, Bud Hibbert, had a photo of Mickey on his desk,
recognized him, and called me. I called
Savich and Sherlock. They've finished interviewing Boozer Gordon. I don't want
to call Barbieri; she's probably still flat on
her stomach, high on codeine."

"Actually," Harry said, "I'm with her
now, and she's doing okay. She's got to
get dressed, but we'll be there as soon
as we can."

"Good. Ask Eve to requisition a Chevy
Suburban out of the marshals' pool, that
way the five of us can ride up together."

Harry punched off his cell. He looked
up to see Eve standing in the doorway to
the kitchen, unmoving, her face set.

"You heard what Cheney said?"

She nodded. "I didn't want to believe
Mickey could be dead, it hurt too much, so
I tried not to think about it." She swallowed. "But I knew he had to be. Harry,
he's dead, just—dead. That monster murdered him."

Harry said, "Yes, the monster murdered
him. But we've got two kids who saw

him. We've got witnesses, Eve. Cheney wants us to go up there. We'll catch him; you know we will."

She turned to go into her bedroom, saying over her shoulder, "I can't stand this, Harry, just can't stand it."

Harry thought of Mrs. O'Rourke, thought of Mickey O'Rourke's teenage daughters, thought of the uncertainty they'd been living with for the past four days, the soul-eating fear, and now they had to face the death of a husband, a father.

When Eve came out, she was dressed in her black and red, her hair in a ponytail, no makeup on her face. Her eyes were puffy from crying.

He walked to her and lightly rubbed his fingertip over her cheeks. "I'm sorry, Eve. Believe me, I know how you feel."

28

Near Nicasio, California
Forty-five minutes northwest
of San Francisco
Sunday afternoon

Harry turned the U.S. Marshals' Chevy Suburban west off Highway 101 on Lucas Valley Road, drove about ten miles, then turned right on Nicasio.

Sherlock looked out over the rolling hills of cattle and horse country. "The hills are still all gold and brown, even with the rain."

Cheney said, "The rain was a little late this year. By March, the hills will be as green as Ireland." He saw Harry turn the windshield wipers on intermittent, and said, "I hope we stay with this light mist. A full-on downpour would really make things difficult." He waved a hand as Harry curved left. "There's Nicasio, one square block, really. Its claim to fame is the 1871 red schoolhouse. It's a historical landmark."

Harry said, "The Nicasio Reservoir is up ahead. You'll see this area is a real mix, with a few exclusive, expensive homes sitting next to farm country and to old hippie hangouts."

Eve said, "Hard to believe we're so close to the gazillion people living in San Francisco."

They were all thinking, *We're talking about the ridiculous weather and the scenery because Mickey O'Rourke is dead.*

Harry pulled in to what looked like a makeshift parking lot, climbed out of the Chevy, and opened a gate. "Here it is. Ranch Road." And he got back into the SUV and drove through the gate. He followed the narrow, dirty road through trees and fancy horse pastures and hills dotted with cows. They came across a white Crown Vic with a green sheriff's ID on the side, parked at the edge of the road.

Bud Hibbert, the Marin County sheriff, was tall and runner-lean, with a full head of iron-gray hair that glistened with a light film of rain. He had a craggy, weathered face that announced he sat squarely in his fifties, and dark, smart eyes that looked like they'd seen about everything.

"How'd the FBI get hold of a U.S. Marshals' SUV?" he asked, nodding toward the big black Suburban.

"I'm Deputy Marshal Eve Barbieri," Eve said, and shook his hand. "I'm their procurer." She introduced everyone, and Sheriff Hibbert introduced his three deputies, all from Civic Center Main Station.

Hibbert said to Cheney, "I got the particulars you sent out on Federal Prosecutor Mickey O'Rourke Friday afternoon. When we realized the body was O'Rourke, I pulled our guys back immediately to preserve the crime scene for you. You've got a forensic team coming?"

Cheney nodded.

Sheriff Hibbert said, "The two kids who saw the killer—we knew they weren't blowing smoke because Rufino Ramirez's dad is a deputy sheriff in our Point Reyes Substation.

"We haven't seen this kind of thing around here, Agents, since the trailside murders. It's already all over town."

Hibbert raised his face. "It's been raining on and off all morning. I'm afraid I can feel more coming. No choice, let's do this," he said, and turned toward his cruiser and said over his shoulder, "Deputy Sheriff Ramirez took his boy, Rufino, and his friend, Eleanor, back to his house; then he called the other parents over, so they're all together, waiting for you. How far behind you is the forensic team?"

Cheney said, "They're only a few minutes out. I called Joe Elder, the forensic team leader, told him you'd have a deputy waiting here for them at the same place where you met us."

Sheriff Hibbert nodded, climbed into his Crown Vic, and led them slowly past a few more dirt tracks before turning left at the fourth, which threw them into a mess of thick oak and bay trees. Soon they saw half a dozen more cars pulled onto the grass along the dirt tracks, their passenger sides pressed up against the trees. The tracks narrowed to a dirt path.

The sheriff pulled over, got out of his Crown Vic, and waved them forward. He said, "We figure the killer parked some twenty feet down this trail; that's where we found tire tracks, nice and clear before the rain picked up. Our guys are taking the tire casts now. He carried O'Rourke's body about a hundred feet farther into the woods. This is private land, but you can't see the house from here."

They followed him along a narrow trail, the trees so thick overhead it looked like twilight in the woods. There was no wind to speak of, but the air was pregnant with rain, and a light drizzle continued to fall. When they reached a small clearing, Sherlock looked up, hoping to see a bit of sun, but she knew that wasn't going to happen. She hoped heavy rain would hold off for a while longer to give the forensic team time enough to set up some cover.

Marin County officers circled Mickey O'Rourke's grave, talking, drinking coffee. Savich saw the hole was maybe three feet deep, deep enough to keep Mickey O'Rourke hidden in this desolate spot for decades, if it hadn't been for those two kids. He wanted to meet them. He nodded to the deputy, then leaned down and pulled back a white tarp. They stared down into Mickey O'Rourke's bone-white face and the obscene red slash across his neck. The deputies around the grave looked on with them.

Eve couldn't bear it, just couldn't. She swallowed, turned away. She said, "Ramsey is going to hate this. Why did he have to die?"

There was no answer to that.

They all turned around at the sound of footsteps coming up the trail.

"That'll be our forensic team," Cheney said, and waved when he saw Joe Elder.

"What are you standing in our way for!" Joe yelled, still from a distance. "Move your carcasses, let us through."

Joe was nearing retirement now. He was impatient with fools, impatient with everyone, as a matter of fact, and would generally snort at anyone in his vicinity.

They listened to him bark out orders to his team of two men and two women, snarl at the deputies who happened to get into his space, and shout for some coffee for him and his people.

There was silence when they at last lifted Mickey O'Rourke out of his grave. Eve crossed herself, a habit ingrained from her childhood, and said a prayer. She looked over at Harry, whose face seemed to be carved from stone. His hands, though, were clenched at his sides.

Since there wasn't anything more for them to do, Sheriff Hibbert led them to the Ramirez house. It was a mile away off another dirt road, a small clapboard house set pressed against a knot of bay trees.

They heard the two kids' high, excited voices before they got through the front door. After introductions and their assurances no one would browbeat the kids, Julio Ramirez led them in from the kitchen.

They were eleven years old. Emma's age, Sherlock thought, and skinny as skateboards. They looked both scared and excited, just like their parents. Eleanor looked a great deal like her mother, small and fine-boned, quite unlike her father, lucky for her.

Rufino was a good-looking kid, the image of his deputy father. A future heartbreaker, Eve thought.

It took about ten minutes before Deputy Ramirez convinced the other parents to adjourn back to the kitchen and wait. Finally they got the kids settled at the ancient mahogany dining room table, each with a soft drink and within easy reach of a plate of chocolate-chip cookies provided by Eleanor's mother.

In another few minutes, they gently got Eleanor and Rufino to the point in their story where their explorations took them near the clearing.

Keep it light, Sherlock thought. "You two were smart not to call out to him."

Rufino said, "We almost did, then Ellie grabbed my arm and pointed. We both saw the shovel and the big mound of earth. Ellie nearly peed her pants, she was so scared."

Ellie punched him in the arm. "Yeah? Well you did, too, Ruf."

Sherlock grinned at both of them. "I can sure understand that. Can you tell us what the man was wearing?"

Eleanor said, "A raincoat, it was brown, and he was wearing a Giants ball cap. It was drizzling."

Rufino said, "We were trying to find a double rainbow, but we didn't. We never saw his face because he had his back to us. He was pounding down a big pile of earth, then he pulled branches over the—"

"The grave," Eleanor said, and squeezed Rufino's fingers. "It was really gross."

Rufino said, "And we knew right away it was a grave and we knew this man wasn't good, so we were real quiet."

Eve thought, *You're both alive because he never realized you were there.* There was no doubt in Eve's mind the man would have killed both children and buried them with Mickey O'Rourke. Her ponytail swung forward as she leaned toward the kids. "Did you see any part of his face? Like his profile?"

"No," Rufino said. "We were always behind him. His boots were real dirty. His feet were small, like my dad's."

Harry asked, "Was your impression that he was tall? Short? Fat?"

"He was kinda tall," Ellie said without hesitation, "and he wasn't fat, but not as skinny as Ruf's dad."

"Was he about your dad's height, Rufino?" Eve asked.

Rufino wasn't sure; the guy was pretty far away. He knew the deputy marshal was disappointed, but he didn't want to make anything up, and she smiled at him when she realized it. He smiled back. Yes, indeed, a girl slayer, Eve thought again.

She said, "Did he seem old to you? Young?"

"Old," both kids said at once.

"Older than your parents?"

Neither child was sure about that. To these kids anyone over twenty was old.

Cheney said, "Then what happened?"

Rufino drank the last of his soda and wiped his hand across his mouth. "After he put some branches over the grave, he leaned down and picked up the shovel."

Ellie said, "He said something, then he walked away."

Harry felt his heart pick up. "Did you hear what he said?"

Ellie said, "Yes, sir, but it didn't make any sense to Ruf or me. It was something like RIP and then a name—Mickey I think. We were afraid to move, so we sat there for another five minutes."

Rufino said, "We heard a car motor start, it was a long ways away, but we heard it. We figured he was leaving so it was okay to move."

Ellie said, her small voice trembling, "It was horrible. We sat there and stared at those branches and all that black earth and knew there was a dead body under the ground."

Rufino leaned over and patted her back. "It's okay, Ellie, it's okay."

Cheney said, "Let me tell you, kids, you're both heroes. Without you, the man you saw buried would probably never be found. And you've really helped us."

Rufino patted Ellie's back again. "Since you're a girl hero I guess it's okay for you to be scared." The little girl stopped shaking.

Another chocolate-chip cookie each, and everyone at the table knew the kids were tapped out. They were still excited but wrung out. They all went out into the kitchen to thank the parents and tell them how incredible and smart their kids were. Sherlock studied Rufino's dad—maybe five feet ten inches, give or take, one hundred fifty pounds, give or take. Was Sue the taller of the two?

When they returned to the grave site with Sheriff Hibbert, they stared down into the empty hole. The rain had picked up, and the dirt was fast becoming mud and sliding into the hole. "*RIP, Mickey,* that's what he said over Mickey's grave." The sheriff looked at each of them. "I really want you to nail this bastard."

There was a moment of silence. Sherlock said, "The killer matches the general description of Ramsey's shooter. More or less."

Harry said, "If it is the same guy it's got to tie in to the Cahills. But it could be a woman, this Sue, I suppose." He pushed one of his fists into his palm.

Savich nodded. "Okay, we don't know exactly when O'Rourke died yet, but my guess from seeing the body is he was murdered fairly recently. Did the killer head back from the hospital after his attempt to kill Ramsey on the elevator to where he'd stashed Mickey O'Rourke in order to kill him?"

Yes, he had, Harry thought, and nodded.

Eve turned to Sheriff Hibbert. "So he might have stashed Mickey O'Rourke somewhere near here. You have any ideas about that, Sheriff?"

Sheriff Hibbert nodded. "Deputy Ramirez told me there's an old farm shack in the woods near here, on property that belongs to a new house a developer built some six years ago. As for the shack, it's been deserted for years. Let's go see."

They fell in behind the sheriff's car and soon turned off another dirt road onto a rutted path. They slowly made their way about fifty feet until they couldn't go any farther.

Sheriff Hibbert leaned out the window. "We can't see the new house from here because the dirt road—Mason's Cross— is set at a ninety-degree angle in the middle of a bunch of oak and bay trees. We've got to walk the rest of the way to the shack."

They climbed out of the Suburban into

the drizzling cold rain and mud and trudged after the sheriff for about twenty yards.

Hibbert stopped. "There it is."

They stared at a dilapidated wooden shack, probably older than Sheriff Hibbert's parents.

29

Sheriff Hibbert motioned them back. He opened the creaking wooden door, his gun drawn. They heard him suck in his breath.

He stepped back, his face set and pale as death in the dim light. "You're not going to like this."

The shack was a single room, maybe twelve by twelve, the floorboards rotted through. Part of the roof had caved in, probably years before, and rain flooded in. A single metal cot was shoved against the back wall, beneath some remaining roof. There was a dirty blanket hanging off the bed, nothing else.

The blanket and the mattress were soaked with blood, dried black. There was blood splattered on the wooden floor planks, even on the walls.

Cheney pulled out his cell phone. "Joe? We found the kill site. I need you to bring a couple of your people over to us." He handed Sheriff Hibbert his cell.

"Ask Deputy Millis to show you the way. The shack is off Mason's Cross Road. You'll have to walk a ways." He handed the cell phone back to Cheney.

None of them said any more. They all knew Mickey O'Rourke had spent the last three days of his life tied down to that cot, alone, knowing in his gut he was going to die. And he had. He may have wanted to die at the end. By the look of the shack and the spattered bloodstains, he'd been beaten. For information?

It was difficult to step back, cut off the rage and sadness, to force their minds to focus on what was in front of them. Sherlock said, "There's a chance he left fingerprints."

Eve said, "He hasn't missed a single trick so far, but he never expected anyone to find this shack. So maybe you're right."

Harry asked Sheriff Hibbert, "Do you have any idea how long this shack has stood vacant?"

"At least twenty years, maybe longer. I haven't heard of anybody staying out here since I've been sheriff. We get some homeless people squatting in our abandoned buildings now and then, but not here, because it's too remote." He looked up at the boards sunk in on the crumbling ceiling. "It'd be safer to camp under a tree." He looked toward the bed. "How I hate this smell, the smell of death."

Cheney took one last look around the room, and said, more to himself than to the rest of them, "It's up to me to tell Mrs. O'Rourke her husband's dead. I'll take a chaplain with me." He sighed. "As if that will help." He looked up. "This guy doesn't deserve to walk the earth." He paused for a moment. "I know a woman didn't do this. If this was Sue, then Sue is a man."

It was odd, Eve thought, looking out the Suburban window as Harry drove them back to the city, how the ride home always felt quicker.

She listened to the windshield wipers clapping steady as a metronome, the rain, now that they weren't getting soaked standing in it, oddly soothing, somehow comforting.

She saw Cheney's eyes were on his hands, clasped in his lap. He had to be thinking about Mrs. O'Rourke and the girls and what he would say to them—it couldn't be the truth, at least not all of it.

Harry looked stiff, mechanical, as if he was afraid to express anything for fear he'd yell with it. Savich and Sherlock, too, were without expression, but Dillon was pressing his wife's open palm against his thigh. She wondered how much horror they'd seen. Too much, she thought. What were they thinking?

Eve felt a wave of despair, not just because of the bloodbath they'd found in the shack but because it was the naked proof that some people were simply evil, some people were simply missing all compassion or any human feelings at all. How else could this monster have killed Mickey so brutally?

RIP Mickey. She wanted to kill him herself.

She met Sherlock's eyes. Sherlock said, "How's your back, Eve?"

She snapped back from the edge. "Thanks to Harry the Hands, I'm feeling fine." She added, "Harry was at my condo this morning, and let me tell you he's got the greatest hands. I think he even got a moan out of me, it felt so good."

No one said a word.

Where had that come from?

Eve cleared her throat. "What I meant to say was that he massaged my back with muscle cream and—"

"Let it go, Eve," Harry said. "No one thinks there were any prurient thoughts in your head or mine. Your back is purple and green, and you were hobbling around like a crippled old deputy marshal retired lady."

Insanely, Eve wanted to laugh.

When they arrived at the Federal Building, Cheney said, "I'm going to pick up the chaplain in my own car and drive over to see Mrs. O'Rourke. As for the rest of you, it's Sunday. Take some time off, try to let go of all this. We need all your brains ready tomorrow morning. We can bank on hearing from forensics and the medical examiner first thing." He paused for a moment. "Wish me luck."

They did, all of them grateful they weren't walking in his shoes today.

Eve said her good-byes and went walking in the rain. She realized her mistake a couple blocks later when every step made her back hurt. She saw a taxi, and, miracle of miracles, it stopped for her. She directed the Ukrainian driver to Saint Francis Church on Larkin, a fixture in her Russian Hill neighborhood for nearly a hundred years. The rain was coming down heavier when she opened the side door and slipped inside. It was warm and dim and ancient. She breathed in the soft air scented with incense. She always felt safe here. She sat awhile, absorbing the quiet and gazing at the many symbols of hope that surrounded her, hope she knew was embedded in the very walls. She eased forward on the pew and sent a prayer of gratitude that Eleanor and Rufino were alive. She prayed to find this man who'd wantonly killed Mickey O'Rourke, who'd tried to kill Ramsey. She didn't pray that she would kill him; she didn't think she should push God on things like that. And she prayed for Mickey O'Rourke's soul.

When she walked back to the vestibule, she saw Father Gautier standing by the big closed double doors, arms crossed over his chest, an umbrella open at his feet to dry. He was St. Francis's longtime pastor, always soft-spoken and patient. Father Gautier gave her a long look. "I hope you found what you needed, Eve. I noticed you weren't in church today. Is something troubling you?"

She told him that Mickey O'Rourke, whom Father Gautier had known as his parishioner far longer than she had, was dead, a violent death. She gave him no details.

He took her hand as he closed his eyes a moment. He whispered, "I am so very sorry, for his family, for all of us. *Requiem in pace.*"

They stood quietly for a moment, then Father Gautier said, "You're wet," and his voice held a touch of humor, bless him.

Eve said, "Not so much now. It's so very warm inside. I think I'd like to stay that way."

When Father Gautier left her, she pulled

out her cell. "Harry, sorry to call when you're just getting home. Would you come get me at Saint Francis Church on Larkin? It's not too late, and I could use the company. I can make us something to eat, if you like."

"If you're up to it, so am I," he said.

30

**Judge Sherlock's home
Mulberry Street, Pacific Heights
San Francisco
Sunday evening**

Sean was lying boneless against Savich's shoulder, Savich stroking his back. He'd fallen asleep between his grandparents in front of the TV watching Sunday Night Football.

He took Sean to the second guest room next to his and Sherlock's bedroom, gently eased him down on his back on the twin bed, the crib long stored away in the basement. He pulled the dinosaur sheet and two blankets over him, since Sean liked to be warm when he slept. He kissed him, breathed in his kid smell, and straightened. He felt the light touch of Sherlock's hand on his arm.

"He's so beautiful, so perfect, and we made him," she whispered. "Isn't that amazing?"

Savich turned and hugged her. He said against her ear, "I was thinking that right now it'd be good to be as innocent as Sean." He closed his eyes and pressed his face against her hair. "I can't get Mickey O'Rourke's face out of my mind, or that farm shack where he was beaten and murdered." He hugged her more tightly. "Life is so fragile. You're here, then you're not, and it's final, no going back, no changing anything at all."

She held him, stroking her hands up and down his back and said against his cheek, "Dillon, I've been thinking about what Cheney said—that a woman wouldn't have killed Mickey O'Rourke like that. I don't see it, either. Not only was the killing savage, she would have had to carry O'Rourke back to the car, a good distance from the shack, and then she would have had to carry him an even longer distance to bury him. Remember, Ellie and Rufino said after he left O'Rourke's grave, they heard the car start up from a good ways away? Sue is slightly built. Even with superior upper-body strength, I don't see how she could have managed. O'Rourke was a big guy—taller than you. What does it mean?

Savich said, "It means our Sue isn't a woman."

31

Hyde Street, Russian Hill
San Francisco
Sunday night

Eve's back hurt so badly when they arrived at her condo she didn't think she
could walk a step until Harry's hand
cupped her elbow. "Harry's hands are
here to minister to you so you have a
chance at some sleep tonight. First,
though, you need a long, hot shower. I
don't want you getting sick."

"I can make you some coffee."

"I'll make it while you shower. After you're dry and warmed up, I'll see to your back. I'll call Feng Nian Palace and get us some Chinese delivered. We can stretch out in front of the TV, watch what's left of the football game, and munch on egg rolls."

After her shower, Eve walked into the living room to see the Patriots' QB Tom Brady complete a pass to Wes Welker and gave a small cheer. "I think Wes Welker would make a great marshal," she said. "He's strong and fast, and you can tell that brain of his is high-voltage." She grinned down at Harry as she tossed him the tube of muscle cream. She carefully sat beside him on the sofa, eased her robe off her shoulders, and leaned forward. Her hair was loose down her back. He looked at her hair for a moment, then shoved it over her shoulder and began smoothing the cream over her back. He stroked her until the final whistle blew. She really didn't want him to stop, but finally she said, "Your hands will cramp up. I'm fine now, thank you. I can't believe how stiff I was. Goodness, it's almost nine o'clock. Are you hungry yet?"

"Dinner should be here any minute. You feel okay?"

"Better," she said, "much better." She realized her robe was still down. She quickly shrugged it back up, closed it, and tied the belt. She turned to face him, lightly laid her hand on his arm. "You're very kind, Harry, thank you."

Harry was silent for only a moment, then said, "Sherlock told me about Mrs. Howell's homemade pizza for her son, Boozer, how delicious it was at eleven o'clock this morning. I was thinking we eat too much pizza—so we're having Szechuan. That okay with you?"

"It's great. Do you know I can't imagine an amateur trying to find a vein in my arm and poking that needle in a dozen times? It's too bad the guy had his face and head covered up."

Harry said, "Yeah, but we were real lucky today—if those kids hadn't seen him, we'd still be looking for Mickey O'Rourke."

"Yes, forever. Hey, what do you want with your fried rice? A beer?"

Harry asked for water. He watched her walk to her kitchen. She looked looser, walked more easily. He said, "I called Cheney while you were in the shower. He said Mrs. O'Rourke was brave, that was the word he used. I guess he was expecting her to fall apart, but she didn't. She told him she wanted to be the one to tell her daughters. The chaplain stayed, but Cheney's home now."

"I hope I don't ever have to tell someone their husband or wife is dead. By violence."

"Agreed. I called Officer Mancusso and asked him to unplug the TV and call if Ramsey happens to find out something. He said he'd alert the nursing staff to keep quiet as well."

"That's good, Harry. I'll tell you, Molly looked so beaten down, so afraid for Ramsey today, that she shouldn't have to handle any more tonight."

"We should be okay until morning now," Harry said.

Eve handed him his water. "I'm thinking our killer has been making a few mistakes. Like the kids seeing him today. You know he never wanted Mickey O'Rourke to be found. And he failed to kill Ramsey twice."

Harry took a drink from the Pellegrino bottle. "I can't help but think he's not altogether sane." He stopped, shook his head. "Just shoot me. I don't know what to think anymore, but I do know this has got to be a huge hit for him. Any time now he's going to listen to the news and hear about Mickey O'Rourke being dug up. So what does he do now?"

Eve said, "Good question. He isn't going to give up, that's all I'm sure of. If Savich is right, he's in the spy business. I don't imagine you can survive very long doing that unless you're real careful. But he hasn't been careful, has he, at least with his two attempts on Ramsey's life?"

Harry said, "He tried to be with burying Mickey O'Rourke; just bad luck for him there."

"We'll find out from forensics tomorrow if he left any prints in that shack. And if Sherlock is right that he's spent time in prison, we'll have him."

Eve took a pull of her beer. "Why did you and your wife divorce?"

The doorbell rang. The food.

She said, "Give him a big tip, Harry, I'm really hungry."

They were eating hot-and-sour soup when Eve said, "I'm sorry I asked you about your wife. I didn't mean to. It popped out."

"My ex-wife," Harry said mildly, and finished off the bottle of Pellegrino.

"Nevertheless, it's none of my business. I've only known you for a matter of days. Isn't that amazing? So much has happened, it seems much longer."

He said nothing, but she was right, it felt very odd.

Eve sat back against the sofa and immediately sat forward again at the stab of pain in her back. "I hate not having control. My dad's the same way. I'll tell you, Mom had to belt him lots over the years when he tried to be her camp commandant. I'll bet they've both lost count.

"My four brothers are all grown up, and they laugh at him now when he tries to throw his weight around." She drank the last of her beer. "My dad's amazing. He reminds people of Tommy Lee Jones, though the two marshal movies came out before he started his service there."

"Service where?"

"In Chicago. Didn't you know, my dad's

the U.S. marshal in Chicago? He's served as marshal there through two presidents."

"I thought the marshal changed out with every new administration."

"Once in a great while, an appointed marshal is so well regarded he's left in place. My dad says he's trained the toughest hard-asses in the United States Marshal Service right there in Chicago. He says they take no grief, since they have a responsibility to Tommy." She paused for a moment. "He's very good, my dad."

"How does your dad treat you?"

Eve gave him a big smile. "You heard Dillon talk about the power of the ponytail? Works on my dad every time."

32

San Francisco General Hospital
Monday morning

Ramsey blamed himself, Eve saw it clearly on his freshly shaved face, just as she'd known he would.

"It's obvious to me that by suspending the trial, I alerted the Cahills or whoever is working with them that I suspected something going on with Mickey's prosecution. If only I'd held off that day, let the pretrial motions continue until I could talk to him privately, he might still be alive."

Eve said, "It isn't like you to sit back and watch a train wreck, is it, Ramsey? You did what was appropriate, what your experience and your training told you to do. Who could have known what would happen?"

Ramsey plowed right over her, shaking his head back and forth. "No, no, I should have thought it through better. I should have realized that with the death penalty on the table, whoever was controlling Mickey wouldn't draw the line at anything. It's my fault they killed him, no one else's."

Eve said patiently, "Ramsey, say Mickey had succeeded in manipulating you, and you had ruled to dismiss the federal case against the Cahills. Do you think they would have let Mickey live? I think you know as well as I do after what happened that Mickey was dead the minute they threatened his family. If he'd come to you, maybe it would have turned out differently, but he didn't."

Slowly, he shook his head. She hated it. He looked defeated. "I should have approached him differently, gotten him to confide in me—if he'd told me, I could have made sure he'd be safe. And his family."

She lightly tapped her fist against his arm. "Stop this, Ramsey, you're pissing me off. A monster hiding in a human skin did this. No more blaming yourself or I'll have to punish you for it when you're well again."

He didn't smile. "I've been thinking about why they shot me, of course. I'm a judge, and if a judge is doing his job, he's providing an even playing field to give the jury the best chance of arriving at the truth, not to influence the jury in any one direction.

"So why me? Most of my pretrial rulings had been in the Cahills' favor, in fact. And the bigger question—why did they try to kill me again after the trial was dead in the water, at least in my court? We were done with each other, so why?"

He looked at each of them. "The only answer I've come up with is that they think Mickey may have talked to me before they could grab him, told me something dangerous for them, either about the case itself or implicating whoever had threatened him. That would also explain why they tried to shoot me again on Saturday, while they could hope I was still too ill and drugged to have spoken to anyone."

"That's a reasonable scenario, Judge Hunt," Harry said. "We're certain someone was working with the Cahills, probably a professional. And the man—we're calling him Sue for the moment—might have a great deal to lose if he's exposed. As a matter of fact, Sue did try to find out if Mr. O'Rourke told you anything before he kidnapped him, but O'Rourke didn't have any information to give him, and so he ended O'Rourke's life."

Ramsey said, "So whoever this Sue is, you can be sure the Cahills are up to their earlobes in this with him; there's simply no other explanation." He paused for a moment, his eyes narrowing. "Molly already knew Mickey was dead last night, didn't she? She knew, and she kept quiet about it."

Eve said, "No, I didn't tell Molly."

"The TV didn't work, either. I wondered why not. What'd you do, Agent, unplug it?"

"I asked one of your guards to unplug the TV, Judge Hunt," Harry said.

"I hate lying here feeling helpless, everyone guarding me, shielding me. I'm pretty sick of it." He smacked his fist on the bed and swallowed.

Eve waited a moment until he had himself together again, then looked him straight in the face. "I had nothing to do with it. It was all Harry's idea."

What moxie. Harry had to work hard to keep the laugh in. She was a piece of work, fast on her feet. He couldn't help but admire that. She'd succeeded in distracting Judge Hunt. Harry saw incredulity, disbelief, and then humor in his eyes.

Harry said, "Yes, sir, it's true. I ordered Deputy Barbieri to keep her mouth shut, and I told everyone here in the hospital to keep this from you or I'd have them all fired."

"But still—" Ramsey said, but Eve overrode him. "You want guilt? Give me a big share, okay? I allowed you to very nearly get killed in the elevator only two days ago."

Ramsey frowned at her. "Get real, Eve."

"I will if you will. Listen, we all do our

feeble best, and sometimes things simply don't go the way we planned or we prefer. Did your recovery take a hit from that fiasco Saturday?"

"No, the elevator business didn't faze me, Eve. Dr. Kardak even told me I was such a superb physical specimen he felt comfortable taking out the chest tube this morning. They took away my morphine pump, too. I'm on oral pain medication now, and I'm thinking a lot more clearly." He looked from Eve to Harry. "You two are quite a team, aren't you?"

"We're not a team," Harry said. "That's a vicious rumor."

"That's right," Eve said. "If we were a team, Harry would be saluting me by now."

"In your dreams," Harry said.

Ramsey didn't laugh. He knew how bad it would make him hurt. He said, "So you think Sue is a code name for a man? That simplifies things, doesn't it?"

"It's a start," Harry said. "All we can do is keep digging."

"If we were a team, Ramsey," Eve said, "you could count on me telling the boy here where to dig."

A laugh came out this time. Ramsey closed his eyes and took some light shallow breaths against the stabbing pain in his chest where the tube was removed. Slowly, too slowly, he eased. He said, "Emma's performance is in a week and a half. I keep telling my body to get over it and stop whining at me. I really don't want to miss it." He managed a smile. "Do you know what a pain it is to have to lie here and let people come in and out and torture you? Amazing that the hospital makes you pay them for it." He realized he had come full circle. "Sorry for the complaints. I'm a loser. Just belt me."

"Nah," Eve said, "not until you have a prayer of belting me back." He was exhausted, Eve saw it, knew Harry saw it, too. Not only exhausted, he seemed flattened emotionally, like Molly. She knew he'd think about Mickey O'Rourke's murder and blame himself for a very long time.

She watched Ramsey close his eyes. He said, barely above a whisper, "You've got to find the worthless son of a bitch who did this."

She took his hand, squeezed it. "We will, Ramsey, I swear we will."

There were two marshals and two SFPD officers nearby, two outside and two inside the room. Of course they'd been listening. She knew they'd all discuss the O'Rourke murder with Ramsey after she and Harry left. Perhaps they'd come up with something. She knew the deputy marshal who was stationed outside Ramsey's room was smart and committed to keeping Ramsey safe. Not a single sign of trouble, he'd said when they'd arrived to see Ramsey. She hoped it stayed that way.

She said to the guards standing by the window, "Hey, has Judge Hunt talked you into playing poker with him yet?"

Ramsey groaned.

"What, you haven't stripped them of their paychecks, Ramsey?"

"No, not our paychecks," Officer Mancusso said. "We told him he'd have to fix parking tickets for our wives."

Ramsey said, "I tried to tell them I couldn't fix a thing since I'm a federal judge, not a state judge."

Mancusso winked at her. "We don't believe him. We figure a federal judge has got friends everywhere."

"If you win, Ramsey, what will you get from them?"

Ramsey didn't open his eyes. "I'm thinking maybe they can get one of their buddies in Contra Costa County to ticket my chief judge's boat in Discovery Bay. He's having way too much fun on *Cyrano*—his big bad cabin cruiser—and drives way too fast. Scares the crap out of the fish. He deserves a couple of tickets, and he needs to spend more time in here commiserating with me."

Mancusso said, "I heard the chief judge has friends everywhere, too, sir."

33

Federal Building
Thirteenth floor
San Francisco
Monday morning

After the forensic team leader Joe Elder and the M.E. Dr. Martin McClure had left the conference room, one back to his beloved lab, the other to his sanitized and very quiet morgue, Cheney summed it up. "So all we have from Joe is a smudged partial palm print that may be identifiable and we know isn't O'Rourke's." Cheney clicked off his second finger. "The M.E.

confirms Mickey was tied down and beaten during the two days before he died early Sunday morning. The killer sliced Mickey's throat with a sharp knife at least six inches long, not serrated, right to left, suggesting he's left-handed. And last, Sheriff Hibbert let us know the tire tracks were made by a worn Goodyear All Weather, a popular replacement tire for a whole lot of SUVs. So we haven't got a lot."

Savich said, "Nothing from Hammersmith about the Dodge Charger he's been looking for?"

"He's had no luck with that," Cheney said. "And no useful leads yet from any of the hotels in the city on the man—or woman—who was driving it."

Savich said, "After what the killer did to Mickey O'Rourke, we should stop talking about a woman. We all think you're right, Cheney. It's a man who killed Mickey O'Rourke."

Burt Seng said, "Still, guys, it could have been a very strong woman. Hey, Eve here could carry lots of dead weight."

"Not that much," Eve said.

Dillon said, "Mickey O'Rourke weighed

two hundred and ten pounds, and everyone has described the perp as slender, not very big, so it's got to be a man, a very fit man."

Harry said, "I agree; even the ponytail couldn't have managed it."

Eve said, "I know I couldn't, so it's a man. For sure. Now, I don't think Cindy was putting us on, either, about the name Sue—it was too raw, too fast. I don't know who this Sue is, but I agree, she can't be O'Rourke's murderer. Maybe an accomplice, but not the killer."

Sherlock said, "Boozer Gordon described a man, too, not a woman; there was no question in his mind. So, yeah, good-bye, Sue."

"Without those kids," Harry said, "not only wouldn't we ever have found Mickey O'Rourke, but, bigger yet, we still would have been trying to fit our killer into a female body."

Cheney said, "I say we buy those kids tickets to a Forty-niners game."

Savich repeated slowly, "If Sue is an accomplice, was she with the killer when he beat Mickey? Did she question him? Did she tell him to slice Mickey's throat?

If so, then why wouldn't she go with him to bury him? As his lookout, his helper, whatever? But she didn't." Savich stopped cold. He looked very thoughtful, then, without another word, he started quickly typing on MAX's keyboard.

Sherlock cocked her head at him, since she knew that *Eureka!* look well. He'd thought of something, something big. She said, "We've been working on a bit of information Boozer Gordon gave us. When the man was putting on plastic gloves to draw Boozer's blood, Boozer noticed two rings on his fingers. The diamond pinkie ring sounds like the one Mrs. Moe described the shooter wearing when he rented the Zodiac. As for the other one, Boozer said it looked sort of 'religious' and actually asked the man if he was a priest. The man said no, he'd won it in a poker game. But still it could be an easy lie. Since it was an odd sort of ring to wear, it could have significance, it could be important."

Eve said, "Priests don't wear rings, not in the Catholic Church, though bishops do."

Sherlock nodded at her. "We sent a police artist to meet with Boozer and get a sketch of the ring. Here it is, to the best of Boozer's memory."

While everyone looked at the drawing, Sherlock said, "Even though it's pretty rough, we sent the sketch back to the Hoover Building. Given all the ecclesiastical rings I looked at on the Internet, Boozer's description of the ring isn't far off. We should know soon if our people can find anything." But Sherlock didn't look hopeful.

Harry pointed to the sketch. "The ring does look faintly religious. I hope you're right and it's important to this guy, for whatever reason."

"Well, well, would you look at this," Savich said. He looked down at MAX again for a moment, then smiled at everyone. "In all the talking we've done about Sue, we've assumed Sue is an American woman because it's an American name, short for Susan. But it occurred to me to ask if there are names in other languages that sound like Sue, since this case revolves around espionage. I ran it as a search through MAX, and it turns out there are names in Chinese that are pronounced *Sue*, or close to it. The closest one is a family name, written in English as *X-u* or *S-u.* Either way, since it's a surname it can be a man or woman's name, but no matter, I'd say Xu is a man and very probably Chinese."

Cheney rose straight up, slammed his fist to the table. "That's got to be right! It fits too well not to be. It all makes sense now. The Cahills had a Chinese handler named Xu who probably recruited them to get access to Mark Lindy's classified information. Question is, why is Xu still in the country? Why is he still around more than eight months after the Cahills were arrested?"

"Maybe he's trying to clean things up before he checks out," Harry said.

Eve said, "To stay here over eight months, he'd have to be an American citizen, whether he's working for the Chinese or not, or have excellent fake papers."

Harry said, "And the reason he's still here is because the Cahills know exactly who he is, and they could announce his identity to the world at any moment they liked."

Savich said, "Say Xu is an agent for the

Chinese. They can't be happy with him that the simple retrieval of information of Mark Lindy's data—meant to be done with stealth and alert no one it was even taken—turned instead into the very messy murder of a U.S. citizen, one working for the federal government. Imagine if it got out that Chinese intelligence was responsible, and the press got ahold of it— heads would roll. This Xu's continued usefulness to his employer, maybe even his life, might depend on the Cahills keeping their secrets. He had no choice but to stay here."

Cheney said, "So Xu had to try to get the Cahills off, or make them think he would, to prevent them from giving him up."

Cheney said, "I wonder if the CIA already suspects Chinese involvement? If so, they probably beat us to this Xu name days ago."

Savich said, "I'll speak to Billy Hammond at the CIA again, give him a heads-up. They're much better placed to follow this up quickly, if they haven't already."

"Will he tell you the truth?" Eve asked him.

"I suppose it's a vague possibility. On the other hand, Hammond was a stone wall when I asked him what kind of intelligence the Cahills were after on Lindy's computer."

"It's possible they don't know," Eve said. "I mean, who knew the Forty-niners would be having a winning season?"

They were interrupted by a knock on the door.

"Come," Cheney called.

The door opened to Agent Andre Devereau. Behind Andre stood Molly Hunt.

"She needs to see you, Cheney, so I brought her back." Cheney nodded, and Agent Devereau closed the door behind Molly.

Eve was on her feet. "Molly? What's happened? Are you all right?"

Molly was wearing jeans and a sweatshirt, sneakers on her feet. Her vivid red hair was wild around her head, no makeup on her face. She looked like a teenager.

She said to Eve, "A phone call came in a half-hour ago. You told me never to pick up, and to record every call, and I did. I didn't want to stay there and wait, so I came right over. Eve, call my home number. The voice mail access code is one-five-five-nine."

Eve picked up the landline and punched the speakerphone. She dialed Molly's number, and they all heard it ring, heard her punch in the code. There was the date and time, then a muffled gravelly voice.

"Mrs. Hunt, the mole on the back of your left thigh is very sexy. I'm thinking you and I will get together after your murderer husband is underground. It will be you and me and Emma. She can teach me to play the piano, and I can teach her—other things. The murdering bastard won't be with us much longer, Molly—may I call you Molly? I'll come for you, I promise."

Eve knew if she even breathed deeply everyone would hear it as she pressed the stop button.

Molly stood as pale as the morning fog snaking over the bay behind her, her hands clenched at her sides. But when she spoke, her voice was calm. "I can't figure out why he called Ramsey a murderer."

"He said it twice," Sherlock said. "Does he believe Ramsey is a murderer because he was presiding over a death penalty trial—namely, the Cahills'?"

Eve walked to Molly, placed her hands on her shoulders. She looked her right in the eye. "Molly, how could this guy have seen you naked?"

Molly ran her tongue along her bottom lip. "The bathroom has a large window looking out at the ocean, right beside the Jacuzzi. Ramsey and I like to—" She broke off, swallowed. "There are blinds, but we never use them. There are no neighbors to look in, after all, and it's a direct view to the ocean and the headlands beyond."

Harry said, "Too far from the water to see a mole, even with binoculars. So he may have managed to sneak up to the back of the house and look in on you without your seeing him. It could have been any time, even before he shot Ramsey. Think, Molly. Do you remember anything—maybe a shadow you couldn't identify, a flash of movement out of the corner of your eye?"

Molly shook her head. "It was raining last night while I was bathing. When I looked at the window, I only saw the raindrops streaming down the glass, nothing else, I'm sure."

"He could have managed to get to the window unseen by the deputies guarding the house," Eve said. "It's a big property, with lots of ways in, if one climbs the cliff or sneaks through Mr. Sproole's yard. It's a huge risk to take, though. It's more likely he saw you a week or more ago. When he was planning to shoot Ramsey."

Sherlock said, "Molly, did you tell the marshals?"

Molly nodded. "They weren't happy. They checked around the house right away, but they didn't find anything. You know the rain was heavy."

Molly stared at each of them in turn. "He's going to kill Ramsey unless you find him. How many more times can he fail? He was promising me, you heard the certainty in his voice. He's going to kill Ramsey."

Savich hated the despair in her voice, and he snapped her back. "Molly, have you taken a bath every night since last Thursday night when Ramsey was shot?"

She started. "Well, no. I've been so exhausted, I've hopped in and out of the shower, but last night—" She gave a hoarse laugh. "Last night I needed to calm myself down, get it together for the children. I soaked for a good thirty minutes. And maybe he was outside, watching me, and I didn't know it—I was lying there, my eyes closed, and I was so thankful Ramsey had survived the elevator attack—" She looked at them blindly. "I know he was there watching me, all the time, *he was watching me.*"

And in everyone's mind—*Could he have gotten to her last night, broken into the house without alerting the marshals outside?*

Sherlock said with infinite calm, "He's not going to try to take you. His whole purpose is to terrify you, to scatter your focus, and our focus. The best thing for your peace of mind, and for ours, would be to take you and the kids to a safe house for the duration."

Cheney nodded. "I can arrange it."

Molly said, "That's like in the movies. I can't believe any of this, it's all so surreal, and Ramsey—" She broke off, pulled herself together, cleared her throat. "All right. Good. I'll try to make the boys think it's a mini-vacation, maybe down by the zoo? We'll need to transport Emma's piano, since she plays at Davies Hall in a week and a half."

Harry said, "It'd be less risky to rent one, bring it to the safe house."

"No, that wouldn't work. Emma's piano—it's been her lifeline since Ramsey was shot."

Cheney said, "Don't worry, we'll figure it out."

"Thank you. I'll head home, then, and get everything ready. But what if he's watching the house? What if he sees us leave? And follows us? He'll know you're taking us away; he'll know it."

Savich said, "No, Molly, he won't know where you're going. Listen to me, this guy isn't some kind of superman who knows all, sees all. He's only one man, and we've done this before. Trust me, this is going to throw him off his game."

But not for very long, Eve thought. They had no idea whether his game included continuing trying to kill Ramsey, or even what his game was. Not that she would say that to Molly. He knew they would all hear his phone call to Molly. If he thought about the consequences at all, which, of course, he had, she knew they were going to have to be very careful while moving her.

Molly slowly nodded. "I don't want to tell Ramsey about this. There's nothing he can do. I can't stand worrying him more when he's helpless. It would destroy him to know he can't protect us. All right, I'll get Emma out of school now."

34

Crandall Building
California Street
San Francisco
Late Monday morning

Damn her eyes, I'm one of the most famous defense lawyers in the world. How can she do this to me?

Milo Siles mashed the elevator button once more, then another couple of times for good measure. The elevator doors opened, and he stepped in. Eight other people surrounded him, most taller than he, and he felt the familiar punch of claustrophobia. He closed his eyes and thought about the .38 he'd left in his glove compartment. He'd managed to wheedle a permit for it, not an easy task in San Francisco. It was a good thing he'd left it there or he might have shot the selfish cow and her greedy moron of a lawyer. How demeaning it was to be forced by a lamebrained judge to meet with a lamebrained mediator on the twelfth floor of the Crandall Building, in *her* lawyer's conference room, to listen to *her* lawyer demand half a million dollars from him every single year for the rest of her selfish self-centered life, plus the house in Claremont, plus the shares in the vineyard in Sonoma, plus support for their two boys until they were eighteen.

Half a million dollars. A year.

Milo was so angry at his soon-to-be ex-wife's outrageous demand, he'd nearly out-shouted his own divorce lawyer. And that officious cow of a mediator had counseled that they all take a deep breath and sit back and close their eyes for a moment. And then what? Sing "Kumbaya"? He wouldn't be surprised, not in San Francisco.

He'd taken that deep breath and closed his eyes anyway, and that did help him relax, because what he saw was a huge number of zeroes flashing in front of his eyes—the ten million dollars or so he had stashed in his holding company in the Grand Cayman Islands. No way Marjorie or her lawyer would find out about that. He'd been very careful through the years that it couldn't be traced to him, not by anyone.

He grinned to himself. You never knew, when you went the extra mile to make some real money in this business, if you might have to make a quick exit. This trial with the Cahills was a disaster, but at least it had pushed his nest egg up to that nice round number, more like the nest omelet he'd always wanted. He should never have taken the risk of defending the Cahills' worthless butts after they screwed up and got themselves indicted for murder. The case was hopeless from the start. He should have known that for all that money there would be risks far beyond keeping the Cahills quiet and cooperative, making his motions, and sitting back to wait. Well, he'd done everything as agreed, and he deserved that money. It was Marjorie's overspending that had pushed him into it, wasn't it?

He pictured his wife staring at him across the table, her eyes narrowed beneath her dark brows, which always needed plucking. It made bile rise in his throat. He'd supported her lazy butt for seventeen years, and what had she done to earn it? Be a housewife? As in be the loving wife who tended the house, took care of the children, maybe cooked the occasional dinner? That was a joke. Marjorie had a maid, a cook, and a gardener— and a nanny when the boys were younger. She did nothing at all useful, spent her hours on herself and on her idea of playing, whatever that happened to be. She'd probably had a half-dozen lovers, all of them buff and twenty years younger than she was, he knew it to his gut, and it was *he* who had paid for them. When he'd stormed out of that ridiculous meditation session with her lawyer, the lead-faced dyke who didn't make any bones about hating him, Marjorie had come up behind him and whispered in his ear—easy for her to do, since she was two inches taller than he, the cow—"I know more than you think, Milo, about this Cahill trial, about how you've cheated your firm. Think about it, dear. Five hundred thousand dollars a year is a lot better than sharing a cell with Clive."

He'd turned on her, his mouth working with no coherent words at first. "I let you do what you want, what's in this for you?"

She laughed. "Let me paraphrase Nicole Kidman when they asked her how she felt about splitting up with Tom Cruise—I don't have to wear flats any longer."

He'd nearly decked her.

Tom Cruise wasn't that short, and neither was he.

Milo would have smashed his fists against the elevator doors, but he couldn't lose it since there were too many people looming over him in the elevator. Marjorie was divorcing him because he wasn't tall enough for her?

He had to get hold of himself. She'd overheard a conversation with Clive? He couldn't remember any such conversation, but obviously he hadn't been careful enough. Well, she'd keep her mouth shut. If she spilled to the cops, then the Feds would seize all his assets under the RICO Act and she wouldn't see a bloody dime. Maybe sharing a cell with Clive would be worth it, knowing she'd have to get a job, maybe selling bagels in one of those outdoor kiosks at her favorite mall.

Milo walked a block over to the Mason Building, which housed his law firm, and directly into the underground garage to his new Beamer parked next to the express elevator. He admired its sleek lines for a second, still got a kick out of how the door opened for him with his key fob still in his pocket. As he squeezed in, he saw Marjorie's smiling face again, her smile so big she showed the gold tooth in the back of her mouth she'd never bothered to change out. He smacked his fist on the dashboard. This wasn't his fault; none of this was his fault. He was a good provider. And he would still send his boys to Princeton, his alma mater.

He buckled his seat belt and settled smoothly onto the sinful dark gray leather seat and pressed the magic button—

that's what his youngest son called the ignition. No, he wouldn't worry about his sons. They'd get over this. They were old enough to understand. He would make them understand.

His baby roared to life. *Calm down, calm down. So what if you give the witch half a million dollars a year? You can afford it.* But it was his hard-earned money, and she would spend it on those vacations she was always taking by herself, with the boys, with her frigging friends. Never with him after the first five years. All right, so he was usually busy; he had to support his family, didn't he? He had no interest in being one of those idiot tourists who walked around with a guidebook in their hands, always pulling out their cell phones to take stupid pictures no one cared about.

He backed out of the garage and eased into traffic. He crossed the Golden Gate twelve minutes later, and headed north toward Bel Marin Keys, to the beautiful little clapboard house he owned, with its own private boat dock and its one inhabitant, Pixie. She would make him feel better. She listened to him, really listened, and she knew he was suffering today. She cared about his feelings and what his wife was doing to him.

It wasn't raining, but it was cold and overcast, and promised rain. He was glad he'd gotten the coupe and not the convertible now that it was getting toward winter. This was San Francisco, after all.

35

Federal Building
San Francisco
Monday afternoon

If Bill Hammond at the CIA was to be believed, the CIA hadn't made the connection that Sue could be a Chinese name
spelled Xu, hadn't even known for sure
that a foreign government was behind
the attempted theft of Mark Lindy's materials. He assured Savich the CIA would
of course follow up on that possibility,
search out every Chinese national with

diplomatic cover whose name sounded anything like Xu.

Savich doubted the two CIA operations officers who'd come to San Francisco some eight months before to conduct an extensive investigation had left not even knowing a foreign government was involved, let alone which one. It really didn't matter now, Savich thought, since the game had changed. Now that they had a name, the CIA would be back in the investigation, trying to crash the party and take the cake. Savich figured he had one last shot at the Cahills before CIA operations officers arrived. They were the only ones who knew Xu, the only ones other than Xu who knew what had happened to those files off Lindy's computer.

He sat with Eve again at the same scarred table in the interview room. "I'm glad you're still wearing a ponytail," he said to her as the guards brought Cindy and Clive Cahill in.

The first thing out of Clive's mouth when he saw them was, "The guard said you wanted to see us again, Agent Savich. You wouldn't believe—or maybe you would believe—what kind of language Milo Siles used when he found out we'd talked to you without him on Friday. He tried to make us promise we'd never do that again. But Cindy and I—we're beginning to wonder a bit about Mr. Siles, and that's why we agreed to see you without him."

It's about time you're finally realizing Mr. Siles isn't in your corner. Savich said, "Tell you what, Clive, after we talk, you and Cindy can consult with Mr. Siles if you feel the need, how's that?"

Clive and Cindy shared a look, and Clive slowly nodded. "No harm in listening, at least until you bore us." He looked at Eve. "You're quite the little hero, aren't you, doll? It's all over the news how you saved Judge Hunt's life, threw yourself on top of him in that elevator and took three bullets in the back. How good are the Kevlars nowadays? You sore?"

Eve smiled at him. "You bet."

Cindy said, "A pity the guy wasn't a better shot and splashed your brains all over the judge."

Eve turned her smile to Cindy. "My

brains are relieved that didn't happen. It's true, I'm still a bit sore, but you, on the other hand, are still wearing chains and brushing your teeth with your fingers."

"Nah," Clive said. "This is a class joint. We even got toothbrushes, but you have a point, they're not electric."

Eve said nothing more. She didn't want to tangle with either of them, at least not yet.

Cindy noticed Savich was looking at her and leaned slightly toward him. "Isn't that sweet, Clive? Little Miss Sunshine with her bouncy ponytail doing her good deeds. She saves a life, then visits us poor put-upon prisoners again with her sidekick, Mr. Tough Guy."

Savich said, "Actually, we wanted to thank you in person for blurting out the name Xu. So how does he spell that? *X-u?* Or *S-u?* *S-o-o,* maybe? At any rate, he's Chinese, and he's your handler. We know he's fluent in English and no one has yet pegged him as Asian, so he's either very good at disguises or he's an American. Is he American?"

Cindy and Clive didn't say anything.

Savich continued. "It's only a matter of time before we find him. If we do that without your help, you won't have anything left to trade."

"I don't remember any Xu," Cindy said. "Xu—who is that, Clive, do you have any idea?"

"Not a one, sweetie. You look beautiful today. I've missed you." He started to lean over to kiss her, but there was a firm fist smack against the glass window in the door and he pulled back. What would the guards do, Eve wondered? Come in and physically distance him from her so he couldn't reach her? Probably. The guards couldn't know when violence would erupt, and wouldn't take that chance.

Savich said, "You know we found Mickey O'Rourke, your federal prosecutor, dead yesterday."

"We heard about that," Cindy said. "Gossip moves at the speed of light in prison, makes my old neighborhood look like slo-mo. Imagine O'Rourke getting himself killed. I didn't find out too many details, because the cops on TV are keeping a lid on it. Only that he met with *foul play.* I've always thought that phrase sounds wussy, don't you, Agent Savich?" She said it again: "Foul play—like they're going to hand out some kind of football penalty.

"Clive, did you hear about poor Mr. O'Rourke getting whacked? That idiot man who preened and strutted around in court and only finally managed to get himself in big trouble with the judge?"

Clive nodded, his lips seamed. "How did he die?"

Eve said, "Xu cut his throat."

Clive's hand went unconsciously to his neck; his fingers lightly rubbed against his skin. "That wasn't very nice."

"No, it wasn't." Savich sat back and regarded the two of them. "You can't think this is part of some master plan to get you out anymore. It seems to me Xu is snipping off loose ends, killing anyone who might know who he is. Do you want to know who the big whopper loose ends left are?" He suddenly sat forward, pointed at one, then at the other. "You and Cindy."

The Cahills' eyes met briefly, then

Cindy laughed. "That's a stretch, isn't it, Agent Savich? Unbelievable, that's what it is. We've been in this lovely facility now for eight months, fourteen days—"

"Thirteen days," Clive said.

Cindy shook her head. "You know I believe thirteen is unlucky, Clive. Nope, this is the fourteenth day. Being here means we're safer than you two are driving on Highway 101 at rush hour. Do you know, if I were this mythical Xu you talk about, I wouldn't be too worried about your catching me, any more than you could catch a box of smoke."

"Smoke—did Xu describe himself that way to you?" Savich said.

Cindy smiled broadly. "Oh, I don't know any Xu. That's only what I say—I mean, he is leading all of you around by your noses, isn't he?"

Eve said, "Xu has managed to get away so far. But smoke? When we take him down we'll ask him how he wants to style himself then."

Clive said, "Yep, the guy sure made you look like incompetent morons. Oops, I guess I shouldn't say that, should I? You might order up the waterboarding."

Eve leaned forward. "You might as well know we wounded him"—*Well, not quite, but close enough*—"we have his DNA, and when we match it we'll know exactly who Xu is. You know the CIA will have his prints, even if Xu is a brand-new alias for him. As Agent Savich said, it's only a matter of time." And Eve sat back, crossed her arms over her chest, and continued, "The CIA is coming back soon to talk to you again." She gave an elaborate shrug. "Waterboarding? I hear they don't use that anymore, old hat now. The CIA has much better methods.

"You know they've got a lot of motivation to find out everything you know, since Mark Lindy's project was highly classified. They won't even tell us about it. Believe me, everybody wants to catch this guy before he leaves the country. So Agent Savich and I have been talking with the U.S. attorney, and he's willing to make you an offer if you tell us what you know."

The Cahills were silent again, but there was something in the air between them. Fear? Of Xu getting to them?

Savich picked it up. "Suppose for a moment you get out by some quirk, even on bail. Xu would have every reason to kill you."

Eve shrugged. "Of course, if you wait until the CIA gets here, they could bollix everything up. Or Xu could be captured or killed. Either way, we wouldn't have anything to offer you then."

Cindy Cahill yawned. Her wrist chains rattled as she raised her hand to pat her mouth. She froze. Too bad the rattling chains always ruined a good performance.

Cindy said, "Agent Savich, we don't have any idea what you're both talking about. We're United States citizens, and we haven't been convicted of anything. You can't think we believe the CIA is going to haul us off to Guantánamo Bay?"

"And we didn't steal anything," Clive said, his voice parroting Cindy's tone, as convincing as his lawyer's. "Cindy and I have maintained our innocence through-out this debacle. We know nothing of this Xu or O'Rourke's murder or the two at-tempts on Judge Hunt's life. We don't know anything at all. We're in jail. Get over it."

"I'm getting bored, Clive, honey," Cindy said.

"Me, too, sweetie," Clive said, "but, hey, at least we get to see each other."

Eve knew they weren't getting anywhere fast. It was time to get down and dirty. She said, "Surely you two are smart enough to realize you could be convicted on half the evidence the prosecutors have. You are both going down, and that means all the way down to a lethal injection."

Clive smiled at her. "I thought you said the CIA was going to haul us away, never to be seen again?"

Eve turned to Cindy. "Tell me, Cindy, do you have any idea what you're going to look like in five years? Ten years? In fifteen years, right before you get the needle in your arm?

"Let me tell you what I've seen. You'll probably exercise for another year to keep your body in shape, but you'll be fighting a losing battle. They feed you lots of carbs and fat, and you'll gain weight because there's not much else to do in prison but eat. After a while, you'll stop exercising, I mean, why keep it up? Who is there to admire you? A bunch of women who could view you as too pretty and hate your guts and hurt you?

"Your skin turns pasty in jail because there isn't much sun available to you, and no good beauty creams. In five years, you'll be a fat slob and anyone you know now who sees you will hardly recognize you. Clive will, and because he might still care about you, in theory, he'll try not to gag.

"When they finally put that needle in your arm, you'll be a ruin, and they'll be putting you out of your misery. You'll end up only a name and a carcass to be disposed of."

Eve kept quiet and waited. They were crude threats, but they were all she had left. She listened to Cindy Cahill's pumped-up breathing, watched the appalling comprehension in her eyes before she managed to smooth it away. But Cindy couldn't veil the rage that followed. It beamed out of her eyes like a flashing beacon. She said, "I hope Xu cuts your face up before he kills you, bitch."

"That's not going to happen, so listen up. Tell us about Xu and what he has, and you won't have to worry about him, or about dying in here."

There was a heavy lump of silence, while the two of them looked at each other. Clive gave Cindy a small shake of his head.

Eve felt Dillon's hand pat her knee. He said, "You know what I admire about you, Clive? You're a real gamer. You know how to spot the perfect mark; you know how to manipulate your mark into doing exactly what you want. You picked out Cindy, didn't you, because you knew you could mold her to be exactly what you needed?"

Clive said, "Then I'm smart enough to know when I'm being gamed, right, Agent?"

"Sure you are. There'll be lots of games in prison, Clive, but you won't win many of them; you won't even get to play because you'll be the game. The inmates will recognize you fast enough as a *GQ* sort of guy who's used to the good life and sees them as a bunch of low-life ya-hoos. Believe me, they'll detest you on sight. They'll make you very sorry you look good, Clive.

"The chances are they'll make you their

bonus buddy, at least for a while, as long as you're looking good. After that, it depends on how bored and sadistic they are."

Eve heard the tension in Clive's voice. "Come on, that sort of thing doesn't happen anymore. I've been here eight months. No problems like that. Sure, there are disagreements among the inmates, but nothing violent, nothing sexual."

Savich shook his head at Clive. "This is local lockup, Clive, not a big bad federal prison where you're headed. Did Milo Siles try to convince you that if you're found guilty, you'd be headed to one of the federal country clubs for B felons? If he did, he lied.

"No, you're going to a place designed for people like you—violent felons and cold-blooded murderers, there to mark time on death row.

"You're a thinking man, Clive, I told you I admire that. But you're not a tough guy. You won't be able to protect yourself. And you won't have any money to buy yourself out of bad situations.

"Actually, I doubt you'll even last to the end of all your appeals unless they put you in solitary. At least you wouldn't get a hunk of soap pushed down your throat in solitary. On the other hand, who wants to spend the rest of his life in a concrete box by himself?"

The only sound in the small room was the hitch in Clive's breath.

Clive cleared his throat. "What sort of deal are you offering?"

Cindy hissed at him, but Clive didn't look at her.

Savich said, "The death penalty's off the table. You'll get twenty-five years, but it will be in a kind of prison you can look forward to walking out of instead of being carried out in a green body bag."

Clive looked at Cindy, but her eyes remained on Savich's face. "This is bull, Clive. Don't listen to them, they're playing us." She said to Eve now, venom pulsing in her voice, "When I get out, I'm going to kill you if it's the last thing I do."

Eve's eyebrow shot up. "What did I do to you? I've told you the truth, nothing more, nothing less." Eve sat back,

CATHERINE COULTER

touched her fingers to her ponytail. "Do you hate me because I look healthy and clean, and my breath is fresh and I can drink Starbucks coffee every morning if I want to?

"Get off your high horse, Cindy, I'm not the one here who murdered Mark Lindy. Tell us the truth, and you might survive to see the light of day outside of a prison."

Savich watched Clive lean again toward his wife, but at the bang on the door window, he pulled back. He licked his lips. They were dry and peeling. *Not that handsome now, are you, Clive?*

Cindy Cahill rose to her feet, her chains rattling. "I know twenty-five years is way too long. You bring the prison time down with the possibility of parole and we'll think about it. Clive, keep your mouth shut."

He nodded at his wife, but Eve saw him swallow convulsively. *Good.* He was scared, as well he should be.

So was Cindy; she was simply a better actress. Eve wondered if Dillon could get the federal prosecutor down even more. She was of two minds on what should happen to these two violent, greedy people, but protecting Ramsey trumped everything else.

Savich watched the guards walk them out. He doubted either of them would be speaking to Milo Siles about the offer.

36

Saint Francis Wood
San Francisco
Monday afternoon

Emma hovered around the three big men as they tenderly eased her prized ebony Steinway out of the moving van, positioned it onto the big roller board they used for pianos, and carefully pushed it from the driveway onto the side flagstone walkway.

The drizzling rain had stopped for a while, which was a relief, since Molly knew Emma would have tried to plaster herself on top of the waterproof tarp over her piano to make sure it stayed dry.

As for Molly, she was relieved to see the pinched look gone from Emma's face. When Emma had come into the principal's office at her school on Lake Street, her face had been frozen with fear until she'd seen Molly standing there, smiling. Still, Molly had said immediately, "Your dad's okay, Emma." She'd pulled her shaking daughter against her and said again, "He's fine, I promise you. Now, I've decided it's best for us to leave our home for a little while. We're going to stay in a lovely house in Saint Francis Wood. Remember, we've driven through the neighborhood and admired all the older houses, and the big yards, just like ours?"

Emma raised her face. "They're afraid the man is going to try to kill us, aren't they?"

So much for sugarcoating the truth. "Everyone wants to make sure we'll be safe. That's all there is to it."

Emma said with great patience, "Mom, I'm nearly twelve. Tell me what's happened."

Molly nearly lost it then, but she wasn't

about to tell her daughter about the message the man had left on the machine. "Nothing happened. I only want all of us to be safe."

"You trust me to take good care of the boys, but you won't tell me the truth? So I'll know what's going on? So if something happens I won't be surprised?"

Good point. "It's possible a man came onto our property last night. Everyone wants us out of there until they catch the man."

"The marshals didn't see him?"

"You know how many ways there are to sneak close to our house. He may have climbed up the cliff, and there'd be no one to see him unless he went around to the front of the house. It will be much easier for everyone in the house we're moving to."

Emma squeezed her mother tightly to her. "It's all right, Mom. We'll get through. The boys will think it's a cool game. I'll help."

Molly had hugged this precious human being tightly in return, whispered against her hair, "We're bringing your piano."

Those few words had earned her a quick smile from her daughter.

Molly watched the men maneuver Emma's piano to the base of the three front steps of the large Mediterranean house.

Savich looked at Harry, and they tried to join them in carrying the piano up the steps, but the foreman held them back. "Thanks, gentlemen, but we can't have you hurting yourselves. We've got this."

One of his young assistants, who had a tall red Mohawk, said between grunts, "It's the insurance he's worried about. You're right, though, this freakin' sucker's heavy."

Emma hung back, ever watchful. Molly was standing inside the doorway, one eye on the twins, who were examining every inch of the living room, and the other on Emma. The Steinway had never been moved an inch since it was reverently placed in their home in Sea Cliff five years before. This was a huge deal for Emma, and on top of everything else. How could Emma function? How would she react? Could she still see herself playing in front of a huge audience at Davies Hall in nine days? Molly saw her smile at Red Mohawk, who was grunting big-time, just for her, and hoped.

Once they carried the piano into the entrance hall, Red Mohawk grinned down at Emma. "Your mama said you're a big deal, that you're so good you even play with the San Francisco Symphony. That true?"

Emma never knew what to say to this sort of question. She was aware her mother was watching her, ready to speak for her, but she knew she was old enough to answer for herself. "I'm not playing with the orchestra this time. I'm playing by myself—George Gershwin's *Rhapsody in Blue,* a week from Wednesday. I don't know if there are still tickets left, but you could ask. What's your name?"

The young man laughed and touched his bush of hair. "You can call me Mohawk. Let me see the size of your hands." Emma held up her hands. The young guy studied them, placed them palm to palm. "Unbelievable," he said.

The foreman said, "Do you know what my name is? I'm Sam Davis, but there's no relation."

Emma stared at him. She didn't have a clue what he was talking about.

"Sammy Davis Jr.; he was one of the Rat Pack," he said, but Emma was still in the dark.

He grinned at her. "Ask your dad or maybe your granddad; one of them will know."

Once they lifted the piano back onto the roller board, Emma trailed behind them as they steered the Steinway through the doorway into the long living room.

"Here," she said, "in this corner, wide part of the case out."

When the piano was placed exactly, Red Mohawk brought in her piano bench and set it just so in front of the keyboard.

Emma looked at each man in turn. "Thank you for taking such good care of my piano."

Red Mohawk said, "Play us something if you really want to thank us."

Gage, whose hand was now being firmly held by his mother, shouted, "Emmie, play them the theme from *Star Wars*."

Cal shouted louder, "No, the theme from *Jaws*!"

Emma grinned at her little brothers, sat down, and played "Nobody Does It Better." There were whistles and applause, and a couple of boos from Cal and Gage.

When the movers left, Emma took Gage and Cal upstairs to show them their new bedroom, the twins chattering away in the twin talk they spoke when they didn't want anyone to know what they were saying.

Molly waved her hand around the living room. "This is very nice. However did you manage to get us this beautiful house on such short notice?"

Savich said, "The house is for sale. When the owner found out Judge Dredd needed it as a safe house for his family, he offered it to us immediately."

"It has some of the feel of our home," Molly said. "Built a long time ago and beautifully remodeled." Her voice hitched, and she added quickly, "Come along, I'll make us all coffee. Tea, Dillon?" She motioned away Sherlock. "No, let me do this. At least I still have control over making coffee."

When they were all seated around the authentic-looking fake Chippendale dining room table, Molly said, "The red-and-cream walls blend so well with this rich furniture. It makes this room oddly peaceful. Thank you all so much for coming here with us. It makes this all less difficult."

Sherlock said, "The backyard is fenced in, so the boys will be fine. The owner is sending over a jungle gym for Cal and Gage, said his granddaughter's outgrown it."

Savich's cell phone rang, and he left the room to answer it.

Sherlock said, "We're hoping for a phone call from Clive Cahill, telling us he's ready to deal. It's been nearly an hour since Dillon and Eve talked to them."

"Not Cindy?" Molly asked.

Sherlock shook her head. "Dillon thinks Clive's the weak link in this chain, or maybe he's the more realistic."

Harry nodded. "Eve said her money's on him as well. I know she has all her digits crossed. She wanted to be here, but she's meeting Marshal Maynard, going over plans for Judge Hunt's protection. Last time I saw she had her cell phone attached to her ear."

Molly asked, "Do you think the Cahills will talk?"

Sherlock said, "We'll know soon. We tried to reach Milo Siles, their lawyer, but his secretary told us Milo was in a divorce mediation session with his wife and her lawyer this morning and hasn't returned to the office yet. She let drop he was probably in a rage and she'd bet he'd turned off his cell until he calmed down. Still, Dillon tried to call him, but it went right to voice mail."

Molly said, "What do you think is going on?"

Sherlock said, "Since Siles was angry, it could be as simple as his sitting in some bar somewhere sulking."

When Savich walked back to the dining room it was to tell them it was Cheney, who'd gotten a call from his buddy, Marin County Sheriff Bud Hibbert.

It wasn't good.

37

Bel Marin Keys, California
Late Monday afternoon

A chill, thick mist cloaked the golden Marin hills in gray. They hit heavy rush-hour traffic on the approach to the Golden Gate Bridge. Harry passed Cheney the emergency light bar, and Cheney stuck his arm out of the window and plopped its magnetic base on the roof. Traffic, thankfully, made way for them as best it could. Harry always got a kick out of using a magic blinking light bar, made him feel like Moses parting the Red Sea.

Cheney said, "Let me give you some background on Pixie McCray, some of which I learned from Milo Siles's secretary. Pixie was divorced, no kids, and she was a legal secretary for Mifflin, LaRochette, and Kent, a firm Milo has litigated against many times over the years. That's how they met. We don't yet know how long they've been together, but I found out Milo bought Pixie's house about four and a half years ago. He bought a Sea Ray Sundancer to go with it, a fast luxury yacht that even has a swimming platform. It's parked right on his own private dock on the lagoon."

"Pixie—a charming name," Sherlock said. "And now she's dead, along with Milo Siles, just because he was visiting her."

Savich said, "I wonder if Milo's wife knew about Pixie."

Cheney said, "Even though his wife was using photos to get more leverage in the divorce settlement, according to Siles's lawyer, my guess is neither of them cared much about what the other was doing for the past five years or so. That's from Siles's divorce lawyer. He said Milo left really mad about his wife's demands at the mediation session, and that's the last anyone saw him."

Sherlock asked, "How did Xu find out about Pixie McCray?"

Cheney cut his eyes to her. "Funny thing is, it wasn't a big buried secret. The house in Bel Marin Keys is in Milo's name, and so is the Sea Ray Sundancer, both easy to find out."

Sherlock said, "I gather this house and boat weren't part of her demands?"

Harry said matter-of-factly, "Milo Siles's wife is obviously having an affair, too, maybe even a long-term affair, like her husband, so they seemed to treat it as no harm, no foul."

Sherlock closed her eyes for a moment. How could anyone live like that? Were Milo Siles and his mistress, Pixie McCray, dead because the Cahills had told him too much about Xu? Had Milo tried to blackmail Xu? Or was it simply because he'd known who Xu was and what he'd done that had signed his death warrant?

She said, "We need to keep checking on whether Siles had any hidden accounts, see if he got himself killed because Xu paid him to keep his mouth shut."

Savich nodded. "If Milo hid any money in his own name, he was pretty sophisticated about it. It could take some time, but MAX will find it eventually."

Sherlock said, "I'm hoping we don't find any accounts. That would mean Milo wasn't so stupid as to imagine he'd come out of this whole-hide if he was dealing with Xu."

And Pixie McCray, who probably hadn't known anything, hadn't done anything to anyone at all, was dead, too.

Cheney kept the lights flashing until they turned east off 101 on the Bel Marin Keys exit. They drove through an industrial area, then wetlands, and finally past some palm trees lining the road on both sides. The closer they moved toward San Pablo Bay and its myriad waterways, the heavier the fog became. The roadways crisscrossed around the lagoons, the fog blending with the water like a surrealist painting. The rain picked up and the gloom deepened. It was nearly dark now.

Cheney said, "On a sunny day, this is a beautiful area, fairly affluent, with hundreds of homes sitting either on a lagoon or on Novato Creek. All the lagoons have access to San Pablo and San Francisco bays, as you can see from all the boats. I have a friend who lives not far from Pixie's house, on her same street. I wonder if he knew Pixie McCray. Maybe he's even seen Milo Siles at her house."

Cheney turned left off Bel Marin Keys Boulevard onto Calypso Shores. The houses were set close together, the landscaping mature and well maintained, a great place for both families with kids and retirees. Cheney pulled Eve's Suburban up to the curb about a half-block from Pixie's house, the closest available spot. The houses blocked the view of the lagoons and the boat docks, but they could see the water at the end of the street, and the lock where boats came through. They huddled under umbrellas and walked quickly to the house. There were half a dozen Crown Vics, a couple of them haphazardly parked in the driveway, others against the curb, one up on the lawn. The county coroner's van and the county's Crime Analysis Unit van were parked in the middle of the street, blocking traffic.

Neighbors were standing around, staring and talking, looking generally horrified, huddled beneath umbrellas and awnings as the rain beat down.

The white wooden house was a single story with a big solar panel on the roof, built some thirty years ago. It still managed to look stylish, its three palm trees in the front yard adding a bit of tropical charm.

Sheriff Bud Hibbert met them at the front door. "I'd just as soon not have seen you guys until the Christmas party. What this guy did, how fast he moved—it's frightening. They're in the bedroom."

They left their umbrellas on the front porch and walked around two forensic techs and a sheriff's deputy through the country feminine living room and a small country kitchen with a connected eating area, and down the carpeted hall to the end of the corridor.

Sheriff Hibbert asked for the photographer to stand back for a moment and motioned them around the big king-size bed. It was a god-awful scene, Sherlock thought, so much blood. There was always so much blood. She sometimes wondered how a human body could hold that much blood.

The sheriff said, "I haven't let them touch the bodies. The crime scene's just as it was when a deputy arrived after we got a call from a neighbor who heard Pixie's dog carrying on and came to see what was happening."

None of them really wanted to, but they looked closely at what had once been two living, breathing people until Xu had slit their throats.

The sheriff said, "All their clothes are in place, so no sexual activity had begun even though they were lying on the bed. Look at the blood splatter, the way their bodies ended up when they died. Siles's head has nearly fallen off the near side of the bed, and she's fallen nearly off the other side of the bed. I've been trying to figure out exactly what happened."

Savich pointed at Sherlock. She was standing quietly at the foot of the bed, and he knew she was putting it all together in her mind, using her special gift to picture what few people could see at a crime scene.

"Sherlock?"

She said, "He came in quietly, saw them. He was fast, silent, and smart— even managed to lock Pixie's terrier outside without alerting them. Milo was first. He grabbed him by his hair, jerked his head back, sliced his throat—again, right to left. Not even a second, that's all the time it took. He let Milo fall, reached over him, grabbed Pixie by her hair, jerked her head toward him, then back so violently it snapped her neck. When he sliced her throat he must have been staring down at her, watching her eyes as she realized she was dying. The coroner might be able to determine which of those things killed her, not that it makes any difference.

"You can see the dried tears on Milo's cheeks. He was crying, his head probably against Pixie's shoulder. She was— comforting him."

Sheriff Hibbert stared at Sherlock for a moment. He said slowly, "Yes, I can see that now. Thank you."

Cheney said, "Milo came to her for comfort. And he got her killed."

Sheriff Hibbert said, "Let's back out now, let the coroner and the CAU people do their jobs."

Sherlock paused. "The CAU?"

"Yeah, the Crime Analysis Unit; that's what we call our forensic section."

Sherlock said, "Of course. We're from the CAU in Washington, the Criminal Apprehension Unit."

Sheriff Hibbert said as he walked them to the back of the house that gave onto the waterway and the boat dock, "The neighbor—Mrs. Dee Kotter—saw Pixie's terrier, Bob. He was locked out of the house, and that surprised her, since it was raining. She knocked on the door, found it wasn't locked, and found them. She told us Milo was a twice-a-week fixture at Pixie's house, her longtime boyfriend. He was always polite, spoke to the neighbors who spoke to him, and made Pixie happy. She said it was sort of a joke with Pixie, always saying why marry a man and put up with the toilet lid being up all the time? Better to have him visit, orderly and planned, and that was the way she liked it. The neighbor didn't know Milo was married.

"Mrs. Kotter took Bob. Last time I saw her, she was petting him, kissing him over and over, and crying.

"It's nearly dark, so canvassing the neighborhood is tough. And the damned rain doesn't help. We don't believe it was raining when the killer got here, so hopefully someone saw a stranger, a car, something.

"We also have men over on Caribe Isle—that's the spit of land across the water—interviewing everyone along the street. There's a small park at the end of the spit, and a narrow beach with a nice view of the back of all the houses along this street, including Pixie's house.

"Even though there was a break in the rain, I don't know if anyone was in the park or on that skinny beach. So far, we don't have anything."

Savich cursed. Sherlock was so surprised she nearly tripped over a Christmas cactus on the wide back porch.

Savich said, "I just realized, Xu's got two major loose ends left—the Cahills. You know he's going after the Cahills. Ramsey, at least, is safe from him for the moment."

He got Eve on the first ring.

"Barbieri."

"He's going after the Cahills next. I

know in my gut he's got a pipeline into the jail. Xu has to know they're going to flip on him now he's killed Siles. Eve, get over to the jail, get them to safety."

When Savich punched off, he said, "She's going to bring the Cahills to the twentieth floor, put them in one of the pre-court holding cells."

They stood under the wide porch and looked out over the water to Caribe Isle, listened to the waves bumping against the dock. It was dark and miserable, the rain coming down in torrents. A deputy sheriff strode through the rain from the neighbor's yard, a black umbrella over his head.

He shouted, "Sheriff, we got a winner!"

They'd found an old gentleman on Caribe Isle who'd been walking on the narrow beach beyond the small park. He had a straight view to the back of Pixie McCray's house and her dock. He was chewing on his pipe since he didn't smoke anymore, he told the deputy, hurrying because he knew the rain was going to start up again, and that wasn't good because Purlie, his bulldog, hated to do her business in the rain. He said it was nearly four o'clock when he saw a small outboard motorboat come through the lock, turn left, and motor to Pixie's dock. He saw a man climb onto the dock and go into the house.

Did he see the man leave?

Nope. Purlie was through doing her business, and it started drizzling again, so he took her home.

Xu had come by boat, just as he'd done the night he'd motored the Zodiac to Sea Cliff and shot Ramsey.

They went to speak to Mrs. Dee Kotter, Pixie's neighbor, but she was in shock, numb. She was crying again, holding Bob close, both of them shivering in disbelief and horror at what had happened, here, in Bel Marin Keys, and nothing ever happened here.

38

San Francisco
Monday night

Xu stood beneath the striped awning of Morrie's Deli on Seventh Street, looking through the rain at the Hall of Justice across the street, and waited. It really didn't make any difference that he was there because there wasn't anything more he could do. But even if he couldn't control what would happen, he wanted to be close.

He hated feeling impotent. He'd had no choice but to put his trust in people he hardly knew to carry out his plans, too often a recipe for disaster. His Chinese trainers had dinned into his head over the years never to give anyone else a task that was critical to a mission. And nothing could be more critical to him than Cindy and Clive Cahill dying tonight.

It was at moments like this that he wondered what his life would be like if he had stayed Joe Keats, the name he'd picked for himself when he was eighteen and tired of having Xian Xu mangled and then mocked as a girl's name by the uneducated idiots in Lampo, Indiana. No one ever mispronounced Joe Keats. Except for some of the braying asses he'd trained with in Beijing, who thought it shameful that he, with a Chinese father, had taken on an American name.

He drew a calming breath. He had done what he could, and if his plans went south, he was ready to run, from the FBI, even from Chinese intelligence, if he had to. He would survive.

Joyce Yang, the girl who'd turned him to the dark side, she'd say and laugh her husky laugh that made him mad with lust, and why not, he'd been only twenty years old. He'd loved her with everything in him, at least in those long-ago days before she'd betrayed him with a mid-rung operative, Li Han, in Chinese intelligence, and Xu had cut her throat and buried her deep near her precious hometown of Beijing, where he knew the choking sand from the Gobi Desert would score her grave until her bones were uncovered in the years to come, a fitting place for her, he'd thought at the time. As for Li Han, a man who looked like he was supposed to—Chinese through and through—Xu had left him with a slit throat in an alley in one of the many nasty parts of Beijing where murder was as common as girls selling themselves for a bowl of rice. Would their kids have looked Caucasian like him or like their mother, a full-blooded Chinese?

He looked at his watch. Nine-twenty on this dark rainy night in San Francisco. Soon he'd be drinking scotch at the Fairmont Hotel, watching the football wrap-up of the Monday-night game on the big flat-screen TV in the sports bar.

He whistled, realized he didn't have enough spit in his mouth. For twelve years he'd survived—indeed, he'd thrived—working undercover in the American section of Chinese intelligence. They had taken to calling him *mingzing*—the star—because of what he'd accomplished for them. He'd learned to be ruthless in the way they respected, and yet he was charming enough to talk people out of their paychecks. Maybe his black hair was a bit too glossy and coarse, but no one would question that he looked entirely American, just like his mother, Ann Xu, who'd been an American history teacher at Lampo High School. The principal, fat Mr. Buck, hadn't made fun of him like his peers had, since Xu was the school system's expert in cyber-security. Buck even managed to get him a computer science scholarship to Berkeley. Xu wondered sometimes what Mr. Buck was doing these days. He smiled now. No way Mr. Buck, the bulwark of American conceit and smugness, could know his prized student had killed three students on his watch. Even then, Xu had been good at making people simply disappear.

Joyce poked into his memory again, those beautiful almond eyes of hers, whispering her flawless English in his ear how it would astound her trainers that he could so easily pass for a Caucasian. Like him, she'd been born in the U.S., not twenty miles from Berkeley. Ah, those days at Berkeley, hoisting up the Chinese flag, screaming with other protesters about the brilliance and honor of the Chinese people and the profligacy and corruption of Americans. He'd learned over the years, though, that it was the Chinese who had the market cornered in corruption. He wasn't like the Chinese, he wasn't corrupt, he carried his assignments out promptly and professionally—but now he was watching in disbelief as his life spiraled into the crapper in the span of five short days.

He'd failed in his mission—his *anli*—his superiors had told him, because he'd chosen defective tools, yet they'd happily approved Xu's plans when he'd assured them Cindy Cahill could focus her attention on Mark Lindy and he'd be stuttering to do whatever she wished. And he'd been right, Lindy couldn't resist her, just as his handlers couldn't resist trying to get their hands on the latest generation of the Stuxnet worm Lindy was working on. Even the original Israeli worm had infected sixty percent of Iranian computers and slowed down their production of nuclear fuel for years. Having the access codes to Lindy's work was as important to their industrial security as having the hydrogen bomb.

But his superiors had ended up being right about those two losers, Cindy and Clive Cahill. To cover themselves, they said they'd known Lindy would be too smart and too cagey to fall for a Mata Hari, that he'd be as careful with his passwords as the devil with a bowl of ice cubes.

Xu remembered as clearly as if it had happened today when he'd gotten a call from Cindy more than eight months ago, hysterical, screaming—Lindy was dead, that it wasn't her fault he'd been called in by some sort of incident response team and they'd questioned him about accessing private networks that Lindy knew he hadn't accessed, and he'd accused her of calling up the Stuxnet program on his computer. She'd called in Clive, and he'd held Lindy down while Cindy had poured the poison down his throat. Idiots, both of them, asking to be caught, and they had, of course.

All his superiors in Beijing had wanted was to have him steal the information and leave the country, with no one the wiser, if possible. They blamed him that a high-ranking American cyber-intelligence officer had died. They made it clear they wanted no more killings, and so he'd made a deal with the Cahills, hired Milo to keep them quiet, gotten O'Rourke in line, and waited.

Until everything went to hell. O'Rourke had panicked, ready to spill his guts to that damned judge when he'd suspended the trial. He'd fixed that problem, but he still couldn't be sure how much Judge Hunt knew, or suspected.

From the moment he'd slit O'Rourke's throat, he'd been on his own. From that point on, the Chinese would be more likely to have him killed to prevent his arrest than to help him. Perhaps if he succeeded tonight, the Chinese would see he'd acted in their best interest as well as his own.

It will be all right, Xu, you'll see, it doesn't matter that those silly kids are making fun of you, my darling, that just makes them stupid. And his mother had rocked him when he was small, and he'd believed her, but he'd started to feel a simmering rage, a rage that seemed to encase him like a tunnel, and he knew he wanted to kill them all for mocking him. When Xu was fourteen, one of the bullies with a brand-new driver's license had died in an auto accident, or so it was ruled. He remembered his mother had looked at him as if she knew what he'd done, but she'd said nothing. But he remembered now, she was watchful, always watchful after that. He'd been more careful with the other two bullies.

Xu shook his head, wondering why he'd think of his mother now, wondering, too, if she would rock him now, tell him he was smart, that he'd figure his way through this fiasco, and everything would be all right. Had she known then he would kill again? And again?

As for his father, he was grateful to the loser for two things—he'd forced him to learn Mandarin and had sent him to Beijing to visit his grandfather before the old man dropped over dead during Xu's last visit when he was seventeen.

He looked down at his watch again, saw a streak of blood on his left wrist. How could he have missed it? He scrubbed his skin until the dried blood flaked off. Was it Milo's blood, or the woman's? What was her name? Pixie, that was it, like some lame rip-off of Tinker Bell.

No matter. Soon Billy Cochran would be dispatching Clive Cahill to hell. He knew Cochran as an angry man who'd killed before, a three-time felon set to transfer out to San Quentin in the morning. Cochran had very little to lose, and was enough of a veteran inmate to know how to kill Clive without being caught. Cochran had been eager enough to accept the offer Xu had made when he'd visited him—he was leaving an aging grandmother who needed money badly. Cochran was vicious enough and would feel no remorse, but there was always the question of whether he could pull it off.

He'd been caught three times, after all. Xu wished he could do it himself, but it wasn't possible.

Nine-twenty-nine—one minute until Cochran killed Clive. Xu himself had set the time. That was when the TVs were turned off and the prisoners were herded to the showers before they returned to their cells for the night.

Nine-thirty exactly. Cochran should be smoothly slipping his shiv into Clive's back to penetrate his heart, and he'd fall dead without a sound, leaving trails of his blood to mix with the water going down the shower drain. Cochran would be gone in the morning, and there was no missing that fool. Xu looked through the big window into Morrie's Deli and thought about a corned beef on rye. He realized he hadn't eaten all day, but not yet, not just yet.

Cindy's death might be more problematic, and a pity, really. He thought of the last time he'd had sex with Cindy, what a delight she was as she slid her fingers beneath her thong and shimmied it down her legs. Yes, a pity. Once, a long time

ago, he'd thought they might work together again.

The best he could find was a scared
little Asian woman, maybe five feet tall,
and one hundred pounds. She'd spoken
to Cindy to gain her trust; he'd made sure
of that. He'd found Lin Mei himself, out
on bail, and he'd found she had a little
boy. She didn't have Cindy's physical
strength, and that might be a problem if
Cindy spotted the blade at the last second. Still, he had more faith in Lin Mei
than in Cochran. She was an immigrant,
and he'd been right to think she'd believe
him absolutely when he looked her directly in the eyes and told her in fluent
Mandarin her son would die if she failed
in her task.

It was nine-thirty-five now, and it was
over, one way or the other. He looked into
the rain-soaked night and imagined fire-
works, bursting balls of sparkling red
shooting out of the top of the Hall of
Justice.

He prayed the whole nightmare was
over.

He pulled his collar up on his Burberry

rain jacket and walked down Seventh Street toward the Bayshore Freeway, where his Audi was parked in a safe underground garage.

As he cranked the engine he realized he'd forgotten the corned beef on rye. It was a cop deli, too, probably delicious.

39

Harry Christoff's house
Maple Street
San Francisco
Monday night

Harry pulled his Shelby into the driveway, cut the engine, and turned to face Eve. She had asked him about every detail of the crime scene in Bel Marin Keys. They had fallen back on talking about the brutal murders as dispassionately and profes-sionally as they could, but it was difficult.

Eve said, "At least Savich should have a real shot with the Cahills tomorrow morning. We've got them isolated in the marshal holding cells, out of contact. They shouldn't find out about Milo's murder until Savich springs it on them. There's a good chance one of them will talk, since Xu killed their lawyer this time, their only contact with Xu and the person they've been pinning their hopes on to get them out. What's left for them to try?"

Eve opened both her car door and her umbrella, and ducked under it. She stepped onto the driveway and took her first good look at Harry's house. Even in the dark with the rain pouring down, she could see enough to be surprised at how big it was, probably worth a bundle even in this depressed market. She liked the shake roof and the big windows that gave it a colonial sort of feel even without the columns. She ran through the rain from Harry's Shelby to the front door. A bright porch light was a welcoming beacon. There were even ferns hanging from under the porch ceiling, still looking perky, though it was nearly Thanksgiving. She imagined the tree-filled yard would be spectacular in the spring and summer.

"I like your house; it's the showcase of the neighborhood, isn't it? You'll have to tell me how you snagged it."

He gave her only a curt nod. It was odd, Eve thought, but Harry had seemed a bit unwilling to bring her here, but, as she reminded him, he'd been to her condo, and now it was time for her to see his digs.

His wife's digs, he'd said, not looking at her.

Since she'd left the Suburban at the marshals' pool at the Federal Building, he'd offered to take her home. She knew he hadn't realized he would be making a stop first.

"Everything is beautiful. You have a gardener, don't you?"

He nodded. "His name is Mr. Sanchez. He's been with me six years, comes once a week. His son helps him now." He paused for a moment as he stuck his key in the front door, looked over his shoulder at her. "I just realized I don't know his first name. He's always been Mr. Sanchez to me. His son goes by Junior Sanchez." He smiled. "Not Sanchez Junior."

He pushed open the door, turned off

the alarm, and stepped back for her. "Come on in."

Eve shook out her umbrella and slipped it inside a copper umbrella pot. She stood in a small square entryway with a mirror on the wall above a curvy modern table for mail and flowers, but the beautiful Italian cachepot was empty. The gardeners didn't work inside. He pointed her to the living room, where a big easy chair, an ottoman, and a big-screen TV were displayed front and center, and a pile of newspapers had been tossed in a haphazard stack on the floor beside the chair. Sure, there was a sofa, chairs, and a coffee table, all with an Italian country flavor, but it was obvious he never sat there. Other than the pile of newspapers, nothing else was out of place. No beer cans, no running shoes. Two *Sports Illustrated* magazines sat on the coffee table. She gave him points when she saw that neither one was the swimsuit issue.

Still, everything was so "guy," she had to smile. She looked at the walls, saw they were covered with framed travel posters—of Lake Como, the Alps, Parliament on the Thames—all in full color, inviting you to step right in. She waved toward the posters. "Do you like to travel, Harry?"

"Yes."

She turned to him. "Only a simple yes? No explanation, like whether you've been to all these places and which one is your very favorite in the whole world?"

"That would be Lake Como, I guess. The hiking is great around there. I like Inverness for hiking, too."

She said, "I've never been to Inverness."

"It's stark, usually cloudy, often raining, and almost, well, painfully real. Would you like some coffee?"

She checked her watch. "I'd be a moron to drink coffee this late. You have nonfat milk? Splenda?"

He had both.

Eve watched him grind coffee beans, then measure the ground coffee into the filter and dump water in from the sink tap.

Harry said, "Funny what Savich said about Billy Hammond, his friend at the CIA in Langley. He wouldn't verify anything at all about the information Xu obtained or was after, even though he's known Savich for a hundred years, give or take. That kind of secrecy, it's enough to make you gag in your soup."

"At least he apologized," Eve said. "It must be incredibly sensitive stuff if they're putting tape over his mouth. I'll bet they already know exactly what was accessed, since it would be recorded on their servers. They just don't want anyone else to know, though, even us."

"According to Savich," Harry said, "they weren't much interested in interviewing the Cahills. They probably know the Cahills didn't know about the information Xu accessed, or how valuable it is. But maybe they know enough to help us find Xu."

"That's all we want from them, really," Eve said.

Suddenly he was staring at her as they stood in his kitchen, listening to the coffee perk, shaking his head.

"What? Do I have rain still dripping off my nose?"

He said, "The first time I saw you I thought you looked like a homecoming queen from somewhere in the Midwest,

someone who should be frosting cup-
cakes for her kid's birthday party. I wondered, how can she possibly be a deputy
U.S. marshal?" He shook his head again.
"You're so damned pretty." Then he
waved his hands, as if he were trying to
wave away his words.

Since it was obvious to her that Harry
wished he'd kept his mouth shut, Eve
waved her own hands at his kitchen cabinets. "You said you liked my kitchen.
I had it remodeled last year, you know. I
found a really good contractor who came
in on budget and on time. You want her
name?"

"Nah, everything works fine. Once in a
while the sink clogs, but that's no big
deal."

She grinned. "You're right. Nothing
wrong with cooking in the 1940s. Now
that I think about it, if you wait another
couple of years, all your kitchen appli-
ances will be back in style as retro, except maybe for those green-tinted
cabinets."

He handed her a mug of coffee, gave
her nonfat milk from the refrigerator, and
dug out a couple of packets of Splenda

from his stuff drawer. As she stirred her coffee, she said, "What you said, Harry— do you know my brothers are always saying the same thing? They still call me Miss Suzie-Q.

"When I told my dad I wanted to be a U.S. marshal like he is, though, he looked at me up and down and said, 'That would make me very proud, Eve. It's a great career choice for you. You'll be one of the best.'" She paused for a moment, looked down into her coffee mug. "Yes, that's exactly what he said, straight up. I've never forgotten." She cleared her throat and drank some coffee. "This is very good, Harry. Do you cook?"

"When the need arises. What did your mom say?"

Eve took another sip of her coffee, enjoyed the zing of caffeine, though she knew she'd be cursing herself at two a.m. "When my dad told her what I wanted to do, she laughed. And laughed. She was happy. I saw her kiss my dad and shake her head and say something about the apple not falling far from the tree.

"I look just like my mom, you know. It's

funny what you said, Harry, because my mom was a college cheerleader. And I can still see her cutting our birthday cakes at our big kid parties, hear her singing at the top of her lungs, leading all the kids in a sing-along. I might add that everyone adored her. She was so beautiful, so bouncy and fun. She still is."

Harry said, "So you fell pretty close to both trees. And your dad's the U.S. marshal in Chicago?"

"Yep. Like I told you, he's an anomaly. He's served under two different presidents now, unlike most of the ninety-four marshals countrywide. Tell me about your folks, Harry."

He shrugged. "They live in London—well, they do for most of the year. They love to travel, always have, and they took me with them. I guess they gave me the travel bug."

She could only gape at him. Parents lived in Harrisburg, Pennsylvania, for heaven's sake, or Minneola, Florida, not London, England. "Why do they live in London?"

He looked like he wanted to tell her to

leave it alone, but he said finally, "My dad's a financier. It sounds old-fashioned, I know, but that's what he says he is."

"What does he finance?"

"Well, he runs Willet, Haversham, and Bayle."

She let out a whistle. "They're so big even I've heard of them. They're worldwide. And they survived the bankers' rape of the world with fairly clean hands, from all I've read. Your dad's CEO?"

"Well, not really. He's the chairman of the board. Actually, he pretty much is Willet, Haversham, and Bayle."

"But your name's Christoff."

"Willet and Haversham are his first and middle names, the middle name from his own father, and Bayle is his best friend. They picked the name because Dad liked the sound of it, all snooty and English, like one of their ancient law firms."

"So your dad is Willet Haversham Christoff? And what's your full name?"

"I'll tell you on my deathbed."

"That bad? Does your name sound like an English duke? All right, I'll wait. Do you have any brothers or sisters?"

"I'm an only child."

"All right, I'll keep pulling hen's teeth. Your mom?"

"Sylvia is my mom. She's a fashion consultant."

She stared at him. "You're kidding."

He shrugged. "She'd take one look at you and want to haul you off to be photographed for *Vogue*. And she'd be right. The camera would love you, she'd say. You've got great bones."

"How would you know that?"

"She took me with her on photo shoots, showed me all the subtle clues in a person's face, actually. I've found it all very useful to a cop."

"With that background, why'd you want to be a cop?"

Harry said, without hesitation, "My uncle Roy, my mom's brother, is FBI. When I was six years old he told me I had the heart of a cop. He was right."

Harry's cell rang. "Yeah?"

His face remained impassive, but his eyes hardened. "We'll be there in twelve minutes."

"What?"

"You put the Cahills in a holding cell in the Federal Building, right? Someone evidently cleared the Cahills to go back to the San Francisco jail. Cheney called, found out they were transferred at eight-forty-five tonight."

"No, that's not possible. I mean—what happened?"

40

Hall of Justice
Women's jail
Monday night

Cindy Cahill shook her hands to regain some circulation as plump mean-as-a-snake Annette in her too-tight uniform trousers unlocked her wrist chains. "Welcome home," Annette said. "Hey, you weren't over in the Federal Building for very long. What was that all about?"

Cindy shook her head. "No one said a word, dragged me and Clive over there, then brought us back."

"Your hubby okay?"

"Clive would be thriving if it was World War Three." She and Clive had been taken to the holding cells on the twentieth floor because Savich had wanted to scare them, and not about the CIA, either, but about Xu, as if he'd have a chance of getting into the jail and killing them. Of course, no one had said that, but she'd known it to her toes. Why hadn't that bitch marshal Barbieri told her what this was all about? Because Barbieri was only a drone, and drones kept their mouths shut, if they even knew the answers.

As she knelt down to unfasten the ankle chains, Annette said, "Maybe this moving you around has to do with your lawyer being murdered up in Bel Marin Keys this afternoon. Both him and his girlfriend."

Cindy's heart stopped, her breath caught in her throat. She put her hand out to the wall so she wouldn't fall over. Milo was dead? Murdered? Of course Xu had killed him, she knew it, and that meant he was cleaning house: O'Rourke, Judge Hunt, Milo—she and Clive were the last ones left. Well, Judge Hunt was alive, but why Xu gave a crap about the judge was a huge question in her mind, since he had nothing to do with anything. Had Milo tried to blackmail Xu into giving him more money? Could he have been that stupid? Or was Xu ready to leave the country? He didn't want to take the chance of anyone finding out his name or anything about him?

And now she and Clive were the only ones left who could tie him to anything at all. It was bad enough Xu had murdered O'Rourke, but she'd believed he'd had to, since O'Rourke had screwed everything up and alerted the judge. It even made sense to her. Both she and Clive had believed Xu would find some other way to get them out. But to murder Milo? Even though in the last couple of days both she and Clive had begun to have doubts about Milo, he'd always calmed her, always made her feel like she was in charge. And he always reminded her that Xu was backing them, the man who had all the money and would spend as much as it took. Xu wasn't bad in the sack, either.

Now he'd murdered Milo.

"Hey, you hadn't heard? That's amazing. The lieutenant burps and everyone in this place knows a meatball sub was delivered before he's finished it off."

"No, I hadn't heard," Cindy said, and she thought, *Screw the twenty-five years.* She suddenly didn't care how old she'd be when she got out of prison. At least she'd have a chance of getting out. Were she and Clive really safe here? If Xu really wanted them dead, could he somehow make it happen? She felt fear so corrosive it was like her stomach was turning in on itself.

"I need to use the phone. I need to call Agent Savich at the FBI."

Annette gave Cindy her patented "I can do whatever I want with you since I'm the boss" look and shook her head. "Nope, sweetheart, you can make your call to Agent Savich during business hours tomorrow. This isn't a hotel. Come on, time for you to shower and get your butt to bed."

"But it's urgent; it's a matter of life and death—"

Annette simply sneered at her. "Like I said, Cindy, this isn't a hotel. Let's go."

Cindy knew Annette wouldn't budge, and so she bowed her head and followed her to the showers. She'd call Savich first thing in the morning.

She didn't pay attention any longer to the guards seeing her naked; it hardly even registered. There were several other women in the showers before lights-out, some of them sullen and quiet, others usually loud and foulmouthed. She'd learned to avoid the two or three bullies, to stick with those who stayed quiet and left her alone.

How could she get Savich to agree to fifteen years now he knew she was terrified of Xu?

She managed a bit of lather out of the crappy soap bar as she considered what she'd say to Savich. Better to leave Clive out of it, let him deal on his own. She'd known yesterday Clive wanted to tell Savich and Barbieri everything he knew, down to Xu's sock size. And she'd stopped him. Had that been a mistake? No, no, tomorrow morning it would be fine. She knew Savich would interview Clive separately soon enough after her to make sure she'd told him the truth.

She'd still try to bargain for fifteen years. No more, fifteen years. It wasn't a lifetime of years. She could get through it, she *would* get through it. If only Mark Lindy hadn't found out what was happening and freaked out—

Cindy put the bar of soap back on the shelf and turned to see a tiny Asian woman she'd noticed hovering in the background since yesterday, always deferential and polite to her, trying to get Cindy into a conversation. What was her name? She couldn't remember. The woman was standing naked in front of her, something in her hand. In a blur Cindy saw it was a blade. She jumped back, but she wasn't fast enough. The blade sank into her chest even as she slipped and fell on her back onto the wet tiles. She stared at the woman, whispered, "Why did you do that?"

The woman said, "For my son. I'm sorry."

Xu, she thought. Xu had done this. Her last thought was of Clive. Was he dying, too?

41

San Francisco General
Monday night

Clive Cahill was dead, and Cindy Cahill was fighting for her life in surgery because of a stupid mistake, and it was all her fault, no one else's.

Eve sat in the waiting room with Harry, playing the "if only" game—if only she'd stayed longer with the Cahills at the holding cells on the twentieth floor of the Federal Building, if only she'd thought to read the Cahills' transfer papers from San Francisco jail carefully enough, Xu would never have found them.

No, Miss Brilliance had looked with only one eye and half a brain at the transfer papers, never seen the error that had to be there that returned the Cahills to the San Francisco jail instead of leaving them right here. She had only glanced at the paperwork, really, then trotted out with Harry, excited to think she'd finally see his house. She hadn't even thought to double-check; no, she'd happily hopped into Harry's Shelby and gone with him without another thought about the Cahills' safety. *Her fault.* She'd fire herself if she were her own boss.

Cheney walked into the surgical waiting room with Sherlock and Savich behind him. Before Eve or Harry could open their mouths, Cheney said, "We don't know yet who got to Clive. It was clean and fast, and before anyone knew anything, the guard heard a yell and there was Clive lying dead on the shower floor, a shiv lying beside him in bloody water.

"They found an Asian woman by the name of Lin Mei standing over Cindy, crying, still holding a bloody homemade blade. Lucky for Cindy she stuck her in the chest just once with it, then jerked the blade right out."

Eve said, "Did she say why she did it?"

Savich said, "Lieutenant Clark in the San Francisco Sheriff's Custody Division spoke to her while the EMTs were transporting Cindy Cahill to the hospital. He said her voice sounded like she was drugged or in shock, that she couldn't seem to speak above a whisper. She told Clark a man who looked American told her in fluent Mandarin in the calmest voice she'd ever heard that he would slit her son's throat if she didn't stab Cindy Cahill to death. He handed her a photo of her son shooting baskets in a friend's driveway. He even told her where she would find a blade to stab her with tonight—in a drain next to the women's shower. She said she didn't have a doubt he'd do exactly what he said if she didn't kill Cindy."

Sherlock said, "It seems so unlikely, but we know now that Xu looks American. No one who's seen him thought he looked Asian, but he was always wearing glasses before. So it means he's Chinese American, with Causasian features."

Eve said, "So Xu visited this woman in prison?"

Savich shook his head. "Clark told me that Lin Mei had been out on bail until yesterday. Then she showed up after missing her court date, on purpose, it looks like, told by her court-appointed lawyer, who told her she'd see a judge in the next couple of days and be rebonded. Xu approached her while she was working at her job at the bakery at Whole Foods. He waited patiently until she was on break and stepped in front of her."

Savich shook his head. "Do you know she was arrested for kiting a check for her brother to get him out of trouble with a Chinese gang because she didn't have any money? Now she'll be up for murder."

Eve said, "Hopefully attempted murder with mitigating circumstances. Didn't she think about what would happen to her and her son if she got caught?"

Cheney said, "Caught? She never tried to hide that she'd stabbed Cindy. She was paralyzed by what she'd done, that she'd just tried to kill another human being. Lieutenant Clark said after she described what she'd done and why, her eyes rolled back in her head and she fainted. When she woke up she didn't say another word. He said he asked her over and over why she hadn't come and spoken to one of the guards, but she only looked at him with great sadness. He had her brought here to the emergency room."

Eve looked up to see her boss, Marshal Carney Maynard, standing in the doorway. He looked tired, she thought, and unhappy, and she couldn't blame him at all. Maynard said, "There aren't any nurses around who know anything about Cindy Cahill. Is she still alive?"

"She's still in surgery and hanging in," Eve said. "That was all the OR nurse could tell us. She said when the surgery's done, the surgeon will come out and speak to us. It's nearly one a.m., sir, you didn't have to come." *Of course he had to come, you idiot. He's here because of you.*

Maynard said, "I did have to come, Eve. Cindy Cahill is here because my people screwed up."

Nice way of putting it. "No, sir, your people didn't screw up. I screwed up, and I'm singular," Eve said, and looked him straight in the eye. "Let's do this in front of everyone, I deserve it."

Marshal Carney Maynard eyed her back and frowned. "How do you figure you suddenly rule the world, Deputy Barbieri?"

"Sir, the truth is I only glanced at the transfer papers. I should have studied them as carefully as I would if they had been papers bringing Qaddafi's body to the U.S., but I didn't."

Maynard waved a hand to cut her off. He was more frazzled than tired, and here was Barbieri desperately trying to shoulder all the blame. It'd be easier if he could heap it all on her head, but he couldn't. He said, "Since the proverbial buck stops with me, Deputy Barbieri, I'm the one responsible. I knew the importance of this transfer, but I was watching the Monday-night football game. This was the classic definition of a snafu. I'd hoped never to have one with such disastrous results under my watch, but it's happened, and now we all have to deal with it.

"So dial it down, Eve." He laughed. "We've given our FBI contingent a fine show. Here's what happened. Turns out we had a new deputy driving the prisoner van. His partner didn't look closely at the paperwork, and so they did the run they normally do. They drove Clive and Cindy Cahill straight back from one of our holding cells to the San Francisco jail. That simple. No, Deputy. You did your job. I didn't do mine."

Sherlock said, "No one wins in a blame game, Marshal Maynard. Not even the FBI contingent."

Nurse Camp looked in from the doorway. "Dr. Elba is tied up and asked me to speak to you. Cindy Cahill is out of surgery. Dr. Elba thinks she has an even chance, though she's still oozing blood because of a clotting problem she's developed from all the bleeding. We moved her to recovery. You won't be able to speak to her until morning, all right?"

Harry asked, "Could you please find out about a new patient for us, a Mrs. Lin Mei, probably having a psychiatric evaluation?"

Nurse Camp said, "Not in my bailiwick, Agent. The people at the reception desk can help you find her."

Eve thanked her and watched Savich dial Bill Hammond at the CIA. They could hear a man's voice loud and clear: "Are you nuts, Savich? It's four in the damned morning!"

Harry and Eve looked at each other, knew they didn't want to hear this conversation, and left the waiting room. They took the elevator to the fourth floor to check on Ramsey before they left the hospital. It wasn't the same elevator. That one still had crime tape plastered over the doors on every floor. Eve didn't think she'd ever want to ride that particular elevator again in her life.

42

Judge Sherlock's home
Pacific Heights
Tuesday morning

Judge Corman Sherlock said to his son-in-law the next morning across the breakfast table, "You're frustrated, Dillon, and no wonder, after last night. How about I give you my membership card for the Pacific Heights Club over on Union Street and you get a good workout? I can call Mr. Eddie, he's usually there, and he's been looking forward to mixing it up with you. He outweighs you by a good twenty pounds, all of it muscle. Even though he's older than you, he's one tough bald bugger."

Savich hated to say no; he couldn't think of anything he needed more than a sweaty hard workout. He shook his head. "I've got to take a rain check with Mr. Eddie. Lacey and I have to get over to the hospital as soon as we can. Cindy Cahill's awake, more or less, and this is our first chance to talk to her."

Five minutes later, after Sean had demolished a bowl of Cheerios and started to rag on his grandmother about the visit to the zoo she'd promised him, even though the zoo wasn't open yet, Sherlock started up their rental car for the ride across town to San Francisco General Hospital.

Savich booted up MAX as they drove toward Market Street. "Cheney is already working on getting a sketch of Xu from Lin Mei. He said he'd have it out to Hammersmith about now, but it doesn't look like he's posted it yet. I wonder how Cindy will react to it."

"I only hope she'll be able to talk to us,"

Sherlock said. "Cheney said she wasn't doing well."

"If she can, I know in my gut that now she'll tell us everything she knows about Xu, since he tried to have her killed."

He sat back for a moment, closed his eyes. "Until Xu murdered Milo Siles, and his game plan became clear, it was a nightmare trying to predict him. Sometimes he was controlled and logical, sometimes not. What he pulled off last night was an act of desperation, beyond his control. He was lucky it worked out as well as it did."

Sherlock turned onto 101 South. "Ripping up an elevator ceiling, throwing down a smoke bomb, and firing down on a bunch of marshals and Ramsey sure wasn't a logical, controlled act. I still can't figure that one out."

"I can't, either. It's so over-the-top and out of character for him. Why was he so desperate to kill Ramsey in such a crazy way? Bottom line, he's a spy, probably has been for quite a while, and a spy's first watchword, it would seem to me, is discretion. He buried Mickey O'Rourke in a spot no one would ever find, just bad luck for him that those kids were there.

"But then he murdered Milo Siles and Pixie McCray in broad daylight when he could easily have been spotted. He's all over the place."

Sherlock said, "I think with Milo it boiled down to eliminating anyone who could hurt him as fast as possible so he can get out of Dodge. It was desperation, like you said. I think if he'd thought he had a choice, he'd have waited until he could get Milo alone, bury him deep, like he did Mickey O'Rourke. I'll tell you, Dillon, it gives me a headache."

Savich grinned at her. "I'm hoping Xu is deluded enough or desperate enough to make a try to kill Cindy in the ICU. I doubled her guard. She's as well covered as Ramsey. If Xu shows up, we'll get him, no doubt in my mind."

"You know he's got to try. The last thing he wants is for her to talk to us, and he's got to know she would talk, since he tried to have her killed."

"Ah, here comes the sketch."

Sherlock looked over at MAX's screen at the man's face. "Not very distinctive, is he? Not a single Asian facial characteristic except maybe for the thick black hair. Green eyes, and a thin, longish face. What age would you say, about thirty-five?"

Savich said, "Yeah, that's about right." He stared at the man and found himself wondering how Xu had hooked up with the Chinese government, and why he'd become a traitor to his country of birth. *Does he feel more Chinese than American? Or is it all about money?* Savich knew neither was the whole of it. Fact was, though, Xu was a psychopath who happened to be half Chinese and had found a perfect fit getting paid to do what he took pleasure in.

43

San Francisco General Hospital
Tuesday morning

They found Cindy Cahill in the surgical
ICU only one cubicle away from where
Ramsey had fought for his life, shot by the
same man who'd ordered Cindy killed.
Officer Colley looked them over from be-
side Cindy's cubicle and smiled at them.
He'd also done a guard shift when Ramsey
had been here.

"Good to see you, Agent Savich, Agent
Sherlock. Agent Christoff and Deputy

Barbieri have been waiting inside for you for a couple of minutes. There've been lots of doctors and nurses in and out. I think she's in trouble." He held up his cell phone to show them the sketch of Xu. "Just got it." He nodded to Sherlock. "No sign of him. You can bet they'll strip-search any guy who looks like him before he leaves the lobby, ball cap or not."

Cindy looked white as death, her eyes closed, her eyelids bruised, her hair matted down. There was a plastic oxygen mask over her mouth, and when she breathed, it was with effort, as if it was hard work for her. The single sheet pulled over her was stained pink where it touched her chest, and looked to be draped over a maze of gurgling tubes, packings, and pressure dressings, some of them stained pink as well. One of her IVs held a bag of blood that was slowly dripping into her arm. Without makeup, without a show of her usual attitude and the force of her personality, she looked young and vulnerable, and gravely ill.

Savich nodded to Eve and Harry. "Has she been asleep since you got here?"

Eve shook her head. "She's awake, but she hurts and she's dopey from all the drugs they're pumping into her. The doctor told me he didn't know whether she'd make any sense or not."

Sherlock said, "All we can do is try."

"Ah, there's an eye opening." Eve leaned over her. "Good morning, Cindy. You want to blink at me so I know you're there?"

Cindy Cahill blinked. "I'm here," she whispered.

"Are you in pain?" Savich asked.

Incredibly, she smiled. "It doesn't feel like I'm swimming in Bali with the sun beating down on me, if that's what you mean. I've always wanted to go to Bali, but I don't know if I'm going to make it there now. Do you know she apologized to me after she stuck that knife in my chest?"

Everyone felt a pang of pity until Cindy whispered, a heap of venom in her voice, "I even went out of my way to talk to that skinny little bitch. I mean, I didn't have anything better to do, so why not? And all she did was yak, yak about her son, as if I cared." The real Cindy, attitude and all, had snapped back into focus, as ill as she was.

Harry grinned. "Sounds like you're getting back to normal, Cindy," he said, and kept his fingers crossed she'd stay with it.

"I won't be back to normal ever. Look at me. At least the bitch didn't kill me."

"Her name's Lin Mei," Sherlock said.

"Who are you?"

"I'm an FBI agent."

Cindy said, "I like your hair. I once had red hair, well, more auburn, really, but I didn't curl it like you do yours." She cut her eyes to Eve. "What I hate is blond ponytails. I mean, it's so dated, like a woman trying to regain her girlhood. It's pathetic."

Eve said, "The reason Lin Mei tried to kill you is because Xu threatened to murder her little boy if she didn't."

They all saw how quickly Cindy computed this, even as sick and drugged as she was. "Poor kid's dead now. I mean, since I'm alive, it means Mom failed, and Xu will find that out fast enough."

"Her boy is being protected," Sherlock said. "He'll be fine."

Eve continued, "Do you know Lin Mei's in shock and here in the psychiatric unit?"

"She's probably faking it. I hope she goes down hard for this." They saw a hand clench. "I actually pretended to *listen* to her! I actually paid her some attention, and this is how she repays me."

Savich said, "I'm sure you agree she was smart to pay more attention to Xu. She didn't think the police could protect her son from him."

"All right, so she was smart to believe him. I mean, he shot Judge Hunt, murdered Mickey O'Rourke and poor Milo, the greedy idiot. Wait—" Sudden panic bloomed in Cindy's eyes. "Clive. Where's Clive?"

Savich hadn't wanted to go there, not yet, but Cindy's face was flushed, her eyes focused on him. He didn't have a choice now. He said, "Xu hired a prisoner to stab him in the shower, just as he had Lin Mei stab you. Clive didn't make it. I'm sorry, Cindy."

Cindy's face went perfectly blank. She tried to shake her head at them but couldn't seem to make her head move. She closed her eyes and didn't make a sound, except for her labored breathing. Tears seeped from beneath her eyelids and streamed down her white cheeks.

Eve thought, *So Cindy hadn't been simply using Clive after all.*

Savich said, "You can't help Clive now, but you can help yourself. I've got that offer from the U.S. attorney for you, Cindy. Are you ready to tell us what you know about Xu?"

Cindy whispered, her eyes still closed, "Is it fifteen years, like I wanted?"

"Yes, since Xu's now a serial killer, fifteen years is on the table if what you tell us helps us find him."

"You got that in writing?"

"There hasn't been time, Cindy, and we don't have much of it now. He could be leaving the country as we speak."

"Can I trust you, Agent Savich?"

Savich leaned down close to her face. "You can trust me."

Cindy opened her eyes and studied his face. She whispered, "Xu's first name is Xian, *X-i-a-n,* but he'd always been called Xu, said it was easier than Xian. He's a lot younger than Clive, but he didn't tell me his age. I teased him enough for him to tell me he was from Indiana, got out of there when he was eighteen. He said he changed his name to Joe Keats, but when he was working, he was Xu. I don't know if he's using Joe Keats now, since I never saw his passport. I think he's got lots of aliases."

"Does this look like him, Cindy?" Savich showed her the sketch of Xu on the cell phone.

"That's not too bad. He's handsomer, though, really pretty green eyes. He did tell me he got his eyelashes from his mom, Ann."

"Do you know where he's staying?"

"No, he never told us that. He showed up when he wanted to. I think he moved around."

"What was Xu after from Mark Lindy's computer?"

"He never told us that, either. He said the less we knew about it, the better for everyone. Lindy did tell me he was an expert on computer worms and viruses, stuff like that. He bragged to me once when he was lying on top of me after sex that he was one of the major designers of the worm that shut down Iran's bomb plans."

An alarm went off on one of the electronic monitors Cindy was connected to, and a nurse and resident rushed into the cubicle. "Please leave now," the doctor said. "She needs some help."

The four of them were hurried out of Cindy Cahill's cubicle. They stood motionless outside the cubicle. "Is she going to die?"

No one had an answer for that.

Savich punched the elevator button. They said nothing more, waited until they were inside. Savich said, "Since there's nothing we can do about Cindy, I need to sit down somewhere, run the information she gave us on Xu through MAX."

As they walked to the cafeteria, Eve said, "I want her to make it, I really do. I'll admit I was surprised she was so upset about Clive. I always thought she was using him, like he was some sort of father figure to her. It's all just so—useless."

Savich shook his head. "I'd say they had a mutual dependence, strange as it was."

Eve nodded. "I also think she had a bit of contempt for him, since she knew very well Clive was weaker than she was—but yeah, she depended on him, he was always there for her. I wonder what will happen to her now."

44

San Francisco General Hospital
Cafeteria

Sherlock set down her coffee cup as she looked over Dillon's shoulder. Xu had been born and raised in Lampo, Indiana. He was the son of a Caucasian mother, Ann Xu, a history teacher at Lampo High School, and a Chinese father who had first immigrated to the Gulf-side town of Paxico, Florida, before moving to Indiana and buying a gas station.

At eighteen, Xu and his parents had left Lampo for a long summer vacation at

Bronson Lake, fifty miles from Lampo, Mrs. Xu had told neighbors.

The family had simply never returned. The gas station Mr. Xu had owned remained vacant; the history position at Lampo High School had been filled when Ann Xu hadn't returned for the fall term. No one ever heard from the son. Cursory inquiries were made, but there was simply no sign of the Xu family after they'd gone on vacation. They were eventually forgotten, since no one knew of any family on either the mother or father's side to contact.

Sherlock said, "Do you think Xu killed his parents?"

"Oh, yes," Savich said. "There's no trace of Xu after that. If he changed his name legally to Joe Keats, we'll find him."

The critical thing was that they had Xu's first Indiana driver's license, with a photo taken of him when he was sixteen. Dillon had already sent the photo to the image-processing lab at the Hoover Building to have it updated to show how he would look now, nearly twenty years later. They were waiting for the aged picture now, ready to compare it to the sketch Lin Mei had given the police sketch artist, and then would forward it to Hammersmith and his team as soon as it arrived.

"His features really are Caucasian," Sherlock said, looking at the driver's license. "Look at those green eyes. There doesn't seem to be any resemblance at all to his Chinese father, except they are both on the slight side. He's a good-looking kid, isn't he?"

"Look closely," Savich said. "He's already got an arrogant tilt to his head, and there's a dead-on look in his eyes, staring you right in the face, like he doesn't care what you think or about much of anything."

A message notification popped up, and they were soon looking at the same face, though more filled out, lines about his mouth and eyes, yet his eyes were more intense, and still had the same dead-on look, easily recognizable. Savich forwarded it to Hammersmith, waited a few seconds, and called him on speakerphone.

Savich said, "Griffin, did you get that picture of Xu I sent you?"

"It's going out over the network now. I was wrong about Xu moving from the Atherton B-and-B to a middle-of-the-road motel on Lombard or down by the wharf or any of the motels in the Tenderloin. We've checked; he ain't there.

"I'm still convinced, though, he's got to be close by. I don't think he knows we've identified him yet. It could be he's staying at one of the most exclusive hotels, like the Stanford or the Fairmont or the Mandarin, figuring we wouldn't expect that. I'm thinking the Fairmont."

"Why the Fairmont in particular?" Sherlock asked.

A pause, then Griffin said, "A feeling, just a feeling. No guarantees."

None needed, Savich thought.

"Also, from what we know about him and his contacts, he's not short on money, so why not be comfortable?"

"Then why did he stay at that bed-and-breakfast in Atherton when he first arrived to kill Judge Hunt?"

"I don't know. I've realized he's not so easy to figure out." Griffin sighed. "Until he killed Mickey O'Rourke, I had him pegged differently. We'll canvass all the hotels we can, this time with Xu's photo in hand. We'll have them put up his photo behind the registration desks. He might still be wearing that ball cap and sunglasses—well, there's nothing we can do about that except give them a heads-up."

"Griffin, do me a favor."

"Sure, Sherlock, whatever you need."

"Be careful, Griffin. He's a very dangerous man. Please don't forget that."

"I will. Listen, I could be all wrong about the Fairmont."

"They tell me that doesn't happen often," Savich said. "Call when you get something."

When Eve and Harry got off the elevator on the fourth floor, Eve looked up the hallway at an SFPD officer and a deputy marshal, on their feet when they spotted them.

Once inside Ramsey's room, Deputy Marshal Haloran said quickly, "What's going on?"

Eve said, "I really made a mess of it, Joe."

Harry squeezed her arm. "She means Cindy Cahill is pretty bad off. But she may have finally given us something useful. We'll know soon."

To Eve's surprise, Ramsey was reading a spy novel, and wasn't that perfect? She wondered what Savich would find out about Xu, the spy and cold-blooded murderer who wanted Ramsey dead.

She leaned over and kissed his cheek. "You look really hot, you know that?"

He also looked tired. But he was back, all hard, dark edges, and the killer smile, Judge Dredd in the flesh. "I look hot? That makes you as much of a liar as my wife. Happy to see you, though, liar or not." He paused. "Eve, I can tell by looking at you that something's happened. What?"

Eve said, "Cindy Cahill told us the man who's been trying to kill you is called Xian Xu. He's Chinese American, born in Indiana, and looks as WASP as you do. Dillon and Sherlock are trying to track him down. I don't suppose the name means anything to you?"

"Not any more than the name Xu by

itself," Ramsey said. "If they can find him, maybe I can start making some plans to get out of here and back to work."

"We should get him now, Judge Hunt," Harry said. "He won't come after you again." Ramsey stared from Harry to Eve, considering that, and Eve said, "Hey, do you think you'll be going home in time for Thanksgiving?"

Ramsey became aware that the pain meds were tugging on his brain, and evidently his hearing as well, because he thought in that moment that Eve had a beautiful speaking voice. He forgot about Thanksgiving, forgot everything but her voice. He stared up at Eve. "You ever have voice lessons?"

"Me? Goodness, talk about playing a rusty saw. That's what my vocal cords feel like. Ramsey, have you had your pain meds recently?"

"Well, yes, a couple of minutes ago. You're lucky I'm still awake."

She took his hand, squeezed it. "Hey, Haloran. If you want to play more poker with Judge Hunt, now's the time."

———

Sherlock and Savich were seated in the security office off the lobby, Griffin on the phone. He sounded so hyper she hoped he wasn't driving.

"We've got him! Amazing what a difference that picture made."

Sherlock said, "Let me put my cell on speaker, Griffin. Okay, make our day."

"Xu's here at the Fairmont Hotel. The registration clerk on duty recognized him after studying the photo. She was used to seeing him in sunglasses and his ball cap, but this morning, he came trooping out of the restaurant after he'd had breakfast and asked the concierge a question. She said good morning to him. He said good morning back to her and smiled. She added he had a very nice smile. So it appears our Mr. Xu either forgot his sunglasses or he didn't care this morning about hiding his face from prying eyes. Maybe he doesn't intend to stay much longer."

They cheered loud enough for Griffin to grin. The guard at the hospital video console turned toward them and toasted them with his coffee, since they looked ready to high-five the world.

Sherlock said, "Griffin, you're a genius. I worship at your feet. Tell us everything."

"He's not at the hotel now. The registration clerk told us the last time she saw him, he was headed toward the hotel front doors."

Savich asked, "Griffin, did the registration clerk say he was carrying anything, like luggage?"

"I didn't ask her. Hold on." Two minutes later, Griffin came back on line. "She doesn't remember seeing him carrying anything."

Savich said, "If he believes Cindy is dead, he may think his job here is done. He could have put his luggage in his car before he went in to breakfast. Griffin, speak to the concierge. Find out what question Xu asked."

Griffin was back on the line in a minute. "The concierge who spoke to Xu is off-duty. I'll try his cell to see if he remembers what Xu wanted. I'll get back to you."

Savich said, "Griffin, stay around the lobby. If Xu comes back, call us, but don't try to apprehend him, okay? How many agents are with you?"

"There are two of us."

"Make sure you all look like happy tourists. Cheney or I will call you."

When he punched off his cell, Savich said, "I'm thinking keep it simple. We wait for him in his room, that way there's no chance of any bystanders getting hurt."

Sherlock cocked her head at Dillon. "Do you think he's leaving for good?"

"I don't know. He's careful and he's smart. He didn't check out when he left the Fairmont this morning, but if he's got luggage with him in the car, he may not go back."

"I would bet he knows Cindy is alive by now, and of course Ramsey is, too. Do you think he's giving up on it all, running?"

"Nothing he does would surprise me. There are only three places we know he might go—back to the Fairmont, one of the airports, or here, the hospital."

"He's got to know we're ready for him here, Dillon, and that Ramsey and Cindy Cahill are well protected," Sherlock said.

"So was Ramsey in the elevator. Call Eve, have her alert the deputies with Ramsey. Something big is going to happen today. We just don't know where."

They were walking toward the parking lot when Savich got a call from the ICU.

Cindy Cahill had gone into convulsions. She hadn't made it. She was dead.

45

San Francisco General Hospital

Xu walked at a brisk pace through the San Francisco General Hospital campus to Potrero Avenue. He turned right and walked to Twenty-second Street, where he'd parked his Audi on a quiet residential side street.

The San Francisco air was fresh and chill, clouds scuttling across a gray sky. Finally he could take a second to look at them and breathe a sigh of relief. He grinned. He'd taken a huge risk coming to the hospital, and now that Cindy had

had the grace to die, he hadn't had to take the even greater risk of trying to kill her himself.

That little scrap of a woman, Lin Mei, had ended up a murderer after all.

He'd worried at it like a dog's bone. Cindy would have had every reason to talk to the FBI now, and if she had told them what she knew, they would eventually have found the Xian Xu who became Joe Keats. The National Security Agency would have no record of a Joe Keats or of his connection to Chinese intelligence, but he could never have been Joe Keats again. He would have become an international fugitive wanted for murder, dependent on the Chinese for his very life, if they chose to let him keep it.

Had Cindy managed to speak to the FBI agents he'd seen leaving the ICU before she died? He couldn't be sure, but it was unlikely. She'd had major surgery; she'd had a tube down her throat until this morning. If she'd been conscious at all, it wasn't for long. He'd heard the frenetic beeping from the monitors, watched the staff rush to her cubicle. They'd been in there a long time. When they'd come out, he knew she was dead by the expressions on their faces.

Cindy had gone to meet her maker, whoever that was, and she'd taken his secrets with her. He thought about her death, wondered if she'd even known she was dying or if she'd been too drugged out to even recognize what was happening to her. To his surprise, Xu saw his mother's face, saw her heaving for breath as he'd stood there, a bloody knife in his hand, watching her in the kitchen of their small vacation house, grabbing her throat because she couldn't breathe as she sank to her knees on the floor.

He walked faster. His mother's death was long ago, long over and done. He'd been trained to block out memories that were of no use to him, to focus on what was important, and immediate, not wallow in the past, reliving moments he couldn't change. His immediate task was to get back to his superior in Beijing, Colonel Ng, a tough-as-nails little man with a gold tooth in the front of his mouth. He would have to rehearse carefully, convince Ng that there were no more witnesses to hurt them, that Ng's cyber-intelligence unit could not be tied to anything that had happened. Xu had, after all, brought them a great prize, the latest American Stuxnet research, or a good part of it. Who could fault him if he'd had to dirty his hands, so long as they were all safe? In the end they would do as they wished, of course, but he hoped they would find him too useful to waste.

After eight long months, things had finally turned around for him, and he no longer needed to stay. After he picked up his luggage at the Fairmont, he and his Audi would make the six-hour trek to LAX. No way was he going near SFO airport. He momentarily pictured himself waving good-bye from thirty-three thousand feet on his way to Honolulu to the idiot FBI agents still looking for him.

Xu was whistling when he reached his Audi ten minutes later. He fobbed open the door and slid in. He paused for a moment, staring out the windshield. The sun had peeked out from behind the clouds, full and hot. He loved this beautiful city, with its swirling pristine fog that rolled in through the Golden Gate and left again. No one should live in Beijing with the lung-rotting pollution and its sandstorms blowing in from the Gobi Desert that turned the sky brown, choking its people even through the masks they wore. Crowds of people, endless millions of them scrabbling to survive in a city where buildings seemed to go up every second, so poorly constructed they began to fall apart around you the next day—that is, if some unscrupulous local officials didn't evict you first.

As he drove north toward the city, he thought back to his college days at Berkeley, where he'd protested with all the vigor and ignorance of youth against the cause du jour, usually a variation of the theme of America as a decadent wasteland. He smiled now at how he'd lapped it up, with Joyce's help, both of them ardent young Communists. Except Joyce had been more, so much more. He hadn't realized until he'd lived in Beijing that the Chinese government at all levels could give the bozos here in America lessons in corruption. His idealism had died there, drowned in all the bureaucratic inanities and the fraud that permeated everything. He'd watched groups protest, watched them shout their pitiful truths, watched them get the Chinese government's boot on their necks. How could you continue to believe in a society in which you couldn't even trust the food you ate, or the air you breathed? The only people you could trust in China were your own family, and he had no family left.

During his year-and-a-half stay in the area, Xu had come to hope he could live there, though it would surprise his masters that he would leave behind the splendid apartment they'd given him near the Forbidden City. Perhaps in a year or two, when all of this was behind him, he could think about working for himself. He had a reputation in some important circles. He would see.

He honked at a driver who cut in front of him as he turned onto California Street. He knew the locals thought the traffic here was insane, and he snorted a laugh. Even L.A. couldn't compete with Beijing, the traffic-snarl capital of the world, with its endless streams of bicycles weaving in and out of traffic on the overcrowded roads. Once he'd even seen a skinny little kid pedaling away on top of a thick stone wall.

He looked at the people walking on the sidewalks, most of them with phones attached to their ears, most of them busy with the little problems in their little lives. They had no idea what was going on in the world around them.

It was time to go back to Beijing and make his case. He hadn't contacted them since he'd taken O'Rourke, and now he decided he'd wait. Best to do it in person.

Xu felt a taste of fear in his mouth. It was viscous, foul, like the pumping blood from Mickey's throat spraying the walls of that miserable little shack.

He started whistling again. He'd be in and out of the Fairmont in ten minutes, no longer, and on his way to LaLa Land.

46

Fairmont Hotel
California Street

Xu left his Audi with the valet. He'd be back in ten minutes, he told her, pressing a ten-dollar bill into her hand. Pretty girl. He walked through the elegant hotel lobby, with its yellow granite columns, scattered huge palm trees, and sculpted seating arrangements spread throughout, and arrived at the elevators. He punched the button for the sixth and top floor. There were two couples in the car with him who obviously knew one another, the men carrying shopping bags, the women flushed and happy and chattering about lunch.

Both couples got off at the fifth floor. He wondered if they had views as incredible as his. He'd miss seeing the Golden Gate in the distance, and the downtown beneath him to the east, a tight knot of multifaceted buildings shining with reflected light in the bright afternoon sun.

He got off the elevator and walked down the beautifully carpeted hallway to his suite at the end of the wide corridor. He didn't see a soul except a maid standing beside her cart in front of the door across from his suite. He didn't recognize her, and he always made a point of knowing who was around him when he was in an unfamiliar place, staff included.

She looked up at him, smiled and nodded, then said, "Is there anything you need, sir?"

He shook his head and thanked her. He watched her sort through a stack of towels. There was something about her he couldn't quite pinpoint that was a bit— off. Was she new? Was it simply because she was working a different shift? Or had he simply not seen her before? He smiled back at her. "You having a good day?" he asked.

"Oh, yes, it's splendid today, after the rain," she said, and turned her back to him to open the room across the hall.

Something was definitely off, but what was it? They couldn't have found him, simply couldn't have. But he hadn't stayed alive for the past twelve years by taking chances. He carefully eased a small canister out of his jacket pocket, slipped his finger through the ring and pressed it against his thigh. When he slid his key card down the slot, the green light flashed and the door opened, quiet and smooth, as it always did. He let the door open a crack.

He stepped into the very modern living room of his suite, with its view of the city spreading out before him.

A man's voice yelled, "FBI! Hands in the air! Now!"

"Don't shoot me!" he yelled. He flung his hands into the air, and let the safety ring remain on his finger as the canister crashed to the floor. There was a deafening blast, and thick smoke billowed like a black curtain in front of him. A sheet of flames burst out hot and high, and Xu was down, rolling. He'd closed his eyes as he'd hurled the canister and turned his head away, but he still saw lights, felt his eardrums throb from the deafening noise.

He heard shouts, heard bullets flying around him through the flames and smoke. He knew they couldn't see him any more than he could see them, even less if they were still blinded by the light with their ears ringing. But they'd know if they didn't do something fast they'd burn to death. He felt a bullet sting his arm, ignored the shot of pain, crawled to the front door, and rolled out into the hall. His last view of his suite was through a wall of flames, the FBI agents yelling to one another from the other side.

He jumped to his feet to face the maid, who was raising her SIG. "Freeze!"

A shout and three more bullets came through the smoke, striking the wall behind her close to her head, and she flinched. He kicked the SIG out of her hand, backhanded her face, knocking her to the floor, and took off down the nearest stairs. His left arm hurt like the devil, but he took two, three steps at a time, hoping he wouldn't go flying on his face. With his useless arm, he'd break his neck if he did. He forced himself to slow and straighten his clothes before he reached the lobby, and took a second to regain his breath. He saw blood had soaked through his jacket sleeve. It was a dark material, thankfully, it wouldn't be all that apparent at a glance, but it hurt, really hurt. He knew he should be applying pressure, but there wasn't time.

He forced himself to walk, not run, across the lobby and toward one of the smaller front doors. The fire alarm went off, the people in the lobby started looking around uncertainly, wondering what to do while the staff took their places to usher them to the doors. Very soon there would be pandemonium, he would see to that, enough craziness that even the FBI agents would be too busy trying to save their own butts and protect all the innocent bystanders to care about catching him. He heard a shout from behind him over the alarm bells. "It's Xu! Stop, FBI!"

He kept walking as he reached into his

pocket and pushed a preset number on his cell phone. There was a loud explosion, and soon there were screams and the sounds of people running—the chaos was beginning, and the FBI agents waiting for him in the hotel lobby would be drowned in the stampede.

He held his arm as he walked quickly to the valet station. He saw his car, but the girl wasn't there, no one was, none of the bellmen, none of the valets. He saw her then, but she was dashing back into the lobby, yelling something to the doorman. Where were the keys to his Audi? He didn't see them, and he couldn't wait. He had to get out and grab a taxi, and where was a taxi stand?

He didn't register the dark van parked across the street until the van door slid open and a redheaded woman jumped out. He saw a gun pressed against her side. Another fricking FBI agent, he thought, and she was running right at him.

Xu took off, weaving through the growing crowd of panicked people clogging the sidewalk. He heard sirens in the distance. How had the FBI found him? How?

Cindy, he thought, she'd been able to talk.

He could hear her, knew she was gaining on him. She was a woman, and if she made the mistake of getting too close, he could kill her in an instant. He could nearly smell her now. He heard angry, panicked voices as she shoved people out of her way.

Sherlock heard an explosion. Her heart stopped as she looked up to the top floor and saw a window flying outward, sending shattered glass raining down, smoke and flames gushing out after it.

It was Xu's room. What had he done? Eve, Harry, and Griffin Hammersmith had been in that room waiting for Xu, and Agent Willa Gaines outside in the hallway, dressed as a maid. Were they still there?

Sherlock couldn't believe it was Xu she saw coming out through the luggage door of the hotel. She saw people running out of the hotel behind him, heard yells, felt the rising panic.

She jerked open the van door and jumped down. Two agents monitoring the hotel exits shouted after her, but she paid no attention. She ran full speed after Xu. He was fast, but there were so many people around, all of them excited and looking up, wondering what had happened.

He disappeared for a moment. She stepped around a couple of tourists, saw a blood trail on the sidewalk. Good, he was hurt. Who else was hurt? *Stop it. Focus.* Sherlock saw him again, holding his arm as he ran. She took a flying leap past two civilians who stood in the middle of the sidewalk gaping up at the flames and landed on his back, her arms around his neck. The force drove him to his knees. He was larger than she was, and stronger, even wounded, but she was well trained, her adrenaline level off the charts. She had to flatten him, get his face against the sidewalk.

She struck her fist as hard as she could against his wounded arm, and he howled. He fell to his belly, yelling in fury and pain, cursing, trying to flip her off him. With his good arm, he tried to grab her to pull her beneath him, but she didn't let that happen.

People were standing around them

now, looking to see what was happening, but not understanding. "Keep back!" she yelled. "FBI! This man set the bomb in the hotel!"

Sherlock raised her SIG, shoved it against the back of his head. Xu froze. Sherlock leaned down beside his ear. "Give me an excuse, Xu, come on, twitch or move your finger, anything. Let me blow your brains out."

"How did you know?"

"We're FBI. You're not." She leaned back and clipped a handcuff around his right wrist. "And it turns out you're not as good as you thought you were. You have the right to remain silent. You have the right to—" She grabbed his wounded arm and was pulling it back, Xu yelling in pain and fury, to fasten them together, when her brain registered the sound of a shot and a spear of sharp bright light before everything went black.

47

Something was wrong. Savich double-parked the Taurus and ran toward the FBI van across from the Fairmont, where he knew Sherlock and two other agents were positioned. He heard the explosion, saw the glass bursting outward from the sixth floor, followed by gushing smoke and flames.

And then he saw Sherlock through the throng of panicked people, barreling through the crowds, shoving people aside. She was after Xu, and Sherlock was catching him. Savich watched her leap forward and tackle him. They disappeared from sight.

He shoved people out of his way, yelling Sherlock's name. Then he saw her astride Xu's back, cuffing him. Suddenly there was a loud cracking sound from somewhere behind him, a rifle shot, he registered it in an instant, and he saw her head bloom red. His heart froze in his chest. Xu threw her off and scrambled to his feet, one handcuff dangling off his right wrist, and disappeared into the crowd.

Savich couldn't believe what he'd seen, simply couldn't accept it. He had to get to her, had to see her smile at him and tell him it had all been a dream, nothing more. Above the mayhem he heard a ferocious growling sound he realized was coming from his own throat. He saw frightened faces staring at him, but he ignored them. People dove out of his way. His vision narrowed to an arrow of misting red, like blood—no, not blood. He'd get to her, he'd find it was all a mistake, that what he'd seen was a lie his own brain had spun together, nothing more than that.

When he burst out of the last scattering knot of people, he saw three teenage boys huddled over Sherlock, protecting her from the stampede.

He grabbed one of the boys' arms, pulled him back. "I'm FBI. Keep the people away—you, call nine-one-one."

Savich stared down at all the blood streaming down her face, matting her hair to her head. She was lying on her side, utterly still, and he was afraid in the deepest part of him that she was dead. He couldn't breathe, couldn't think. He was afraid to touch her, afraid that when he pressed his fingers against her throat there would be no pulse, there would be nothing, and it would mean she was gone. His fingers hovered, then finally touched the pulse point in her neck, pressed in. He felt her pulse. Yes, she was alive. He ripped a sleeve off his white shirt and pressed down on the blood streaming from her head. His hands were steady and strong, but his brain was a wasteland of chaos. But she was alive. Nothing else mattered.

One of the boys asked, his voice shaking with a mixture of fear and excitement, "Is she dead?"

Savich barely registered the question. It was outside of him, not important, only she was important. He could see he was pressing on a deep gouge the bullet had made along the side of her head. But how deep? There was so much blood with a head wound, too much. He pressed down harder on the wound and put the fingers of his other hand against her bloody neck to find her pulse, to reassure himself again it was there. He touched her vivid hair curling over his hands, wet with blood.

He said, more to himself than to anyone else, "She's alive." Saying the words helped to make them real.

One of the boys said, "The nine-one-one operator said everyone in the city is rushing to the Fairmont."

"*Billy, what are you doing? What is going on here?*"

"Mom, we're okay. We're helping the FBI. One of the agents got shot."

Savich blocked out the parents' voices, leaned close to Sherlock's bloody face. "It's okay, sweetheart, you're going to be fine. You've been shot—well, let me say it's more than a graze, but still, the bullet didn't hit your brain." He pressed his cheek against her bloody hair, and thanked God the shooter's aim wasn't true. He wondered for only an instant who the shooter was.

"Savich! Where's Sherlock?"

It was Eve. Billy's parents pulled him and the other two boys out of the way. Eve fell to her knees beside her.

Savich raised his face, now nearly as bloody as his wife's. "I saw the explosion blow out that window in Xu's suite. Are you all right?"

Eve waved that away. "Your face—"

"It's Sherlock's blood," he said.

Eve said, "Is—is she okay?"

He made himself nod. "The bullet didn't kill her. She's alive, but she's out—" There weren't any more words. He pressed his shirtsleeve hard against the wound, his eyes not leaving her face.

He didn't care about Xu, didn't care if the Fairmont burned to the ground, only about Sherlock. *No, get yourself together, Sherlock's alive. You have to take charge, there's no one else.* She'd captured Xu and then someone else had shot her. Who? It didn't make sense; Xu was alone, always alone. Wasn't he?

He looked over at the three boys, Billy's parents standing protectively behind them, and Savich registered that Billy was as redheaded as Sherlock, tall, gangly, and skinny as a plank. He nodded at them, and manufactured a calm, steady voice. He said to Eve, "These boys protected Sherlock from the crowd. Get their names." He managed a smile at Billy's mom.

"Ma'am, your son is a hero, all three of them are heroes. Thanks, all of you."

He looked back down at Sherlock. "Eve, where's Harry?"

"He went after Xu."

No more words; he never looked away from Sherlock's face until Eve touched his arm. "The EMTs are here, Dillon. Let them take care of her."

48

EMT Nathan Everett lightly touched Savich's shoulder. "You all right, sir? Yes, okay, I see now it's her blood. You need to let us take care of her now."

Savich raised his face to a man he'd never seen before in his life. "She's going to be all right."

"Yes, sir, yes, she will," Nathan said, and turned to direct two other EMTs to bring a gurney.

Eve pulled Savich to his feet. He watched them lift Sherlock onto the gurney. She looked nearly lifeless. No, she would live, she had to. "I got the boys' names and addresses."

Savich forced himself to focus on Eve's face. "Are you okay, Eve? And Harry and Griffin?"

"Yes, we were just rattled."

"Have Harry and Griffin gone after Xu?" He looked at her face, really registered it for the first time. "You look like you've been in a war."

She nodded. "All three of us do. The fire and smoke was from an incendiary device, but we made it through. Xu even had a bomb rigged in the room. Luckily, we'd gotten out before he blew it."

The crowd melted away from Sherlock's gurney as they rolled her to the ambulance. Savich walked quickly after her. He said over his shoulder, "Who shot her? It sure wasn't Xu, since I saw her cuffing him. So who was it?"

"We'll find him," Eve called after him, as he climbed into the ambulance with Sherlock and they shut the door.

It was slow going getting through the snarled traffic, the gawkers milling around, but finally the ambulance pulled onto

Market Street on the way to San Francisco General.

Savich held her hand between his, never looking away from her face.

"I know it's a lot of blood, sir," Nathan said, "but head wounds are nasty like that."

"Yes, I know," Savich said. "I've seen them before."

He watched the EMT check her pupils again and look at her head wound. He prepped her arm and slid a needle into a vein at her elbow. "My name is Nathan. The bleeding from her scalp has stopped. She needs this IV in case we have to give her medication. She's getting saline now, nothing more."

Savich nodded. "My name's Savich. Give me an alcohol pad and I'll wipe the blood away."

Nathan Everett wanted to say *No, you shouldn't touch her,* but he saw the big man with only one shirt sleeve, his black leather jacket on the floor beside him, was desperately trying to keep control. "Sure, here you go. But stay away from the wound; we don't want it to start bleeding again."

He watched Savich lift up her hair and wash it with sterile dressings Nathan had soaked in saline from a plastic bottle. He was gentle, his touch light. After a half-dozen dressings, he got most of the blood cleared from her hair.

Nathan handed him another dressing. "You need to wash your face as well, sir."

Savich did as he said. *So much blood,* he thought, as he wiped his face.

Thank goodness, Nathan thought; the wound wasn't as bad as he'd feared. It was a deep gouge along the side of her head. But was her skull fractured? Her brain injured? Was she still bleeding inside her skull from a lacerated artery? Nathan didn't know, but he did know the bullet had passed only a few millimeters away from exploding her head open. Nathan swallowed. The important thing now was that she wake up soon. The sooner she woke up, the better the chance she was still the person she was. He said aloud what he was hoping for. "It isn't fatal, but she needs to wake up. Are you an FBI agent?"

"Yes, I'm Agent Savich, Dillon Savich."

"You work with her? Is she an agent, too?"

"Yes, she's an agent. I live with her as well. She's my wife."

Nathan nearly fell over backward when he said that.

"You're kidding."

Savich only shook his head. He listened to the ambulance siren blare loud and insistent as traffic pulled over in front of them. Odd, but he hadn't heard the sirens before now. He wiped a streak of blood off her face. She was pale, nearly as white as Sean's two percent milk. It looked obscene. It nearly broke him.

Her eyes opened. She looked dazed, like a prizefighter who'd gone too many rounds.

Savich leaned in close, his hand squeezing hers. "Sherlock?"

She blinked, licked her lips. "Why are you up there, Dillon? Or why am I down here? What happened?"

"You don't remember? It doesn't matter. You were shot, but you'll be fine."

She looked confused, as if she hadn't understood what he'd said. "Dillon, my head really hurts."

"I know, but we're nearly to the hospital

now. You had a small accident—nothing, really—only a small hit."

"A small hit?"

Nathan said, "That's right. Try to stay awake. That's right, can you focus on my face?"

"Her name's Sherlock."

"Sherlock, what color are my eyes?"

She didn't say anything, simply closed her eyes again.

Nathan saw Savich's face go blank and said quickly, "She woke up, she was herself, and that's an excellent sign. Six more minutes and we'll be there. She's not going to die, Agent Savich."

For the first time, Savich looked and actually registered the face of the man beside Sherlock. He was in his early forties, on the heavy side, with pockmarked skin, deep brown eyes, and a reassuring smile, but most important, as he'd spoken, Savich hadn't seen any lurking doubt in his eyes.

Nathan cleared his throat. "Who shot her?"

"I don't know," Savich said. "I don't know much of anything except there was a bomb in the Fairmont and she caught the man who blew it up and someone else shot her."

Nathan said, "Was the man a terrorist?"

A terrorist? "No," Savich said. "He's a very careful, very well-prepared man who deserves to be in shackles." He added, never looking away from Sherlock's face, "I hope no one died in that hotel."

Sherlock jerked, took a hitching breath.

Savich felt her hand tighten briefly around his fingers before she let go again. He clasped her hand tighter, and his own breath hitched. He was terrified.

He felt Nathan's hand on his shoulder. "I do, too, Agent. We're here, sir."

49

San Francisco General Hospital
Tuesday afternoon

Fifteen minutes later, half a dozen FBI agents rushed into the emergency room, thankfully not at all crowded, Cheney at their head. Savich was standing by the registration desk, speaking quietly to a nurse.

Cheney forced the words out: "Eve said it's a head wound. How is she?"

Savich looked at Harry, Eve, and Griffin, with four other agents whose names he didn't know crowding in behind them, some of their faces and clothes blackened with soot. One of them had blood smeared on his shirt. His or someone he'd pulled out of the hotel?

Virginia Trolley and Vincent Delion came running in behind them.

Savich said, "She's awake. I'm not with her because they're doing a neurological exam and the doctor said there wasn't room and since I couldn't add anything useful, I needed to be out here." He nodded to the nurse. "Nurse Blankenship is going back and forth, telling me exactly what they're doing and why."

"How bad is it?" Virginia Trolley came up to put her hand on his shoulder.

Savich said, "The bullet gouged a trench along the left side of her head, above her left ear." He touched his fingers to his own head to show them. "If it had been a couple of millimeters to the right, she'd be dead." Savich felt his throat close. He swallowed. He stood as stiff as a fence post, trying to get himself together. "She was a little groggy when I left her, but she seemed okay. They were shaving off a square of her hair so they could put stitches in." Odd, but saying those words nearly broke him. He said nothing more. He knew he needed to stop to keep control.

Nurse Blankenship looked from Savich to the group, and said to all of them, "As I told Agent Savich, the fact that they're ready to stitch her scalp so soon is great news. They're not taking her to CT right away, and that means they're not worried about a skull fracture and her neurological exam must be normal, or nearly so."

"Is there something wrong with her exam?" Savich asked.

Nurse Blankenship hastened to say, "No, sorry—I only meant she's had a concussion, that's all. I tell you what, I'll go back in and check on them again, so you'll know what to expect, okay?"

She smiled at them all, walked quickly down the hall into Sherlock's cubicle, and returned in under a minute. "They said she'd be going for a CT scan in a few minutes, just to be sure. The doctors say the odds are good the scan will be normal and that she'll be staying for only a day or two, that she'll make a complete recovery with only a small scar for a souvenir.

"Now, if all of you would repeat to Agent Savich that his wife should be up within the week, I would appreciate it." She patted Savich's arm and excused herself.

There was a collective sigh of relief. Harry studied Savich's face, saw he'd finally accepted Sherlock wasn't going to die. Savich turned toward them, focused again. "What information do you have? Do you know who shot her? Do you know what happened to Xu?"

Harry said, "A couple of Virginia's officers who were positioned two blocks up on California ran into a young guy waving his fists and yelling after a white Infiniti that was fishtailing down the street. Xu had jerked open the guy's car door, clouted him in the head, and shoved him into the road. We've got an APB out on the car and the license plate number.

"Xu is hurt. One of us"—Harry nodded toward Eve and Griffin—"shot him in the suite from behind a wall of flames. Agent Gaines, our maid in the hallway, said Xu was shot in the upper arm and bleeding pretty heavily when he took off down the stairs. He broke her nose but didn't kill her. When she got herself together, she came in to help us get out, a good thing, since Xu had left a bomb to detonate when he got clear. Griffin's singed a bit around the edges; we all are, inside and out, coughing a bit, but nothing worse.

"We followed Xu's blood trail down the stairs to the lobby, and we were in the stairwell when he detonated the bomb. There was pandemonium in the lobby, but we didn't stop to help, we ran directly outside to find Xu. You were already there, leaning over Sherlock." Harry looked at the others. "That's all we know."

Agent Kain, who'd been one of the agents manning the van with Sherlock, said, "Sherlock spotted Xu. She didn't say a word, jumped out of the van and took off. We ran after her fast, but there were people clogging the road and the sidewalk. Then that window blew out on the top floor, and people were screaming and trying to escape the flying shards of glass. When we got to you, Savich, you were with her along with those three teenage boys."

A second agent said, "She had him flattened on his belly with one of the cuffs already snapped on when we heard that single shot. It sounded like a rifle, which meant it could have been fired from anywhere behind us. We'll have a trajectory as soon as they get forensics out there."

Savich said, "But who? Xu didn't know we'd be there at the Fairmont waiting for him. How could he have arranged for someone with a rifle to be covering his back?"

Cheney said, "I don't know, Savich, but how likely is it that a brand-new player suddenly shows up when Sherlock has Xu down and nearly restrained and then, for whatever reason, shoots her?"

Savich slammed his fist down on the counter. "She had him, it should be over, but now he's in the wind again. And it must be that Xu isn't flying solo."

"The Chinese?" Eve asked.

"It's possible," Savich said, "but I don't see the Chinese doing this. In their position, I would have shot Xu, if anyone, not Sherlock."

Virginia Trolley said in a voice that could cool boiling water, "We've got half the force out near the Fairmont. Someone must have seen him, seen something. Keep the faith, Dillon."

Cheney said, "It's a mess at the Fairmont, the streets blocked with fire trucks and police cars. We moved your Taurus, Savich, not to worry. So far, Sherlock's the only one they seem to have ambulanced out. There were only cuts and bruises, from what I could see."

"The media were already there when we left," Eve said. "It's national by now, since it's the Fairmont Hotel in San Francisco. They've got everything going for them with this story—a bomber they're calling a terrorist and an FBI agent shot in the head."

Cheney's cell rang. He glanced down and frowned. "It's KTCU." Savich watched him think for a minute, then answer. He turned away from them as he said, "Agent Stone."

Almost immediately, Cheney said, "Yes, yes, but I'm not there. What do you know for a fact, so I'll know if I can add anything?"

Smart, Savich thought, *pulling information from the media for a change.*

Cheney punched off his cell, rejoined the group. "That was the anchor of the six-o'clock news. He told me only a corner suite on the sixth floor of the Fairmont was badly damaged. Naturally, he had no idea it was Xu's suite. I didn't tell him I already knew from my own people it was completely gutted, a lot of smoke and water damage on that whole floor, but he did tell me the fire's out.

"The anchor wanted to know if a terrorist was holed up in the Fairmont and if he managed to shoot the FBI agent in the street. He wondered if the FBI had bombed the suite to get the terrorist to come out."

Cheney grinned at them. "Where do they get this stuff? Like the FBI carries grenades around with them in their holsters. I told him I was only now finding out anything, and to give me an hour."

Eve asked, "What will you do when he calls back?"

"I'm going to give him our photograph of Xu to put on TV. Given the bomb was at the Fairmont, you can bet everyone will be watching the news to find out what happened, which means everyone will know what Xu looks like by tonight. If the media wants any more than that, I'll tell them to talk to the police commissioner."

"Many thanks," Virginia said.

Cheney said, "Now, tell me about the bombs, Harry. Was the first one a hand grenade?"

Eve wondered how the devil Harry would know, when Cheney added, "Harry was in Special Forces before he joined the Bureau."

Harry said, "It wasn't a conventional grenade or some of us would be dead, Xu included. There was no shrapnel, too much boom, and too much blinding light. It was a flash-bang. We used those suckers a few times in Afghanistan, when the situation called for something debilitating but not fatal, like cleaning out an enemy nest.

"Flash-bangs are powerful, they're effective, and they're pretty small. I'll bet Xu carried one around in his pocket, in case he ever found himself in trouble.

"I'm thinking he must have suspected something wasn't right when he got to his room at the Fairmont; maybe our agent in the hall spooked him. Anyway, he must have had the canister in his hand when he opened the door to the suite. He threw it at us, and there was a deafening noise and a blinding light. I knew what it was, but that didn't stop my ears from buzzing or help me see any quicker, and, of course, it hurt.

"There was instant fire everywhere, walls of it, and that was Xu's doing, too. Flash-bangs make a great incendiary device if you wrap them in an accelerant, like Sterno in a Ziploc bag, and duct-tape the bag to the canister. It would make the canister that much bigger, but not too big to carry in a jacket pocket. The Sterno ignites and gets blasted in all directions. It's a potent weapon.

"Since Xu knew what was coming, he had a second to turn away, prepare himself. We didn't, but we did manage to fire through the flames even though we couldn't see anything. Luckily, one of us hit him."

Nurse Blankenship returned and nodded to Savich. "Agent Savich, your wife will be going to CT now, before she's admitted to her room. You can go with her. She'll be out in a second."

"There she is," Eve said.

Sherlock was lying on a gurney, a white sheet pulled up to her neck, what looked to be rolls of cotton bandage wrapped around her head. There were streaks of blood at its edge, probably from her hair. She looked pale. "Give us a moment," Savich said to the orderly and nurse.

He slipped her hand out from under the sheet and squeezed it. "Sweetheart, are you awake?"

She whispered, "Yes. I was only resting my eyes." She looked around at every-one. "All of you guys are here? Hey, is this some kind of party? Is it my birthday?"

Savich knew she was trying to make a joke but was too woozy to pull if off. He said, "Yes, it's a party, and you're the guest of honor. After you get this dinky head scan to make sure your brains are in good working order, we're going to cut you a slice of your birthday cake."

Her eyes dropped to half-mast, her voice faded, but Savich, who knew her as well as he knew himself, heard the whisper of humor when she said, "I sure hope it's carrot cake."

"Yes," Eve said, "with butter-pecan ice cream."

Savich leaned close. "After the scan, the doctors want you to camp out here for a couple of days. Is that okay with you?"

She closed her eyes, and her voice was starting to fade out. "I don't think I want to stay here, Dillon. The light's too bright and I don't know anybody and my head hurts. Well, maybe I'll stay if you stay with me and bring me birthday cake." She attempted a grin. "I'll share it with you."

Savich smiled. "You know what? I'm going to see if you can't camp out with Ramsey. Would you like that?"

"I like Ramsey," Sherlock whispered. Her words sounded like they were floating up from the bottom of a well.

Harry said, "Sherlock, do you remember chasing Xu down? Tackling him?"

"Yes, of course I remember Xu. I got him on his stomach, and he was bleeding all over the place and I was cuffing him and then—" She frowned. "I saw a really bright light, it was beautiful, and then, all of a sudden, I was here getting stitched up and waiting for my birthday cake. Do you really think they'll let me camp out in Ramsey's room? I've never heard of anything like that before."

"I'll see if you can sit with him by the campfire."

"Please tell me Xu didn't get away. Please."

Eve said, "He did, but not for long. Now neither will the man who shot you."

Sherlock couldn't say anything because it was suddenly all too much. She closed her eyes again and breathed deeply. The orderly said, "We need to get her to CT now, Agent Savich. You'll have to clear it with admissions if you'd like her to stay in the Taj with Judge Dredd. You really know him?"

There was a bit of laughter, which felt very good to everyone. Cheney said, "I think it's a great idea, her rooming with Judge Hunt. Dr. Kardak might go for it, if only to keep even more law enforcement officers out of the hospital. There's already a battalion of marshals and SFPD officers hovering on that floor. We can fit her in without adding a single man, and still be sure she's safe."

Eve said, "Ramsey can get her into their poker games. Does she play?"

Savich smiled at Eve. "She's a killer at Texas Hold 'em."

Cheney said, "Okay, listen up, everyone. There's no way Xu gets away from us. We'll have his picture all over the news in an hour. He's wounded, and he needs medical care. He's in a stolen white Infiniti with an APB out on him. All he's got with him is what he was carrying in his pockets. A passport, if he's lucky. But he's not going anywhere until he gets his wounded arm taken care of. That's got to be where we focus."

But it wasn't Xu who had shot Sherlock, Savich thought.

50

San Francisco General Hospital
Tuesday evening

Sherlock's head thrummed to a steady beat. If she tried to move her head, it felt like electric jolts were frying her brains. The stitches felt like they were pulling her scalp too tight. On the other hand, she was alive, and breathing trumped everything.

Savich had kept her parents away with the promise she'd be home tomorrow. Really it was Sean who'd kept them away. Her parents had looked at him and known to keep still, and put on a good show. Savich told her he'd lied clean, telling Sean his mother was staying with Molly and Emma because they were scared. Sean had listened thoughtfully to this smoothly delivered lie, Savich told her, and said, "But Papa, I want to protect Emma. Can't I go over and stay with them, too? We can have cocoa and I can show Emma *Flying Monks,* my new computer game."

Sherlock's mother said, "But Sean, you promised to go with me to the movies tonight to see *Rory and the Last Duck,* don't you remember?"

Torn between impressing Emma with his computer game and the movie, Sean was seriously conflicted until his grandfather said, "Your grandmother promised to buy me kettle corn, Sean; that's my favorite. Yours, too, right?" and so Sean's conflict melted away. He did think to ask, "Papa, are you coming with us?"

No, Savich told him, he was going to help his mother make Emma and Molly and the twins feel all secure, but not to worry, he'd be back to tuck Sean in. Since Sean was five years old, matters of life and death and hospital stays with a huge white bandage around a parent's head weren't about to be a part of his reality. When they'd wheeled Sherlock into the room, Molly had been there with Ramsey. She was horrified at what had happened, and question after question came pouring out until she saw Sherlock had gone quietly to sleep, providential, since the last thing she needed was Molly hovering over her.

When Sherlock woke up, the nurse gave her two Tylenol, a net, the nurse told her, to keep her safe, the only pain meds she would be getting for now. Hence the dull roar in her brain when her dinner was delivered thirty minutes later.

A fillet of sole sat in the center of a hospital plate, with half a lemon on the side, and vegetables. Who wanted vegetables when you felt down and out? When you could have been dead, your head shot off? No, you wanted ice cream, and a birthday cake, not runny chocolate pudding. She said to Ramsey, who sat in his bed eight feet from hers, "How are you surviving on the hospital food?"

He smiled, having seen the limp fish on

her tray. "Since I'm Judge Dredd, one of the nurses asks me every day what I would like for dinner. The chef either makes it himself or picks it up on his way in to the hospital."

"That's not fair. Nobody asked me what I wanted to eat. What did you get for dinner?" Despite the hot wire slicing through her head, she leaned up. "I see now, it's a big steak, medium. And a baked potato. This isn't fair, it's not right. Can I have a bite?"

Ramsey looked at the steak left on his plate, looked over at her, and said, "Nah, I'm far more in need of red meat than you are, Sherlock. I've got to build up my strength. Getting shot in the chest trumps a little head wound any day. Eat your fish and leave the real patients to chow down the meat and potatoes."

Deputy Morales said from the window, a hamburger halfway to his mouth, "We were nice as could be to the nurse, but she kissed us off, said we had a per diem, and we should order in what we wanted for ourselves."

Savich appeared in the doorway, carrying two big pizza boxes. "Ramsey told me you'd try to steal his dinner, so here you go, sweetheart, enough for you and your guards and maybe one slice for Ramsey, if he's still hungry." He studied her face. She was still pale, but she was sitting up, with the bandage wrapped around her hair, looking faintly ridiculous. Today he liked ridiculous; it was a great look.

Soon there were four guards standing around the two patients, all chowing down on pizza, including Savich's vegetarian pie. Savich stood at the foot of the bed knowing he should eat, but his thoughts of what had happened wouldn't let go of his brain. He couldn't imagine eating, and so he stood there, watching her, listening to their chatter and laughter fill the room. Everyone was distracted, and that was a good thing.

The pizza tasted wonderful and settled nicely in Sherlock's stomach, despite her headache. She saw Dillon wasn't eating, and she wanted to tell him she was all right. He leaned down to kiss her, and she saw the fear lurking behind his smile as he said, "I'll be back after I've tucked Sean in for the night."

She took his hand. "Will you bring my birthday cake?"

"So you remember that, do you?"

She smiled at him. "Don't forget the butter-pecan ice cream."

There was a knock on the door. A young cop none of them had ever seen said, "Agent Savich? I'm Officer Holt. I found a folded piece of paper on the sidewalk where Agent Sherlock was shot. I took it immediately to Lieutenant Trolley. After she read it and dusted for prints, she told me to bring it to you right away." He handed Savich the paper. "You can see it has your name printed on it, nothing more. No one has any idea who left it."

Officer Holt looked over at Sherlock. "Hello, Agent Sherlock. I'm glad you're okay." He looked then at Ramsey and swallowed. "Sir, all of us are glad you're going to be all right," and he swallowed again.

Without thought, Sherlock turned her head to see how Ramsey was reacting to this show of adoration, and froze at the jolt of pain in her head. She managed to smile at him when Ramsey thanked Officer Holt for his concern, but her focus was on Savich as he unfolded the piece of paper.

"What's in the note, Dillon?"

He looked up, his brow furrowed. "Remember last Thursday, that note delivered to me at the Hoover Building?"

Sherlock said, *"For what you did you deserve this.* What about it?"

He handed her the note.

51

It was quiet, the light dim in the hospital room. Sherlock and Ramsey lay quietly, waiting for the sleeping pills the nurse had just given them to pull them into sleep. The guards by the windows were reading by shrouded reading lights. Savich hadn't returned yet from tucking Sean in. They'd brought in a cot for Savich.

Sherlock said, "Ramsey, I was going to wait until Dillon got back, but I don't think we should put it off. We need to talk about this other person in the mix, this man who shot me—he was already here in San Francisco, waiting, I suppose until he had the setting he wanted. Shooting me—it was revenge, Ramsey. It's got to be revenge. Against Dillon."

No sleeping pill could compete with what she said. Ramsey's brain snapped to full alert. "I gathered you thought that, from that bizarre note, but I don't understand. You don't think the man who shot you has any connection to Xu, that they don't have anything to do with each other?"

"It's possible, I suppose, but I don't think so. Everything Xu has done is business to him, a matter of survival, but for the man who sent Dillon that note, it's personal; something in the past is driving him. *For what you did you deserve this.* How do you like that for over-the-top drama? He wants to terrorize us; he's taking pleasure in it."

Ramsey turned toward her, immediately regretted it, and held himself very still. He hated the sharp pain, but he hated more having to lie like a slug, helpless and impotent. And he hated having to be shaved and bathed each morning because he wasn't strong enough yet to take his own shower. He reminded himself both he and Sherlock were lucky to be alive. He said, "So shooting you was revenge against Savich. But why here, why now? And why you, rather than Savich himself?"

"Well, there's more to it than that, Ramsey." She looked up to see Dillon slip into the room through the partially open door, saw the guards move quickly, then throttle back.

Savich nodded to the guards, said quietly, "This was his second note, Ramsey, that's what Sherlock was going to tell you. What did you call it, Sherlock? His second notice of doom? He sent me one before he shot you."

Ramsey tried to take it in. He said slowly, "You're saying I was this madman's first victim? You're saying he shot both Sherlock and me to gain revenge against you?"

Savich nodded. "The first note was delivered to me last Thursday at the Hoover Building. That night, Ramsey, at midnight, you were shot. We didn't connect the note to you until tonight, when he proudly sent us the second identical note after shooting Sherlock.

"We couldn't ever be sure of a motive for Xu to try to kill you in the first place. All of us wondered why shoot the judge? But his connecting your shooting to the Cahill trial, making it seem the Cahills were responsible, I'd say it was fortuitous for him. Shooting you succeeded in getting Sherlock and me to fly out to San Francisco, and that wasn't fortuitous, it was planned. He's been watching us ever since."

Ramsey said, "But if the man was in Washington delivering the note to you, he'd have had to move fast to get to San Francisco and set everything up to shoot me from the beach below my house the same night. There wasn't enough time."

Sherlock said, "He wasn't in Washington. He paid a young auto mechanic to deliver the note to the Hoover Building on Thursday. We found the guy who did that and brought him in, but we couldn't track down the man who'd paid him."

Savich said, "In fact, we know he was here in San Francisco, studying you and staying at a B-and-B in Atherton for about a week, enough time to do the reconnaissance he needed of your habits, your home, for planning the Zodiac rental, all of it. What's terrifying is that he would have succeeded if Molly hadn't called out to you at the last moment."

Ramsey said, "So my being shot the same day I shut down the Cahill trial, the same day Mickey O'Rourke disappeared, it was all a coincidence?"

Savich said, "Yes, and one he took advantage of. The shooter was following your trial closely enough to decide that Thursday night was the perfect time to shoot you to throw us off making the connection to the note for a while. He couldn't have scripted it better."

"Like Dillon said, he'd already been here a week before any of that. And he had to have been to Washington before he came here, checking out the neighborhood around the Hoover Building, learning enough about Teddy Moody to pick him out as his mark."

Ramsey said, "Why didn't he leave a note with me, so you'd know this was his revenge, like he did with you?"

Sherlock said, "I imagine he was getting a real kick out of the confusion he'd created since we immediately connected your shooting to the Cahills. I guess when he shot me, he was ready to take the credit."

Ramsey said, "And that leaves us the big question. Why me? We've been friends for a long time, Savich, but there are other people closer to you. That must mean the shooter has a connection to both of us." After a moment, Ramsey said, "This is the same man who tried to kill me again in the elevator on Saturday, the same man we believed was Xu."

Sherlock said, "And that was an act of someone who's driven or unbalanced enough to take such a risk. Very unlike Xu." She closed her eyes for a moment, not in pain but in thought, though sleep was pulling on her. She became aware of Dillon stroking her forearm, his touch light and comforting. She continued. "It all makes sense now. Xu was very hard to predict, even to understand. How could we profile a man, reconcile everything he had done, when he was two very separate men whose motives couldn't be further apart?"

Ramsey said, "Then that telephone message to Molly, that wasn't Xu, either."

Savich said, "No. The phone call was meant to terrorize, like the notes."

"It was a spur-of-the-moment dig at me, and my family?" Ramsey said.

Savich nodded. "That, yes, and more than a little unhinged, like that photo he left of you as Judge Dredd X-ed through under the hydrangea, and the blood he left in the elevator shaft. The man makes plans, but he's not rational. He's deranged."

Sherlock said, "The thing is, Ramsey, he took lots of time to plan this all out, to learn all about you. Lots of time—and that's the key. We think he was in prison, where he'd have nothing but time to spend in the library. He told the young man who delivered the first note to Dillon to call him the Hammer. That's a prison moniker."

Ramsey said, "Do you think it's someone I put away?"

There was silence in the hospital room, the two guards at the window listening intently.

Savich said, "Maybe, but it's got to be as much about me because he picked me to send the note to, and he shot my wife. I don't know why he went for you first, Ramsey. Forgive me, but if I'm to be blamed I would have thought he'd have gone for Sherlock first, but he didn't. It was you."

Sherlock said, "There's got to be a good reason he went for you first, Ramsey. We have to figure out what it is."

Ramsey said, "It means he's carrying a load of rage at me, maybe more than he has against you, Savich. It could be over something he thinks we did to him together."

Sherlock only nodded. Her head felt like a weight was pressing her down. "Yes, but what?"

Savich said, "We'll have to find out, but not tonight. You both look ready to fold your tents. Get some sleep."

Savich leaned down and kissed Sherlock's mouth. "Sleep well, sweetheart. We'll get this all figured out in the morning. Ramsey, don't snore so loud you wake her. I'll be back in a moment," and Savich followed Deputy Babcock and Deputy Cluney out of the room. Deputy Babcock said, "This is hairier than my mother-in-law's legs. Two killers, not just this Xu character. Have you told Marshal Maynard?"

"Cheney will."

"Barbieri called a few minutes ago, said they'd found the Infiniti on one of the winding streets above Sausalito. Sounds like he was on his way to find a doctor to take care of his arm. I hope Xu hasn't invaded someone's home. I can't imagine a doctor would have a fully equipped office in his own home, but I guess he'd have enough stuff to help him with an arm wound. I sure hope he hasn't killed anyone."

Savich said, "I hope Xu won't think it's prudent."

"We'll find out soon enough, either way," Babcock said.

Savich said, "Xu's got to be somewhat panicked. No, don't listen to me, I'm too tired to think straight. He's survived this long by staying cool and always using his brain. Everyone is focused on small medical offices and walk-in clinics, especially those with a Chinese clientele. He probably knows some doctors who cater to people at the Chinese consulate, take care of their families. I wonder if we can find out who those doctors are."

"Probably already done," Babcock said, "I wonder how he expects to get out of here?"

Officer Cluney said, "I would drive out of California, maybe to Utah or Nevada, stay away from the airports for a while."

Savich said, "You're probably right, if he's well enough to drive that far. Now that his cover is gone and we know he didn't shoot either Ramsey or Sherlock, it's the second shooter we have to guard against."

Cluney said, "If they don't know each other, how lucky is that for Xu?"

Babcock said, "I'll bet Xu's putting him in high on his nighttime prayer list. Agent Savich, you can relax. With four of us around the clock, how could this second guy possibly believe he could get to either Sherlock or Judge Hunt in here?"

"How? Remember the elevator?" Savich snapped his fingers. "He came this close to killing Judge Hunt. Don't forget, this guy prefers the elaborate over the simple and straightforward. The more convoluted and intricate he can make his plans, the bigger the rush he gets."

Babcock said, "But he's failed twice. Doesn't he realize that we all know now he's the danger and not Xu?"

Savich said, "But the only reason we do know is because he led us right to it, by shooting Sherlock with Xu in sight, and by leaving that note. Now he wants us to know."

Babcock said, "I don't understand why he doesn't simply wait. Say a month, even another year. If it's revenge we're talking here, what's the rush?"

Savich said, "That note was a challenge, and he'll see himself as a failure if he doesn't get it done before we get him. It's payback for him, and it will be fast, whatever he does."

"It won't matter," Babcock said. "Everyone guarding Judge Hunt and Agent Sherlock knows exactly what we're dealing with now. He won't get near either of them."

But when Savich drew the single blanket over himself on the cot, he wasn't so sure. He wasn't about to let Sherlock out of his sight.

If they were right and the man had been in prison, what was he in for? Murder? Who was his payback for? A son, a friend, a brother, maybe a mother? He and MAX would find out.

52

San Francisco General Hospital
Wednesday morning

Sherlock touched strands of bloody hair at the edge of the white bandage wrapped around her head that made her look like she'd walked out of a war zone. She wanted to do something about that before Dillon returned. She said to the nurse, "When can I get this white towel off my head? When can I wash my hair?"

"Actually, you look sort of cute with the white towel," Nurse Washington said, patting her hand. "Once Dr. Kardak examines you, we'll get your hair washed and change out the dressing for an adhesive strip that will cover your sutures. So how are you feeling, Agent Sherlock? Any headaches, dizziness, nausea? Were you able to sleep?"

Sherlock said, "The headache's better this morning; it comes and goes. I felt a little dizzy when I first stood up. That's about it."

"Have you felt disoriented at all? Any mental side trips? Ah, here's Dr. Kardak, to look at both you and Judge Hunt."

Dr. Kardak said good morning to her and to Ramsey, then took her chart from Nurse Washington and hummed in approval as he read it. He looked up at her. "I heard Nurse Washington ask if you had any disorientation, any mental side trips? An interesting way of putting it, yet perfectly clear."

"Harry Potter World might be fun, but no, I haven't been taking any trips in my head. My orientation's fine."

Dr. Kardak nodded, pulled the curtain around them for privacy, and leaned down to plant his stethoscope on her chest. "You've had a mild traumatic brain injury," he said. "You can expect the symptoms you're having—what we call the post-concussion syndrome—to last a week or so, maybe longer. Now, I'm going to need your patience because we're going to repeat the neurologic exam you had yesterday and ask you a few questions to test your memory, okay?"

"As long as we don't forget to wash my hair," Sherlock said.

When Dr. Kardak finished, he straightened, studied her face silently for a moment. "Your balance, your strength, your reflexes, your memory, everything looks good. I have to say, Agent, you're the luckiest patient I've treated in some time. Your scan from yesterday looks normal, except for your scalp injury. To be shot in the head and sustain no structural brain injury or bleeding, no cracked skull, no visible swelling, is amazing. I would think, though, that most people who've had your experience might consider a career change."

Sherlock said, "I realize I was incredibly lucky and I am immensely grateful for that. To be honest here, what happened at the Fairmont, well, I guess you could say it came out of the blue, so there was no way to do my job and avoid it." She grinned up at him. "It could have happened to anyone."

He said, "In that case, Agent Sherlock, I hope your luck continues for your next three lifetimes. As for your husband, I must tell you the man's a wreck, but, naturally, he believes he has to appear calm and in control around you. My prescription is for both of you to take a break and hug each other really tight, all right?"

Sherlock nodded and felt a stab of guilt. With so much flying around them, they couldn't take a break, but she surely could hug him. She said, "Yes, I can do that."

"I want you to rest this morning, and by that I mean no chatting up Judge Dredd here. If you're not sleeping, you're to lie here nice and calm and quiet. I'll leave the curtain between the two of you so you're not tempted to talk shop. With a bullet wound such as you've had, I like to repeat the CT scan to make sure there's no delayed swelling or bleeding. I doubt there will be. If everything looks good I want you to continue resting this afternoon, let your brain and body settle and heal. Depending on how you feel, we can talk this afternoon about whether we'll have the pleasure of your company through Thanksgiving, Agent Sherlock. How does it sound if we plan to release you Friday morning?"

"No can do, Dr. Kardak. I've got a five-year-old son who doesn't need to see his mother lying in a hospital bed. I'd like to leave this afternoon."

He studied her face for a moment. "Five years old, you say? What's his name?"

"Sean. He's the image of his papa. He plans to marry three different girls. He's also planning on working three jobs so they'll all be happy."

Dr. Kardak chuckled. "Sean sounds like my kid Peter, all mouth and laughter and boundless energy. There aren't any girls yet on Peter's somewhat limited horizon." He looked toward the curtain, called out, "Judge Hunt, how long have you two known each other?"

"More than five years," Ramsey said from behind the curtain. "When I first met Sherlock, she was three months pregnant, throwing up whenever anyone in her hearing said the word *pregnant.*"

"Oh, goodness, I'd forgotten," Sherlock said. "I remember belting Dillon a couple of times when he let the word slip out."

Dr. Kardak pursed his lips. "I'm going to mention that to one of my shrink friends." He rolled his eyes. "He's a practicing Freudian therapist. I shudder to think what he'll have to say." He studied Sherlock for a moment longer. "Very well, if nothing unexpected shows up, you may go home, but you're to rest, let everyone wait on you. You are not to bake even the sweet-potato casserole, you understand me?"

Sherlock nodded. "I won't even make my sausage stuffing. Promise."

"You may, however, eat as much as you want." He pulled the curtain open and nodded toward Ramsey. "As for Judge Dredd here, he gets to enjoy our hospitality for a while longer. I understand there's to be a Thanksgiving feast here in the room tomorrow. The floor staff can't talk about much else. The chef told my assistant he was even preparing a surprise for your dinner. I'm thinking I might drop by, see if there are any leftovers. Maybe watch one of the football games."

When he left ten minutes later, Sherlock heard Dillon speaking to Dr. Kardak outside in the hall. When Dillon came into the room, he was smiling and carrying two cups of coffee. Sherlock held her arms out to him.

53

San Francisco General Hospital
Wednesday morning

Molly sat beside her sleeping husband, her hand resting lightly on his forearm. He looked thin, she thought, even with all the extra meals the nurses brought in for him. He wasn't eating enough, despite their efforts. It was the pain and dependence and niggling fear, she imagined, fear for her, and for Emma, and for the boys.

Molly laid her cheek against his shoulder and wondered for the dozenth time who the man was who had shot him. Who hated him, and Dillon, so much?

At least Sherlock was going home after her brain scan. Molly looked at the big hand of the clock on the wall. Sherlock would be back soon. Deputy Marshal Ray Rozan was with her, her Kevlar vest, Sherlock called him. As for Savich, he hadn't budged an inch from her side until the phone call. The call was short. When he'd punched off his cell, he'd looked at his wife and she'd told him with no hesitation, "Go. I'll be fine with Deputy Rozan." That was it. Molly knew the call had to be urgent to make him leave Sherlock. She admired Sherlock's restraint. She hadn't asked him what had happened, and he hadn't said a thing.

Molly thought Sherlock looked perfectly fine to go home when they'd helped her into a wheelchair for her CT scan. Having all the dried blood washed out of her hair and the clunky bandage replaced with a strip of plastic tape had made a huge difference.

Molly looked toward Officer Lamar Marks standing beside the window, staring down into the parking lot. Was he thinking about Thanksgiving tomorrow? She knew he wasn't on duty tomorrow, since he had three kids and a truckload of relatives coming to his house. Another SFPD officer had volunteered. He'd eat very well for it, she thought, smiling.

But maybe Officer Marks was thinking about the same thing Molly was: *There were two separate killers.* It was difficult to accept that that could be possible, yet everyone had always wondered, *Why would Xu shoot Ramsey?*

"Molly?"

She looked up to see Dillon standing in the doorway.

"Sherlock's still getting her tests?"

She replied in a whisper, "She should be back soon, Dillon; that's what the nurse told me. Ramsey's sleeping, which is excellent. What happened? Who called you?"

He smiled at her shotgun questions, motioned for her to join him at the door. "A Chinese physician was found murdered early this morning in his office in Sausalito. There was ample evidence Xu had been there yesterday. We understand the doctor closed his office that afternoon, sent everyone home. Xu was probably there already, demanding treatment. Given all the blood in the examining room, Xu was in bad shape." He paused for a moment. "Dr. Mulan Chu was a primary-care doctor that Xu knew somehow. Perhaps he'd treated Xu before. It's a pity Xu got to the doctor before he got the warning we were sending out."

Molly said, "Why would Xu murder the doctor who'd saved his life, a doctor he knew?"

"We're thinking Chu found out what Xu had done at the Fairmont. Virginia said there'd been a call from his number to the police department asking to speak to someone about the Fairmont fire, but the caller hung up. We're thinking Xu overheard Dr. Chu dialing the cops, and that's why he killed him."

Ramsey said from behind them, "Do you think Xu is out of control, Savich?"

Savich and Molly walked back to Ramsey's bedside. Savich said, "No, I don't. I think he did what he believed he had to do to save himself. I think all Xu wants is to get out of Dodge, and he's doing whatever he has to do to accomplish that. He's not insane or going on some sort of mad killing spree. Not that it matters to Dr. Chu or his family."

Savich looked over at Officer Lamar Marks, who looked like he'd been punched in the face. Savich knew exactly how he felt, since he'd felt the same way when Delion had first told him. Officer Marks said, "Xu better hope all he needs is this one doctor visit."

True enough, Savich thought.

Officer Marks said, "He could still end up in an emergency room somewhere."

Ramsey said, "Lamar's right. If he's that bad off, then he'll need more medical attention."

Molly said, "Even if he can weather through it, Xu could still be stuck in bed for another week, Dillon." She brightened. "Maybe he could die."

"He's certainly lost enough blood. Dr. Chu couldn't have transfused him in his office."

Officer Marks said, "No one saw him at the doctor's office? No other staff, patients, passersby?"

"We have nothing so far. We do know Xu went to Dr. Chu's clinic within an hour of his getting shot. The ME estimated Dr. Chu was dead within a couple of hours after that."

"I wonder where Xu is holed up now?" Officer Marks said.

Savich heard some voices in the corridor behind him and quickly turned. He expected Sherlock, but it was a couple of orderlies. Where was Sherlock?

Savich bolted from the room and ran to the nurses' station.

54

Sherlock was tapping her fingers. Why in heaven did everything take so long in a hospital? Well, okay, so she'd been sitting here in the patient waiting area only about ten minutes, but still. Where was a nurse, or the tech to wheel her in and get this business over and done?

She didn't even need another brain scan. She sincerely hoped it wouldn't include an injection. Her head was aching again, a slow series of dull thuds. She wanted to get out of here; she wanted to be able to kiss Dillon silly and hug Sean to her, have him pat her shoulder and ask her to play a computer game with him that it would be her responsibility to lose with dignity and guile.

Deputy Ray Rozan stood near the radiology waiting room door, his eyes always on the move, studying anyone for the slightest interest in coming within six feet of her. He was on edge, all the guards were, what with two maniacs out there. But it wasn't Xu, it was the other unknown man that scared him. They had only a sketch and a description of him: slender build, an American, maybe older, but no one was really sure. Whatever his age, he'd been capable of that mad spree in the elevator on Saturday.

Ray looked over at Sherlock, knew she wanted nothing more than to go home. He watched her pull her cell phone out of the pocket of a dark blue bathrobe with lots of dog hair on it that Savich had brought in for her along with her cell. He'd heard Savich had returned the previous night to sleep on a cot not two feet from her hospital bed. Rozan wondered if he'd told her why he'd been called away. He probably hadn't, since she didn't look upset, only a bit anxious. And hurting a little, too, from the fixed expression in her eyes. Her hair looked better without the blood—a soft riot of curls now, so thick it nearly covered the small bandage over the head wound. It was hard to imagine the person in that bathrobe tackling Xu and bringing him down.

"You want me to go see what's holding up these yahoos, Sherlock?"

She glanced down at her watch. "We can give them another couple of minutes. We'll make it fifteen minutes, tops. I think I'll call Dillon, see what's happened."

Rozan said it aloud: "Xu killed a physician, the one who treated him."

She nodded. "Yes, I was told." She closed her eyes against the stark knowledge of it. She'd been so close, she thought. She'd had Xu flat on his face against the sidewalk. If only she'd had time to get the other cuff on him. If only.

"We're ready for your test now, Agent Sherlock." Sherlock looked up to see a tall, lanky tech standing beside Deputy Rozan, wearing scrubs, a mask over his nose, green booties on his feet. He had a sheaf of papers in his gloved hand.

Deputy Rozan said, "I need to see your ID."

The man turned, clearly startled. "Are you her husband, sir?"

"No, I'm Deputy Rozan. She's in my care. Show me your ID, please."

"Well, you can see my name tag, and here are the orders for Agent Sherlock's CT scan, signed by Dr. Kardak."

"Why don't you have a hospital ID?"

"It's in my locker. I usually wear it, but no one ever asks for it."

"Then show me your driver's license."

Savich burst into the waiting room, saw the tech, masked, standing too close to Rozan, and raised his SIG. "Get back and drop to your knees!"

The man dropped Sherlock's chart and fell to his knees on the floor. Savich, panting hard from running, stood over him.

The man looked up at him, obviously terrified. "Who are you? What did I do?"

Rozan said, "He didn't have his hospital ID, and I'd just asked him for his driver's license when you, ah, came in, Agent Savich."

"Lose the mask," Savich said.

The man pulled the ties loose. The

mask fell off his face. "My name's Terry Lempert; see, my name's on my name tag. Why are you pointing that gun at me?"

Savich put his SIG back in his waist holster.

A nurse came to the door. "What's going on here? Goodness, Terry, what did you do now?"

Sherlock said calmly, "Officer Rozan is my guard, and this is my husband. I guess you'd say he's part of the guard detail for me. He thought this man was a threat to me. Do you know him? Can you verify he's supposed to be here? To take me in for a CT scan?"

The nurse looked toward Rozan.

"Yes," Rozan said. "Can you identify this man for us?"

She said, "I've known him for nearly ten years. It's Terry Lempert. He's been known to flirt with pretty patients, though, and I thought he'd gone over the top this time." She watched the husband pull Terry to his feet.

"Very funny, Kaitlyn," Terry said, dusting off his knees. "I wasn't doing anything, really."

Savich said, "Sorry, Mr. Lempert. You

really should consider wearing your ID, given all that's happened here the past week."

Lempert said, "Yeah, oh, yes, right. You nearly made me mess myself."

"He didn't shoot you," Officer Rozan said, and smiled, shook Lempert's hand. "You'll be fine. You did good."

Savich walked to where Sherlock sat smiling, of all things, in her wheelchair. She laid her hand on his arm. "My hero."

"Terry, go get your ID. Then you can take over Jonah's case in room three. Jonah can deal with Agent Sherlock. Next time, don't wear a mask when you fetch a patient. I've told you it freaks them out." She shot a look at Savich. "And their husbands."

Savich rested one hand lightly on Sherlock's shoulder. "Sorry, Terry," he said. "But if anything happened to Sherlock, I'd lose my job."

Terry was very pleased to take over Jonah's case, even if it was a ninety-year-old curmudgeon from Fresno who did nothing but cuss at him.

55

**Skyline Motel
El Cerrito, California, east
of the Richmond Bridge
Wednesday afternoon**

Xu was trying to sleep, but it was hard, since he felt like crap. After leaving Dr. Chu's clinic yesterday afternoon, he'd barely made it across the Richmond Bridge and was glad to find this hole-in-the-wall motel near the highway. He wished he'd made it farther, but it was impossible, not until he was stronger. He had not taken enough oxycodone to kill his pain entirely because he couldn't allow himself to get completely helpless. It was what a stupid man would do, and he hadn't survived by being stupid. He would make peace with the grinding pain.

Xu knew what this pain would be like, since he'd been shot once before. One of his trainers in the army compound outside Beijing had accidentally shot him in the leg, the blind moron. He remembered his trainer Mr. Yeung had actually cried over him, which was the only reason Xu hadn't tried to kick his stomach through his backbone.

His arm would heal, Dr. Chu had assured him several times, and he'd be well enough to fly anywhere in three or four days. Xu knew from his other gunshot wound that he wouldn't have full use of his arm for several months. At least the bullet hadn't shattered any bones on its way out of his arm.

Dr. Chu had known not to ask what had happened when Xu showed him his wound and his gun. He'd calmly sent his office staff home before he ushered Xu into one of the clinic exam rooms, helped him out of his blood-soaked jacket and his shirt, and settled him on the examining table. He'd asked absolutely nothing while he'd worked on him, but Dr. Chu had known. The doctor had given him intravenous morphine and Versed. Xu had watched him as he began silently cleaning out and suturing his wound. Xu had floated away, only vaguely aware of what Dr. Chu was doing. He remembered lying stretched out on Dr. Chu's examining table until he thought he could drive safely. He'd asked to take a Windbreaker with him he'd seen on a hanger in a hallway, and Dr. Chu had helped him put it on. It was large enough to fit over his arm without too much pain and zip over the bandage, since his shirt wasn't salvageable. Dr. Chu had told him to wait while he brought him antibiotics and pain meds from his office. He hadn't realized Xu had followed him down the hallway and could hear him speaking.

He heard Dr. Chu say, "I need to speak to the police about the fire at the Fairmont today. I know what happened."

Xu had no time for thought. He'd

stepped into the small office, aimed his Beretta at Dr. Chu, who heard him and looked up and threw the phone at him as Xu pulled the trigger. Xu watched him slide down behind his desk. He heard a voice on the phone saying, "Sir, who is this? What do you want again? You said you knew about the Fairmont fire?"

Xu hung up the phone, took some antibiotics and oxycodone, and walked out of the clinic.

It was too bad about Dr. Chu. Xu appreciated what the doctor had done for him. The doctor was collateral damage, and he'd still be alive if he'd had better judgment.

The FBI knew who he was and knew what he looked like; they had to, since they'd found him, probably through Cindy. He'd been too late after all. His passport and his visa were useless to him, but he knew where he could get others. At least they didn't have a clue where he was now or where he was going to be soon enough. It was then he realized, paralyzed for a moment, that neither did he. He'd dumped the white Infiniti on one of Sausalito's curving streets and hot-wired a dark blue Honda parked nearby. He should have gone farther away to find a car, but he'd simply been too weak.

Xu pulled the cheap motel blanket up to his neck, settled his wounded arm on one of the skinny pillows. First he had to heal. He could hardly fly to Beijing into the arms of the Chinese, not now, even if a false passport got him through customs. The Chinese would sever all connections with him now and deny he ever existed, no matter how valuable the information he'd gotten them from Lindy's computer. They might even kill him if they could.

Xu forced himself to lie perfectly still on the rock-hard mattress, yet the pain in his arm continued to drum a steady tattoo. He wanted nothing more than to go to sleep, but the instant he closed his eyes, he was back at the Fairmont, watching each and every scene play through slowly. So be it. He examined each decision he'd made, an exercise his trainers had taught him early on. He thought of the flash-bang he'd long carried with him. He'd never really believed he'd need it, but his training had always pushed precaution, and that piece of insurance had paid off in spades. It had been a while since he'd used one, but he hadn't forgotten. That and the bomb he'd set up in his room had saved his life.

Should he have gone out the hotel through the back service entrance? No, there would have been FBI agents out there waiting for him, away from the crowds. He'd done the right thing there, too, getting whole-hide out of the lobby by mixing with the tourists who were running around like berserkers after he blew up his little surprise.

He let himself relive the awful pain he'd felt crashing down to the sidewalk when the FBI agent had tackled him and smashed her fist against his wounded arm. He felt again the humiliation and panic when she'd snapped the cuff on his right wrist and began reciting his rights to him, close to his ear, the bitch.

Even after all his training, perhaps because of it, there'd been no way he could have foreseen that agent chasing him down. It wasn't just any damned FBI agent, no, it was a woman, and it shouldn't have happened, wouldn't have happened if he'd been whole. He should have turned to face her, used his training to snap her skinny neck or his Beretta to shoot her dead, before she'd gotten him down.

A woman bested me. He looked down at the handcuff that still circled his right wrist. How to get the damned thing off? It would have to wait. He'd figure something out, he always did.

And someone had shot the bitch. It had looked to Xu like she was dead, a shot through the head, but of course he hadn't checked, just shoved her off him and run.

Who was he? Was it the same idiot who had shot Judge Hunt at the wrong moment and blown the Cahills' trial apart? Had he shot the agent purposefully to save Xu? Why?

Who was he?

When the knock came on the door of his motel room, Xu grabbed his gun, gasped at the rip of pain through his arm, and shouted, "Go away!"

Another knock.

Xu raised his Beretta, aimed it at the motel door. "Who is it?"

A hard rasping smoker's voice called out, "I'm the one who saved your bacon."

56

Xu stared at the man standing in front of him, his back to the motel door. He was wearing a Giants baseball cap, sunglasses, a loose blue Windbreaker, jeans, sneakers, and gloves. He smiled at Xu, not moving since Xu's Beretta was steady on his chest.

"Who are you?"

"I already told you, I'm the one who saved your bacon. Good thing I followed you here from that doctor's office in Sausalito, since it looks like you're going to need some more saving."

"How did you find me?"

"Well, now, I've got to admit I had a bit of luck there. My car was near that white Infiniti you stole—nice job, incidentally, yanking that guy right out, no muss, no fuss, and you were out of there. I lost you for a while because of all that snarled traffic you caused at the Fairmont, but then I thought about it and decided you'd probably headed to the Golden Gate, so I did, too. And there you were ahead of me, going through the tollbooth. I followed you off at Spencer Avenue, watched you leave the Infiniti and steal the blue Honda. Then I sat back and waited for you just down the block from that doctor's office.

"Yeah, I heard the gunshot. You killed the guy. Why? He saved your bacon, too."

Xu's arm hurt from holding the Beretta steady, but it didn't matter. The Beretta didn't move. "I overheard the moron calling the cops. I had no choice."

"Good to know you don't just go around shooting folk for no reason."

"No," Xu said, "there's always a reason. Then you followed me here?"

"Sure, not a problem. I was surprised you made it so far the way you were driving. Gotta say, you sure don't look so hot. You've still got some blood on your face from when that agent planted you on the sidewalk."

There was blood on his face? What did this guy want? Xu said slowly, "But that was yesterday afternoon. Why did you wait until today to knock on my door?"

The man said matter-of-factly, "The Feds might have been following you or you might have had some other help coming. I had to wait, seeing as how I'm not too fond of the cops myself. You know, there's a chance the clerk in the dinky motel office might have seen the blood on your face, and if he did, he must have wondered. Surely he wondered. If he sees your photo on TV, he'll know."

"Nah, the kid doesn't know anything; he was too busy playing video games when I checked in. I don't even remember a TV."

"Like I said, you don't look too hot. Do you want another pain med? Once we get you feeling better, we can decide where to go. Look, if I'd wanted you dead, I wouldn't have shot that agent off your back. I'm not here to hurt you. You're already in bad shape. I'm here to help you. Stop pointing that ridiculous gun at me."

Xu ground out the words "Why would you care?"

"I'm thinking we're a lot alike."

"That's crazy."

"Nah, I kill because I want to, and you kill because you have to. See? Not so different."

Xu stared at the guy for a long time, and nodded. "The pills are on the night table."

The guy shook two pills out onto his gloved palm, handed them to Xu, waited until he swallowed them, and gave him a glass of water.

Xu still didn't pull down the Beretta. He motioned the guy to step back, then held himself still and waited for relief.

"I see from the number of pills still in the bottle you've been going light on the pain meds. Not a bad idea, given who could come through that door."

"Take another step back. I don't want you so close to me."

Xu watched him take two steps back.

"Why did you kill that FBI agent who was on my back?"

"Well, you see, when she knocked you down, she was out there in the open. I had a nice clear shot, and I took it."

"You're saying it wasn't about me? You wanted to kill her?"

"Oh, yeah, I wanted her dead, but I figured what I was seeing was pretty interesting, so why not see where it led me? Hey, kill one bird and save the other."

He opened his mouth, but the man raised a gloved hand. "No reason for you to ask me any more right now. Maybe if we become BFFs, I'll tell you everything."

The medication was numbing the pain in his arm but blurring his brain as well. Xu said, "Were you the one who tried to kill Judge Hunt?"

The guy nodded. "I thought I nailed the bastard, but he turned at that last second. Can you believe the rotten luck? But still, it was a good shot, he should have died."

"But he didn't. Did you try to take him out again in the hospital?"

Xu would swear the guy puffed up with pride.

"I gave that plan a lot of thought, even got me some blood from a patient in the hospital to smear on the walls of the elevator shaft to drive the Feds nuts, but—"

Xu interrupted, "It was a ridiculous plan." He stopped talking at a fierce jab of pain, held himself perfectly still, waiting for the meds to kick in and kill the pain once and for all. This idiot who'd shot through an elevator hatch wanted to help him?

Xu said, "I want to see you. Take off those sunglasses and that ball cap now or I'll drill you between the eyes."

"Okey-dokey, fair enough, but ready yourself. You're in for a big whopper surprise."

The ball cap and the sunglasses came off. Xu stared, so stunned that for a moment he didn't feel the pain in his arm.

"Got you, didn't I?"

Xu could only nod.

"Fact is, I mean, who can you trust in this sad world?"

"You," he said. "Maybe I can trust you. You're as bad as I am."

"No, you're wrong about that. I'm worse."

57

Judge Sherlock's home
Pacific Heights, San Francisco
Wednesday evening

Sean was teaching Cal and Gage how to play *Flying Monks,* the latest computer game his grandmother had presented to him when they'd first arrived. It was always a treat for Sherlock to watch her five-year-old teaching younger children, and three-year-old Cal and Gage looked utterly absorbed, nodding and all serious about the rules Sean was laying on them.

Flying Monks—another new game Sherlock would have to master.

She caught herself thinking that kids were so different now, an observation probably made by every single generation in man's long timeline. She smiled to herself. Time always passed, and everything always changed. No kid today could imagine the world without a small device called a cell phone that would soon do everything but make them Kool-Aid. And now you could ask your phone a question and it would answer. But people, she thought, people themselves never changed.

Cal shouted, "I got you, Gage. I've moved up two ranks. I'm flying! I'm a Major Monk now."

Sherlock felt bone tired, and was trying not to show it, but she didn't mind, because she'd succeeded in fooling Sean. She'd hidden her bandage well enough— thank God for all her curly hair—and he'd accepted her being gone Tuesday night, inquiring only if Emma had wondered why he hadn't come to see her. Sherlock had lied to him cleanly. "Of course Emma wanted to know where you were, Sean. I told her you'd promised yourself to your grandparents and you'd never break a promise."

"You didn't tell her I went to see *Rory and the Last Duck,* did you, Mama?"

"Nope."

"She doesn't know Grandpa and I ate two buckets of kettle corn, does she? I don't want her to think I'm a pig."

"Nope."

Sean looked thoughtful, an identical expression to his father's. "There's so much to do, Mama. Sometimes I just don't know."

His grandmother had walked in then with a freshly baked plate of chocolate-chip cookies, and Sherlock forgot to ask him what he just didn't know.

She sensed Dillon behind her and heard his deep voice. "Here, sweetheart." He leaned down, kissed her mouth, and handed her a cup of hot tea. "Drink it down. Then I'm thinking it's time for you to hang it up for the night."

"But—"

"Dr. Kardak said you'd give me grief

and I was going to have to be the enforcer. You've done well, stayed nice and quiet all afternoon and evening. Now it's time to let your brain and your body knit themselves back together while you have pleasant dreams." He paused for a moment. "I'm thinking I have some good ideas on how to help you make that happen."

She took a sip of tea, looked up at him. "You're going to read me a bedtime story?"

"I could, but I hadn't planned to."

"I wonder what you could possibly have in mind?"

He smiled at her. "You finish your tea and we'll see. Molly called, said Ramsey misses you since you were a civilizing influence on all those males around him. She'll be here with Emma soon to pick up Gage and Cal. Ah, if you like, I can remove Sean before Emma comes in."

"I'll watch Cal and Gage," Evelyn Sherlock said. "I've got the power as long as I've got these chocolate-chip cookies."

Sherlock said, "Maybe it'd be good to take Sean upstairs, otherwise he'll be so

excited about seeing Emma it'll be difficult to get him to bed."

Half an hour later, Sherlock was lying in
bed, the pill Dillon fed her quashing the
remnants of pain in her head.

Now, what else did her husband have
in mind, as if she couldn't guess? She
heard him singing a country-western tune
in the bathroom, a song James Quinlan,
a fellow agent and musician, had written
about a man who loved wild broncos,
wilder women, and black gold. When he
came into the bedroom a few minutes
later, he was wearing only pajama bot-
toms, slung low on his hips.

Sherlock thought she'd swallow her
tongue. "Don't move, please."

He obligingly stood still, arms at his
sides, backlit in the bathroom doorway,
smiling at her. "I missed you scrubbing
me down."

"Me, too." It was true. As a shower
mate, Dillon was a keeper.

"How's your head?"

"What head?"

He was grinning when he came to stand
over her. "Life's been a tangle, hasn't it? I

say we take a small break from the madness. What do you think?"

It was amazing how good she felt in that moment. This was probably the best idea she'd heard in a very long time.

58

**Eve's condo, Russian Hill
Tuesday night**

"You've got a burn just there." Harry lightly touched his fingertip to a red spot on Eve's neck.

She never looked away from him. "I could put some more burn cream on it, or maybe you could kiss it and make it well."

"Not a good idea," he said, and took a step back from her.

Harry, Eve, and Griffin had been treated by the EMTs at the Fairmont, had been pronounced good to go, had been debriefed at the Federal Building, and had showered and cleaned up at Harry's house before he'd brought her back to her condo.

Eve felt punch-drunk, both hyped and exhausted. The weird thing was, this potent mix had her seeing Special Agent Harry Christoff with new eyes. The new eyes really liked what they saw.

Harry knuckled his own eyes. "I keep seeing Xu coming into the suite, and then I hear Griffin yell for him to get his hands in the air. Then everything happens so fast, all at the same time—the explosion of bright light and that god-awful noise, and fire everywhere.

"I still can't believe Xu was carrying a flash-bang. And he knew exactly what to do with it."

Eve said, "I want to learn how to use one. Talk about effective; my ears didn't stop ringing for an hour. It was as if that light slapped right into my brain and I was as good as blind for five minutes."

Harry said, "Xu certainly came prepared, you have to give him that."

Eve said, "I don't have to give him a damned thing. However, I wouldn't mind shooting him in both knees. I guess you'd have to be in the military to learn how to use a flash-bang."

Harry said, "No Flash-bang Escape Weekends for civilians?"

"Not that I've heard of. You want a beer?"

He shook his head.

Eve waved him into her living room, eased herself down onto the sofa.

Harry sat in the chair opposite her and gave her a brooding look over his steepled fingers. "I'm wondering if the State Department can get the Chinese government to tell us anything about Xu now that he's blowing up hotel suites and killing people."

"I doubt they'd even own up to knowing who Xu is. If we pursued it, accused Xu of being a Chinese spy, they'd claim he was probably an innocent bystander the FBI was trying to nail as a scapegoat. I'll bet the State Department will back off, without more proof, and even then—"

Harry tapped his fingertips together. "I keep asking myself—is there anything we could have done to stop him?"

"If we hadn't been blinded and mule-kicked, we could have put a dozen bullets in his chest. That would have ended things nicely. At least one of us got him in the arm. I wonder which of us it was. I don't suppose the medical examiner will want to examine our weapons?"

"If it got out that the M.E. was going to check our SIGs, there'd be a pool started up to see which of us had popped Xu."

She got up, went into the kitchen. She called out, "You want some Fritos and queso dip?"

Harry laughed. "Sure, why not? I can't remember the last time we ate."

Eve brought in a tray with a huge bag of Fritos and a bowl with the queso dip, steaming from the microwave, and set the tray on the coffee table. "Well, come on over and sit next to me unless you want to drag that chair over."

Harry dragged over the chair opposite the coffee table.

Eve gave him a long look. "I usually like it when a guy is scared of me, but you? You won't sit next to me on the sofa, you won't even give me a mother's kiss on my neck to make my owie better again."

"Mama didn't raise me to be stupid."

She scooped up dip onto a big Frito. "Do you know I overheard Cheney saying you weren't a nasty git any longer, only nasty."

"When did you hear that?"

"At the hospital last Friday morning. I was standing in the corridor outside the ICU when you and Cheney came waltzing in."

"What I really am is a mild-mannered agent, only no one will believe me. Okay, maybe it's true I haven't been too much fun for the past year and a half."

"Amazing, we only met last Friday."

"We've seen each other on the elevators, in the Federal Building garage."

"Yeah, well, you pretended you were this tough guy who shaved himself with a hunting knife. Hard to reconcile that image with what all of us deputy marshals know to our guts, namely, that FBI agents are all wimpy clones made in the FBI factory."

"Oh, yeah?"

"It's common knowledge."

"You want to know what FBI agents think about the fricking Marshal Service?"

She grinned at him. "Nope."

When he opened his mouth, she raised her hand. "You asked and I answered, so keep quiet."

He said, "The few times I've seen you, I always thought you were too pretty to be a marshal, since nearly all of them are ex-military buzz-cut hardnoses. And look at you—you wear that black-and-red getup with your butt-kicker boots so you can be one of the boys. Have you found they take you more seriously?"

He was spot-on about that, she thought.

"It's the boots that win the day," she said. "No one messes with the boots."

"The fact is, though," he continued after eating a Frito, "the unmarried FBI agents keep trying to figure out how to get your attention. Word is, you never give any of us the time of day."

"Nope, you're all pantywaists. Who wants to hang around a pantywaist with wingtips on his big feet?"

"Yeah, yeah, blah, blah. You know what it is about you—it's that blond ponytail and those big blue eyes, makes all the guys want to take you home to Mama."

"The blond ponytail wouldn't have anything to do with it. Nope, Mama would admire my black boots."

He laughed. "Maybe."

She studied his face a moment and liked what she saw—the hard planes, the sharp cheekbones, and his eyes, green-as-the-Irish-hills eyes. There was an in-bred toughness in him. She said, "You know, the past five days have made me understand a little why there were so many wartime marriages. Men and women thrown together in extraordinary circum-stances—I guess to survive they needed to reaffirm they were alive by making con-nections, by making another human being matter to them so they were able to ig-nore death, if only for a little while."

Harry said, "Nah, it doesn't work like that."

"What? Hey, that was all sorts of philo-sophical and you say 'nah'? Haven't you heard of the bazillion wartime marriages?"

"I think regardless of how people meet, they're either meant to be together or they're not." He ate his Frito, then quickly dipped another into the dip. "I'm starving and I hadn't even realized it." He toasted her with it. "Thanks for the best Frito I've had in a week."

"Nothing beats a Frito. So you weren't such a nasty git before your divorce a year and a half ago? It was the breakup that made you into one?"

"I've always been nasty. The git thing, that's all Cheney."

"That's why your wife left you?"

He paused with a Frito an inch from his mouth. "No."

She cocked her head at him, said slowly, "No, that isn't what happened, is it?"

"Why do you think that isn't what happened?"

She said, "I've known you only a short time and one thing I see very clearly is that you're not nasty. You're an honest man, Harry. You say you'll do something and you do it. You don't make excuses when things don't go right, and you don't expect to hear any. That's clearheaded, and it's tough, but it's not nasty.

"Well, maybe when I first met you I wanted to punch your lights out because you were posturing like a rooster. I think you enjoyed getting my reaction, you liked rubbing my nose in it, liked reminding me I was *only* the protection detail, not a member of the investigation team." She ate another chip, never looking away from his face. "Not that I really mind posturing for the fun of it, mind you. You know one of the things I like best about you? You're funny, you make me laugh. You have a good outlook, Harry."

"I was shot three years ago in an aborted bank robbery."

"Where?"

"At the Bank of America on Chestnut."

She threw a Frito at him. "No, on your body? Where were you shot?"

He gave her a faint smile, stood up, and pulled out his shirt. She looked at a four-inch scar on his left side over his lower ribs. It had to really hurt, she thought. She'd never been shot, only punched a couple of times. She kept looking at him, couldn't seem to drag her eyes away from that hard disciplined body.

He said as he quickly tucked his shirt back in and sat back down, "She freaked, and couldn't get past it no matter what I said. Our three-year marriage went downhill fast when I refused to resign from the Bureau. Bottom line, it was her ultimatum."

He picked the Frito she'd thrown at him off his sleeve. Then he looked at it in his hand and carefully laid it down on the tray. "I'd always heard it's nearly impossible for cops to stay married—but I'd never thought about it, since my parents have been married forever. I mean, we were both good people, weren't we? I was in love, and so was she. Before I asked her to marry me we talked about the high divorce rate among cops. I gave her all the stats, quoted a couple of articles. She scoffed at the idea that she— who had just passed the bar—could possibly be swayed by any of that. I told her my hours could be crazy and she said her hours wouldn't always be her own, either, but she was nothing if not levelheaded, she'd have no problem dealing with the chance of violence bumping into our lives.

"To be honest, the entire time we dated, it was more or less nine-to-five for me. I went out of town only a couple of times to do some undercover, but it didn't impinge much on our time together. But the threat, the reality of violence, it was always there, always lurking, and I knew it. I simply ignored it.

"I'll tell you, Eve, it sucks to be a cliché."

She wouldn't want to be a cliché, either. He was right, what had happened to them was all too common, and maybe why she hadn't ever set herself up in the marriage market again. "You want a beer now?"

"Sure." He got up with her to go to the kitchen. "Sorry to unload my sorry history on you. I didn't mean to. Actually, I have no idea why it popped out."

"Thank you for telling me."

"How old are you?"

"I'll turn twenty-nine on the twenty-sixth of January."

"You ever get close to getting married?"

"Yeah, I was married, right out of college. It wasn't long before I realized I wasn't going to be the last notch on the moron's belt. Truth is, after the moron, I don't think any guy could make it past my dad and my brothers. They'd make hash of him." She rolled her eyes. "They told me after my little misadventure—

that's what my brothers called my brief marriage—if any guy did me wrong again they'd bury him deep, never to be found."

She got a couple of beers out of the refrigerator, handed him one. They clicked bottles and drank.

Eve said, "You ready to kiss my owie now and make it well?"

"Yes," he said, putting his beer on the counter, "I think I am."

59

Judge Sherlock's home
Pacific Heights
Early Thursday morning
Thanksgiving Day

Sherlock opened her eyes to see Dillon standing over her.

A big smile bloomed because, quite simply, how could it not? Sherlock yawned and stretched. "What time is it?"

"A bit after six a.m. How are you feeling?"

Sherlock queried her head. The wound itself throbbed a bit, but there weren't any voices inside her head screaming punk rock, and that was good.

"Like a million bucks. You tell a great bedtime story, Dillon. Every bone in my body is humming 'Ring My Bell.' What in heaven's name are you doing up? Helping my parents with the turkey?"

"No, Molly is keeping the turkey to herself. Your mom's in the kitchen, though, making sausage stuffing for you carnivores and a nice cornbread stuffing for me. I woke up a couple of hours ago, realized we'd all overlooked something, and went to work on MAX."

She studied his face. "You know who he is? The man who shot me yesterday? The man who tried to kill Ramsey twice?"

He climbed into bed beside her, pulled her against him, and kissed her hair. "It's all pretty straightforward once you look at it the right way."

He was big and warm, his heartbeat steady against her chest. "What do you mean, 'the right way'?"

"Remember, it was you, Sherlock, who suggested a long prison stay fit the bill, someone who'd had time on his hands to plan the bizarre attacks on Ramsey. And we knew the person who had that note delivered to me at the Hoover Building had joked to Ted Moody about calling him the Hammer—prison slang."

She nodded.

"And Dane and Ruth have been checking inmates released since the first of this year, looking to find a father or a brother, someone with a relationship to one of our cases who was out now, who could be looking for revenge."

Sherlock said, "Ruth told me she and Dane were going nuts, that they couldn't find a prisoner who fit the profile."

Savich said, "There's a very good reason for that. I realized the one case that remotely connected Ramsey to me was more than five years ago, though I wasn't all that involved. Remember Father Sonny Dickerson, the pedophile who kidnapped Emma?"

Sherlock clearly remembered the obsessed ex-priest who'd sexually abused Emma until she'd escaped and Ramsey had found her and hooked up with Molly to save her. So much violence, so much deception, and it had all ended in Dickerson's murder in the hospital. And now

Dillon knew. Sherlock snuggled closer, waiting. She enjoyed a good punch line as much as he did.

"I did a search on all of Father Sonny's relatives. His father's dead, his only other sibling, a brother, is dead. There was only one relative left who wasn't dead, and that's Sonny's mother, in jail for killing her husband. She's the Hammer."

That was a kicker. "You're kidding me—Sonny Dickerson's mom shot me in the head?"

"Yes. We all believed it was a man, of course, since everyone who saw her— from Ted Moody, who brought us that note in the Hoover Building, to the lady who rented her the Zodiac—described a man. We even heard what we all thought was a man's voice on that telephone message to Molly, never doubted it was Xu.

"She's got a gravelly voice she's learned to control, and she knows how to disguise herself as a man. She let us believe all the attempts on Ramsey's life were Xu until Tuesday, when she shot you with Xu on the ground under you." Sherlock came up on her elbow. "I just can't get over it— Father Sonny Dickerson's mother. But,

Dillon, why didn't her name pop right out when Ruth and Dane did their search, no matter if she's female?"

"Because her name is Charlene Cartwright. Like I said, she was in jail for ten years for the murder of her husband, evidently a miserable human being who not only abused Sonny and his now-deceased brother but also his wife, Charlene. She snapped and shot a dozen bullets in his face with his own gun.

"From the court transcript I read of her trial in Baton Rouge, I think her shooting him was justified. I don't know why her lawyer didn't plead self-defense, but he didn't. He went for the SODDI defense— Some Other Dude Did It—but the jury didn't buy it, and no wonder, since there was so much evidence against her. They wanted her to serve hard time, and so she did. She was given fifteen years, paroled after ten.

"Father Sonny was murdered when she'd been in prison for about five years, so she had ample time to figure out who to blame and how to carry out her revenge."

Sherlock said, "Why did she target

you? Of course I remember most everything about the case, but you were hardly
involved."

"That's why I didn't make the connection sooner. When I found her, I realized
that she saw me as making it all possible
because of the facial-recognition program I modified from my friend at Scot-
land Yard. Remember we didn't believe
the sketch we inputted into the program
would pay off? But it did, the program spit
Father Sonny out right away."

Sherlock said, "So Charlene read about
the facial-recognition program, saw your
name and your connection to Ramsey,
and decided you were the one who fin-
gered her son, that without you, he
wouldn't have been caught, which is totally wrong. Father Sonny tried to take
Emma again in Monterey. In the end,
that's what brought him down."

"Yeah, but we're talking a very angry
woman here."

"Angry but irrational," Sherlock said.
"She used you as her focus, the hub of
the wheel. She was going to punish you
by killing those who mattered to you, as

you had hurt her by supposedly killing her son."

"Looks like. I guess there was no way she could know Father Sonny kidnapped the wrong little girl when he took Emma since he was ordered killed by Emma's grandfather for it. She must have believed Ramsey killed him, that I and everyone else protected him, covered it up, and that's why he was number one on her hit list."

Sherlock recited, "*For what you did you deserve this.* I wonder how many lines she played around with before she came upon this one. It sounds highfalutin, doesn't it? Like God is going to smite you and you deserve it. Why isn't her name Dickerson?"

"It was a common-law marriage, and she kept her maiden name—Cartwright. She served her ten years in Louisiana Correctional Institute for Women in Saint Gabriel, outside of Baton Rouge, until four months ago when she was paroled, completely rehabilitated, and, citing her exemplary behavior, willing to do whatever was asked of her, according to the warden himself. She was, naturally, a clerk in the prison library, spent many hours in there 'studying,' according to the parole board records."

Sherlock said, "And I was second on her list after Ramsey? To hurt you?"

Savich nodded. "She must have decided to put Ramsey on hold, since she realized there was no way she could get to him again in the hospital, not after the elevator debacle."

He shook his head. "I can't get over her preparation for that attempt. She even took Boozer's blood, remember, because she wanted us to think she was wounded, and that she was a man. She wanted to play with us."

"And Boozer described a man as well."

"Well, we thought Xu was a woman for a very long time, what with that Sue name mix-up. Turns out we were wrong on both counts."

Sherlock said, "That stunt in the elevator. Amazing, what she did."

"She failed, thanks to Eve and Kevlar."

Sherlock said, "Dillon, how do you know it was Charlene, though? I mean, for sure?"

"There were samples of her handwriting in the trial record. They matched the notes she sent us. And she's wanted in Louisiana again, for cutting out on her parole officer two months ago."

Sherlock said, "She must have been following the FBI van, no other explanation for why she was there and ready to shoot just when I was out and visible at the Fairmont."

"She would have had no idea you'd jump out of the van and go after Xu. That part of it was lucky for her."

"Lucky for both of them," Sherlock said. "And isn't that a happy thought?" *If her aim had been a hair better, I'd be dead.* Sherlock's hand was a fist on his chest. He felt her fingers tangle in his chest hair. He pressed lightly, flattening her palm.

Savich said, "I've got her photo. It will make a huge difference knowing who we're looking for. You know, Charlene doesn't look like a killer, not really. I saw two photos, one before her trial and one taken two years ago. She didn't look beaten down anymore, like a battered wife. She looked fierce, the set of her head and shoulders was proud, like she was on a mission for justice, like some old Joan of Arc."

Sherlock pushed off the covers. "Let me see."

"No, you stay put. I'll bring MAX in here to show you." He felt her hand moving over his chest. He leaned down, kissed her.

"No, don't bring in MAX just yet," she said against his jaw. She kissed his throat. "Not yet."

60

San Francisco General Hospital
Judge Hunt's room
Thanksgiving

Nurse Natalie Chase was divorced. Even though her ex was a real loser, she'd loved his name, and since she didn't have any kids by him, she'd kept it. Thank heaven his gene pool wouldn't continue through her. She had no close family, only a couple of cousins who lived in Boston, so she always volunteered for holiday shifts. She liked holidays; there was usually something special going on, and she didn't have to be alone. This year she'd been invited to a Thanksgiving feast like no other she'd seen in a patient's room, with Judge Hunt and his crew. They were breaking more visiting rules than she cared to think about, but nobody was worried about it, not since it was Judge Dredd and it was Thanksgiving.

Sure, she had to keep an eye on all her other patients, but most of them were with family, chowing down on turkey and dressing if they could. Even her elderly patient with Alzheimer's was with his daughter, who was snacking on turkey and stuffing while she kept vigil. No one was alone today.

It baffled and angered Natalie that someone would want to kill Judge Ramsey Hunt. He was genuinely nice, a treat to the eyes, and, like everyone else taking care of him, she was thankful today of all days that Judge Dredd was doing so well. Another three or four days, she thought, and he should be well enough to go home. Home, maybe, but not back to his normal life. Not while there was a killer who might try for him again. She couldn't imagine living with that, couldn't imagine what his family was going through, knowing that a madman was still out there, waiting for another chance.

At first the TV news had showed a picture of a man, Joe Keats, who'd escaped from the Fairmont a couple of days ago, as the man who'd shot Judge Hunt. And today they were showing the picture of a woman instead, who was supposed to be the shooter. She looked, Natalie thought, a bit like her own mother.

Would there be another picture tomorrow? The news didn't seem to have any idea why she tried to murder Judge Hunt and the FBI agent, but she knew that by the end of the day there would be talking heads arguing over every detail on TV and plastering the Internet with so many opinions even the mullahs in Iran would see them. She could already recite the words: "Anyone with any information about the whereabouts of either of these people—"

SFPD Officer Gavin Hendricks waved his hand in front of her face. "You look a million miles away. Another slice of turkey?"

She shook her head at him, smiling. He'd been guarding Judge Hunt for the past three days. He was a tall black man with a pitiful excuse for a goatee, she'd told him, and he'd laughed and said it was his father's fault. She said, "If I eat any more I might pop a button, and that wouldn't be cool at all. What if an emergency turns up? What if a patient sees me with my pants button popped open? It wouldn't inspire much confidence."

"You're sure, Natalie?" Molly Hunt called out. "We've got lots."

"Thank you, Molly, but if I ate another bite, I'd have to find a bench to sit on because my butt would be too big for a chair."

Gavin laughed. Natalie saw Molly turn to her husband and touch his arm and then his cheek. She did that every few minutes. A lioness always watching.

The room should have been pandemonium with all the visitors—four guards, Judge Hunt's family, three kids, and a slew of FBI agents. They'd wheeled out the second bed and taken advantage of the largest patient room in the hospital to set up several folding tables provided by the cafeteria, spread a tablecloth over them, and crammed in a dozen chairs. It was a wonder to see in a hospital room, Natalie thought. The table looked like a family dinner, with everyone in fine spirits, except that many of them were wearing guns and darting their eyes to the door if anyone approached.

Agent Sherlock, the FBI agent who'd been her patient just yesterday, was forking down some of the incredible sausage stuffing, laughing at something her husband said to her. *Lucky, lucky woman,* Natalie thought. Did she realize how near she'd come to death?

Not the time for grim thoughts, Natalie told herself. She looked back over at Officer Hendricks. He was coming her way, two slices of pumpkin pie on small Thanksgiving paper plates, with whipped cream on top. "I've decided both of us will trust our buttons not to pop," he said, and held a slice of pie out to her.

She considered turning it down, but naturally, she didn't. "Thank you, Officer Hendricks."

"Make that Gavin, ma'am."

"And you can call me Natalie."

He sat down beside her, and they ate pumpkin pie and chatted about nothing in particular until the football game came on. Gavin forked down another bite of pie, closed his eyes, and hummed. "Oh, man, that is fine. I hear Emma Hunt made the pie. Emma's a whiz on the piano and a good cook. I'd say the kid's got it made."

They looked over to where Emma sat beside her father, her small white hand on his forearm.

Her two little brothers, Cal and Gage, seriously cute identical twins, sat at the large table, currently hemmed in by three large adults and another little boy, Sean Savich. He would grow up to be as handsome as his dad, Natalie thought, looking from him to his father, Agent Dillon Savich.

"Emma Hunt's playing with the San Francisco Symphony next Wednesday," Gavin continued, took another big bite of his pumpkin pie, and shook his head. "Hard to believe. Look at those small hands. What is she, eleven, twelve?"

"She's eleven, Judge Hunt told me. He's so proud of her he would pop his own buttons if the hospital gown had any. All he can talk about is being well enough to go to see her perform next Wednesday."

"He'll make it," Hendricks said. "The man's strong, he's got an iron will. I've gotten to know him. You know, I keep seeing him jumping down from the judge's bench in his black robes, flattening those yahoos who invaded his courtroom."

"I remember that. Goodness, everybody does. It was an incredible thing he did," Natalie said. Her wrist pager beeped. She smiled at Officer Hendricks—Gavin—rose, and thanked the cooks for feeding her an extraordinary dinner.

Natalie paused in the doorway for a moment, and looked back. She marveled at the bonhomie and goodwill they were all managing, even with that woman lurking in everyone's mind, out there making more plans for murder. Even if the goodwill was paper-thin, it was valuable. She gave a last smile to Gavin.

Natalie took care of the emergency—Mr. Pitt in room 306B was hyperventilating at the news his grandson had happily delivered about his marrying a Las Vegas dancer—and walked back to the nursing desk. She studied the photo they had of Charlene Cartwright again. Soon this woman's face would be more familiar to people than the governor's. The woman had once been pretty, Natalie thought, but now she was beyond that, an odd thing to think, but it was true. She touched her fingertip to the smoker's lines fanning out from her eyes, the deep scored lines about her mouth. There was a message in the woman's eyes, wide pale green eyes, flat as a stagnant pond. Those eyes scared Natalie to her toes. The message was, quite simply, both the promise of death of anyone she wanted gone and the acceptance of her own death, should it be demanded of her.

She realized she'd seen eyes like Charlene Cartwright's once before during a six-month stint in a psych ward. She hadn't wanted to think about what was going on behind those eyes.

Ramsey was asleep, finally, an exhausted sleep that worried Nurse Natalie Chase a bit, but then she managed a reassuring smile at all his family hovering around his bed. "Don't worry. His vital signs are fine. His football team lost, that's what flattened him."

They all smiled and eased.

When Dr. Kardak came in a moment later to have the small slice of pumpkin pie he'd been promised, he looked down at the sleeping Ramsey. "I'd say he had too much fun." He looked over at Sherlock, lifted her hair off the butterfly strips she'd pressed over the sutures, and, thankfully, left them alone. "Still feeling well, I take it, Agent Sherlock?"

"Fit as a fiddle," she said, then, "I always wondered why a fiddle was fit? I mean, what does health have to do with a musical instrument?" and Dr. Kardak, forking down a bite of pumpkin pie, swallowed and smiled. "Not a clue." He looked one last time at the sleeping Ramsey, nodded to the rest of them, and left.

Sherlock was tired. She wished she could curl up next to Ramsey and take a nice long winter snooze, but she knew it wasn't to be.

Savich said, "You look burned out, sweetheart. You ready to go home to bed?"

"Are you offering another bedtime story, Dillon?"

He lightly touched his fingers to her cheek, studied her exhausted face. "I think it's got to be sleep without dessert for you tonight." He turned to Eve and Harry, who were studying Charlene's photo.

Eve said, "A woman, all the time it was a blasted woman. I mean, it was okay for Xu to be Sue for a while, but Charlene Cartwright is giving our sex a bad name. And look at us, Sherlock, you've got an aching head, and I'm still nursing the bruises she shot into my Kevlar in the elevator. Do you think she's nuts?"

Savich slowly nodded. "She is now. Before she married her husband? If I had to venture a guess, I'd say no.

"You're right to be worried about Charlene. Xu has no more reason to be here that I can see, unless he's too weak to drive. Either way, he'll be out of the picture for a while unless we're lucky enough to find him.

"Charlene's a different matter. We are her purpose, her focus. She needs this fight or she might as well float off the planet, that or kill herself. But you know, I really don't think she'll give it up until we bury her." He pulled Sherlock close, closed his eyes for a moment.

He said, "All of us know that informants solve most of our cases. Since her photos are everywhere, we've got to hope she stays close."

61

Skyline Motel
El Cerrito, California
Nine o'clock Thursday night

Charlene looked through the glass into the small motel reception office. Her luck was holding. Only one skinny guy was inside, and from the description Joe had given her, it was the same guy who'd been deep in a computer game when Joe had checked in. He said he remembered the kid's name because it was so weird. Okay, she'd told him, but Jerol wasn't as weird as Xu, and she was going to call him Joe. He'd smiled up at her. And she'd started singing Johnny Cash's "A Boy Named Sue."

She didn't know where she was taking Joe just yet, but it was too dangerous staying this close to the city any longer, now that his photo was plastered all over the TV. She figured he needed another couple of days before he'd be good for much, not that she needed him to help her, but he was smart, had lots of experience. If he could learn to trust her, maybe they could stay together for some time, like she'd planned to stay with Sonny. She'd be with Sonny now if not for that little kid, Emma. What a snooty name that was. Wasn't she to blame, too, for Sonny's being dead? It wasn't Sonny's fault he had this problem. The kid shouldn't have run away from him, selfish little cow, when she knew—Charlene shook her head to get her brain back on track. She was losing herself more often now in her thoughts. She'd think something, and then the thought seemed to grow and change, to branch out in all directions, like a spin-off of a TV show.

She focused on Joe, and her brain

seemed to flip a switch. He really knew these FBI agents, he told her, knew how they thought, knew what they'd do in any given situation. He'd stayed one step ahead of them, no problem, just as she had. *But you didn't know about that little redheaded agent who slammed you down on your face, did you? Without me, the train would have left the station—you'd be on it dressed in shackles and handcuffs.*

He knew that as well as she did, so she didn't say it out loud. He'd thanked her twice already, and it came easily to him. She found him charming. She'd known Joe for such a short time, and she already liked him a lot better than she'd ever liked her miserable husband, bad memory that he was. Joe said he liked the big diamond on her pinkie finger, and she'd laughed, told him it wasn't real, told him it was as fake as her vicious long-dead husband who'd given it to her and that's why she wore it, to remind her of that wonderful day she'd shot his face off. And he'd asked her about the other ring she wore that looked like it belonged to a religious order. She'd fallen silent, fingering the ring, then said, "It belonged to my son, before Ramsey Hunt murdered him." And that's when he'd asked her to tell him the whole story.

When he'd finally fallen into a restless slept last night, she stretched out on the bed beside him and listened to him breathe. She realized she hadn't slept beside a man in a very long time. It felt strange to hear another's breathing so close beside her. He woke her up once when he started talking in his sleep. And now she knew something about who and what this man was—not only a killer, as she was, but mixed up with the Chinese— a spy, maybe? And he was piss-in-the-pants afraid of them. *I end up with the weirdest people,* Charlene thought. Her son was kind of weird, of course, but he wasn't stupid, he was—off. He hadn't deserved to die, hadn't deserved to be murdered by that miserable judge.

Her familiar rage kicked in, made her mind hiss and crackle. It wasn't right what happened to Sonny. What had happened to him was the real crime. Imagine a federal judge murdering a man in his hospital bed? And every one of those crooked cops had covered for him, nothing but sympathy for him because of pathetic little Emma. Emma—Charlene hated that name now. She figured the kid and her mom had moved to a safe house after she'd left that phone message for little Molly, since when she'd last driven by, the house was empty. She'd find them, follow the kid from school, maybe.

Emma, Emma, Emma, the name drummed louder and louder in Charlene's brain. *Get it back, get it back, focus, focus.*

She blinked, again focused on Joe. He'd been thrashing around, a fever, and she'd fetched him three aspirin and some water, and cupped his head. He never opened his eyes, but she already knew his eyes showed a life ancient with violence, far more than she could imagine. As she'd looked down at him in the dim motel room light she realized he might have made a fine son. There was something about Joe Keats, whose real name was Xu—maybe his will to survive, she wasn't sure—but he impressed her. Regardless of what he was or what he'd done, he was a man who didn't whine or complain or strike out. Well, she'd see about striking out.

He healed amazingly fast, she'd thought, when she'd tended his wound earlier. The flesh around the wound was pink, and healthy-looking. She hadn't seen any blood crusted around the stitches. And now Joe was sleeping. He'd sworn to her he could drive. She'd told him he should get rid of that blue Honda he'd lifted in Sausalito. As soon as they were away, he'd told her—best not to leave it at the motel. Well, if he got himself killed because of that stupid car, it was his business. She was driving her own car, bought and paid for in Stockton from a little old man going into a nursing home.

The bell tinkled when Charlene pushed open the door and strolled into the motel office, cash in her hand. Jerol was sitting behind a counter loaded down with piles of brochures for local sights. Joe was spot-on about him—Jerol was playing a computer game, all his attention on some military figures fighting on the screen, its gunshots, loud bangs, and booms punctuated by his grunts and cheers.

Joe's Beretta was snug against her side, just in case, since you never knew when some snake might up and try to bite you.

She spotted an ancient TV propped up on a portable serving table. It was tuned to a local news channel. The weather report was segueing into the news. The spit dried in her mouth. Her photo appeared on-screen followed by Joe's. The volume was turned low, but she could hear the newsman talking about Joe. *Hurry, get checked out or the moron might look up, see the photos, and call the cops.* She moved to stand squarely between the kid and the TV.

"Hey, I was looking at that bad guy on TV."

Well, that settles that, she thought, feeling the Beretta warm against her palm. *No choice now.*

She smiled and said, her voice loud to drown out the TV, "Hey, do you have any brochures on Six Flags Discovery

Kingdom up in Vallejo? That's the new name of the place, right? I'm thinking my friend and I would like to check it out tomorrow."

"Who's your friend?" Jerol Idling said, his voice impatient. He'd been close to scoring another hundred points and needed only one more good kill, but he'd happened to look up at the TV when she came in and there was a photo of some guy and they were blaring how danger-ous he was, how he'd set off the Fair-mont fire and murdered some people, and the weird thing was, the man looked familiar. Jerol knew he'd seen him, but where?

Charlene studied his face as she said, "My friend's name is Joe—" She stalled. What had Joe called himself when he'd checked into this place? Cribbs, that was it. "I'm with Joe Cribbs. He's in two-seventeen."

Jerol wanted to see the man's photo again on the TV, but this woman was standing right in front of him. "Mr. Cribbs didn't say anything about a *friend* com-ing." His mom hated guests coming in unannounced ever since six college students had snuck into one room to spend the weekend. He'd been only seventeen at the time, but he still remembered the mess they'd made. Not that this old lady was likely to make a mess, not like those beer-guzzling yahoos, but still. "When did you show up?"

Rude little bugger, Charlene thought, leaned toward the kid, showing him a cleavage she'd learned to make by pushing in her elbows and leaning over. She could push them nearly to her tonsils, and there weren't that many wrinkles. The two truckers in Bakersfield she'd tried it out on were distracted quickly enough. "Last night. So you got any brochures?"

"Yeah, we even got brochures for mud baths in Calistoga if you want. Is Mr. Cribbs feeling better? He looked pretty bad when he checked in yesterday. I mean, he was all hunched over, and I knew he didn't feel good. Do you know, he looks kind of like—"

Charlene said quickly, "He's fine, only a flu of some sort."

"Hey, aren't you a little old for Mr. Cribbs? I mean, like his mother?"

Well, now, that's quite enough out of you. Charlene raised her hand and shot him in the face with Xu's Beretta. As she fired, she jumped back. She didn't want his blood to splatter on her clothes.

62

Judge Sherlock's home
Pacific Heights, San Francisco
Thursday night

Savich punched off his cell. He watched Sean happily playing an NFL video game with his grandmother, who knew squat about football, and he was winning. He wondered if Sean was smart enough to be on the 49ers' side in the game and not the Redskins'. He leaned down and said quietly to Sherlock, "Cheney said they're getting about fifty calls an hour on the hotline with sightings of Xu and/or Charlene. The SFPD has provided some manpower to sift through the calls, since the field office hasn't the staff to do it."

"At least we can discount the calls that have Xu walking around, since he isn't," Sherlock said. She rubbed her hands over her arms.

"Cold?"

"No, I guess someone walked over my grave. I wonder where that saying comes from. It's pretty gruesome."

"But descriptive. What did you feel?"

"I'm worried that something bad's going to happen, Dillon. Soon."

He didn't say anything. He pulled her to her feet, then sat down and brought her down on his lap and held her. He knew she was right, something bad had to happen, with two armed and desperate people out there, their pictures all over TV.

After they got Sean bathed and buttoned into his Spider-Man pajamas, they got him down but, unfortunately, not out. He couldn't stop talking. He was too excited about how he'd stomped his grandmother at NFL football. He had, to Savich's surprise, gone for the Patriots. Savich finally sang him his favorite song of all time, guaranteed to put him out by the end of the first verse—"You've Got a Friend in Me" from *Toy Story.*

Sherlock was grinning when Sean's eyes closed. "Every time," she whispered.

They were getting ready for bed when Savich's cell rang.

"Savich here."

He was quiet, listening, his expression unchanging, but Sherlock saw his eyes darken. The bad something had happened.

She looked down at her watch. It was an hour and a half short of midnight on Thanksgiving night.

63

Skyline Motel
El Cerrito, California
Friday, one minute after midnight

Eve looked at the cluster of cop cars surrounding the motel office, parked at all angles throughout the lot. The few motel guests were grouped together, talking, probably trying to figure out what had happened. They knew enough, Eve thought, looking at the M.E.'s white van. They just didn't know who had shot Jerol.

After they'd spoken to Mrs. Idling, Eve and Harry had come outside, primarily to

get out of the way of the El Cerrito forensic team and the M.E. She said to Harry,
"I hate this. That young man is dead because he must have recognized Xu on
TV. But what I don't understand is why Xu
came back to the office and shot him.
Why not simply leave? Why even come
to the office in the first place?"

Harry said, "Maybe Xu couldn't be sure
about him, didn't want to chance him
making a phone call. The kid was another
loose end." He watched them wheel
young Jerol Idling out, already zipped
into a green body bag. Savich and Sherlock and Cheney followed. They were
speaking to the El Cerrito police chief,
Glenis Sayers.

Eve said to Harry, "When Chief Sayers's detectives arrived at the scene, they
found the name Joe Cribbs with the license plate number that Jerol had written down for him next to it. When they
matched it to the blue Honda that was
stolen in Sausalito on Tuesday, they called
her. Bless her, she called Cheney right
away, so it's thanks to her we're in the
mix at all."

They watched El Cerrito police officers crowding around the chief, one of them with his arm around Mrs. Idling's shoulders. She was plastered against him. They could hear her sobs from where they stood. Life can be snuffed out from one moment to the next, Eve thought. It was horrible and scary, and true for each and every human being on this earth.

Harry nodded. "There isn't any doubt it was Xu. Everything fits. Mrs. Idling never saw him, but she knew a guy had paid cash to check into room two-seventeen on Tuesday. Jerol told her the guy seemed sick, favoring his arm when he checked in, said the guy seemed really out of it. The Joe Cribbs signature in the ledger is pretty illegible, as if written with the wrong hand. Remember Xu is left-handed, and he was shot in that arm. I'll bet ballistics matches the bullet to the gun that killed Dr. Chu."

Eve said, "But that doesn't help us tonight. Maybe Xu doesn't know we've got him made, doesn't know we're looking for that blue Honda he's driving. I wish Mrs. Idling hadn't dismissed the shot she heard as a backfire for those precious minutes before she came over to investigate."

Harry said, "The corker is she saw two cars skidding out of the parking lot, with the door to Mr. Cribbs's room standing wide open."

Eve said, "It means he was too sick to ditch the Honda, but he wasn't too sick to call someone to the motel to help him. He's been here a day and a half. He could have called the Chinese for help. You think that second car was driven by a Chinese connection?"

Harry shook his head. "That doesn't sit right with me, doesn't feel right. But you know, if not the Chinese, then who? And was that other person the one who shot Jerol?" He thought about that, but no answer stepped up. He said, "That second car, Mrs. Idling is sure it's an older Corolla. Since there was no license plate matching it in the register, it wasn't anyone who was staying here, legally, at the motel. If they're smart, they'll leave the Honda somewhere and we'll have no way to trace them."

Eve said on a sigh, "Whoever it is, it's a game changer. With help, Xu can go anywhere he wants now."

Cheney called out, "Harry, we need you over here."

64

Harry Christoff's house
Laurel Heights, San Francisco
Saturday morning

Eve kicked back, put her booted feet on the ottoman. She was wearing the same clothes she'd worn yesterday, and she felt grungy. She leaned her head back against the sofa back and said, "My head hurts."

Harry stood over her, a cup of coffee in his hand. "You ate breakfast an hour ago so it's okay to drink another cup of this fine brew. Then we'll talk."

Talk? That opened her eyes. *What did*

he mean, talk? Eve didn't want to talk—a *guy* talk about two adults enjoying sex and no commitment? No, that wasn't Harry. Harry was honorable to his feet. Like big statue-of-David feet. No, Harry felt guilty because he'd made love to her and now it was morning and somewhere along the line he'd realized she expected more from him, and so he regretted ever pulling down her blue bikini panties. How was he ever going to explain that to her so she didn't shoot him?

She stared at him, unblinking. He hadn't said a word while he'd chowed down on his cereal, one of those health-food brands she'd never heard of, while she'd slathered strawberry jam on her toast. Not a single word about how incredible she was and it was the best night of his life, and how about now let's get naked right here, on the table? Would she climb up on the table? Yes, she would.

She continued to stare at him. To her eye, Harry radiated guilt.

Eve drank a bit of coffee and watched Harry walk to the chair opposite and sit down. He looked indolent and loose, his legs stretched out, crossed at the ankles, and he steepled his fingertips together. *Tap, tap, tap.*

Maybe she was wrong, maybe he didn't feel guilt about having sex with her, wanting now to shoulder the blame, to claim all the fault. Maybe she was wrong. Instead, maybe he was feeling cocky he'd scored with her. Was that better than his feeling guilty about seducing her? *Seducing* her? What had happened between them—what was it last night, three times? Talk about a busy two-way street.

Harry said in a brooding voice, "You're so pretty, it drives me nuts."

Pretty? He was beginning his guilt speech by telling her she was *pretty* and it drove him nuts? No, what she was was a mess. She needed a shower, she needed a couple of multivitamins, she needed to have Harry tell her it wasn't just because she was *pretty* that he was attracted to her; what she wanted him to say was something very different, like it was her insides that turned him on, and he didn't for a single instant feel guilty about making love with her, and he wanted more, he wanted—Eve pulled out her cell. "I want to speak to my dad."

"Why now?" His left eyebrow shot up. He still looked, she thought, loose and relaxed, indolent as a lizard, and she wanted to smack him.

She managed a credible sneer. "What do you care? Oh, I see, if Daddy asks me where I am, I'll have to confess to him I'm currently only twenty feet from a guy's bedroom, wherein lies a rumpled bed, and the guy's name is Harry Christoff, and sorry, Dad, he's not in the U.S. Marshals Service, he's a dippy FBI agent."

Harry grinned at her. "I love to listen to you spit out a hundred words without taking a breath. Actually I'd like to speak to your dad. Don't you think it's about time? He really doesn't like FBI agents?"

About time? To apologize to him for seducing his daughter, but, hey, it happened, so let's move on? She studied his face, took another slug of her coffee, and carefully set the cup down on a magazine to spare the shiny wood surface. He wasn't smiling. In fact, he was holding himself very quiet, his eyes focused on her face. No way was she going to let him speak to her dad. She said between seamed lips, "I was thinking you don't really like women except to sleep with them to add another notch to your belt. But that's not it—you feel guilty, right? You're sorry you seduced a colleague. Were you thinking about apologizing to my dad? And then you'd like me to just go away so you can forget it ever happened."

Harry couldn't help himself. He smiled at her. What was her idiot talk about his not liking women? About his feeling guilty he'd slept with her? He felt calm and steady, better than he'd felt in so long he couldn't even remember when or why. *Well, Eve, the truth is making love to you made me remember that life is really a very fine thing indeed. You think I feel guilty because I made love with a colleague? Don't you realize you're my entire bloody army of salvation? Bring on your daddy.* He said, "I'm now a reformed git. Here's to the power of the ponytail." He picked up his coffee cup, said slowly, feeling his way, "You think I took advantage of you?"

She thought about that for a moment. She had to be honest here. "Maybe not every time."

Harry wasn't about to dwell on each glorious time; he'd shake himself out of

his chair and that wouldn't put the focus where it belonged. "That ponytail of
yours—it's a big draw, Barbieri. I look into
those big blue eyes of yours, listen to you
smart-mouth me, and I find myself thinking I'd like to see that ponytail at the
breakfast table for, say, the next fifty years,
or so. Yeah, at least fifty years. I come
from healthy stock, and so do you." There,
he'd spit it right out, and waited.

*Oh, no, no, that wasn't a guy's guilty
speech or a cocky speech. What this was
was way too fast, way too much, even
with his light hand and that intent look in
his eyes. Beautiful eyes, he had. No, wait,
stop it.*

What was he saying? Eve couldn't get
her brain around it. He wanted to see her
ponytail for fifty years? Across the breakfast table? As in marriage? Eve jumped out
of the chair, grabbed her jacket, and was
at the front door in under thirty seconds.

He called after her, "What about calling
your dad?"

"He doesn't need to know yet what
kind of deep trouble I'm in."

"Can you tell me about this deep trouble? Maybe it concerns me?"

She shook her head and was gone. Harry didn't go after her. He listened to her engine rev, heard her back too fast out of the driveway, and hoped she didn't knock over the azalea pot he hadn't brought in yet for the winter.

Harry sat back in his chair and smiled. Sitting across the breakfast table from Eve for fifty years. It sounded fine to him, more than fine, it sounded like he'd wake up smiling a whole bunch of mornings. He loved her brain, her smart mouth, her courage, and, well, her gorgeous athletic body as well, and her gorgeous athletic body's enthusiastic reaction with him was something to make a guy grin like a fool for a millennium.

He sat back and closed his eyes, wondering how long it would take her to come to grips with what they could be together, given a healthy chance. She'd thought he was going to give her the guy talk about not wanting it to be more than sex? How could she ever think that? *Well, there's your history, stupid.*

He drank the rest of his coffee, set the cup on his knee. He closed his eyes and leaned his head back. He caught himself when Xu's face intruded clearly in his mind's eye. He was not that far away, and who was with him? The El Cerrito police had found the Honda downtown, but no trace of Xu or his companion.

There had been hundreds of calls yesterday, but nothing helpful in finding Charlene Cartwright, either. It was a manhunt now, pure and simple. Until the end played out, Judge Hunt, Savich, and everyone in their path was in danger. He had to get showered and shaved, get himself to the hospital.

As he lathered his face, he wondered what he could do that would really count. Other than chase Barbieri down and kiss her stupid and convince her it wasn't only sex for him.

He thought he'd ask Savich to write a country-and-western song about a girl with a swinging blond ponytail and shit-kicker black boots.

Time to get yourself together, Barbieri.

65

San Francisco General Hospital
Saturday morning

Dr. Kardak straightened over Ramsey and nodded, looking, truth be told, very pleased with himself. "You're healing very nicely, Judge. Your tube tract is closed and your lung sounds good, barely a crackle or two left. You're very lucky that bullet didn't wreck your lung, or worse. I see you've cut back on your pain meds, and you're smiling. I couldn't ask for more. Our chef said you were eating more of his wonderful meals.

"All in all, you keep improving like this, and you're going to have a front-row seat at Emma's performance next Wednesday." Maybe not front and center, Dr. Kardak thought, though he didn't say it aloud. With any luck at all, Ramsey should be able to sit upright for an hour or so.

Ramsey heard a cheer from the guards at the window as Dr. Kardak left. He grinned over at them. Both of them spent Thanksgiving here; in fact, they had both been with him for more than a week now, and he'd been cogent for at least four of those days. He knew just about everything important about all the people who were taking care of him and was wondering how he could pay them back. SFPD Officer Gavin Hendricks and Nurse Natalie were really hitting it off, and maybe he'd played some part in that. They made a nice couple.

He felt clearheaded again, he felt in control. He was able to think in a straight line without having to deal with pain trying to jerk him off the path. And his thoughts led him right to Father Sonny Dickerson's mom. Her name was Charlene Cartwright, and she had to be in her sixties. What kind of a person that age could hatch a plot like this and execute it? He tried to imagine her motoring a Zodiac to his beach, being a good enough shot with a sniper rifle to have killed him dead if he hadn't turned, and then using that sling shot with that absurd photo of Judge Dredd attached to it. Harder still to imagine her climbing down on the roof of the elevator, pulling up the ceiling hatch and firing down at him and escaping— she must have kept herself in very good shape in prison. Her audacity amazed him, even as a mother avenging her son. Father Sonny was a son who didn't deserve even a passing thought, much less a full-blown vendetta. Didn't she know full well that he'd been an obsessive insane pedophile? The fruit must not have fallen far from the tree, he thought. Charlene had to be as crazy as her son in her own way. He opened his laptop and began researching Charlene Cartwright's criminal record. He wanted to know everything about her, her murdered husband, and her children.

She'd planned and plotted for five years. Amazing. Thank the good Lord she'd failed. At least until now.

66

San Francisco General Hospital
Saturday morning

Sherlock sat in Dr. Kardak's small office on the fifth floor, waiting for him to come back from morning rounds and give her a final check. Thankfully, she didn't have to worry about having the stitches snipped out of her head, since he'd told her they would resorb by themselves. She'd sent Dillon on to see Ramsey, saying, "I'll be fine. There's no reason for us to sit here and twiddle our thumbs together. You've got a lot on your plate—go deal with it.

Send up a guard if someone's bored; otherwise, I'll come to Ramsey's room when I'm done."

Savich had gently lifted her hair and lightly touched his fingertip to the small bandage. "I'll send a guard. You will not go anyplace without someone covering you like a blanket." He'd stared at her for a moment, kissed her hard, and left.

Sherlock knew he was still reliving those moments when he'd thought she was dead, but what could she say? She refused to think what she'd feel and do if Dillon had been the one shot. She pulled out her cell and called Ruth, who was in Maestro, Virginia, with her husband, Dix, and her two stepsons on this fine Saturday morning.

Ruth said, "You guys have sure got yourselves in the middle of a big curdling mess out there. You swear to me you're all right, Sherlock?"

"Yes, don't worry, it was only a little tap on the head. Talk to me, Ruth, about Charlene Cartwright. What do you know?"

"Dane flew to Baton Rouge last night, then drove to the Louisiana Correctional Institute for Women in Saint Gabriel this morning. He said the warden was goggle-eyed to hear what sweet, good-natured Charlene had done. He had to admit that yes, it was true, Charlene had worked out in the gym like a trouper for the past five years or so, and was in excellent shape for any age, really, and remarkable for someone ready for Medicare. Dane didn't tell the warden she'd styled herself the Hammer. He should be about through with his interview with an inmate who was supposedly Charlene's best bud, so you should call him in a couple of minutes. You swear you're okay?"

After reassuring Ruth about herself and Judge Hunt and how he and his family were holding up, Sherlock dialed Dane, who answered on the third ring. "Hi, Sherlock. I just finished up a very informative interview with Charlene's confidant, Maria Conchas, so your timing is perfect. Let me search out a private place." He came back on a couple minutes later. "I'm in a supervisor's office. Maria's a piece of work, in prison now for eight years for shooting her neighbor for looking in at her sleeping through her bedroom window, or so she claimed. 'And I was naked, the nasty peeper!' Quote/unquote. Maria put the guy in a wheelchair for life with a bullet in his spine. Her punishment is another two years, after which she can waltz out of here on two strong legs.

"Moving right along. Maria and Charlene spent long hours discussing life and men and how the Big Bad brought you down until you took charge and decided to do something about it. Maria said Charlene wasn't shy at all, in fact, enjoyed talking about what she was going to do to FBI Agent Dillon Savich when she got out. She called him 'hateful bastard,' the one who was responsible for her boy's death, namely, Sonny Dickerson. Do you know she made Maria call her the Hammer? Said Charlene could turn so mean it scared her to death, but never in front of the guards.

"Now, I wondered why Maria was so eager to tell me everything about Charlene's plans, since she had been, supposedly, her best friend. Maria told me she looked up Father Sonny Dickerson in their newspaper files and found out what he'd done five years ago before he'd died, well, before he'd been murdered. *Good rid-*

dance, she'd thought. She couldn't believe Charlene wanted revenge for that
'crazy pervert,' as Maria called him, even
if Charlene was his mother. She told me
she knew to her gut after reading about
Sonny and what he'd done that Charlene
had to be mad as a hatter to want to
avenge him. Charlene said this to Maria,
and I wrote this down, 'I'm going to get it
done. I blew off that vicious jerk's head
who made my son the way he was, didn't
I?' She was talking about her husband.
Maria said she believed her and we
should, too.

"I asked her if she knew about the note
Charlene sent to Savich. She laughed,
said Charlene worked on different word-
ings for three months before she was
happy. Maria recited the note in a dramatic voice, *For what you did you deserve
this.* Maria said she even tried her hand at
some variations, but Charlene didn't like
anything she came up with. Maria shook
her head and said to me, 'I mean, who
would take that idiot threat seriously? Talk
about sappy.'"

Sherlock said, "So she said Ramsey's
name?"

"Yes, Maria said Charlene told her about some 'nasty bugger' judge she was going to kill, too."

"Was there anyone else on her hit list after she killed Ramsey? Had to be someone close. I mean, to make Dillon pay a stiff price, this person had to be close, right?"

"I'd say so," Dane said, "since it was you, Sherlock. I know we were all hoping it was random, that any FBI agent would have filled the bill—but it wasn't random, and I doubt you really thought that for a minute, not really.

"Charlene wanted you dead because you're Savich's wife, the most important person in his world, just as Sonny was to Charlene.

"Yes, I know it doesn't make much sense, since Savich was three thousand miles away when Father Sonny was killed, but Charlene didn't care. If not for Savich and his fancy technology, her precious boy would never have been caught. She thought Sonny would still be flying high and free, and she would be there with him, together again."

Sherlock said, "Dane, even if there

hadn't been a match in the facial-recognition program, Father Sonny wouldn't
have cut his losses, disappeared, and
flown free. He'd have done just what he
did do—gone after Emma again, and
that's why he was caught. Identifying him
through the sketch was only a shortcut,
and not a very important one."

"Didn't matter. Maria said when she
pointed out to Charlene that Sonny had
to get caught sooner or later, Charlene
threw a ten-pound free weight at her.
Maria gave me a manic grin, said she'd
never argued with Charlene again after
that. I wanted to ask her why she hadn't
figured out sooner that Charlene was off
her rocker, but I didn't, since Maria's train
isn't exactly running on the tracks, either."

Sherlock said, "But that whole deal at
the Fairmont; how could she possibly
have found out I'd be there?" She paused,
added, "I just gave myself a head slap.
She was following me, of course."

"Yep, probably for a couple of days,
waiting for her chance. She must have
thought God was in her corner when you
leaped out of that FBI van and took off

after Xu. I'll bet she was already in position and she took her shot."

"I never saw her, Dane, never noticed. How good an agent does that make me?"

"Have you forgotten that no one even considered there was another shooter besides Xu out there, and certainly not an older woman? You know Charlene was very careful. She knew you were in the surveillance van, knew something was going down at the Fairmont."

"How long was she out of prison before she shot Ramsey, Dane?"

"Nearly six months. Maria told me Charlene planned to rob a couple of stores to get herself a big enough stake, then she was going to take shooting lessons. This probably all went down close to Saint Gabriel, but far enough away not to connect her. When she was ready, she skipped out on parole. I'd have to say she got good at the firing range, but not good enough to kill you."

"With me, that's true, but with Ramsey—she wouldn't have failed with Ramsey if he hadn't been just plain lucky.

"Is there someone else on her make-Dillon-pay list?"

She realized Dane didn't want to say the name aloud, she could hear it in the pulse of silence. She felt her heart speed up because she knew, of course she knew. She waited. Finally Dane said, "After you, Maria said Charlene was going to kill Sean. 'An eye for an eye,' she told Maria. She wanted Savich to suffer as much as she'd suffered. A son for a son. And that's why I was going to call you right away if you hadn't called me first."

Dr. Kardak walked in, smiled and apologized for making her wait, but Sherlock was already on her feet, halfway out the door. "I'm sorry, but I can't stay. Later, Doctor." And she ran out of his office.

She heard him call after her, "I guess if you can sprint like that I shouldn't be too concerned about you."

Two hours later, Corman and Evelyn Sherlock and grandson Sean were in the Sherlocks' SUV, headed for a visit to Yosemite National Park.

67

San Francisco General Hospital
Saturday morning

Harry wasn't at all surprised to see Eve sitting next to Ramsey's bed when he arrived at the hospital. He hadn't had a chance to speak to her since she'd taken off like a launched rocket out his front door that morning. His first thought was that she looked gorgeous wearing her signature red and black, her U.S. Deputy Marshal badge sparkling on her jacket whenever she moved, her blond ponytail swinging. Harry couldn't seem to remember the last time he'd felt, well, this light, like gravity wasn't quite pulling him down to the ground. Despite all the scary violence going down around them, despite Eve's wariness of him and of them that morning, Harry realized he was grinning like a loon at the two guards who'd seconds before looked ready to tear out his throat before they'd realized who he was.

He looked at Molly and Emma sitting on the other side of Judge Hunt's bed, all their focus on husband and father. The two guards, at ease now, moved again to stand in front of the big window.

Eve, who'd been speaking to Judge Hunt, looked over at Harry, saw him smiling at her, and froze like a deer in the headlights. She rose, her black boots bringing her nearly to his eye level to make herself more of a force, Harry thought, and she snarled at him, "A little late, aren't you, Agent?" She got a surprised look from Emma.

Harry, all bonhomie, said, "I finally came to see if Judge Hunt is ready to bribe me to take him home."

"I'll get my wallet," Ramsey said, pretending to reach for it. He caught a brief punch of pain in his chest and laid his head back against the pillow again. "Maybe tomorrow morning would be good. I'll have to make sure Molly doesn't steal my money, though."

"I have your wallet along with your vast fortune of about sixty bucks," Molly said. "You can forget any bribes, no one'd take that pitiful amount of money, not when they'd have to face Eve. And me."

"Maybe I can pay in favors," Ramsey said.

"Yeah, yeah," Eve said, "like anyone in this room is going to end up being tried in front of a federal judge."

He laughed, regretted it immediately, and felt Emma grasp his hand.

Emma said to Harry over her shoulder, "Dad says he's going to be at my performance next Wednesday even if they have to helicopter him in."

"If need be, I'll fly the helicopter," Harry said, patted Emma's shoulder, nodded to Molly, and walked past Eve over to the guards. SFPD Officer Gavin Hendricks and U.S. Deputy Marshal Jimmy Purcell looked alert and serious as a gun barrel staring you in the face. You couldn't ask for more than that. "Everything quiet?"

"Yeah," Jimmy said. "Believe me, anything on two legs gets past the two guys outside, we'll throw them to the floor, strip-search them, male, female, you name the species, we'll strip it."

"And search it," Gavin added.

Harry answered their questions about what was new, what was happening and what wasn't, took a call from Savich and said to everyone in the room, "I'm doing guard duty for Sherlock while Savich spends some time with you, Ramsey. Then he's scheduled to call Disneyland East and update Director Mueller."

Harry was whistling as he left Judge Hunt's hospital room, but he couldn't stop himself from looking back. He met Eve's eyes, smiled at her, and would swear she was looking back at him like he was a big New York steak, and she was starving. That look, he thought, was surely an excellent sign. He spoke to the guards sitting outside the room, and walked toward the stairwell. As he took the stairs two at a time toward Dr. Kardak's fifth-floor office, he decided the time he was assigned to be with Sherlock was his best shot at being there if something happened, since Sherlock was right at the eye of Charlene's storm. There was no way she could get to Ramsey, and Sean was safe, on his way to Yosemite. Despite himself, he really wanted a chance at Charlene, then he wanted to haul Eve to Carmel for long walks on the beach, longer nights, and no sleep. Then maybe she'd agree to think about spending lots more time with him, maybe she'd even come around to giving a nod to a future. Why was she wary of him? Because she didn't see him as a good risk? He would convince her he was. He was reliable, he kept his promises, he wasn't a pig, and he even knew how to cook. Yes, his work could be dangerous, but Eve understood that, and he would have to worry about her as much as she'd worry about him, since she also carried a gun.

Yeah, he might get an ulcer worrying, but she might get one, too. Only fair. They'd share that worry, like Savich and

Sherlock already did right now. Sherlock and Savich were solid, and Eve and Harry could be, too. They even had a little boy, Sean. A kid? Now, that was something to think about.

He raised his hand to knock on the door when Sherlock opened it. "Hi, Harry, I heard you coming. You walk heavy, so I knew it wasn't Charlene with an ax in her hands. You didn't see Dillon? No matter. So Dillon volunteered you to stick close." She shook her head. "Thing is, Dillon's very protective, but I really don't think—"

Harry looked at her beautiful serious face and its halo of rioting red hair and raised his finger to touch her mouth. "Stop. I'm here. Think of me as your overcoat. Is Sean safe?"

"Yes. He was so excited about his surprise trip to Yosemite, he was whooping and hollering around the house. Bless my parents. Dad simply called the chief judge and postponed his upcoming drug trial for a couple of days. Sean's safe."

Sherlock studied his face. "I apologize for trying to brush you off. Let's chalk it up to an idiot moment. I'm very glad you're here. And now that I look at you,

Harry, I'd swear you look like you're about to burst. What's happened?"

He was that transparent? He shook his head. What was happening between him and Eve was nobody's business. It was private business, his business, and when he decided the time was right, he would make it Eve's business too. He said, "Eve is running scared."

"Not for Ramsey, I hope. He's better guarded than the president."

"No, she's scared about us. Maybe she thinks I'm a sucky risk."

Sherlock marveled. No matter how grim a situation, people still found each other. It was, she thought, one of the very fine things about being alive. She patted his arm. "Nah, you're not a sucky risk. Your first wife didn't have the guts to deal with your job, so you cut her loose. That was the right thing to do. It's time now you let yourself move on, Harry.

"If anything, Eve's probably scared her dad and her brothers will freak that she's allowing a pantywaist FBI special agent to spend quality time with her, as opposed to one of their own—a mighty macho U.S. Marshals Service deputy."

Harry blinked at her. "You think?"

Sherlock nodded solemnly. "I'd say from the way she's been looking at you lately, you don't need to worry."

And Harry realized his private business was now lying on the floor in front of Sherlock. Why had those words, his own business, popped out of his mouth? Was Sherlock right? He remembered Eve's snarl in Judge Hunt's room.

Sherlock lightly touched his arm. "Nice jacket," she said. "Harry, stop worrying, it'll work out okay. I've seen that look before. All of us pantywaist FBI agents will write you references for her family if you need them. Eve's something else, isn't she? She really impressed Dillon in those two Cahill interviews."

He didn't want to say anything more, he'd said too much already. His lips were now zipped. He said, "Savich was right, she's sharp, she's intuitive. I love her cheerleading ponytail, Sherlock, and her big heart. She's got a huge heart. Do you know, after my divorce I swore off women for as long as I drew breath, and would you look at what happened? I'm thinking about long walks on the beach a week after first seeing her. Is that insane or what?"

Sherlock wanted to laugh, she really did, but she saw he wasn't joking. She said calmly, "All I know is both you and Eve are smart and honorable, and that your heart's as big as hers. You've got a lot going for you. She wants you, Harry, and one reason is because you're sexy. And look at that Shelby you drive, that car's nearly as sexy as you are. Seriously, Eve will be fine. She just needs some time. Like you said, it's only been a week. Her family will be ecstatic once they meet you. You know that as well as I do."

He wasn't going to say another word, never again was he going to spurt all his thoughts out like a shaken soda bottle. "When I left Judge Hunt's room, it's true, she looked at me like I was a steak."

Sherlock laughed. "Talk about a positive sign. Harry, come sit by me and let me tell you what I've found out about Charlene."

Dr. Kardak came in ten minutes later to hear Sherlock say, "You wouldn't believe Sean, Harry. He made his grandparents both promise to let him use their cell phone cameras so he could take lots of photos of El Capitan in Yosemite to show his three girlfriends. Hello, Dr. Kardak. Sorry for the delay."

"I'd like to meet this pistol," Dr. Kardak said waving away her apology. "I hope there aren't any more emergencies, Agent Sherlock, and you won't be haring out of here again."

Harry rose to excuse himself, but Sherlock smiled up at him. "Nah, Dr. Kardak won't make me take off my clothes to see a head wound. Harry, please supervise, make sure he does things right."

And so Harry watched Dr. Kardak push back Sherlock's hair, remove the small bandage with a light hand, and probe around the stitches.

He did a quick neurologic exam, asked her a few questions, and pronounced her free of him. He looked down at his watch. "That took all of five minutes, and no emergencies to interrupt either of us. Call me if you have any concerns, Agent Sherlock, and do let me meet that son of yours sometime."

Sherlock was glad to be done with it all

as they walked to the elevators. Done with the medical part, that is. Harry watched everyone, checking out any man or woman who even looked in her direction. They were far from done with the rest of it.

Sherlock said, "The hotline is getting reports of Charlene sightings from Fresno up to Redding and reports of Xu from as far away as Montana. They're following up on as many leads as they can.

"One thing worries me, though, worries me a lot. We still don't know who was driving that second car that screeched out of the Skyline Motel Thursday night."

Harry had fretted over this loose thread as much as Sherlock had. Everyone he knew was thinking about it. "No. We don't have a clue."

"According to Maria Conchas, Charlene is a guided missile. My gut says she won't stop until she's shot down. Probably she couldn't call a halt even if she wanted to. She's got herself hardwired."

Harry said, "Charlene Cartwright's crazy. Xu isn't. I don't know who's more dangerous."

"I guess I'm more afraid of crazy, since Charlene's the one who shot me and Ramsey."

Sherlock saw the same tech who'd had the misfortune to come into the CT waiting room on Wednesday walking toward them, whistling. He saw her, saw Harry, who was staring at him as if he was measuring him for a hole in the ground, and stopped in his tracks.

What was his name? She finally remembered. "Mr. Lempert, it's okay. This is Agent Christoff. Harry, this is Mr. Lempert. The thing is, Harry, last Wednesday Dillon was a little hard on Terry." The use of his first name brought him back, and he even managed a tentative smile. He came one step closer to her, shot a glance at Harry, and cleared his throat. "You're looking good today, Agent Sherlock. You must have come from Dr. Kardak's office."

He darted a look at Harry. "I'm not a killer—well, unless I feel threatened, that is." He cleared his throat when Harry didn't change expressions. "That was a joke, Agent. Really."

"And a good one, Terry," Sherlock said,

and patted his arm. "I've got to tell you, I sure hope I don't have to see you again for a while—professionally, that is."

She spotted a women's room near the elevator and excused herself. "Harry, maybe you want to message Deputy Marshal Barbieri? See if everything's okay on the steak front?"

He grinned. "I'll message Eve after I see you're safe upstairs." He stuck his head in the door, didn't see anyone. He walked in, looking beneath each of the three stalls. He saw two feet in sandals with bright red toenails, young feet. He watched one of the feet tap to the sound of music he couldn't hear. Okay, then. When he came out he said, "I'll be right here if you need anything."

As Sherlock stood at the counter washing her hands, a woman came in. Sherlock automatically went on alert until she got a look at her. She was older, quite heavy, a scrub nurse in a loose green top and pants, down to the green booties covering her shoes. A surgical mask hung by its ties around her neck. She wore a name tag. Harry wouldn't have let her in otherwise, Sherlock thought. A green scrub hat was perched on her thick black hair. She wore black-framed glasses.

"Hey," the nurse said, looked around, then walked toward a stall.

The nurse was suddenly behind her. Sherlock felt a gun pressing into the back of her neck. A deep voice hissed hot rage in her ear, "How did you find me, bitch?"

This wasn't Charlene Cartwright; she knew her photo as well as she knew her own. She willed her fear and her pounding heart to the back of the bus. "Xu, I can't believe you came here. Why? Are you trying to get your manhood back?" She felt her breath clog in her throat. Was this the way to play him? What would he do?

She heard a sneering laugh. "I wondered if I'd ever get the chance to be alone with you, with that big guy outside following you around. But you had to visit the bathroom, didn't you? The only reason you got me on the ground was because I was hit real bad."

Good, he was talking to her, trying to justify how she had gotten him down. She sneered back. "Yeah, an arm wound's all you had, nothing to write home about. And you're still whining? I thought above all, Xu, that you were a professional, that you were doing only what you had to do to clean up the mess you'd made. But look at you, here, trying to show me up."

His left hand moved up to grab her throat. He whispered next to her ear, "You and your people destroyed my life by finding me when it shouldn't have been possible. You're going to be my prize at the end of this wretched assignment. Tell me now. How did you find me so fast?"

She held his hot eyes. "Turns out you're not so special, Xu. Our profiler guessed you liked to treat yourself well and thought the Fairmont would be right up your alley. Before she died, Cindy told us about Lampo, Indiana. We found you within two hours of accessing your old Indiana driver's license."

His hand was shaking.

Pedal back. "Would you look at you now, Xu, no one would guess who you are. And you've succeeded in getting me alone. Who made you the ugliest nurse in the universe?"

Sherlock hadn't realized her voice had

risen. He moved the gun fast, shoved it against her ear. He hissed, "Keep it down. If that bodyguard of yours comes in here, I'll blow his head off. You want him to die with you?"

She shook her head, whispered, "No, I don't want him to die. I don't want to die, either."

He laughed.

68

"You want to know who helped me?"

She nodded at the fat bedraggled scrub nurse with coarse black hair and puffed out cheeks and smeared dark mascara looking back at her. He met her eyes in the mirror, used his nose to push aside her hair and whispered against her ear and the Beretta's gun barrel, "No one looks at ugly people. That's what she told me."

"Who?"

"Crazy Charlene. She told me this getup was my best chance of killing you."

Charlene? For a moment, Sherlock couldn't get her brain around it. "Charlene was driving the second car out of the motel parking lot?"

He grinned at her, worked the gun barrel a bit deeper into her ear. "She found me, took care of me. She's crazy as a loon, but the weird thing is, I like her. She's committed. She's got exactly two minutes to get to the roof. Then we can get this done."

The gun in her ear hurt, but it was the fear roiling in her belly that was threatening to bleed panic into her brain. *No, you can't let fear kill you. Time, you need time.*

She whispered, "Charlene is here? Did she kill Jerol Idling at the Skyline Motel?"

"Yep. That gunshot brought down the house, and so we had to move out fast. I thought my arm was going to fall off running to the car. That's when I first thought of killing you, of watching the light go out behind your eyes. I gritted my teeth and knew before I left I'd come for you." He shoved the Beretta in hard. She couldn't help it; she made a small yipping sound of pain.

She didn't look away from his face next

to hers in the mirror. He was standing so close she felt his hot breath on her cheek, saw his flat, dark eyes, eyes that had watched dispassionately as he'd killed. She knew she'd see death in them if she looked closely, knew she'd see her own death. She thought of Dillon, of Sean, of a stranger walking through the bathroom door and Xu calmly shooting her. She said, "Why isn't Charlene here wanting to kill me?"

"Charlene's got other plans. I promised her I'd provide a nice big distraction soon so we can both take care of business."

"Charlene won't get near Judge Hunt."

"Goes to show what a tiny little imagination you Feds have." His voice lowered. "You don't have much time, so I might let you in on it. You won the first round, I'll admit it, but the game goes to me."

"Why would Charlene follow you? Take care of you?"

He kept his voice low, whispered, "Charlene apologized to me for not killing you, but I didn't mind. It meant I'd get to kill you myself. All the others, they were just business, but not you. You're my bonus."

Ramsey's safe; no way can Charlene get to him. "What's your distraction?"

"A nice big boom, like at the Fairmont, but you won't hear it, you'll be dead. You think Charlene's going for that judge? Even though her brain visits Disneyland a lot of the time, Charlene realizes Judge Hunt is a no-go for now. She's willing to let the judge lie in bed, suffer for his sins. She's going to kill another man she blames for her son's death, and that's Agent Savich, your husband. Talk about hate, Charlene lives for it. I don't think she can live without it. She seriously wants him dead."

Sherlock's vision blurred, and her heart stuttered. She felt Xu's hand touch her hair. "A pity this pretty hair will be covered with your blood and your brains soon. Say good-bye to your hubby, if you want. You think Charlene's telling him right now to say good-bye to you?"

69

Savich was leaning against the corridor wall, a couple dozen feet from the guards outside Ramsey's room, speaking on his cell to Jimmy Maitland at the Hoover Building. Maitland put him on hold to connect him to the director, who wanted a status report directly from Savich. *Great,* Savich thought, *and what am I going to say? All I can tell you, sir, is that everyone you're worried about is still alive and at large, but there are lots of dead people, too, one of them a doctor who never hurt anyone in his life, and one a young kid who loved video games and worked with his mom in a motel.*

As he waited, Savich decided that as soon as he finished his attempt at raising Director Mueller's spirits he would put an extra guard on Emma. They had kept Sean safe from Charlene, and he would make sure she couldn't turn her attention to Emma. At least right now, she was safe in her father's hospital room.

He'd just finished giving Director Mueller a rundown when a skinny tech came slouching toward him in a long white coat and high-top sneakers. He had thick blond hair on the long side, and a stethoscope around his neck. Savich registered in that second that something wasn't right. Despite all that blond hair, the guy was older than he'd originally thought, lots older. The man looked at his watch, and Savich saw his wrist. It wasn't a man's wrist.

He wasn't fast enough. The man already had his gun jammed into Savich's side.

He leaned close. "No, Agent Savich, I don't think you want to do much more than breathe and accept that your trip through life is coming to a dramatic end. Long overdue, I'd say."

Savich didn't move. He said, "Hello, Charlene. Pretty good disguise, except that all that hair doesn't match how old you are. Why didn't you wear a white wig?"

The gun shoved hard into his side. "Smart mouth on you, but you're right, I could have done better than this wig, but I didn't have much time. Turns out it didn't make a lick of difference, now, did it? I might be older than you, baby boy, but I've got lots of experience handling punks like you."

"No," Savich said, "I don't think you do."

She gave a low laugh as she jerked his SIG out of his belt clip and slipped it into her coat pocket. "Now, don't you move or you're dead where you stand." She leaned closer. "I can tell you want to have a go at me. I read all about your martial arts demos and how everyone oohs and aahs over you, but you move a muscle and I'll shoot you, and then I'll kill those guards in front of Judge Hunt's room, then all the nurses down at the nurses' station. If one of the guards shoots me, who cares? I don't."

The gun jammed hard again against his kidney. Savich didn't make a sound, even though the shot of pain nearly sent him to his knees.

"Now, you and I are going to take a little walk to the stairs at the end of the corridor. We're going to walk up those stairs to the roof. I've given this a lot of thought, and I decided I'd like to see you do a lovely swan dive from seven floors up."

She moved behind him, kept the gun pressed into the small of his back. "Don't forget, I can pull this trigger faster than you can do any of your fancy kicks. You're real quiet, aren't you? You're thinking about going for it? Be my guest. At the very least you'd be strapped in a wheelchair for the rest of your days. That'd be okay, but I'd rather see you lying splattered on the ground seven floors down. You wanna know something really ironic?"

"Yes."

"Your little wife is enjoying herself with Joe Keats—you call him Xu, I think. Only he doesn't look like Xu right now. No, he's a butt-ugly scrub nurse with lots of black hair and glasses. I even put some lipstick on Joe, stuffed his cheeks to fatten them up, strapped a pillow around his middle, smeared on some eye shadow. Think it'll fool your little wife?"

Savich lost the spit in his mouth. *No, Harry will take care of Sherlock. No one's going to get past Harry, but Harry isn't expecting Xu. No, let it go, focus. You've got to get out of this alive before you can get to Sherlock. Pay attention.*

"Yep, Joe called me a few minutes ago. He should have her away from her guard by now, and in a couple of minutes we're going to hear a big honker boom—this floor's going to turn to dust and ashes. That will roust and rumble all your buddies, make them think Judge Hunt's under attack. Joe's good with bombs. Then Joe and I are going to walk away.

"Hey, I wonder if she's bitten the big one yet? He was stone-cold pissed that she brought him down since she's half his size, not to mention she's a woman. She humiliated him. Joe told me a professional has to take pride in his work or he isn't worth spit. She stomped on his pride. A man like Joe shouldn't have to suffer humiliation like that unless he's as mean as a snake like that vicious bastard

of a husband I had to shoot in the face—"
She paused, shook her head. *Stop it, shut your mouth. He doesn't need to know all this, STOP IT.*

She snapped back and focused. "*For what you did you deserve this.* I'd say that sounds real good, don't you? Has a real ring to it. Killing you is going to beat shooting that judge who murdered my boy, because you're the one who made it happen. Keep walking. Up the stairs, boy. Move out."

A nurse called out, "Agent Savich, wait a moment. Judge Hunt asked to speak to you."

Savich saw the gun jerk in her hand and wondered if he or the nurse would be dead before he could answer her.

70

A toilet flushed. Both Xu and Sherlock froze. The stall door opened, and a hugely pregnant woman squeezed out the stall door. She was pulling out earbuds blasting the end of Barenaked Ladies. "Twins," she said. "Isn't that—"

She saw Sherlock, saw the gun, saw the ugly guy who was dressed like a woman and a nurse, and she opened her mouth and screamed as loud as she could, and didn't stop. Xu's gun jerked toward the woman. Sherlock pivoted, brought up her knee hard in his crotch, and slammed her fisted hands down on his wounded arm as the bathroom door burst open and Harry came flying through.

The woman didn't stop screaming, she kept it up, a lovely ear-splitting blast, but those screams were lovelier than the "Hallelujah Chorus" to Sherlock. Xu was trying to raise his arm from the floor to shoot Sherlock or the pregnant woman or Harry, she didn't know which. She kicked him in the head and stomped her boot heel down on his hand, heard the bones crack. The Beretta clattered across the linoleum. Xu was cursing her, an odd mixture of Mandarin and English, and she kicked him in the ribs.

Harry fell to his knees beside Xu, turned him on his stomach, and grabbed his hair, only to have it come off in his hand. Xu's hand came out of his pocket fast, a knife clutched in his fingers. He slashed out at Harry once and again, trying to break free. Harry wanted to kill him, wanted it very much, but instead he jumped back and raised his SIG. "Xu, if you don't throw that knife away and put your hands on your head I will shoot you in one second."

Xu froze. He didn't release the knife.

"You die holding a knife, that's rich." Harry brought his SIG down against Xu's face. "Hey, you got another flash bang with you?" Harry smiled. "Three, two—"

Xu let the knife fall. Harry kicked it against the counter. Harry was cuffing Xu as Sherlock grabbed her cell and punched in speed-dial. Dillon's cell rang once, twice, and kept ringing four times until it went to voice mail. Charlene had him, otherwise he would have answered. She had to get to him, but the pregnant woman was choking, gasping for air, she was so scared looking down at the man lying handcuffed on the floor moaning and cursing. She grabbed Sherlock, hugged her as hard as she could, and began, of all things, to pat Sherlock's back. She cleared her throat. "You're the greatest kicker."

Harry yelled, "Look what I found, a damned detonator." Harry disarmed it. "So much for this part of your plan, Xu."

She'd forgotten the bomb. Sherlock pulled away from the woman. "Thank you. Sorry, I've got to go."

But the woman grabbed her again and kept squeezing. "I'm sorry you can't get closer, but it's twins. I have to wear mules, since I can't even see my feet."

"I know." Sherlock knew the woman was going into shock, and so she said gently, "It's all right now, I promise." Then Sherlock simply lifted her away. In the next second, she pushed out the bathroom door. She shoved her way through the growing crowd of people and yelled, "Get security, fast!"

71

Savich called out to the nurse still walk-
ing toward them, "It's okay. Tell Judge
Hunt I'll be in to see him in a few minutes.
Thank you."

"Smart move," Charlene said out of the
side of her mouth, watching the nurse
give Savich a smile and a finger wave and
turn back to the nurses' station.

"Cute little gal. From the look she gave
you, I think she'd like to fool around with
you. You faithful to your wife?"

Savich saw the nurse turn once more
and look from him to Charlene, puzzled.

Keep going, everything's okay. Keep all your mad attention on me, Charlene.

"Not going to say anything, huh? You're probably not faithful, no guy is, including that dog of a husband I had, and do you want to know what—" She stopped again in mid-sentence. *Shut up, shut up, Charlene.*

Savich opened the stair door and started climbing. What she was saying, it was bizarre, but it was more than that. It was as if her brain suddenly went sky-diving, and she was barely able to bring herself back to focus. Could he use that?

They reached the fifth floor, two more floors to go. Thank God no one opened the doors. He wondered how much longer that luck would hold, kept glancing toward her, looking for his chance. His cell rang, and he felt her jump. He listened to it go to voice mail, then silent.

"Keep those legs moving, Savich. I heard your cell ringing; leave it alone. Two more flights, then we'll get ourselves a nice suntan. It's actually sunny today, and would you believe it this time of year in San Francisco?"

"Yes, it's remarkably pleasant." Savich

could hear her breathing. She couldn't be as fast as he was any longer, no matter how trained up she was. *Only one more floor.* Should he try for her on the stairs?

He took another quick look back. She was walking three steps below him, her gun steady on his back. "What you looking at, Savich? Are you wondering about your little sweetie? I'd have to say there isn't much hope for her, Joe—Xu—is a remarkable man. Can you believe that, a real live spy for the Chinese right here in San Francisco, California? He never told me what he took, only that he'd had some problems. Everyone has problems, I told him, and I took care of him. I like him, he's a gentleman and he said thank you to me for it. So live and let live, I say." She paused, panting a bit, then, "It's sad, though, even though we're supposed to hook up after the bomb goes off, I don't know. I just don't know."

Did she realize she probably wouldn't get out of the hospital alive? She sounded philosophical about it. Let her talk, Savich thought, talking would take more breath and a bit of her attention. He said, "You don't think you'll see him again?"

She surprised him. "Joe asked me to come to Beijing with him, but I can't imagine such a thing anyway. I mean, all those people who don't look like me or talk like me and would probably hate me on sight, you know?"

"Yeah, I know. The thing is, Charlene, I think Joe is in trouble with those people. He's not going to China, no matter what he told you."

"You think he's lying to me? Well, he did say then that he was probably through doing what the Chinese told him to do, so maybe we'll go to Tuscany—that's a real pretty place in Italy where he told me he wants to buy a villa, become a local eccentric, he said, because he has lots of money saved.

"You're slowing down, Agent. Yeah, I can see you're thinking about jumping me. If you try it, I promise I'll shoot you in midair. You got that? I'd rather follow the plan I had with Joe. I mean, we're nearly to the roof, how about it?"

Less than one flight left. They heard a door open down a floor, heard fast footsteps going down.

"Lucky day for that bozo," Charlene

said. She glanced down at her watch again, breathing heavily.

"Here at last. Now we exit. The roof stairs are to the left, down the hall. Shove open the door and don't move."

Savich did as she said.

She was right behind him. He felt the gun pressed against his spine. They walked only six feet to another, more discreet door that led to the hospital roof.

They heard a man's voice.

"Hey, what are you doing here? What's going on?"

72

A young man wearing a nice blue suit came striding toward them, waving his hands. "You're not supposed to be up here. Who are you?"

Savich knew Charlene wouldn't hesitate to shoot him. He said quickly, "I'm Agent Dillon Savich, FBI. We need to check out the roof. We'll be okay by ourselves." *Please believe me and turn around. Go back to your office.*

The man seemed to think about asking to see his ID, but then he shook his head at himself, said, "Hurry it up. No one's supposed to be up here. Security should have told us. Everyone's on edge, I guess. Sorry, do what you've got to do." He flapped his hand at them and walked away.

Charlene said, "Good dresser, but he's got a whine in his voice. I wonder if he's married. Bet he is and his wife can't stand him, probably wants to walk out the door and take some loser lover—" She looked blankly at him for a moment. "Now move it. That's right, you open the roof door."

Another disconnect, Savich thought, but it hadn't lasted long enough for him to make a move. He had to be ready when she did it next. She said, "Another dozen steps to the roof, then there's a door latched on this side.

"I know what you're thinking, but don't do it, not unless you want to live five minutes less. And you really want to live, don't you? Even if your little FBI wife isn't breathing anymore, you still want those five extra minutes for yourself."

He felt the gun shoved hard against his back.

He unlatched the roof door, thought

about jumping out and diving out of her sight, but Charlene grabbed his jacket, stayed close to him.

They stepped out onto the graveled roof together and looked out at the sprawl of San Francisco. The wind was sharp, a chill in the air, but the sun was bright overhead.

"Let's walk over to the edge. See, they've got the thigh-high railing. I wonder what good they think that'll do? I mean, if you want to end it all, you just gotta step right over and then you're flying. Or in your case, you're going to get a little encouragement."

She poked the gun hard in his back. "Walk."

He walked. Savich knew he had to do something or he would shortly be dead. That couldn't happen. He had to get to Sherlock. She was alive, she'd managed to beat Xu, or Harry had, Savich knew it to his gut. He felt her, strong and whole. He saw Sean, so tickled he was going to Yosemite, his arms around his neck, giving him a big wet sloppy kiss before pulling away to go to his grandfather to begin his excellent adventure. *El Capitan* were the last words he'd heard Sean say.

He saw her glance at her watch again. The explosion had to be overdue. How long would it be before she realized it?

73

Sherlock threw open the hallway door on the seventh floor.

"Hey, who are you? You've got a gun!"

"FBI! It's all right," she called to the young man who, after seeing her SIG, stood stock-still. "Did anyone go up to the roof?"

"Yes, another FBI guy and some sort of tech. The roof door's right there."

She ran to the door and pulled it open. Sherlock took the stairs two at a time, un-latched the roof door, and forced herself to lift it slowly. She saw Charlene, wearing a blond wig and dressed like a tech standing not a foot from Dillon, her gun aimed at his chest. He was too close to the edge.

He's alive; thank you, God.

Sherlock climbed out onto the roof, trying not to make any noise. She quietly eased the roof door back down, keeping low. The wind was strong up here, but she could hear Charlene saying, "I can put a bullet in your face and push you over if you'd prefer. Which way do you want it, Agent Savich?"

Dillon said, "Would you like me to tell you who murdered your son, Charlene?"

"Whether it was you or it was Judge Hunt, it doesn't matter. You're both murderers, and you should both be dead, and you will be—" She shook her head, and in that moment, Savich saw Sherlock, fell and rolled as Sherlock yelled, "Charlene!"

Charlene whirled around and fired, but Sherlock had already dropped to the graveled roof behind a ventilation shaft. Sherlock fired three fast shots, and one struck Charlene in her side. She yelled and leapt back.

Savich was on her. He kicked her in the stomach, sending her wheeling backward, but she didn't let go of her gun. She was wheezing and couldn't catch her breath, but somehow she managed to raise her gun and twist around to fire again at Sherlock.

Sherlock fired. She didn't miss.

Charlene Cartwright fell onto her back, breath huffing out of her mouth, blood splattering from her chest, spewing out around her.

Savich came down on his knees over her. "Judge Hunt didn't kill Sonny. Neither did I."

Charlene stared up at him. "Is Joe dead?"

Sherlock said, "No, he's not, but I imagine he'll end up on death row where he belongs. He's not the man you think he is, Charlene."

"He should have been my son," Charlene said, and she stopped breathing.

Savich said slowly, "When they do the autopsy, I'm thinking they'll find a brain tumor. She wasn't right, Sherlock." He rose, gave her a hand, and pulled her up hard against him. "I knew you were okay, I knew I would have known it if you weren't. Harry's all right?"

"Yes." She began feeling his chest, his

arms, dropped to her knees and felt his legs, saying, "I had to get to you. The nurse on Ramsey's floor said you and another guy had gone into the stairwell. I came up as fast as I could."

"I'm all right. Thank you for coming in time." He pulled her to her feet.

Sherlock lightly laid her palm against his cheek and looked at his beloved face. "You would have saved yourself."

Would he? He didn't know. Savich held her for a very long time until the cold wind chilled them.

EPILOGUE

The following Wednesday night
Davies Hall
San Francisco

Molly looked out over the packed hall of beautifully dressed people, the orchestra in their formal black and white, and the conductor, the tall and aristocratic Giovanni Rossini, a charming rooster tail of silver hair rising straight up off his head, lustrous as a new coin under the glittering lights. She watched him raise his baton and listened to the opening chords of Tchaikovsky's Symphony No. 4 fill the vast hall. She couldn't take her eyes off the shining nine-foot ebony Steinway on stage, waiting there for Emma.

She had wanted to be backstage with her daughter, but Emma had clasped her hands between hers and said, "You know it makes me nervous when you're here, Mama. I know you don't understand that, but it's true. Please, you need to be with Dad tonight. He's really tense, and I know his chest hurts. It's the Christmas season, Mama, Dad is here, and everything is wonderful." And Emma had hugged her tight and smiled up at her.

My incredible daughter, Molly thought. She knew at that moment she needn't be worried for Emma. Her piano teacher, Mrs. Mayhew, would be there in any case to keep her calm and grounded. She kissed her daughter, held her small face a moment between her palms, kissed her again and made her way back up to the box to the right of the stage with its perfect view. She knew she had to suffer through a Dvořák and a Mahler before Emma played, and dug her fingernails into her palm. At least she didn't have to worry about the twins, who were at the

Sherlocks' house, stuffing themselves with kettle corn and hot chocolate. As for Ramsey, he looked stoic, but she knew his stomach was roiling with nerves, and she could see the low hum of pain he still felt on his face. He looked thin, she thought, but still a sex god, she'd told him when she'd stood back and looked at him in his formal tux. Both Savich and Harry had helped him dress, a slow, laborious process, with Molly standing in the corner of the bedroom watching, trying not to show how terrified it made her that he was still hurting.

She squeezed his hand. He grinned at her, whispered, "Emma will be superb, you know it." Molly knew he was saying that as much for himself as for her. She forced out a smile and for a moment leaned her face against his shoulder.

The orchestra finished the Tchaikovsky, and Rossini turned to bow and accept applause. Molly turned to smile at Dillon, who had Sean on his lap, and Sherlock and Eve and Harry sitting next to him, and they nodded back at her. She whispered to Ramsey, "We've never had such perfect seats in the hall. It was nice of the

Vincents to lend us their box so all six of us could sit together."

Ramsey nodded, knowing the Vincents were in Paris, where they would most like to be, despite the cold December nights. He remembered squeezing into Notre Dame with them one Christmas Eve years ago along with thousands of other people, and then walking along the Seine to the Pont Neuf, where they'd stopped to buy a bag of chestnuts roasting on an open grill. Perhaps his family could do that together next year.

Rossini's baton came down, and Dvořák's incredible Symphony No. 9, "From the New World," filled the hall. Ramsey settled himself in to listen. He would have a next year now, to go to Paris if he wished. He was so grateful to be alive, here in Davies Hall ready to hear Emma play that he wanted to shout with it.

Molly was fidgeting. Ramsey whispered, "Stop worrying. Emma's a pro, she'll be great."

Molly drew in a deep breath. "You're here, that's all that's really important to Emma, and to me."

The orchestra moved on to play Mahler's Symphony No. 5 in C Sharp Minor, and it seemed to go on forever. Molly would have kicked poor Mahler if he'd been there. Why was he so long-winded? Then it was over, finally. When the applause died down, Rossini turned his charismatic smile on the audience. He said in his charming Italian accent, "We are proud to present Miss Emma Hunt. She will play George Gershwin's *Rhapsody in Blue*. We are also proud and very pleased to see her father, Judge Ramsey Hunt, with us tonight. I was told he said he'd be helicoptered in if need be." Rossini bowed toward their box bringing every eye in the audience to them.

"Miss Emma Hunt." Giovanni Rossini held his hand out to welcome Emma as she walked toward him in her Christmas-red velvet dress, her beautiful glossy dark hair held back by two gold clips, like shiny silk beneath the lights. She wore black ballet flats on her small feet. Her only jewelry was the locket Ramsey had given her for her last birthday, a photo of her and her mother on one side, Ramsey and the twins on the other.

Molly could never adequately describe her feelings when her daughter walked onto a stage. Usually it was a strange mixture of so much pride she could burst with it, and such throat-clogging terror she thought her face would turn blue. And such elation, she thought, that she knew she could leap off the box railing and fly, and finally, utter blank-brained amazement that she'd given birth to this incredible being. She watched Emma take Rossini's hand and smile up at him, then turn to walk to the Steinway grand piano, shoulders straight, lightly running her fingers over its glossy black finish. She sat down in front of the keyboard, moved the bench an inch to the left. Before Emma lowered her hands to the piano, she looked directly at their box and smiled.

She began to play *Rhapsody in Blue,* Gershwin's magical, exuberant, full-bodied, passionate masterpiece. No one who heard it would think an eleven-year-old girl was playing. Slowly, drawn inexorably into the music, Molly began to breathe again and she wondered if maybe she couldn't fly after all. She knew every chord and every run by heart, she'd heard Emma play it so many times. When Emma struck the final chord, she sat quietly for a moment, something Mrs. Mayhew had taught her to bring her back and calm her racing heart, before she eased off the piano bench and turned to face the audience. She bowed.

Molly leapt to her feet, clapping madly, hearing the audience's huge applause as they rose in a standing ovation. If Ramsey had been able to, he would have jumped to his feet along with his beaming wife, and Savich, with a wildly clapping Sean in his arms, Sherlock, and Harry and Eve, but he knew he'd probably tip right out of the box and make a mess of it on the people below.

Emma bowed again as the applause continued, with shouts of "Encore!" She seated herself again at the Steinway. She played variations on a medley of Christmas carols she herself had written, from "Oh, Come All Ye Faithful" to "Silver Bells," which lifted every spirit in the house. When she stood to bow again, the audience rose once more to applaud. Rossini presented her with a deep bow and red roses. Emma looked directly at her father, held out the roses to him, and gave him a bow.

As if choreographed, everyone in the audience turned to look up at his box. The applause, if possible, grew even louder.

When, at last, the audience settled into their seats, there was a single stark instant of complete silence. Sean's little boy voice rang out, loud and clear, from the last seat in the mezzanine to the dressing rooms behind the stage, "Emma, you've got to marry me!"

P.S.

Within an hour of the end of the concert, photos and videos, with sound, appeared on YouTube showing Judge Ramsey Hunt's box in Davies Hall in San Francisco, Sean in his father's arms, nearly falling over the railing in his excitement, yelling to Emma. Within hours it went viral.

To escape the media, Savich and Sherlock took Sean to Disney World in Orlando. Unfortunately, a little girl recognized Sean, jumped up and down, and screamed, "Marry me, Sean!" and it started all over again.